SHADOWS OF THE PAST

PALMA HARCOURT

Shadows of the Past

HarperCollins*Publishers*

This book is fiction. Any relationship between the characters in this novel and any person who exists in reality, including persons who may hold or have held official appointments mentioned in it, is purely coincidental.

HarperCollins*Publishers*
77–85 Fulham Palace Road,
Hammersmith, London W6 8JB

Published by HarperCollins*Publishers* 1996
1 3 5 7 9 8 6 4 2

Copyright © Palma Harcourt 1996

The Author asserts the moral right to
be identified as the author of this work

A catalogue record for this book is
available from the British Library

ISBN 0 00 225421 2

Set in Plantin Light

Printed and bound in
Great Britain by Caledonian International
Book Manufacturing Ltd Glasgow

Prelude

1939

Madame de Mourville regarded her son, her only child, with affection and irritation. Jean-Pierre was eighteen. A clever boy, of moderate height and slight build with dark brown hair and eyes, he had passed his *baccalauréat* with distinction and was planning an academic career after his military service. They were in the main salon of the Château de Mourville which, atop a small hill with forests marching up on either flank, was not grand but quite impressive, and conveniently situated not more than a hundred kilometres east of Paris. The date was important; it was August 1939.

'It is your father's wish,' Chantal de Mourville said, 'and mine.'

'But not mine, Maman. I don't want to go to England to live with these Stanton people. What about my military service?'

'When the papers come we shall say that you are studying abroad. Anyway, they may be irrelevant.'

'What do you mean by that?'

'Jean-Pierre, you may go around with your head in the clouds, but you can't ignore what's going on in Europe, or what's likely to happen. It seems that appeasement has failed. The Germans have occupied the Rhineland, taken over Austria, dismembered Czechoslovakia. It's obvious who will be next. Poland, undoubtedly. If there was any doubt about that, it has surely been dispelled by the signing of the Nazi-Soviet non-aggression pact this month. And don't forget that France and Britain have given guarantees to Poland, though what good they'll be it's difficult to imagine. Poland will fall, and after Poland Hitler will turn his eyes to the West. So in any case it will be war, God help us. We cannot just stand by and let this evil man gobble up the whole of Europe.'

'Phew! That was quite a speech, Maman!' exclaimed Jean-Pierre, as Chantal, her pretty face flushed from her emotion, paused.

A new voice intervened. 'Yes, and a very good one.' Unnoticed by either of them, Jean-Paul de Mourville, an older version of his son, had come into the salon. He and Chantal had been up most of the night deciding what should be done about Jean-Pierre and, after a flurry of telephone calls that morning, a decision had finally been reached. Although normally indulgent with their dearly-loved child, they had agreed that on this occasion they would be adamant.

'All right,' Jean-Pierre said slowly. 'I agree that there may well be war, but does that mean I should run away to England? Ought I not to stay and fight for France as Papa did in the Great War?'

'No,' said his father. 'I sacrificed my future then, I don't intend that you should sacrifice yours now.'

'But –' Jean-Pierre began, and stopped. He couldn't point out that the parallel between himself and his father was invalid. Carefully he avoided catching sight of Jean-Paul's artificial hand; Jean-Paul de Mourville had been a concert pianist with an assured successful career when the war had claimed him. 'But France isn't Czecho-slovakia or Poland,' Jean-Pierre continued. 'France is a great country. The Huns aren't going to sweep through our defences – like a knife through butter. What about the Maginot Line? Doesn't the government boast that it's impregnable?'

'They do, and they may be right as far as I know.' Jean-Paul shrugged. 'But the fortifications don't stretch the whole way. According to my information there's little to prevent the Germans coming in from the north through Belgium. The Belgians, I fear, won't offer much resistance. Then the Hun will have a clear run through to Paris.'

'But Paris won't fall! We'll defend ourselves. Our forces will defend us –'

'They'll try, Jean-Pierre. We'll all try, but personally I haven't much faith in our greatly vaunted forces. In my opinion a lot of good lives will once more be lost, and yet again in vain. We shall ultimately be overrun. I doubt if the British will be able to help us.'

Jean-Pierre glanced sideways at his mother, who almost imper-ceptibly shook her head. It was a signal that he was not to persist. Nevertheless, he couldn't remain silent. Although he knew that his father's deeply pessimistic view of the present situation in Europe was partly founded on past bitterness, he couldn't dismiss it. He accepted that Jean-Paul was a highly intelligent and well-informed man, quite likely to be right in his forecast of the future, and he was appalled.

'What about you two?' he blurted out. 'What will you do? Here in this château you could be almost directly in the path of the enemy.'

4

'I cannot leave the château and the estate, for obvious reasons, and your mother refuses to leave me, so we shall stay here in France. We are not as young as you are, and –' Jean-Paul held up his artificial hand '– obviously I'm no threat to anyone. We shall be all right.'

'Please God,' Chantal murmured.

Jean-Pierre bit hard on his lower lip; he wanted to cry. He knew it was useless to argue further. He would have to go to England and relative safety. It might not be for long.

'If the Low Countries fall and Hitler does conquer France, what then? Won't he invade Britain?'

'I expect he'll have a go, but the Channel may save them, as it has in the past. Dear Jean-Pierre, I don't know – we shall just have to wait and see.'

'And pray,' Chantal added.

'Meanwhile I suggest you ring the bell for Joseph, Jean-Pierre, and ask him to bring us a couple of bottles of champagne. There's no point in keeping it for the Huns.' Jean-Paul smiled. 'If they get here the first thing they'll do will be to loot the cellars. We'll do our best to hide a few of our most treasured possessions, but unfortunately we can't hide all the wine.'

'However, we can certainly drink some of it,' said Chantal, thankful that her husband was sounding slightly more cheerful, even though his cheerfulness was forced.

'Yes, indeed,' said Jean-Paul, 'and when Joseph brings the champagne, we shall drink to Jean-Pierre, to the de Mourvilles and to La Belle France.'

Helen Stanton looked around the room with satisfaction. It had taken considerable thought and effort to rearrange what had been the main guest room at The Elms, and turn it into what she hoped would be suitable for an eighteen-year-old French boy, as somewhere where he could relax, have privacy, study, read, amuse himself. Her eyes lighted on the bookcase, which contained a book on Oxford colleges, a history of England and, chosen by her daughter Anthea, a copy of Alain Fournier's novel *Le Grand Meaulnes*, supposedly to make Jean-Pierre feel more at home.

Helen sighed. She expected he would bring some of his own books, but she had no idea if he would. She had never met Jean-Pierre. She knew nothing of his tastes. Indeed, she knew very little about him. There had been no time for lengthy correspondence, only a desperate telephone call from her old friend Chantal de Mourville, and a decision to be made rapidly.

She hoped it had been the right one. Her neighbour, Margaret Grayson, had told her that she was mad, that a French boy would be a nuisance, chasing after girls, expecting to be waited upon, critical of the food, refusing to accept English ways and with impossible habits.

'He'll be used to wine with all his meals, and he'll complain if he doesn't get it,' she had said. 'Even toddlers are given wine in France. And French table manners are dreadful. He'll clean up his plate with bits of bread after every course.'

Helen laughed, remembering Margaret's shocked tone. She didn't believe a word of it. She was sure that any son of Jean-Paul and Chantal de Mourville would have been brought up with excellent manners; even at their convent school in Paris, Chantal had been fastidious. No, what worried her was that Jean-Pierre would be unhappy living with her family. She and David had stayed with the de Mourvilles a couple of times over the years for brief holidays, though the de Mourvilles had never visited them, and she was aware that life at the château was very different from that at The Elms. The Elms was a comfortable Cotswold house some fifteen miles out of Oxford, with a large untidy garden; it made a good family home, but it was sadly lacking in elegance.

'What's more,' Margaret Grayson had continued, 'there's the question of money. Your two older girls are married and away from home, but you should consider Anthea. It's not fair on her that you and David should lavish money on the foreigner. John and I wouldn't do it. We'd put our own Keith and Karen first.'

Helen sat down on the divan bed. These last words of Margaret's had made her very angry. She had wanted to tell Margaret to shut up and mind her own business, but she was a level-headed woman and had controlled her temper. The Stantons and the Graysons had been neighbours and friends for a long time, their children had grown up together, and it was unthinkable that she and Margaret should have a violent quarrel which might wreck the relationship.

She contented herself with saying coldly, 'There's no question of depriving Anthea of anything. The de Mourvilles have money in England and have made financial arrangements for Jean-Pierre.'

'That's lucky,' Margaret had said. 'And at least the French boy should stop you having to take in any of these evacuees from London that we're threatened with. I gather that most of them have never seen a bathroom and have nits in their hair.'

'Is that so?' Helen hadn't elaborated.

In fact there was no question of the Stantons being forced to have evacuees billeted on them, although they were in a zone reputedly safe from the expected bombing raids. David's elderly mother, who was very frail, lived with them, and the doctors had agreed that it would be impossible to have children in the house. This had been a great relief to Helen but, being a conscientious woman, it had made her more ready to accept the responsibility of Jean-Pierre.

Now she heard the sound of car wheels on the gravel drive, and hurriedly stood up. This would be David, who had gone to Oxford to meet Jean-Pierre. To her surprise she found that she was nervous. What would she do if Margaret proved to be right and the boy was impossible? She squared her shoulders and prepared to go downstairs. She would cope, as she had coped when David had been a prisoner in the last war, and in every family crisis since. After all, she had always wanted a son.

'Here we are,' David Stanton said unnecessarily as he drew up in front of his house. 'This is The Elms.'

Jean-Pierre made no response. He was thankful to have arrived wherever it was. He had had a dreadful journey. In the first place he was struggling with a considerable amount of luggage, and the train to Calais had been full of English holidaymakers hastening home because of the imminent threat of war. They had been noisy and aggressive and, asked by one if he didn't give up his seat to 'young ladies', he had been forced to stand most of the way in the corridor while a triumphant five-year-old took his place.

The Channel crossing – a new experience for him – had been appalling, with high waves and a heavy swell. He had been violently sick and then furiously angry when the boat anchored outside Dover for over an hour until the sea calmed sufficiently for it to enter the harbour. Thankful to be on dry land at last, he had then fallen foul of a customs officer who had insisted that he should open every one of his bags. As a result he had missed the boat train to London, and had at last caught a train that seemed to stop at pretty well every station.

In London, in spite of exhaustive instructions, he had been faced with the complexities of getting from Victoria to Paddington with a truculent taxi driver who had protested at his baggage. Naturally, after all this, he had arrived in Oxford much later than he had expected.

When at length he did reach Oxford, he saw no sign of Mr Stanton on the platform. He collected his bags and carried them in relays out of the station to the pavement, where he sat on the largest case and waited. 'Welcome to England,' he said to himself bitterly.

Eventually David Stanton had appeared, full of apologies. When Jean-Pierre had not been on the expected train, David had telephoned Helen to tell her of the boy's non-arrival. Together they had decided not to alarm the de Mourvilles, but to wait at least for the next train. Then he had gone into the bar, ordered a drink and, getting into conversation with the barman, hadn't noticed the passing time. He was in the lavatory when Jean-Pierre's train came in.

Eventually he found the morose figure on the pavement outside the station. 'Jean-Pierre de Mourville?' he had asked, making it a question though, as the boy got to his feet and gave a small bow, he had no doubt that he had found his French guest. 'I'm David Stanton. It's good to meet you. I'm glad you got here all right. Terribly sorry I wasn't on the platform.'

'*De rien, monsieur.*' Instinctively Jean-Pierre had spoken in French. It was a reflex action, a form of self-protection against the unfamiliar scene around him.

David looked at him curiously. 'You do speak English? I'm afraid my French is of the schoolboy variety.'

'Yes, I speak English, sir – and German.' He had almost no trace of accent.

'Good!' David picked up two of the bags. 'If I take these, can you manage the rest? The car's just around the corner, not far.' He led the way and Jean-Pierre followed obediently. The drive from Oxford was uneventful and almost totally silent. David had concentrated on the road, and as the car swayed around the bends in the Cotswold lanes Jean-Pierre concentrated on not being sick again. But, arriving at The Elms and standing in the driveway, he could no longer contain himself. He staggered to a flowerbed and vomited over a rosebush. It was not, he though ruefully, an auspicious beginning to his stay with the Stantons.

The next morning when Jean-Pierre awoke, with the sun streaming into the room, it took him a minute to remember where he was. Except that he had been sick practically on the Stantons' doorstep he didn't recall much of the previous evening, and by now the nightmare quality of the journey from France had faded. He felt well, but cold and hungry.

He glanced at his watch. The time was ten o'clock and he wondered what he should do. There were no sounds in the house, but voices and laughter came from the garden below, and he realized that his window was open, which accounted for the chilly temperature. He slid out of bed and went to the window, intending to shut it, but curiosity made him pause.

There were three people in the garden, two girls and a man in his early twenties. He recognized Anthea Stanton. She was a tall girl, an inch or two shorter than himself, quiet and rather shy, with fair curly hair and blue eyes; he hadn't taken in more than that at their brief first meeting, before Mrs Stanton had taken him to his room. He had apologized for his sickness, and told her of the frightful Channel crossing. She had been most sympathetic, and agreed at once when he asked if he could go to bed immediately, saying that she would bring him up a light supper. The other two individuals in the garden meant nothing to him, though from their appearance they were obviously related, probably brother and sister. The voices floated up to him. 'Tell us about your Frog then, Anthea. Karen and I are yearning to meet him, especially Karen. She goes to too many films and is sure he's going to be the answer to a maiden's prayer.'

'If you're talking about Jean-Pierre, Keith, he's extremely nice – and better looking than you are, though he's no film star.' Anthea sounded indignant.

'Are you going to teach him English, or is he going to teach you to speak Frog, Anthea?'

'Karen, he –'

There was a knock at the door of Jean-Pierre's room, and he skidded across the floor and slipped into bed as Helen Stanton came in. She was carrying a small tray.

'Good morning, Jean-Pierre. I popped in earlier, but you were still asleep after your journey. I hope you're feeling better this morning. I've brought you some coffee.' Helen smiled at him and, as he sat up, put the tray on his lap before going across and shutting the window. 'Did they wake you – Anthea and the Graysons?'

'Not really.' To Jean-Pierre's surprise the coffee was strong and good. 'Who are the Graysons?'

'Neighbours and friends. Keith has just taken a law degree, and if there isn't a war he's going into David's legal office in Oxford. Otherwise it'll be the army for him. Karen's a doctor's secretary in Charlbury, our local market town. She was at school with Anthea, but ahead of her. Anthea still has another year to go. Their father's a bank manager, also in Oxford. They are nice young people, Jean-Pierre. You'll like them when you get to know them.'

Jean-Pierre thought this unlikely. He was not fond of people who talked of Frogs. He finished his coffee. 'Thank you,' he said. 'I enjoyed that.'

'There'll be more with breakfast in half an hour. Come down to the kitchen when you're ready.'

Helen picked up the tray and made to leave, but hesitated at the door. She was a kind woman and would have liked to say something encouraging to Jean-Pierre, but the news on the wireless that morning had been bad. War was surely now inevitable. There were no grounds for hope. And she thought how awful Chantal de Mourville must feel with her only son so far away.

Jean-Pierre was also thinking of his mother and wondering if he would ever see her again – or his father, or his home.

Ten days later Britain and France declared war on Germany, and this time few believed it would be over by Christmas.

Part I

1943–1945

ONE

'*Ce n'est pas vrai! Rayez cela de vos tablettes.*' Claude Le Sohiér exclaimed stubbornly. 'I could bet my life Jean-Pierre is not a traitor.'

'That is probably what you are doing, *mon vieux*, and our lives too.' Henri Colet was angry. 'We were all right until they sent this *type* to interfere with us. We are a small *réseau*, but we were causing the Huns a lot of trouble.'

'We're a smaller *réseau* now.' Auguste Maque, who wasn't too intelligent, threw back his head and uttered one of his typical high-pitched laughs.

'And we will be smaller still soon if we go on trusting Jean-Pierre,' said Henri. 'In fact, we'll cease to exist. Oh, I know he's been responsible for bringing us equipment and *matériel* – weapons and explosives – that we badly needed, but some of it was dud – *à la manque* – and look at the cost, the men and women we've lost, the safe houses. This last blow, the farmhouse near Alençon betrayed, and the poor Grandins . . .'

The three men were sitting around the ashes of a fire in a hut in north-west France not far from Vire, an ancient fortified town and the capital of this part of Normandy. Henri Colet was the leader of one of the resistance groups that had sprung up in that part of the country, and indeed across the whole of France, and Claude Le Sohiér was his second-in-command. The year was 1943 and long ago most of Jean-Paul de Mourville's prophesies had come true; Paris had fallen and France had capitulated in 1940, shortly after Britain had managed to evacuate a large part of its army from Dunkerque. By 1942 all of France was occupied by the Germans.

Nevertheless, there were growing grounds for hope. Hitler, thwarted in his desire to invade Britain, had turned on his one-time ally Russia, and the United States, attacked by Japan, had declared war on both Japan and Germany. By now, in 1943, there was even talk of the Allies invading Europe, though this was still some way ahead.

13

In the meantime it had been decided to give as much support as possible to resistance groups, especially in northern France, and organizations such as the Special Operations Executive had been established to co-ordinate these efforts. Unfortunately, though there had been a number of successful operations, there had also been disasters.

The French did not always welcome interference. The *matériel* supplied wasn't always useful – explosives without detonators, wrong ammunition and wireless sets missing essential parts. Sometimes drops were made in the wrong locations, to be seized by the jubilant Germans. There had also been several incidents of personnel with the minimum of parachute training breaking limbs on landing. Yet others, because of inexperience or lack of knowledge of the language and the people, had been captured at once.

There was also the constant danger of betrayal. On too many occasions the Germans appeared to have prior knowledge of a drop, so that not only those who landed were rounded up, but those who had constituted the receiving party were captured, and sometimes tortured to reveal further information. Such an incident had occurred recently to members of Henri's *réseau*, or group, and he blamed Jean-Pierre, whom he resented.

'I know things have gone wrong lately,' Claude said mildly, 'but you have no proof that it was Jean-Pierre's fault.'

'Circumstantial evidence.' Henri was firm. 'That last drop was a disaster for everyone except him. He was the only one who didn't end up in the bag.'

'It was a windy night,' Claude protested. 'He was blown off course and landed in a tree a quarter of a mile away. He rejoined us when he could and he was as upset as we were at what had happened.'

'So he says, but why should we believe him? And that German soldier we took prisoner named him.' Henri was beginning to lose his temper. 'Ask Auguste, he was there.'

Auguste nodded. 'Yes, I heard him. Henri asked him if Jean-Pierre had told them about the farm and he said yes.'

The poor Kraut would probably have said anything if he thought it would save his life, Claude thought, but he had no wish to annoy Henri. He compromised. 'Why should Jean-Pierre want to betray us?' he asked. 'After all, he is a Frenchman.'

'French, yes, but not one of us. *Né coiffé* – born with a silver spoon in his mouth – he was. He once admitted to me that he had been brought up in a château. *Merde!* He's just the sort who would be a secret Nazi sympathizer.'

Claude shrugged. He wasn't prepared to argue further with Henri, who was an ardent communist and suspected anyone with more advantages than he possessed. And there was another reason, Claude knew, why Henri disliked Jean-Pierre; he was jealous of him, afraid that his pretty wife, Babette, was attracted to the younger, better-looking man.

'*Eh bien*, Henri,' Claude said. 'Then what do you propose we do about Jean-Pierre? He told us he would be returning to France very soon with replacements for some of the equipment we lost.'

'First we take great care how we receive him. After that, if all is well, we inspect the stuff he's brought.' Henri hesitated. 'Jean-Pierre said he would probably not be coming alone. He hoped to bring a wireless man and perhaps an explosives technician with him, to replace Gustave and Robert. If he does, we must separate them. Then, when we've got Jean-Pierre by himself, we deal with him. It will be easy.'

'What do you mean – deal with him?' Claude asked.

'Shoot him, and throw his body in a ditch,' Henri said.

'Like you did with that German soldier,' Auguste said, and cackled with laughter.

'No!' Claude said, aghast. But he knew that if Henri was determined nothing would stop him.

Jean-Pierre de Mourville lay with Anthea Stanton among the hay in a barn not far from The Elms. They had been lovers for ten months. Jean-Pierre was now twenty-two, and a lieutenant in the British army. Surprisingly, since joining up and after some intensive training and briefings, he had so far spent more than a third of his time in a France that was under German occupation. Keith Grayson, three years older and a captain, had realized what an asset Jean-Pierre's knowledge of his native country and his ability to speak French and German could be to the intelligence unit in which he worked as an aide to one Brigadier Beaumont. He had pulled strings to have Jean-Pierre recruited, dissuading him from joining up with de Gaulle's Free French forces. And at that moment Jean-Pierre was wishing Keith hadn't bothered.

Anthea stirred in his arms and he held her closer. They had made passionate love and he knew they would make love again before they bicycled back to The Elms, which reluctantly he had begun to think of as home. They had so little time together. His leaves were often short and always erratic, and Anthea could never guarantee that she would be able to get away from what she considered a boring office job in 'Ag and Fish', one of the government departments that had been evacuated from London to the Oxford area. All this meant that the two of them had to make the most of what time they had.

'A penny –' Anthea said. 'What are you thinking, darling?'

'I was wishing –' Jean-Pierre stared out of the barn door at the blue-grey sky. He had been wishing that he didn't have to return to his base and wait for one, two, three – however many – days, until the order came through that at such and such a time and place he would be dropped once more into enemy territory.

His last such mission had been a fiasco. He shivered as he recalled standing at the open door of the aircraft with the night air rushing past him. Subconsciously he had registered that the wind was strong, dangerously so, but there was no going back. The supplies had been thrown out, and his companions, a sergeant and a Belgian he had never met before had already jumped.

He crossed himself and followed them. The jerk of the harness as the static line tightened and his 'chute opened had been reassuring, but the next moment a violent gust had lifted him and blown him way off course. He had struggled to steer with the shroud lines, but in vain, and eventually he had landed in a tree some distance from the dropping zone where he was expected.

He had waited, hoping that Henri or Claude or even the foolish Auguste would come to look for him. He hadn't dared to call out. No one appeared. Then he heard gunfire from the direction of the intended dropping zone and after that it had been the Germans for whom he had waited. But they hadn't shown either, and eventually he managed to extract his knife from an inner pocket, cut the parachute harness and drop to the ground. He had fallen clumsily and hurt his shoulder, and when at length he reached the planned rendezvous point, Henri had not been pleased at the fuss Babette made over what was merely a minor injury.

The next day Henri had told him that the Germans had collected the entire supplies that had been dropped that night, but worse, had taken prisoner not only his companions from the aircraft but also the three members of the *réseau* that had gone to meet them. Later Henri reported that they had all been shot. Then had come the raid on the farm at Alençon, the unofficial headquarters of their group. The farmer, his wife and five other members of his family

16

had been taken away, together with a wireless set and a store of weapons that had been hidden in the cellar.

After that he had been left in no doubt of Henri's distrust and hostility and he expected opposition to what he knew had to be done. He had to reach his back-up radio and arrange for a pick-up as soon as possible. The Lysander could come to any one of four or five small fields; he had to hope they had not been compromised. It would touch down for sixty seconds while he scrambled aboard and then take off again. To his surprise, when he explained this Henri had looked at him strangely, as if postponing a threat, and finally acquiesced, though only, he suspected, because the group needed replacement of *matériel* and trained men so urgently.

In Anthea's arms, Jean-Pierre shivered at his memories.

'Darling, what is it?' Anthea shook him. 'I've asked you twice, but you don't answer, just stare into the distance.'

'Sorry. I was thinking, wishing –' He couldn't tell her how afraid he was, not only of the Germans, but of Henri Colet. She would consider him a coward. 'I was wishing my leave would never come to an end,' he said – it was a half-truth – 'so that I could stay here with you for ever.'

'I wish you could,' she said soberly.

She wanted to ask him if he expected to be dropped in France again soon, but she knew what he would say – that he didn't know and he couldn't tell her. He ought never to have told her about going to France at all, but she was glad he had, though it meant that she worried even more at his sudden and sometimes lengthy absences.

Now, sensing his fear – he was wrong to believe that she would think him a coward because of it; she considered him incredibly brave – she slowly began to make love to him again and he responded. Suddenly he laughed.

'I was just thinking that if we did stay here for ever, for ever for us wouldn't be long. We'd freeze to death when winter came or before that die of hunger – unless of course we developed a taste for hay.'

Anthea laughed because she knew it was what he had intended her to do, but she could just as easily have wept. She didn't want to think of death, least of all Jean-Pierre's. She wanted a future with him, if not for ever, at least for a very long time. But she knew in her heart that this was a dream.

★   ★   ★

It was the last day of Keith Grayson's leave too, and for him it had not been a happy one. Marcia, his wife of almost two years, had done nothing but complain, about the boredom of her life in the country, about the sharpness of his mother's tongue, about the constant crying of their baby and about his meanness with money. He wished he had never married her.

He had been a fool. She had tricked him. She had deliberately allowed herself to become pregnant, not because she was desperately in love with him and wanted to marry him, but because having a baby was her one and only means of getting out of the ATS, which she had unthinkingly joined in 1939 and within months had come to detest. And now here he was, in his mid-twenties, saddled with a wife he didn't want and a baby son of whom, he had to admit, he was rather proud.

'For heaven's sake, Marcia,' he said, 'stop griping and go and get dressed. We're due at the Stantons' supper party in half an hour.'

'The Stantons' supper party! What a thrill.' She laughed contemptuously. 'Or are you hoping to get Anthea in a corner and put your hand up her skirt?'

'Don't be disgusting!'

'Disgusting? You didn't think it was disgusting when you did it to me, did you, sweetie? But of course dear Anthea is different. You must be out of your mind if you don't realize she's having it off with that French boy.'

Keith suddenly lifted his hand, but she outstared him and he let it drop. She would have liked him to hit her, then she would have had a real cause for complaint. He turned away. He wondered if she had a reason for what she had said about Anthea and Jean-Pierre or if she had merely wanted to taunt him. She knew he was in love with Anthea, had even proposed to her once and been refused; his mother had told her. Why, he didn't know, except that she didn't like Marcia. It hadn't made life easier for any of them when the air raids on London had forced his wife to live in the country with his parents, though the Graysons both adored their grandson.

'Keith, you'd better listen to what I'm going to say, because I mean it. I'm fed up with this place. I must have a change. I'm going to London for a few days. I know I can't stay at your club, so I'll stay with Karen. She'll be happy to have me. Funny that I should get on so well with your sister, isn't it?'

'What about the baby? You can't take him.'

'No. He'd cramp my style. Your mother can look after him.'

'She's enough to do. With no help in the house and –'

'It'll only be for three or four days, and there's no point in arguing, Keith. I've made up my mind. You'd better break the news to Ma.'

'Marcia, it's not safe. Karen and I work there so we have no choice, but it's not fair on Peregrine that you risk your life gratuitously.'

'Peregrine! He's all you care about, isn't he? Not me! Well, I don't give a damn, Keith. I'm going off and if I don't come back you can get Peregrine a nanny. I deserve a rest from him – and your mother.'

Marcia flounced from the sitting-room, leaving her husband to stare glumly out of the window at the garden his father kept so tidy. It was by no means the first row he and Marcia had had in the last few days, but maybe it wasn't altogether her fault. He supposed it was dull for her, living in the country with no friends of her own and only seeing him at intervals. No wonder she was bored. But she could have taken a part-time job in Charlbury, had she tried, and she could have done a great deal more than she did to help his mother in the house. Perhaps a few days in London would be a good idea.

Oberst Becker sat in his office in the barracks near St-Lô, not far from Vire, which the Germans had taken over from the French. Karl Becker was a man in his fifties, a regular soldier and ambitious, but, having been seriously wounded during the siege of Stalingrad the previous year, he had been assigned to the task of rooting out the pockets of resistance groups in this district, and ensuring that the German hold on this part of the country would remain strong in the event of an Allied invasion. He didn't like his present assignment – he hated this secret world of spies and informants, and much preferred straightforward soldiering – but whatever he was ordered to do he tried to do well and with a fair degree of humanity.

A few weeks ago his main local informant – the baker, Armand Lejeune, whose son was a prisoner in Germany, and who laboured under the delusion that co-operation with the Oberst could buy more humane treatment for him – had helped him to bring off a real coup. He and his men had captured two of three British spies – the third had not yet been found – and all the *matériel* from a drop, as well as the wretched Frenchmen who had been forming the reception party. Under pressure, they had all produced some very useful information. In addition, the aircraft had been badly damaged by his men's gunfire and had probably failed to reach England.

Becker was well satisfied with that night's work, and was now wondering when the next message from Lejeune would reach him; often the messages would arrive, schoolboy fashion, tucked in an aluminium tube baked into the middle of a cake.

TWO

Marcia Grayson stepped out of the shower and, wrapping a large towel around her, went into the guest-room of her sister-in-law's Maida Vale flat where she was staying. She let the towel drop to the carpet and admired herself in the long mirror. She had a beautiful body, long legs, flat stomach – in spite of producing Peregrine – lovely firm breasts. It was a pity, she thought, that Keith no longer admired them. But if he didn't, others would. She stretched luxuriously. She had been three days in London and thoroughly enjoyed every minute of them.

Slipping on a robe, Marcia went into the kitchen. It was half past eleven, too late for breakfast, but she wanted some coffee. Karen had left hours ago for the Ministry of Information where she worked, but Marcia knew where the coffee was kept – real coffee, a present from a friend in Canada, not the ersatz stuff that was available in England. She made herself a pot and sat at the kitchen table drinking it, and thinking about the previous evening.

She had had a wonderful time – supper at the Savoy, dancing at some night-club until after midnight, then back to the mews house that Chuck Carmichael shared with a friend, who luckily was away, more champagne and bed.

Chuck was an American major attached to the War Office with undefined liaison duties. Bill Overton, Karen's boyfriend, had brought him along to make up a four for a small dinner the night she had arrived in London. The attraction had been mutual and they had arranged this date for two days later. He had proved to be a more than competent lover, and he hadn't returned her to the Maida Vale flat till seven o'clock that morning. But she didn't feel in the least tired. She was looking forward to lunch with Chuck.

Having drunk her coffee, Marcia returned to her bedroom and looked through her clothes. She had brought only one suit with her, and there was a stain on the skirt. She wondered if she might borrow something. Karen, she thought enviously, with money from her job and not dependent on a mean husband like Keith, had plenty of clothes in spite of the rationing. Karen had told her she often bought clothes coupons on the black market.

She went into her sister-in-law's bedroom and started to examine her wardrobe. There were half a dozen suits, any one of which she would have liked to own. She chose the one that looked a slightly smaller size – Karen was a little bigger than she was – and tried it on. It was a beautiful mohair suit in her favourite colour of dark green with a silk lining and, though it wasn't a perfect fit, she decided to wear it. She found a hat that was obviously intended to complement it, and was considering the general effect in the mirror when she heard the growl of an approaching V-1 bomb.

These small pulse-jet unmanned aircraft were Hitler's latest form of attack on London. Known as doodlebugs, and loaded with explosives, they chugged along until their engines cut out, when they dived indiscriminately, causing a fair number of casualties and doing a certain amount of damage. But to Londoners who had endured the great bombing raids of earlier years these new weapons had little more than nuisance value – unless they or those dear to them happened to be among the victims.

Marcia heard the noise of the engine grow louder, but paid it no attention. She expected it to pass overhead like the one or two others she had heard during her visit to London. Even when the noise ceased she was not alarmed. It simply didn't occur to her to be afraid.

So it was almost without warning that suddenly the world erupted around her. Ceiling, walls, floor all collapsed amid a huge roaring tumult, and she was falling, falling. She opened her mouth and screamed.

Everything went black. But quite soon, as the dust was still subsiding, she regained consciousness, and now, though she felt no pain, she was terrified. Her head and shoulders seemed to be hanging over empty space, but she couldn't move, she daren't move. Her legs were pinned and there was a heavy weight lying across her chest. Tears coursed down her cheeks. She was sure she was going to die, and her thoughts turned, not to her husband, or her young son, or her parents, but to Major Chuck Carmichael waiting for her at The Ivy where he had intended to give her lunch.

Keith Grayson sat across the desk from his director, Brigadier Beaumont. He hadn't had any contact with his wife since she had come to London at the beginning of the week, though Karen had phoned him to say that Marcia intended to stay over the next week-end, that Bill Overton was arranging a party for her on Saturday, and would Keith like to join them. Keith, who didn't understand how his sister could be attracted to Bill, a regular civil servant ten years older than she was, had refused on grounds of work. He was sure it would be a dull party, and anyway Marcia would not be pleased to see him.

'That last drop was a complete disaster, except that de Mourville wasn't captured – and that was only due to chance,' said Beaumont, who was extremely worried though he was trying not to show it; he hated losing men. 'We can't go on like this, Keith. We'll be running out of *matériel*, quite apart from suitable personnel to send over there. Now we've had a chance to debrief de Mourville, it looks very much as if Henri Colet's group has got a bad apple in it.

'Jean-Pierre says it was quite clear that the Germans were waiting for them with open arms; they knew the location of the DZ, the timing of the operation and all the details. We lost men and *matériel*, and later the Germans raided the farmhouse, which was assumed to be ultra-safe, and arrested the family. God knows what's happened to them,' he added as an afterthought.

'I know, sir, but what do you suggest? Even if we knew the traitor it would be difficult to accuse him, though I suppose it might be possible to arrange an accident for him. Depending on who it was, Henri might even arrange it himself. In the meantime, do you want to cancel the next drop?'

'We can't do that. We can't afford to. We need to strengthen the position around St-Lô, not abandon it,' said the brigadier. 'I've been giving the situation a great deal of thought. It's quite clear we've got to communicate with Henri privately, personally and in secret, without using the radio, so that there's no chance of any interception. And the only way I can see to do this is to send in Jean-Pierre – it's got to be Jean-Pierre, because Henri knows him – in advance of the next drop, to contact Henri and make sure that knowledge of the operation is confined to the smallest possible number of people – people whom Henri knows he can trust. Jean-Pierre might also ferret around and see if he can dig out anything for himself.' The brigadier paused. Then, 'What do you think about Jean-Pierre, Keith? He's had a tough time lately, and I was intending to give him a good rest. But he's pretty well indispensable for this mission. Do you think he's up to it? After all, you know him better than most of us.'

Keith didn't hesitate. A good rest? Bitterly he remembered what

Marcia had said about Anthea and Jean-Pierre; he saw no reason why he should give them an unexpected present of more time together. 'Yes, sir. I believe Jean-Pierre has to go,' he said. 'He's in quite good form really, he knows the ground and, as you say, it would be a mistake to send a stranger at this juncture.'

'Yes. I'm afraid so.' Beaumont wondered if he had been wrong to ask for Grayson's opinion, which was probably not totally objective; he was aware of the undercurrent of ill-feeling between Keith and Jean-Pierre, but had ascribed it to Grayson's veiled dislike of the French as inefficient allies. Of course, it was a dreadful risk. Any drop was a risk. But a dead drop all alone, with no reception –

Beaumont put his head in his hands and stared down at his desk. This was what he hated about his job – sending men and women, some of them very young and none of them professional soldiers, into enemy territory where, if they were caught, they were likely to be tortured and executed. It was a a dirty job, he thought; he much preferred leading his men into battle, and sharing their risks.

He sighed and raised his head. The decision was made. 'Right. We'll let him go, then. I'll brief him myself as soon as you've made the arrangements. We can use the same DZ as last time, because that's the last thing the enemy would expect us to do. The moon will be right if we act quickly.'

'When were you thinking, sir?'

'Early in the week for the solo drop, and two or three days after for the main event. And, even then, at the last moment Jean-Pierre will advance the date he first gives Henri by twenty-four hours, so that if –'

There was an indecisive knock at the door and Beaumont's new secretary, a junior ATS officer, came in. 'I'm sorry, sir, but –'

'What is it?' the brigadier asked irritably. 'I told you we weren't to be interrupted.'

'I know, sir, but –' The girl looked at Keith in desperation. 'There's a phone call for the captain from Miss Karen Grayson.'

Keith frowned. What on earth? Karen wasn't in the habit of phoning him at the office unless it was important. Nevertheless, he said, 'Tell her I'm in conference and I'll call her later.'

'I did do that, sir, but – I'm sorry. I think you had better take her call now.'

Beaumont and Keith exchanged glances, amused at the girl's persistence, and Beaumont said, 'Very well. Put it through here.' The girl, confident that in the circumstances she had done the right thing, withdrew thankfully. A minute later Keith was on the line to Karen.

'Keep it short, Karen,' he said. 'I'm with my brigadier.'

Karen, who had been fond of Marcia and was stunned by what had happened, kept it short to the point of brutality. Keith's immediate reaction was disbelief, followed by intense anger at all the demands that were about to be put on him. His first task would be to go to the hospital where Marcia had been pronounced dead on arrival and deal with the formalities there. Then there would be Marcia's parents to be informed, and his, and the funeral to organize, and after that – What was more, all this would have to be done when he had other more important things on his mind, like the arrangements for the double drop into France, which he suspected from the brigadier's doubts might be Jean-Pierre's last, at least for some while. And there must be no mistakes this time, necessitating his being lifted out at once.

'Bad news?' Beaumont asked tentatively as Keith stared straight in front of him and remained silent. He anger had subsided and he was beginning to think clearly.

'My wife has been killed, sir.' He gave Beaumont a stumbling explanation.

The brigadier was instantly sympathetic. 'My dear chap. I *am* sorry, terribly sorry. What can I say? You'll want compassionate leave, of course.'

'No!' Seeing that the bald negative had startled Beaumont, Keith hurriedly corrected his error. 'No, sir, thank you. I – I would rather carry on. I'll get plenty of support from my family and it will be easier that way, I hope. There will be a lot to do, but I'll just take the odd hour off when necessary, if that's all right with you.'

'Of course,' Beaumont agreed and thought, Poor devil! He's suffering from shock. This has been a bitter blow for him.

The brigadier was wrong and, had he been able to read Keith Grayson's mind, he would have been surprised.

'No, I'm sorry, but I'm busy on Wednesday night,' Anthea said firmly. It was a lie but she didn't care. 'It's quite impossible. Anyway, I thought Karen was coming home early this week and staying on for Marcia's funeral.'

'Yes, she is,' Margaret Grayson agreed. 'But she's bringing Bill – her fiancé – with her. The least we can do is offer him some hospitality, and the chance of a few quiet days in the country, considering that Karen's gone to live with him and his mother in Pinner. She'd have had nowhere to stay in London after she lost her flat if it hadn't been for Mrs Overton's kindness.'

'Well, why can't Karen and Bill babysit for Peregrine together? I'm sure they can be trusted to behave,' Anthea added mischievously.

'Really, Anthea! What a thing to say!' Margaret was annoyed. 'You're becoming a selfish girl. You think only of yourself. Have you any idea what Karen has been through? Apart from the destruction of her flat, she's lost all her nice clothes and some of her most treasured jewellery and possessions and –'

Anthea, thankful that she was on the phone so that Margaret couldn't see her expression, stopped listening. She had heard the litany before, and she refused to be unduly sorry for Karen, who would doubtless acquire coupons to replace all her nice clothes. In her opinion, Karen led an enviable life compared with her own. Most of all she envied Karen the fact that her Bill was in a safe reserved occupation, and not expected to parachute at any moment into enemy-occupied France.

'– the shock of poor dear Marcia's death,' Margaret was continuing. 'She and Karen were close friends. You can't begrudge her and Bill an evening out together without having to worry about bombs and rockets.'

Anthea realized she had missed something. 'An evening out?'

'Yes. We've saved up enough petrol so that they can drive over to Burford for dinner, dropping us off on the way at our bridge evening and picking us up later. It's all arranged, a treat for everyone. Marcia wouldn't mind. She wouldn't want us to mourn for her. She was such a generous person. Of course, now I don't know how we can arrange it –'

'I'm sure you can get a babysitter,' Anthea said, and thought that Margaret's opinion of her daughter-in-law had changed since Marcia's death. 'What about old Mrs Gow? She used to be a nurse.'

'I don't like leaving Peregrine with a stranger.'

Anthea refrained from pointing out that Mrs Gow was scarcely a stranger, as the old woman had started coming in to help Margaret with the housework three times a week. 'Well, I'm sorry, but I can't make Wednesday,' she said.

'I trust you'll be able to "make" next Friday?' Margaret replied sharply.

'Yes, of course.' Friday was the day of Marcia's funeral and, though it meant giving up one of her precious leave days, Anthea had accepted that it was her duty to go.

'It will be a very private funeral. It's so difficult in wartime for people to travel, but Marcia's parents are coming from Yorkshire, and there'll be a few other relations and friends,' Margaret went on. 'We did ask Keith if he'd like to bring Jean-Pierre, but he said it wouldn't be possible. Jean-Pierre's going on a course in the middle of the week. He's always going on courses, that young man. It's a pity –'

'What – what did you say?' Anthea interrupted. 'Jean-Pierre's going on another course in the middle of the week?'

'Yes, that's right. It's a pity the authorities can't think of anything more useful to do with him.'

Margaret Grayson continued speaking for several minutes until she heard Peregrine crying, and ended the conversation. Anthea automatically said goodbye. Again, she hadn't been paying any attention. She had no idea what Margaret had been talking about. Her thoughts were with Jean-Pierre going on another 'course' – another mission probably deep into occupied France, weeks, months perhaps, spent in perpetual danger. She had known this was likely – he hadn't pretended otherwise – but now it was reality, and she was sick with fear.

THREE

Jean-Pierre de Mourville lay on his back in an army cot and contemplated the dirty ceiling of the small room which for the time being was officially his. The room, indeed the whole house which was situated within the perimeter of the airfield from which the Lysander would take off that night, was comfortable without being luxurious. But its biggest attraction was that it represented safety and security, probably the last he would know for some time to come.

He thought about the briefing he had received earlier that morning from Brigadier Beaumont. The brigadier had been kind, almost apologetic, implying that if any other suitable officer had been available he would not have asked Jean-Pierre to undertake the mission. But harsh reality remained. There was no one else. Jean-Pierre was uniquely qualified. Though the brigadier was wording his request so tactfully, Jean-Pierre knew full well he was issuing an order.

Tonight, the weather being right, he would make a solo drop, something he had never done before. The dangers of such drops were apparent. With no reception party, any simple injury sustained on landing could spell disaster.

Then, assuming he was in one piece and mobile, and had not been greeted by an enemy, he would have to seek out Henri, which should not be too difficult, persuade him to arrange in the utmost secrecy for the reception of the next drop by the minimum number of the most reliable members of his group, and suddenly at the last moment bring the time forward twenty-four hours. Would Henri believe him? Would Henri trust him? He had considered putting this point to the brigadier, but it might have seemed that he was making an excuse for aborting the planned operation, and pride prevented him. He couldn't explain that Henri resented him because of his apparent authority and because of Babette – as if he had any designs on the stupid little woman.

And what would happen if, in spite of all precautions, they were betrayed again? Would Henri blame him? Jean-Pierre closed his eyes tightly. He didn't believe that last disaster had been the result of accident, a careless word at a bar, a suspicious wife gossiping to a neighbour, someone intercepting a radio message. He was sure the leak had been deliberate, which meant there was an increased likelihood it would be repeated, whatever care was taken. But he had received his orders, and he would do his utmost to carry them out. Meanwhile it was best, he knew, not to think about the night's drop and its possible aftermath.

His thoughts turned to his parents, as they so often did. He hadn't heard of them for years. All his attempts to get in touch with them had failed, and he had no idea if they were alive or dead, but he prayed for them daily. An only child, and in a sense isolated by their affection, he had always been very close to them, perhaps too close. It had made for a somewhat solitary existence, and made their loss and the presumed loss of his home the more difficult to bear, so that he hadn't adapted easily to a very different way of life in England, in spite of the Stantons' kindness and their efforts to make him welcome – and in spite of Anthea. But not everyone had been kind. He had suffered from Margaret Grayson's sharp tongue, and had never really made friends of Keith or Karen, who often seemed to go out of their way to emphasize the fact that he was a foreigner, a despised Frenchman, not 'one of them'. Even his occasional appearance in a British army lieutenant's uniform with non-regimental General Service badges had not improved matters.

As for Marcia, he had had little contact with her and felt no particular sorrow about her death. He had written formal notes of condolence to Keith and the Graysons, and considered his duty done. He was thankful he wouldn't be going to the funeral, except that it would have meant a chance to see Anthea and talk to her, however briefly.

He smiled to himself as he thought of Anthea. He loved her dearly and passionately, and he knew she felt the same for him. They had agreed they would marry as soon as the war was over, regardless of what might have happened in France, regardless of whether he had a job, regardless of any possible opposition from either family, who might want them to wait. In the meantime, because of their unusual circumstances, they had decided to keep their love a secret and for this reason they never exchanged letters and rarely telephoned. But neither the periods of enforced separation nor the unpredictability of long silences made any difference to their feelings. Indeed, the situation only seemed to increase their mutual attachment for, however much they daydreamed about the future, they knew that their chances of fulfilling these dreams were not high.

A gong sounded and Jean-Pierre pushed himself off the bed and went to wash his hands before lunch. One thing to be said for this place, he thought ruefully, was that the cook had never heard of food rationing, and as this would probably be his last square meal for some while – he wouldn't be able to eat much before the drop – he had better make the most of it. God alone knew where he would be at this time tomorrow.

Not so far away, it was Anthea's lunch hour too. About the same time as Jean-Pierre was going downstairs to his meal, she had come out of the Oxford college which the Ministry of Agriculture and Fisheries had taken over for the duration of the war, and walked up St Giles'. She could have had a substantial, if uninteresting, meal at the cafeteria in the town which was available to temporary civil servants, but she wasn't hungry. She took a precious chocolate bar from her pocket and ate it slowly as she walked. It was a fine day and she didn't hurry. She was thinking of Jean-Pierre, which was not unusual, but since Margaret Grayson had told her he was 'going on a course' he had been constantly on her mind, and she was plagued by unanswerable questions. Was he still in England? Had he landed in France? Was he safe? When would he be coming back? She didn't realize how anxious and insecure she had become until the previous evening when her father, normally a mild man, had rebuked her sharply for being so irritable.

The rebuke had stung and was in part the reason for her present destination, St Aloysius Church, where she hoped to find she wasn't sure what – a few moments of peace, of consolation, perhaps, of feeling closer, if not to God, at least to Jean-Pierre's God. But it was with hesitation that she turned into the entrance. Except on holiday in Europe she had never been in a Roman Catholic Church and then she had been merely sightseeing. The Stantons were not a church-going family and, in spite of Helen's convent schooling, considered Catholicism as unEnglish.

Nevertheless, Helen always made sure that when Jean-Pierre was with them he was able to go to Mass, and Anthea had been impressed, not only by his faithfulness in cycling – even, on one occasion after a heavy snowfall, walking – the miles into Charlbury, so as not to miss Mass, but also by the casual devotion with which he treated his religion.

30

She pushed open the door and went into the church, which smelt of stale incense. She had expected it to be empty, but a priest was busily tidying the altar, a young woman was lighting candles in front of a statue of the Virgin Mary, and two or three people were kneeling in various places, presumably praying. Anthea sat in a pew towards the back of the church and looked about her, at the many statues, the Stations of the Cross around the walls, the red light hanging over the altar. It all seemed strange and foreign to her.

After a while she tried to pray, but found it impossible. She buried her face in her arms and wept. Suddenly she was conscious of someone kneeling beside her and she sat up, startled. It was the young woman whom she had seen lighting candles.

'Hello!' The woman smiled and the smile transformed her rather ugly face; she had short black hair, brown eyes and a wide, humorous mouth. 'I thought you'd come in for a rest, but then I saw it was more serious,' she said. 'Incidentally, my name's Meriel Derwent. I'm twenty-five, unmarried, and at present I work at the Ashmolean Museum.'

Anthea found herself responding to the smile, though she was somewhat overwhelmed by the flood of information she had just received. 'Hello,' she said. 'I'm – I'm Anthea Stanton.' She didn't volunteer any further details.

'I've not seen you here before,' Meriel Derwent continued. 'You're not a Catholic, are you?'

'No, I'm not, but – how did you know?'

'You were obviously not at home. You didn't genuflect. You didn't cross yourself. To be perfectly honest you looked a bit scared until your unhappiness overcame you, and you forgot you were in church.'

'I see,' said Anthea, thinking how much in common this woman would have with Jean-Pierre.

'I live quite near,' Meriel Derwent said. 'I've a small house in Ship Street. Why don't you come back and have a scratch lunch with me – home-made soup and Spam sandwiches? Then if you want to tell me about it, you can.'

'Are you sure?' Anthea had suddenly realized that in spite of her chocolate bar she was now feeling hungry.

'Of course. Otherwise I wouldn't have asked you.' Meriel Derwent laughed. 'Come along!'

Anthea obediently followed the older woman from the church, copying her when she crossed herself with holy water from the stoup. Anthea's spirits had risen. She felt greatly cheered. But if anyone had told her that this was to be the beginning of a lasting friendship between herself and Meriel Derwent and that it would have a considerable influence on her life, she wouldn't have believed it. All it meant to her at that moment was that she hoped she had found someone to whom she could talk without restraint about Jean-Pierre and her love for him.

'Things are going our way at last,' the sergeant said. 'Our chaps have taken Sicily and are streaming up Italy. Musso must be shaking in his shoes. I bet the Eyeties will surrender before long. They've not got the stomach for a fight any more than the French –' He stopped abruptly. 'Oh Gawd! Sorry, sir. I didn't mean – Nothing personal.'

'Not to worry.'

Because of the noise inside the fuselage of the Lysander it was difficult to hear what was being said, and Jean-Pierre hadn't really been listening. He had been wishing the sergeant would shut up and leave him to his thoughts. But he had caught the gist of the remarks and, while he had to admit there was some truth in them – the French had not put up much of a fight in defence of their country – he couldn't help but resent them, especially as he knew they represented a view commonly accepted in Britain. He had once heard Keith say, 'God knows why we always have to fight for the French. We've far more in common with the Germans, Hitler apart. They're our natural allies.' And, like many others, he had wondered how the British would have behaved themselves in 1940 if the RAF and the English Channel hadn't saved them from an immediate invasion.

'You know, sir, I wouldn't want your job for all the tea in China. It must take a lot of guts to do what you do.'

The sergeant, a man of forty with three sons too young to fight, was trying to make amends for what he realized had been an offensive remark, though he hadn't intended it as such. He was a little hurt when he got no response and peered anxiously in the murky light of the blacked-out aircraft at the boy – he thought of the Frenchman as a boy – sitting opposite him.

'You okay, sir?' he asked tentatively.

'Fine, sergeant. Fine, thank you,' Jean-Pierre said. 'I'm just hoping I won't land in a tree like last time.'

'No, no! I'm sure you won't. Lightning never strikes twice, they

32

say.' The sergeant, who was fond of clichés, had remembered that the Frenchman was not only in his charge until the moment he tapped him on the shoulder and shouted 'Go!', but that it was his responsibility to keep him happy until then. 'You'll have no trouble, sir. The weather's perfect. Scarcely any wind tonight, and not too much moon. It should be a piece of cake.'

He wanted to say something more, something really encouraging, but couldn't think what and, to Jean-Pierre's relief, he fell silent until eventually a warning light went on. They were only a few kilometres from the dropping zone. Thankful that the waiting was nearly over, both men stood up, and the sergeant checked Jean-Pierre's harness and clipped the static line hanging from the parachute to the wire running down the middle of the aircraft. He gave it a strong tug to assure himself that it was secure.

A further warning light went on, and the men jostled to the open space where the door of the aircraft should have been.

'All set, sir?' the sergeant said.

'All set, sergeant.'

'Good luck then, sir.' The light went out, the shoulder was tapped, the word 'Go!' shouted and the sergeant watched until the parachute canopy had opened and the static line had parted. Then, as he felt the Lysander turn away, he surprised himself by adding, 'God bless.'

Jean-Pierre had already forgotten the sergeant. He concentrated on making a good landing. The field coming up towards him was likely to be rough and it would be easy to turn an ankle. But there was no wind, he landed without trouble and, freeing himself from the parachute and its harness, bundled them under his arm and ran for the shelter of the trees. Here he paused and listened, but there were no untoward sounds. Nevertheless, he waited until his fast breathing steadied and his heart stopped thumping, thankful that he had arrived safely, the first part of his mission accomplished without mishap. Next he had to bury the parachute, much as he would have liked to keep the canopy for warmth. Then he must find somewhere to lie up for what remained of the night; he knew that a dusk to dawn curfew had been imposed in the district, and anyone found outside during that period was liable to instant arrest. Neither task presented any problem. By now he was familiar with the countryside around Vire and, having stuffed his parachute into a convenient foxhole, he soon located an opening in a thick hedge, into the middle of which he was able to worm his way.

With the help of a pencil torch he inspected his temporary home. It was not the most salubrious of places. Apart from the smell, a couple of used condoms and what looked like the remnants of a dirty pair of knickers confirmed that he was not the first to make use of it. But he didn't care. It was dry, and it afforded shelter from wind and rain that might come with dawn. It was also safe. No lovers were likely to appear at that time; either they had been and gone or they would still be there, waiting like him for the curfew's end.

As for the smell, if it clung to his clothes, it would help to verify his cover – a labourer, according to the papers he carried. With the same intention, though he had bathed before setting out, he hadn't shaved and had purposely dirtied his nails. Now he rubbed his hand over his lower face. The itch of a potential beard was what he hated most of the physical discomforts he was required to endure during these drops into France, and he hadn't got used to it. At least, he thought, it took his mind off the constant fear that gripped his stomach.

Restlessly he shifted his position in an attempt to get more comfortable, and shut his eyes. It was impossible to sleep, but he dozed and the hours passed until at last it was time to crawl out of his hiding-place and set off to walk to Vire and Henri Colet. He would have given a lot to know what kind of reception he would get, and how much he ought to trust Henri.

FOUR

'*Vendredi*?' said Henri suspiciously. 'Are you sure?'

Jean-Pierre shrugged. 'That was the message I was told to give you. Midnight, Friday. The same DZ as before. Replacements for the two who were caught landing last time and for the *matériel* that's been lost recently.'

'*Vendredi*,' Henri repeated as if there were something strange about the day.

'Lucky it's not the thirteenth,' Auguste cackled.

Jean-Pierre looked at him in irritation. The three were sitting in a small room behind the bar-café in Vire that Henri and his wife owned. Babette was serving the early morning customers, while the men drank black market coffee with the usual *marc*, and talked. Henri, surprised at the unexpected reappearance of Jean-Pierre, had ignored his broad hints that their conversation should be private and made no effort to get rid of Auguste.

'After what happened to the last drop, when obviously we were betrayed,' Jean-Pierre said coldly, 'London insists that only the minimum number of your most trusted people should be told – the absolute minimum – and that you should stress the importance of secrecy to those who do have to know. There must be no careless talk in advance.'

Auguste shuffled his feet. 'It wasn't me,' he said, as if Jean-Pierre had accused him. 'I know how to keep my mouth shut.'

'Sure you do, *mon vieux*.' Henri patted him on the shoulder. 'So do we all. It's London that's careless, with their wireless signals, and their supposedly coded personal messages broadcast by the BBC.' He glared resentfully at Jean-Pierre. '*Merde*! They don't care how many French peasants the Krauts kill, do they? We're expendable. Are *you* going to meet the drop, Jean-Pierre, or will you have an important engagement elsewhere?'

Jean-Pierre ignored the sarcasm. 'I shall be there, Henri.' And I shall be watching my back, he added to himself. 'How many others

35

will be needed, do you think, apart from you and – I assume – Auguste?'

'Two more, I'd say, if we're to keep it to as few as possible,' Henri said after a moment's reflection. 'But will that be enough to deal with all the equipment, ammunition and explosives that we're due?' He looked accusingly at Jean-Pierre. 'We'll need Claude's van to move it, if it's really a full replacement for all we've lost, including the stuff at the farm.'

'I doubt if it will be as much as that, Henri,' Jean-Pierre said carefully, knowing that he mustn't get across the man. 'But I agree we need the van. You can't carry much on bicycles and the less time we're on the road during curfew, the less the danger.'

Henri nodded. 'Then there's the problem of what to do with these two English, where they're to stay since we've lost so many safe places recently. What do you advise, Jean-Pierre?'

'Well, their French is very limited –'

Henri snorted. 'Naturally. What could you expect? But I suppose that if they know their jobs we should be grateful, though it's we who have to baby them and we who are put at risk because of their incompetence, not the people sitting on their fat arses in London.'

Jean-Pierre remained silent. He knew there was some truth in what Henri said, but it wasn't easy to find suitable personnel, men or women, with particular skills, willing to be dropped into enemy-occupied territory where the penalty for capture was almost certain death. As far as the Germans were concerned they would be treated as spies; the Geneva Convention didn't apply to them. What was more, the rewards for their efforts were meagre, and mostly they led lonely, fear-ridden lives. It was asking a lot that they should also be expected to speak fluent French.

'*Eh bien*,' Henri said at last. 'We had better get down to business.'

For the next hour, while Henri refilled their glasses from the bottle on the table and Auguste fetched fresh coffee, they discussed what was to be done. On the surface this was in no way unusual, but Jean-Pierre sensed that Henri was very tense, and that there were undercurrents in their conversation. He told himself he was imagining this, that it was his own nerves playing up, or that perhaps Henri had had a row with Babette and was still upset by it. But, as they continued, he guessed that these suppositions were wrong. There was something strange about Henri's attitude to this drop.

Normally Henri would automatically have taken over the operation, made the decisions about who would meet the plane, where

36

the newcomers would stay and where the *matériel* should be cached; and he would have resented any sign of interference on Jean-Pierre's part. But today, in spite of a certain amount of aggressiveness towards London, he seemed content to let Jean-Pierre, if not make the decisions, at least have a major say in them.

Jean-Pierre found this uncharacteristic behaviour disconcerting. The only explanation he could think of was that Henri was expecting another disaster and wanted to ensure that, should it occur, Jean-Pierre would bear the blame for it – and possibly pay the penalty for deceiving the group. On the other hand, if all went well, Henri could always claim the credit later. It was not a good situation. It worried Jean-Pierre and he thought it boded ill for Henri's reception of the news that the drop was to be twenty-four hours earlier than he had just been told.

Jean-Pierre's doubts were realized. Henri was furious, and disbelieving. He lost his temper and accused Jean-Pierre of purposely deceiving him for some obscure reason of his own, of not being dependable, of always thinking of his own skin, of being a secret Fascist. He said he refused to co-operate; Jean-Pierre could take care of the drop, if there was to be a drop – which personally he doubted.

He shouted so loudly and violently that Babette came running into the back room of the café where Henri was conferring with Claude and Jean-Pierre. '*Tais-toi!*' she said, shaking him by the arm. '*Tais-toi*, Henri! Do you want the whole town to know what you're planning, what you're up to?' She gave Jean-Pierre a seductive smile, which wasn't lost on her husband.

Surprisingly this intervention didn't incite Henri to further anger. Instead it produced a great calm. Henri nodded, seemingly in acceptance of the reproof when Babette wagged a warning finger at him, and continued as if there had been no row and he had made no accusations against Jean-Pierre.

'This change means we need some quick action,' he said. 'Babette, send someone to fetch Auguste, will you? He can be useful. Jean-Pierre, you go and tell Bernard his guests will be arriving tonight and not tomorrow. Assist him if he needs help to prepare for them.'

'Right.'

Jean-Pierre wished he could have refused. Bernard was a tanner and cobbler who lived at the other end of the town and was one of

Henri's cousins. It would take a while to walk there and Henri hadn't offered the loan of a bicycle. Moreover, Jean-Pierre expected that as soon as he had left the café, Henri would be on the phone to Bernard telling him to occupy Jean-Pierre and keep him out of the way for as long as possible.

'And I must go and clear out my van,' Claude said. 'It's full of stuff.'

Henri held up a restraining hand to Claude and looked meaningfully at Jean-Pierre, waiting for him to leave. It confirmed his suspicions that Henri was planning something that promised him no good. He couldn't imagine that Henri would endanger the success of the drop and Claude, who liked him, would probably prevent any obvious physical violence, but Henri was capable of setting a trap. It was an added complication that he could have done without, Jean-Pierre thought.

If the sudden advance in the time of the drop had infuriated Henri, the unexpected message giving warning of a drop that very night had equally infuriated Oberst Becker, who had known nothing of the previous arrangement. It was the short notice to which he objected, and which he distrusted, in addition to the fact that the dropping zone was said to be unchanged. He thought of ordering the baker to be brought to the barracks and demanding an explanation from him, but at once changed his mind. Such an action would probably compromise the man whose information had often proved extremely helpful and reliable in the past. Nevertheless, though he might excuse it as an exercise, he didn't want to send his men out on a wild goose chase, if only because it would make them less keen in any future operation. The first thing he must do was check.

He decided to telephone the bakery; he had the number, for use only in case of an emergency, but disliked using it for the line was far from secure. However, he must make sure, and he didn't believe there would be any great danger if he and Armand Lejeune were careful. He dialled and waited.

'*Lejeune? J'ai reçu votre gâteau ce matin.*'

He heard the quick intake of breath as Lejeune guessed who his caller was, and he continued in his heavily accented French to complain that the cake was late. This was greeted by such a burst of French that he had to protest and tell the baker to speak slowly – and carefully.

38

Lejeune started again. Repeating his apologies, he explained that he had baked the cake as soon as he had received the ingredients, and he assured Becker that the ingredients were of the best. The Oberst, he said, should enjoy it. Becker replied that he hoped so – for everyone's sake. It was half a threat, but the German had made up his mind that he would act on the information and with luck bring off another coup.

The dropping zone was a level space of rough grass about five kilometres north of the town. It was surrounded by mature trees, in thick belts on three sides, and a less dense strip on the fourth, beside which ran a country lane, almost a track, which provided means of access.

The group were in Claude's van hidden in the trees between the lane and the dropping zone. They had driven there before the curfew commenced at nine o'clock and faced a three-hour wait, assuming that the aircraft was on time. Waiting like this was never easy. There was always tension as they went to meet a drop or undertake some other operation, but tonight the atmosphere seemed to Jean-Pierre more distraught than usual.

The men took it in turns to leave the van in order to stretch their legs and urinate. There were five of them: Jean-Pierre, Henri, Claude, Auguste and a short ferret-faced man whom Jean-Pierre had never met before and who was introduced as Gustave. It was he who had been driving the van, not Claude, and for some reason this worried Jean-Pierre.

The presence of a single bicycle also worried him. Henri had explained that Auguste would cycle home; there wouldn't be room in the van for them all, with two newcomers and a load of *matériel*. But to Jean-Pierre this had sounded a specious excuse, unless Henri believed they were about to receive an enormous load. And he couldn't rid himself of the suspicion that Henri had set some kind of trap, into which he hoped Jean-Pierre would fall.

This belief was strengthened when midnight approached and they set about their preparations. They pushed their way through the trees and reached the dropping zone. As Jean-Pierre went to the far end to set the shielded flares which would direct the plane, he heard the van's engine start up and the van itself drive off. Hurriedly he completed his task and ran back.

Henri and Auguste, who was now leaning on the bicycle, had set out the other flares, but there was no sign of Claude and the sound

39

of the van's engine had ceased. Either Gustave had turned off the ignition, or he was out of earshot.

'What's going on?' Jean-Pierre demanded of Henri.

'Gustave is turning the van so that we can leave quickly and Claude has climbed up a tree. He'll warn us. He'll hoot like an owl if he sees car lights approaching along the lane.'

Jean-Pierre stared at him. The story didn't ring true. But it was too dark to read his expression and before Jean-Pierre could question him further there was the sound of an aircraft drawing near. '*Vite! Vite!*' Henri said, giving Auguste a shove. 'You know what to do. Go and light those distant flares.'

'And I have my bicycle, so –'

'Just do as I told you, but take care!'

Auguste set off for the far end of the field, trundling his bicycle. Jean-Pierre was already lighting the nearer flares. He didn't understand why Auguste should take his bicycle, but there was no time to ask. The Lysander was now very close.

It came in low, dropping three parachutes which floated down in quick succession, allowing their loads to land lightly. Henri and Jean-Pierre waited. Neither Auguste nor Gustave had reappeared, and there had been no owl hoot from Claude. The plane circled and came in again, higher this time, and two more, larger parachutes blossomed from it.

Jean-Pierre ran. He had reached the nearer parachutist, who was lying on the ground and seemingly in difficulty, before he realized he was alone. Simultaneously, as he struggled to free the man from his harness, he heard the hoot of an owl, and suddenly the field was filled with blinding light.

Two German half-tracks came fast across the rough grass.

Jean-Pierre stood up and lifted his hands; there was nothing else he could do. The Germans were already on top of them.

'Sorry,' he said to the man at his feet. 'I'm afraid we've had it. Are you all right?'

'I think my leg's busted, damn it.'

The other man, who was further from the approaching Germans and had freed himself from his parachute, after hesitating, started to run. It was a mistake. If Jean-Pierre had had any doubts about his own behaviour, which had been instinctive, what happened next justified him. After a cry of *Halte!* there was the quick rattle of a machine gun and the running man stumbled and fell.

40

'Poor devil!' said the man on the ground. 'He was twenty, just a kid.'

Jean-Pierre, who wasn't much older but didn't feel in the least like a kid, said, 'Do exactly as they tell you. It's our best and only hope.'

'Good advice!' A German officer who was obviously in charge had approached and had overheard. He signalled to one of his men to search the captives and take their possessions and when this was done said to Jean-Pierre, 'Put your hands down. Quite apart from the machine guns in my vehicles, I have a pistol on you, so no false move or you'll end up like your dead friend. I won't hesitate to shoot.' And to the Englishman who had given an involuntary cry of pain when he was moved, 'You are hurt?' He spoke good English, with only a slight accent.

'I think my leg's broken.'

'Right!'

The officer issued a stream of orders. His men were highly efficient. They collected the *matériel* that had been dropped. They produced a stretcher from one of the half-tracks and carried the injured Englishman with reasonable care to the vehicle. They also produced a sack for the body of his companion. With a last bitter look around the field, Jean-Pierre followed as the officer gestured to him with his pistol.

As the half-tracks with their prisoners and their booty crossed the field, pushed their way through the trees and headed along the lane, Henri threw down the rope ladder which Claude had earlier attached to a high branch of a tree and the two men very carefully made their way to the ground. Claude unhooked the ladder and wound it up.

'You saw for yourself,' Henri said. 'Now do you believe me when I say that Jean-Pierre is a traitor? It's he who's betrayed us again and again.'

'There's no proof, Henri,' Claude objected.

'No proof? What more do you want? He didn't try to escape like the poor devil they shot. All he did was put up his hands. It was just a show for the other guy. He went with the Huns without any protest. Probably after some drinks, a good meal and a few laughs, he'll manage to "escape". What do you bet? And if he does I'll kill him this time, Claude. I swear I will.'

'Let's go and get our bikes,' Claude said.

But Henri wasn't to be placated. 'If it wasn't for me and my distrust of Jean-Pierre, we'd both be in the bag by now, and Gustave and Auguste with us. As it is, Gustave, warned by your owl hoot, will have driven the van safely back to town by this time, and Auguste will be well on his way.'

'And it would be a good idea for us to follow them,' Claude said firmly as they reached the ditch where they had hidden their bicycles under leaves and small branches. 'It's a long bike ride home.'

FIVE

For several minutes, while the half-tracks reached the road, Jean-Pierre sat in a kind of daze. The attack had happened so quickly that there had been no time to think, but as the drivers accelerated and the vehicles picked up speed his mind began to function again. His thoughts were not pleasant. He knew his chances of survival were slim. There would be prison or a stockade, harsh treatment that could amount to torture, and finally a firing squad – a just penalty for a spy; and he doubted his own courage to face it bravely. That was what disturbed him most.

'Incidentally, I'm Jim Blackstone.' The man with the broken leg introduced himself.

'Jean-Pierre Morel.' Jean-Pierre gave the name on the French papers that had been taken from him.

'A Frenchman?'

'Yes.'

'*Sei' ruhig!*' The soldier sitting opposite them snapped. Blackstone ignored him. 'I was warned that if we were caught the future would be bleak and probably rather short,' he continued more softly.

'Your leg may save you, if it's really broken. The Hun can be quite humane sometimes.'

'But it precludes much action now.'

'*Halt den Mund!*' The soldier waved his machine pistol at them as he told them to 'Shut their mouths'.

'If you'd like to take a chance and fall out of this vehicle when it slows for a corner, Jean,' Jim Blackstone murmured, 'I think I can chuck myself at our Jerry chum here and keep him occupied while you go.'

Jean-Pierre took a quick breath and tried to weigh up the situation. There was only the one soldier with them in the back of the half-track, a small man, but he was armed, and Blackstone, though strong-looking, was injured. However, he himself was unharmed and surprisingly the Germans hadn't manacled him. Moreover this was probably the last chance he'd get. But Blackstone –

'Are you sure? It won't do your cause any good.'

'It's a fair offer. Take it!'

'*Ruhig!*' the soldier repeated the command to be quiet and gestured with his weapon.

They obeyed. They waited. The present speed of the vehicle made any attempt to jump from it suicidal. But the soldier, his authority apparently established, visibly relaxed.

The kilometres sped by and Jean-Pierre began to fear that there might be no opportunity to act on Blackstone's generous offer before they reached wherever they were being taken. He had no idea which way they were heading or where they might be by now.

Then, without warning, the half-track braked so violently that it almost slewed across the road; possibly some animal, a stray cat or dog, had run into its path and the driver had reacted instinctively. There was loud swearing from the front of the vehicle, and in the back the soldier was momentarily off balance.

'Now! And good luck!' Blackstone shouted, and launched himself forward, grabbing for the gun.

Thankful for Brigadier Beaumont's insistence that the people he sent out were in as good physical condition as possible, Jean-Pierre catapulted himself out of the rear door of the half-track. He had assumed that he would find countryside, hedges to shelter his fleeing figure from sight, ditches in which to hide, perhaps a nearby wood. But as far as he could judge in the darkness, lit only by a fitful moon, he was in a town or on its outskirts. At least, he was in a street with houses on either side, a narrow, mean street. All he could do was run, try to distance himself as far as possible from the Germans.

When he could run no further he cowered in a doorway, gasping for breath. If another military truck came along the street he would be done. The doorway wasn't deep enough to afford protection even from blacked-out headlights. But no vehicle approached, the street seemed dead, and after a while Jean-Pierre walked on. He had no idea where he was but, thanks to Jim Blackstone, he had escaped – for the moment. He didn't want to think what might have happened to Blackstone.

Eventually he reached a small square where the buildings were more imposing, and one of them was a church. He could see a cross against the skyline. He prayed that it would be open and he could rest there until daylight and the end of curfew made it comparatively safe to be abroad.

The big main doors were locked. Jean-Pierre leaned against them. For a moment he felt defeated. Then, resolutely, he squared his shoulders and walked around the church in search of a side door. His relief on finding one open was enormous. It appeared to give on to a side chapel, and briefly he knelt in front of the altar. After the shortest of prayers he glanced into the body of the church, which appeared deserted, and then stretched out on a pew. Unbelievably he slept.

The flight lieutenant stood over the camp bed where Brigadier Beaumont spent many of his nights, and where he was now snoring gently. He shook the senior officer by the shoulder. Instantly Beaumont was awake. He sat up and swung his legs to the floor.

'The Lysander's back?'

'Yes, sir.'

Beaumont searched the younger man's face. 'Not good news?'

''Fraid not, sir.'

Beaumont suppressed a sigh. 'Right. Show them into the office.' While he waited for the arrival of the pilot and crew he cleansed the sleep out of his eyes at a washbasin in a corner of the room, and steeled himself for what he feared he was about to hear. After all the precautions that had been taken he could scarcely believe that there had been another disaster, another betrayal. He went through to his office.

'Come in!' he said when the knock came, his voice steady. 'Find somewhere to sit and tell me the worst. I'm glad to see that at least the three of you are all right.'

'Yes. Thank you, sir.'

'What happened, then?'

They told him in as much detail as they could and he listened carefully. It was as he had feared. It had been another trap, another failure, and he had lost two more good men. Or was it three? What about de Mourville?

'You said only one man ran out into the field to cope with the drop?'

'Only one, sir. We couldn't do more than make a single circuit after the two personnel 'chutes had gone, but we're agreed on that. It looked as if this chap went to help the second man we dropped, who seemed to be in difficulties. The first one made a run for it and was shot. We saw him fall, but he could still be alive and in the bag with the others. It's very difficult to tell from a bird's-eye view in dim light.'

'Of course, and you've done well. Go and get some breakfast now, and then have a rest.'

Dismissing them, George Beaumont hoped they hadn't seen how disappointed and upset he was. He supposed he could be wrong. It need not have been de Mourville who had been captured, though, for no better reason than that he was anxious for the Frenchman's safety, he was sure it was. He sighed deeply. He would know fairly soon. De Mourville had access to a radio in Vire, and had promised to report. If there had been no message by noon he could assume that his fears were justified. In any case, Henri Colet's group must be put on the black list; it had already been responsible for the loss of too many men and too much equipment.

Jean-Pierre woke with a start. A few dim lights had gone on in the church, and he could see through the stained-glass windows that dawn was breaking. He sat up. He was cold and stiff and hungry and, as the events of the night came back to him, he shivered. Encouraged by Jim Blackstone, he had taken his chance, but now his prospects seemed little better. He had no papers, no money, not even a watch. The Germans had stripped him of his possessions; all they had left him was a handkerchief. Worse, he didn't know where he was and he had no friends, no one to whom he could turn; Henri and his group was probably his only hope, if he could find them, and even then he wasn't sure that after the previous night he could trust any one of them.

'*Bonjour, monsieur!*'

Jean-Pierre looked up, startled. A priest was standing at the end of the pew. He was a young man, not much older than himself, with dark eyes set in a pale face. He didn't seem particularly surprised by Jean-Pierre's presence.

'*Bonjour, mon père.*'

The priest smiled. '*Vous êtes français? Catholique?*'

Jean-Pierre nodded. He liked the look of the priest, but he wondered how much he should tell him, how much he could trust him, how much it was fair to confide in him. On the other hand, he was desperately in need of help.

'You are in trouble,' the priest continued. 'Can I be of assistance to you? I am Father Vincent.'

'I'm called Jean-Pierre Morel. And yes, I'm in trouble,' Jean-

46

Pierre admitted. 'I am wanted by the Germans. I was out during curfew. I was caught, but I escaped with the help of a – a friend. They will not be pleased – the Germans.'

'And they'll be searching for you?'

'As soon as it's really light, I expect.'

'I'm afraid the church is no refuge. Though some of the soldiers from the barracks come here to confession and to Mass and are not bad men, they won't hesitate to search the church and my presbytery if they are looking for an escapee, and they are thorough as only Germans are thorough.'

'I know. I'll go. I don't want to get you into trouble, father. It's bad enough I should have let my friend – a man I didn't know – risk his life to give me a chance to save myself. But first please tell me where I am.'

The priest looked at him curiously. 'You are in the Église de Sacré-Coeur, in St-Lô. Is that a surprise?'

'Not terribly, father.'

St-Lô was a town about forty kilometres north of Vire, which was encouraging. Jean-Pierre had decided that his best hope was to return to Vire and perhaps seek out Claude or Bernard, who were likely to be more helpful than Henri. But St-Lô was not a place in which to be without resources. He had been briefed that there was a large German barracks just outside the town, which was known to be a centre for anti-resistance activities in the district, and was almost certainly the headquarters of the soldiers from whom he had escaped earlier.

'Come along!' Father Vincent said firmly. 'If a man whom you didn't know can risk his life for you, surely a priest can provide you with breakfast.'

The priest started towards the rear of the church. He had a pronounced limp and for a moment Jean-Pierre was tempted to flee, knowing he could easily get away. But the thought of a hot drink was too seductive and he followed.

He was not to regret it. The priest not only cooked him an excellent breakfast of scrambled eggs – he kept chickens behind the presbytery – but gave him money and an old bicycle.

'Goodbye, Jean-Pierre Morel – or whatever your real name is,' he said as Jean-Pierre prepared to leave. 'God bless you. I'll pray for you, my son. Perhaps we'll meet again some happier day.'

★   ★   ★

Oberst Becker strode up and down his office. He was very angry. He had just learnt the outcome of the ambush of the British drop outside Vire that night and, in his opinion, his men had been incompetent. To have killed one of the spies as he tried to get away was not unreasonable, but to have allowed a man with a broken leg to overpower an armed guard, resulting in the death of both of them, and then let the third spy escape, demonstrated the grossest negligence.

In fact, all they had to show for their night's work were three bodies, one of them a German soldier for whom he would have to account, and a certain amount of equipment. They hadn't taken any of the so-called *résistance*, who must have been there to meet the spies, and they had no one to interrogate. Altogether, it had been a poor effort. He had to admit that he had failed to listen to the Leutnant's plea for more men, but personnel were limited, and the operation had seemed simple. Still –

As to the third spy, the man who had escaped, he had issued orders that the town should be criss-crossed in search of him. Of course it was possible that he had gone to ground somewhere, but he couldn't have expected to land in St-Lô, and the chances were that he was on the streets. In which case they would get him if it meant stopping and questioning every likely suspect. The man had to be found.

It had become a matter of honour with Oberst Becker.

The bicycle which the priest had kindly provided was Jean-Pierre's undoing. Unfortunately it was a bicycle that caught the eye. It had once been green, and the colour still showed in patches beneath the rust. Clearly it had seen better days. But in spite of its dilapidated appearance it worked, and Jean-Pierre had reached the outskirts of the town when he was spotted by a passing patrol car; whether it was its unusual colour scheme – if it could be called that – or the fact that it was a woman's bicycle that attracted the patrol's attention was irrelevant. The patrol car slewed suddenly into the path of the cycle, sending it and its rider sprawling into the gutter.

Jean-Pierre got slowly to his feet as he was kicked. Asked for his papers he shook his head; he knew his only hope now, so slight as to be negligible, was to pretend to be a fool. He let his jaw drop, his shoulders sag. But it didn't work. They didn't bother with questions. They searched him and finding only the few francs the priest had given him, handcuffed him and pushed him into the back of the car.

48

He didn't resist. Resistance would have been pointless. However, he noted with muted pleasure that the bicycle had been left in the gutter. It would soon disappear; even in its present state it wasn't worthless in a war-devastated France and, broken up, its parts could prove useful. This was a relief for, with the bicycle gone, there would be nothing to connect him with Father Vincent.

It took twenty minutes to reach the barracks, where he was escorted into a room that was bare except for a row of chairs, on which already sat three handcuffed men. Facing them were two armed guards. Jean-Pierre took the chair that was pointed out to him and, in spite of himself, his hopes revived. It was possible they had not been looking specifically for Jean-Pierre Morel, but that there had been a general drive to pick up anyone without papers. If this was the case he had been unlucky, but was in a better position than he might have been.

He had no watch and had to guess at the time, but in what he estimated was the next hour two more men were brought in. Then suddenly one of the guards snapped '*Achtung!*' and signalled that they should all stand. They formed a ragged line until the door was flung open and an officer accompanied by an aide came in. Jean-Pierre's heart sank. The officer was the Leutnant who had led the party that had ambushed the drop the previous night. There was no doubt; it was Morel they wanted.

The officer walked down the line, regarding each man with care, as if he might have changed his appearance. It made Jean-Pierre wish he had accepted the priest's offer of a shave, but he doubted it would have made any difference. The officer stopped in front of him and smiled. Deliberately he took off his gloves and hit Jean-Pierre across the face with them, first one way and then the other. They were of heavy leather, and seamed. The blows were unexpected. Jean-Pierre was knocked to the ground, a little blood trickling down his cheek, waiting for the kicks which didn't come.

The officer turned away. He was satisfied. He thought of the insults Oberst Becker had heaped on him because of the inefficient outcome of the night's operation. Perhaps he had deserved them, in spite of his protests at the small size of his force. He had been in charge, had been responsible for losing the English spy whose papers said his name was Jean-Pierre Morel. But at last he had worsted him. The damage was repaired. The man was caught, and he had exacted his personal vengeance.

He said to his aide, 'See that Monsieur Morel is taken to Oberst

49

Becker at once. The Oberst wishes to interrogate him.' And to the guards. 'I am not interested in the others. The police can deal with them.'

He had spoken in German, and Jean-Pierre had difficulty in not showing his understanding and his relief. At least this was a temporary reprieve. He had half expected to be taken out and shot immediately.

SIX

A month passed and nothing was heard of Jean-Pierre de Mourville. Regretfully, Brigadier Beaumont reached the conclusion that he must have been captured and was probably now dead. Contact had at last been established with Henri Colet's resistance group, but this had merely confirmed that de Mourville had been seized by the Germans in the course of an abortive drop. Beaumont now had a choice, either to go on waiting in the vague hope of news or to write that dreaded official letter to David and Helen Stanton.

He had already written to the parents of James Blackstone and Douglas Pierce; Blackstone was said to be missing, believed dead, and Pierce killed in action – half-truths, accompanied by genuine assertions of the men's bravery, which he hoped might bring some comfort to their grieving relatives. But still he hesitated to write to the Stantons.

Jean-Pierre de Mourville had differed from most of his men. He was French, and upper-class French, but he had proved that he could live for long periods under cover as a French workman. He had become, in fact, a professional, showing exemplary courage, and if anyone could survive in impossible circumstances it was, Beaumont believed, de Mourville. But the young man's luck could have run out, or perhaps too much had been asked of him.

George Beaumont was a man who tried to be honest with himself and, though he couldn't have explained why, he accepted that he felt vaguely guilty over de Mourville. It had been against his better judgement that he had sent him back to France so soon. He had partly been persuaded by Grayson. But it had been his own decision. He couldn't blame anyone else.

'Ah, I was just thinking of you,' he said as Keith Grayson came into the office. 'In relation to de Mourville. It's about time I wrote to the Stantons. They're listed as his next-of-kin, until whenever or if ever his own family can be reached.'

'Yes. I agree, sir. It'll be a shock to them, of course, but there's no point in their living in cloud-cuckoo-land. And there's another reason too, which, if you'll forgive me for saying so, sir, I find personally embarrassing. Only last week they received one of those postcards Jean-Pierre wrote for them before he left supposedly for a course in Scotland. How long do we have to go on arranging for them to be posted when there really isn't any more hope? I know they're intended to keep families from worrying, but –'

Beaumont nodded. 'You're quite right, Keith. You stop the post-cards, and collect what few possessions of de Mourville's we have. I'll write to the Stantons this afternoon. It will be difficult to know how much to tell them; I think I shall have to come fairly clean.'

Brigadier Beaumont's letter which, according to his practice, was personal and handwritten, arrived at The Elms on Saturday morning. The Stantons were having a late breakfast. David Stanton – the letter was addressed to him – read it through slowly twice. His grim expression warned Helen.

'What is it, David? Bad news?'

'Very bad.' He handed her the letter.

'Oh no,' she said when she had read it. 'Not Jean-Pierre. He was in Scotland on a course. I don't understand.'

'The letter explains, Helen.'

'I know, but – I had no idea. He never hinted.'

'He was a very brave young man.'

Anthea had heard what her parents were saying, but the words were meaningless. She was trying to concentrate on eating her breakfast, so that her mother wouldn't start asking questions. But her stomach was protesting; she didn't feel well. She was going to be sick.

'Anthea, are you all right?' Helen was suddenly aware of her daughter's distress.

Anthea took a deep breath. 'Yes, I'm fine – my insides are a bit upset. I must have eaten something that disagreed with me. What – what were you saying about Jean-Pierre?'

David and Helen exchanged glances. It hadn't escaped their notice that Anthea and Jean-Pierre had become very fond of each other, though they had no idea how far the attachment had gone, or how much Jean-Pierre had confided in her about his army life.

'I expect this will come as big a surprise to you as it was to us, dear,' Helen said, 'but it seems that Jean-Pierre has been in France.'

Anthea didn't correct her mother. 'And what's happened to him?'

She held out her hand for the letter as if it was her right to read it. For the moment she had quite forgotten that she was about to be sick.

'It's bad news, Anthea,' David said as Helen passed her the letter.

She knew what was in it before she read it, but she read it nevertheless. Now she felt perfectly calm, as if, when they had lain together in the barn or in the fields and made love, she had always known there would be no future for them. It was why they had had to seize every moment of the present.

She folded the letter and put it back in its envelope. 'May I keep this?'

Helen hesitated; she didn't want Anthea to become morbid about Jean-Pierre. 'Yes, all right, dear. Why not? But remember, Jean-Pierre may be safe. The brigadier merely says he's missing, *believed* dead. He could be in a prisoner-of-war camp, and we've not heard yet.'

Anthea was shaking her head. 'No! The brigadier states quite clearly that Jean-Pierre was captured by the Germans, and that can only mean one thing. Jean-Pierre wasn't in France as a British fighting soldier. He was there – he told me – working with a French resistance group. To the Germans that means he was a spy, and as such –' her voice broke '– they will have executed him.'

'Oh, Anthea!' Helen began, wanting to comfort her, but David shook his head.

Anthea pushed back her chair and stood up. 'Excuse me, will you? I don't want any more breakfast. As I said, my insides are a bit upset this morning.'

'All right, dear,' Helen replied; an unpleasant thought had crossed her mind, but she dismissed it. 'I hope you've not got a bug. Remember we're having supper with the Graysons this evening. Keith's home for the weekend.'

'I'd not forgotten,' Anthea said, thinking that she would have to wait till Monday before she could talk to Meriel Derwent.

'*Alors! Tu n'avais pas raison, Henri,*' Claude said.

Henri shrugged. '*Peut-être.*'

The two men, with Bernard and Auguste, were gathered in the room behind the Colets' café in Vire to discuss over their customary *marc* if they might start operations again. Since the failure of the last drop and the disappearance of Jean-Pierre Morel they had lain low, fearful of what the consequences might be, but over a month had gone by, and there had been no attempt by the Germans to round up their group. Confidence was returning.

'Henri,' Claude persisted, 'if Jean-Pierre had been a traitor we would all be in the bag by now.'

'Not necessarily, Claude. It may not have served the Krauts' purpose to take us in. After all, Jean-Pierre could have betrayed us at any time, but he was content with giving away the farm and those others of our comrades.'

'We don't know that was Jean-Pierre's doing,' Bernard said.

'One of the Krauts told us,' Auguste reminded him.

'With a pistol to his head.' Claude was scornful. 'No, if you want my opinion Jean-Pierre is dead and he died soon after he was captured.'

'How do you reckon that?' Bernard asked.

'If he wasn't dead, either he'd have got in touch with us or, assuming Henri's right, the Krauts would have rounded us up. What's the point of letting us go free when they've lost their contact with us?'

Bernard was nodding. 'But why do you say he died so soon? He wasn't wounded, was he?'

Claude answered, 'I say it because, brave though he may have been, I doubt if he could have withstood torture. Could you? *Merde!* I'm sure I couldn't. Think of the stories we hear about the Krauts! No human man could. Of course, they may not all be true, but – we're still here, aren't we? Personally I salute Jean-Pierre Morel.'

'*Moi aussi!*' Babette said, bustling into the room.

'Well, we shall see,' Henri said, which was as far as he was prepared to commit himself.

Helen was pleased that Anthea had made an effort to look attractive for the Graysons' supper party. If she had cried over Jean-Pierre there was no sign of tears now, and she had put on her prettiest dress. Helen saw Keith's eyes brighten as Anthea came into the sitting-room.

'My dears, come in! Come in!' Margaret welcomed the Stantons as if she hadn't seen them for months. 'I've just been putting Peregrine to bed. He really is so sweet. Would you like to go up and see him, Anthea?'

'No, thank you,' Anthea said coldly. Then, realizing how abruptly she had spoken, she added, 'I expect he's asleep by now. I might wake him.'

54

'The little beggar sleeps most of the time,' Keith said cheerfully.

'How would you know?' Margaret demanded. 'You're hardly ever at home.'

'That's not my fault, Ma. As we're always being told, there's a war on,' Keith said.

'There is indeed,' said his father. 'David's just been telling me the bad news about Jean-Pierre. But first, let's have a drink. Luckily, we're on good terms with the local pub.'

After everyone had a glass, for the next few minutes they discussed Brigadier Beaumont's letter, and what might have happened to Jean-Pierre. Anthea contributed nothing. Helen merely said that Jean-Pierre was missing in France, believed dead, and that the details were not known. Keith admitted that there was almost no chance that Jean-Pierre was still alive, and said it would be foolish to hope. He spoke with an authority that chilled everyone except Margaret, who continued to speculate about what Jean-Pierre might have been doing in France when he was meant to be in Scotland, until her husband suggested it was about time they thought about eating.

It was not until after supper that Anthea found herself alone in the sitting-room with Keith. John Grayson had taken David Stanton to his study, and their wives were in the kitchen. Keith came over to sit beside her on a sofa and put an arm around her shoulders. He tried to kiss her, but she pushed him away.

'Oh, come on, sweetie,' he said. 'Give me a chance. Why on earth not?'

'One good reason is that it's only weeks since you buried Marcia.'

'That's not a kind remark.'

'Too bad!'

'Anyway, I hadn't realized that you were so conventional, Anthea.'

Anthea opened her mouth and shut it again. She didn't want to argue with Keith; he nearly always got the better of any disagreement and in any case the point was unimportant. She stood up and started to walk out of the room.

'Anthea! Marcia and I – it was a mistake as we both realized. I've never wanted anyone but you, and now – Don't you think we'd make a good pair?'

'No!'

'Jean-Pierre's dead, my dear. You should be considering the future,' he said softly, but Anthea had gone.

★　★　★

On Monday morning, as soon as she reached the office in Ag and Fish which she shared with a dozen other people, Anthea telephoned Meriel Derwent. It so happened that Meriel had a lunch date with a colleague from the Ashmolean Museum, but hearing the anxiety in Anthea's voice she at once decided to cancel it.

'Okay. One o'clock at my house. We'll have an omelette lunch. I managed to swap my tea ration for some eggs.'

Anthea put down the receiver with relief. Somehow she got through the morning, though she doubted if she had achieved anything of use. She was in Ship Street at five past one.

Meriel gave her one look and said, 'We shall have a drink. I've a third of a bottle of sherry left.'

'Oh, Meriel!' To her own distress Anthea burst into tears. 'Sorry!' she said, snuffling into a handkerchief. 'Sorry!'

'My dear girl, cry if you want to. It's your Jean-Pierre, isn't it?'

Anthea nodded. Before she had been circumspect about what she told Meriel about Jean-Pierre, but now it seemed pointless not to explain what he had been doing in France and, when she had overcome her emotions, the words poured from her.

Meriel was a good listener. She didn't interrupt, but when Anthea appeared to have come to an end she said, 'You must be very proud of him.'

'Yes, I am – very proud, but –'

'You'd rather have a live coward than a dead hero.'

'I suppose so.'

'Then you're wrong.' Meriel spoke with certainty. 'Anthea, you must realize that you're a very fortunate girl. Not many people have even one very special love affair. This way you'll always remember Jean-Pierre with a great joy. The memory will fade a little, but it will never leave you.'

Meriel got up abruptly and refilled their glasses with the remains of the sherry. Anthea was startled, not so much by what Meriel had said as by the emotion with which she had expressed her thoughts, and suddenly it struck her that while Meriel had listened to all her troubles, she had never concerned herself with her new friend's possible problems.

'You too?' she asked tentatively.

'Yes. It wasn't the war, but similar in a way. I met Kieran in Ireland. He was a seminarian on holiday with his family. We had a choice. He wasn't yet committed to the priesthood. We could have

56

married, had children, lived a normal life, but somehow we would always have known it was not right for us, that it wasn't meant to be. So we said goodbye. But it wasn't easy. It took courage – mainly his – a different kind of courage from Jean-Pierre's, but courage all the same.'

'I'm sorry, Meriel.'

'No need to be. I count myself one of the lucky ones too. Let's go into the kitchen and you can make a salad while I cook.'

'Right.' And, as she washed the lettuce at the sink, her back turned, Anthea said, 'Meriel, I didn't come here just to weep on your shoulder. I want help. I'm pregnant.'

'Are you sure?'

'Not positive, but I've missed two periods and I was sick this morning.'

'The first thing is to make sure. I have a friend, a woman doctor, who's very understanding. I'll arrange for you to see her. How – how do you feel about it?'

'In other circumstances I should be delighted. As it is, half of me is happy – after all, the child is part of Jean-Pierre – but the other half –' Anthea thought of her parents' dismay, and the pseudo-sympathy that Margaret Grayson and others would offer. 'I'm scared of all the problems it will create.'

'Yes, my dear, there will be problems, practical and emotional,' Meriel agreed. 'All I can say is that you can always turn to me and I'll do anything I can to help, that is, unless – unless you want an abortion.'

'An abortion? No!' Anthea was appalled. 'I don't care what it may mean to me. The child's all I've got left of Jean-Pierre.'

In spite of the genuine belief of so many people, English and French, Jean-Pierre was still alive, though for how much longer was questionable. He was in a prison cell in the military barracks outside St-Lô, where he had been since he was last captured. He had not been badly treated. He had been interrogated by Oberst Becker, but there had been no question of physical torture, and the mental abuse had been easy to bear, especially when he realized the mistake the Germans had made.

They had failed to count the parachutes after the drop they had intercepted, and because Jean-Pierre had been first sighted on the ground beside Jim Blackstone and because of his perfect English, it had been assumed he was one of three men who had been parachuted into France, and not a member of the French resistance group that had been supposed to receive them.

As a result, when he denied all personal knowledge of the French contacts he had been believed, and the interrogation had centred on the British, their names, ranks, the purpose of the drop, the base in England. Jean-Pierre hadn't found it difficult to satisfy Becker with a mixture of lies and half-truths, and his relief that he hadn't been forced to betray Henri and the others was enormous.

But as his fear of behaving badly under torture receded, his thoughts turned to acceptance of death. Becker had made it clear that as a spy he would be executed by a firing squad, but had given no indication when this might take place, and at first every time his cell door opened Jean-Pierre had expected to be led away to his death. As more and more days passed, however, he became reconciled to the prospect.

His life was tolerable; it could have been infinitely worse. He was fed adequately and hunger didn't bother him. Twice a day he was taken from his cell under escort and allowed to use the facilities of an ablutions room, after which he was given a half-hour's exercise in an enclosed barracks square, where at the far end there was a stain of blood on the ground. One of these days, he thought, I shall be brought out here and shot.

He asked for a priest, but the request was refused. Luckily for him he had always been something of a solitary character, and the lack of companionship didn't worry him unduly. He spent a fair amount of time in prayer, and much more daydreaming, sometimes about his parents and life at the Château de Mourville before the war, but mostly about Anthea Stanton, and what might have been.

SEVEN

Two guards, neither of whom Jean-Pierre had ever seen before, woke him at five in the morning, more than an hour earlier than usual. No light came through the narrow barred window of the cell, but the naked bulb in the ceiling suddenly shone with startling brightness on his face as he sat up. He sensed at once that this was to be no ordinary day. Both the guards were clutching machine-pistols, and neither carried the bowl of gruel that was his customary breakfast. Instead, one was jangling a pair of handcuffs.

'*Komm*'!'

There was no need for the gesture from the older guard. It was obvious what they wanted him to do, and Jean-Pierre got slowly out of his narrow bed. His insides were hollow. Dressing didn't take long. He had only to put on jacket and shoes – he slept in his remaining clothes for warmth – but he stretched out the task as long as possible until the guards showed obvious impatience. Then deliberately he crossed himself and indicated he was ready by holding out his wrists to be cuffed.

He had expected to be taken out to the square where he had been allowed to exercise and where he knew executions took place. But instead he was led along corridors that were quite new to him. He was surprised by the air of bustle and excitement that seemed to prevail throughout the building. Soldiers hurried past him carrying boxes of files. Through open doorways he saw telephones being disconnected, other equipment dismantled, furniture moved. There was no attempt to hide any of this activity from him. Clearly they didn't mind him knowing that the barracks were being evacuated, and he wondered if by any chance the Allied invasion had begun and the Germans were fleeing. He had had no news of the war, nor indeed of anything else that might have happened in the last weeks of his incarceration. But he couldn't believe that the long-awaited Allied attack was the explanation for the apparent panic, if for no other reason than that this was the wrong time of year, too late for a major invasion, which was traditionally launched in the early spring.

Finally, he was led through a door into a courtyard where a varied collection of vehicles was assembled, some of them being loaded with equipment, others clearly waiting for personnel, still others armoured personnel carriers for their protection. It was the nucleus of a military convoy. But to one side, as if not part of it, was a truck, its tailboard down, and it was to this that Jean-Pierre was taken.

He was thrust into the back. The two guards followed him, and by the time he had picked himself up off the floor and found a seat on a side bench, the tailboard was secured, the top flap lowered, and they were moving. As his eyes grew accustomed to the gloom, he saw that there was a third armed guard in the truck and at least half a dozen other prisoners, none of whom was prepared to meet his eye. Two were women.

There were no windows or means of seeing where they were going, and no one spoke except the two guards nearest to Jean-Pierre who carried on a quiet conversation, but their German was heavily accented and Jean-Pierre was only able to catch a little of what was being said. However, he did learn that he had been right; the barracks were being evacuated, though they did not know why. More importantly, Oberst Becker was returning to his regiment and before leaving had given orders that all the prisoners in the barracks were to be sent to detention camps in Germany.

Jean-Pierre uttered a silent prayer of thanks. Either Becker had forgotten the 'Englishman', the spy whom he had promised to have shot, or he had decided to be generous and allow him to be included with those who had probably committed lesser crimes against the Reich. Either way, for the moment it was a reprieve for which he could scarcely have hoped.

His spirits rose and he comforted himself with the belief that perhaps after all he would survive, that he would see his family again, and his beloved Anthea. This belief, though he knew it to be fragile, sustained him through the long and hideous journey that lay ahead.

The truck stopped at a small railway station where the prisoners were removed in pairs and, under escort, were permitted to use the lavatories and, if they had any money, to buy hot drinks from a stall. Jean-Pierre, who didn't have a *sou*, was turning away, when surprisingly one of the guards thrust a tin mug into his hands. He drank gratefully.

Reassembled in the truck, they waited until, perhaps half an hour later, they were shepherded on to the platform as what appeared to be a goods train drew in. They were then herded into the rear van, already nearly full, though there was room for all the prisoners at least to sit on the floor, which was more than could be said for some of the other vans. The doors were shut and locked on them, leaving them in darkness. The guards did not accompany them.

Now the worst part of the journey began. For the next thirty-six hours they were not allowed to leave the van. They had nothing to eat or drink. It was hot by day and cold by night. The smell of unwashed bodies, urine and defecation became unbearable. One man started to shout and bang on the walls until he uttered some odd gurgling sounds as if he were being throttled. Then he was suddenly silent.

The train stopped twice. The first time there was no apparent reason. At the second stop the doors of the van were thrown open – at least this cleared the air – and a soldier appeared and began to read out names. Those who were named got down on to a platform and were led away. No one asked why. The doors were shut and locked again. The train moved on.

Thankful that there was now more space, Jean-Pierre managed to wedge himself into a corner beside the doors. Here a little clean air from outside filtered in, infinitesimally helping to relieve the stench. He was hungry, and cold in his thin clothes, but he was not without hope.

When the train next stopped all the prisoners were made to disembark. One old woman was too ill to move, and was roughly dragged out. A young man was found to be dead; Jean-Pierre suspected that it was the character who had become hysterical and that he had been strangled by a fellow-prisoner. They were lined up on the platform, then marched out of the station, which was scarcely more than a halt, to yet another truck.

This time it was but a short ride to the camp which was to be home to Jean-Pierre de Mourville for the best part of the next two years.

Meriel Derwent's doctor friend had no difficulty in confirming that Anthea was indeed pregnant, and said she should expect the baby early in December. She advised her to tell her parents as soon as possible and Anthea decided there was no alternative but to take this advice, only waiting until the weekend.

61

It was not a happy occasion. There was no indication of any joy that they were about to become grandparents. On the contrary, when they had got over the first shock, they both upbraided Anthea, though Helen was perhaps less shocked than her husband. She remembered the fleeting thought she had had when Anthea had complained of feeling sick at breakfast.

'For God's sake, the two of you!' Anthea lost her temper. 'I'm not the first girl to get pregnant. This is 1943 and there's a war on. It's my bad luck that Jean-Pierre's been killed, or we'd certainly be getting married now. And if you're worried about what the Graysons may say, remind them that Peregrine was a very large healthy baby considering he was meant to be premature.'

'Don't talk to us like that! The Graysons are quite irrelevant.' David Stanton was angry too.

'Why not? I'd hoped you might be understanding and sympathetic, but all you're thinking is that this shouldn't have happened to a daughter of yours. Well, it has and I'm glad, and you'll have to –'

'What is all this shouting and screaming?'

Old Mrs Stanton stood in the doorway, leaning on her stick. She was extremely frail and these days rarely ventured beyond her own suite of rooms on the ground floor of The Elms. There she held court to her family, and was a great strain on Helen's energy and forbearance.

'Well, what's it all about?' she demanded, and when Helen told her she gave a cat-like smile and added slowly, 'You married off two daughters respectably, you can't have expected to succeed three times.' She hobbled to a chair and sat down. She seemed to be enjoying the situation. 'Couldn't one of her sisters adopt Anthea's little bastard?'

'No!' Anthea cried vehemently. 'He's mine and Jean-Pierre's, and I intend to keep him.'

'In that case,' said old Mrs Stanton composedly, 'the first thing you must do is find a good man who'll marry you and accept the child as his own.'

It was a week before these words made any impact on Anthea, a harrowing week, during which Meriel was her only support. She went to the office each day, and was reprimanded twice for poor work. At home she spent as much time as possible in her own room or wandering around the garden. Her parents at last made some effort to be understanding, to reconcile themselves to the idea of a suddenly grown-up pregnant daughter, but because there had been such a gap between her and her older sisters they had always treated Anthea as a child and found it almost impossible to accept the situation fully.

To Anthea's annoyance, her mother, feeling the need to discuss the matter with another woman, confided in Margaret Grayson, who had commented quite innocently that Anthea seemed to be putting on weight. Margaret was less shocked than Helen had been, and expressed sympathy rather than surprise. Perhaps she was mindful of her grandson's early arrival, and suspected – rightly – that Karen and Bill slept together regularly.

'My dear Helen,' she said, 'the young are all the same these days, however carefully they're brought up. They've no sense of morality. It's another part of the price we have to pay for the war. But don't worry too much. It will work out.'

She already had an idea how it might 'work out' and she resolved to take some action which might kill two birds with one stone, if that was not an unfortunate phrase in the circumstances, but she said nothing more to Helen.

The following weekend Keith Grayson, who had had a long and expensive telephone call from his mother during the week, strolled over to The Elms on the Sunday morning. He found Anthea on a bench in the garden, staring into space. It was really too cold a day to be sitting out, but she was wearing a thick coat and appeared not to notice the temperature. She was not welcoming.

'What is it, Keith?'

'I want to have a talk with you, a serious talk.' He sat down beside her.

'Well, here I am. Talk away.'

'Anthea, I'd like to offer you a – a business proposition, you could call it. And I want you to think about it, not turn it down flat.'

'What business proposition?' She sounded uninterested.

'Marriage.'

'Marriage?'

At last he had got her attention.

'That's right.'

'Are you crazy?' she replied at once.

'No. I've thought it over very carefully. Please listen. I'm a young man who intends to go places after the war; I'm already putting out feelers in the property market. I will need a wife, someone to entertain for me, to be a hostess, someone I can trust not to have affairs with other men, or blab my secrets. That trust is important. And, as my mother keeps on telling me,' he smiled ruefully, 'Peregrine needs a mother.'

'What makes you think I'd be a suitable candidate for this – this position?' Anthea was too astonished by Keith's proposal to be other than blunt. 'I'm not an heiress. I don't know any influential people and, as I'm sure you're aware – I suspect your mother's told you – I'm pregnant with Jean-Pierre's child.'

'You happen to be the girl I want. I've put it to you as a business deal because I know you wouldn't want me otherwise. But it's not such a bad offer, Anthea. Let's face it, unmarried mothers don't have an easy time and nor do their children. So think before you turn me down, not only about your position, but also your child's. I'd bring him – or her – up as mine. He wouldn't ever know the truth – I would want that – and there would be absolute equality with Peregrine, I promise. It's not ungenerous, my dear. In fact it's a good bargain, well worth your consideration.'

Before she had a chance to reply Keith got up and strode towards the house. Anthea shivered, suddenly cold. She didn't want to marry Keith Grayson. He was not unattractive physically. He was a clever man, much more astute than she was, and he was ambitious; she had no doubt that he would be successful in whatever career he had planned for himself. That she was not in love with him scarcely mattered in the circumstances.

The real point was that she didn't *like* him. He was full of prejudices; for example, he was against dogs, though he had never been bitten; he was anti-Catholic, though he rarely went to his own church; he was anti-French, anti-Jewish, anti-American, for no reasons at all that she could see. And he made sweeping derogatory statements about people whom he knew only from newspapers or radio. Yet he could be kind, affectionate, generous to those he loved, and she recalled what her grandmother had said about marrying a good man who would take her child as his own.

'But I don't want to marry Keith,' she said to Meriel when they next met. 'I don't want to marry anyone. It would seem as if I were being unfaithful to Jean-Pierre.'

She expected Meriel to support her and agree with her, but she was wrong. Meriel Derwent was a practical woman. She knew from personal experience what it was like to be the illegitimate daughter of an impoverished mother, and she didn't want Anthea and her child to have to face the same prospect. Financially Anthea would be better off than her mother had been, but that would only be a relative advantage.

'I shall always remember the kids following me around the school playground, chanting, "Bastard! Bastard! You're a little bastard!" It's the sort of experience that stays with you for ever,' she said after she had told Anthea her story, 'an experience I wouldn't wish on anyone. But it's your decision, my dear. Whatever you decide it's not going to be easy.'

'Yes, my decision,' Anthea agreed, but she knew that Meriel had been the final influence to cause her to accept the inevitable. She telephoned Keith that evening and told him that she would marry him. She could only hope that she had made the right decision.

Anthea Stanton was married to Keith Grayson on a beautiful sunny day which seemed to mock the occasion. The ceremony took place by special licence at twelve o'clock at the Marylebone Registry Office in London, and can only be described as dreary. The registrar, a woman with a cold, eyed Anthea's fairly obvious shape with casual disdain, as if to suggest that she saw too many such marriages, which were usually regretted later. The best that can be said for the ceremony was that it was short.

Ten minutes after the Stanton-Grayson wedding party had filed into the registrar's inner office, passing as they entered a laughing, giggling collection of young people who made Anthea feel old, and on the way out a middle-aged couple – the man far from sober – they found themselves on the pavement outside the building.

'We'll need a couple of taxis,' said John Stanton, trying to sound cheerful. 'You know where to go if we get separated, don't you?' He was taking them to lunch at the Savoy, the least he felt he could do in these circumstances.

They were only nine in number. It was clearly impossible for Anthea's sister in Australia to travel to England in wartime; the other sister, who lived in Scotland, had decided that she couldn't leave her children, and old Mrs Stanton was too frail to come up to London. But in order to redress the balance with the Graysons, who included Karen's friend Bill, Anthea had insisted that Meriel should be asked and, contrary to expectations, the presence of a stranger eased the situation.

The luncheon party passed pleasantly enough. Anthea and Keith departed by train for a long weekend in North Wales, a brief honeymoon which Anthea found less of a trial than she had feared it would be – Keith was both considerate and kind – and by the end of it she was at least reconciled to being Mrs Keith Grayson.

Five months later Anthea gave birth to a son in the Charlbury Nursing Home. Keith came to see her, but could stay only a few hours; Brigadier Beaumont was suffering from influenza, which meant that Keith was kept extra busy. His sole remark on being shown the baby was that he looked healthy, but he wasn't as big as Peregrine had been when he was born. He raised no objection to Anthea's suggestion that the child should be named John Peter – his own father happened to be called John Peter – and they agreed he should be known as Peter. Keith returned to London a contented man. Everything seemed to be going well for him. He had just been promoted to the rank of major, one or two business deals in which he was involved were developing nicely, he had the wife he wanted, and he didn't mind being congratulated on the birth of a second son.

He was less pleased when he learned that the child had been registered as John Peter de Mourville Grayson. He had his first row with Anthea, a row which ended in him almost raping her – and for this episode she never completely forgave him.

EIGHT

The days passed. The weeks passed. The months passed. Even the years changed, and the seasons followed each other in orderly succession. In the camp there were rumours and counter-rumours. The Allies had landed in Normandy and were sweeping across Europe, taking all before them. The Germans were making a determined stand at a place called Arnhem. Paris had been liberated, had not been liberated. The Russians, after massive battles, had entered Romania and Poland and were on a collision course with the Allies. Hitler had committed suicide.

The last suggestion produced raucous laughter among the guards, who were themselves the sources of many of the rumours; the prisoners had no access to information and were dependent on what they were told or overheard. On the whole they were indifferent to what they learned. One day, it was assumed, the war would be over, one side or the other would have won and they would be sent home – if they could survive so long. Their main preoccupation was keeping alive, and in this place it required a great deal of effort. Besides, for many home was an unknown quantity.

Although the prisoners were unaware of the fact, their camp was a curious establishment. It was not one of those that after the war would come to be called death camps. It was not primarily a concentration camp for Jews. It was a kind of detention centre, with a motley collection of inmates – Czechs, Poles, Russians, a few French, a few Germans who claimed to be Austrians, a couple of Spaniards. It was also curious in that it was mixed, with no determined separation between males and females; some children accompanied their mothers. How they had all come to arrive here, and why, were mysteries. It was best not to ask. Conditions, though rigid and authoritarian, were not extraordinarily harsh. Not many of the inmates actually died from hunger or overwork, though all were weakened and some merely disappeared. Each man, woman or child lived with the constant fear that it might be their turn next.

In a way Jean-Pierre de Mourville was among the lucky ones. He was young, healthy and, thanks to Brigadier Beaumont, in good physical shape. He had also been better fed until his capture than most of the other prisoners, some of whom seemed to have been in various camps since the beginning of the war. And above all, Jean-Pierre had the will to live, a burning desire to see his parents again – and of course Anthea. Whenever he felt despondent, which was not infrequently, he thought of Anthea.

There were few, if any, moral laws in the camp, but Jean-Pierre did his best to adhere to his own code. Certainly he stole, but mainly from the guards, never from the old or sick or those worse off than himself. He lied when necessary to save himself, but not at someone else's expense, unless it was one of the camp bullies. He avoided trouble as much as possible and shunned all sexual intercourse. However tired he was, he always said a prayer each night before going to sleep, and found great comfort in this.

He made few friends, but among them were two Frenchwomen who had both married Germans. Frau Richmann had her son Boris with her; he was a thin, spindly boy of sixteen, who became devoted to Jean-Pierre. They came from Bonn. Herr Richmann had been convicted of dealing on the black market, the family had been separated and they had no idea where the father was, though they feared he was dead. The other Frenchwoman, a Frau Hurler, was older and accompanied by a daughter in her early thirties.

On the day the Allies celebrated victory in Europe, VE Day, Jean-Pierre had a special dispensation to dig Frau Richmann's grave near the perimeter of the camp; she had died in the night. He was watched by a guard and he had no help. For some unexplained reason the inmates were not allowed out of their huts as usual that day. Food was delivered to the door, and relays to the latrines were organized; it was too bad if bowels didn't work to order. From what could be seen on such visits and from the badly blacked-out windows of the huts, there was a great deal of activity in the camp.

Jean-Pierre, an exception to these restrictions while he was digging the grave, sensed an air of excitement, possibly fear – it reminded him of his last day at the barracks outside St-Lô, but he had no means of accounting for it.

He didn't particularly value the temporarily privileged position in which he found himself. The ground was hard, the work was laborious and in spite of the cold he was soon sweating, partly due to weakness. The guard's urging to hurry every time he stopped for breath annoyed him. He had been fond of Frau Richmann.

68

At last he had dug deep enough to please the guard. Frau Richmann's body in its tattered clothes lay nearby. Jean-Pierre lifted it without difficulty – it was almost weightless – and placed it reverently in the grave. Then, before he shovelled back the earth he stood for a moment, head bowed and said a prayer. He crossed himself and grimaced at the guard who swore at him and made threatening gestures with his machine pistol, but for some reason didn't dare to come too close.

As a special concession Boris had been permitted to watch his mother's burial. Now, 'How kind you are, Jean-Pierre,' he said tearfully, wiping his nose on the sleeve of his dirty jacket. 'And brave, to say a prayer.'

'I'm very much afraid it was not the right sort of prayer for her religion, but I don't suppose God minds. Your mother will rest in peace now.'

'Yes. Poor mama! Poor mama!' The boy sobbed. 'You're a good man, Jean-Pierre. I'll never forget you and your kindness to me – and mama. Never.'

'Never is a long time, Boris,' Jean-Pierre said, and thought it could be a short time too. There was something going on in the camp and it probably boded ill for them all.

Jean-Pierre was both right and wrong. The next morning he was woken by a party of fellow-prisoners bursting into the hut and shouting in a variety of languages, 'We are free! The Hun has gone. The gates are open. We can go when we like. The war must be over.'

It was unbelievable, but true. What could have been mistaken for a collection of scarecrows poured out of the huts. Some were laughing. Some were crying. Others were breaking into the cookhouse, looking for any food that might have been left behind. Still others were trying to start a half-track that the guards had obviously failed to start earlier and had been forced to abandon. The atmosphere was one of general hysteria.

Boris was jumping up and down. 'Free! Free! Oh, poor mama, if only she could have lived a little longer. But it's wonderful. The war is over!'

Jean-Pierre didn't have the heart to remind the boy that he was a member of a defeated nation, and that conditions in Germany were unlikely to be easy. 'Where do you want to go?' he asked.

'To Bonn, I suppose.' Boris was not too sure. 'That was where we lived before, as you know, and my papa's family are there.

Perhaps he might even be there himself. You'll come with me, won't you, Jean-Pierre?'

'Boris, I can't. I must go to my own home, try to find my own parents.'

'But how shall I get to Bonn without you? I can't go alone.' Boris was appalled at the idea. 'I'd be lost. I'd never find the place.'

What the boy said was true, Jean-Pierre knew. Boris was sixteen now, but still skinny and underdeveloped, both physically and mentally. He had spent a third of his life in one sort of prison camp or another, always sheltered to the best of her ability by his mother. By himself he would be anyone's dupe, and incapable of survival if conditions outside were anything like Jean-Pierre's imagination. But he was not Jean-Pierre's responsibility.

Although Jean-Pierre's material advantages were as meagre as anyone's in the camp, he believed that alone he would have an excellent chance of reaching France and the Château de Mourville. He could speak German, French and English. He was in reasonably good health. More important, during his time with the Resistance he had learnt to live rough and to make the most of every opportunity that was likely to improve his situation.

Travelling with Boris, however, would negate almost all such opportunities. A physical weakling, not too intelligent – a dependent Boris would be nothing but a burden. What was more, he presumed that somewhere he would come across Allied troops, and the presence of a German boy could prove embarrassing.

'You will come with me, Jean-Pierre. Please!' Boris persisted. 'If you don't I shall die, like mama.'

This was arrant blackmail, and strengthened Jean-Pierre's resolve. Nevertheless, he couldn't abandon Boris. 'Nonsense. Of course you won't die,' he said. 'I'll find your mother's friend Frau Hurler, and see if you can go with her and her daughter. Perhaps we can all start together.'

To Jean-Pierre's surprise, Boris accepted this, and it was with a clear conscience that eight hours later he left the boy in the care of the Hurlers, who were good and capable women. One problem had been that they had no clear idea where they were starting from; the only solution seemed to be to travel westwards. Jean-Pierre suspected from conversations he had overheard among the guards that they were in south-central Germany, perhaps somewhere near Würzburg or Nürnberg. In any case, he decided that if they went towards the west, they couldn't go wrong.

70

That evening they had reached the outskirts of a village, but a party of men armed with shotguns wanted to turn them away. They were not the first arrivals from the camp and others had tried to loot the place, which explained their reception. But, after some argument, the villagers agreed that the two women and the boy could stay there overnight, and thankfully Jean-Pierre continued on his own. He was also lucky in that he had managed to persuade the villagers to confirm his location. His guesses had been more or less accurate; his own best route lay off the main roads and through southern Belgium. It appeared from what he was told that the whole country was in a state of utter confusion – which could only help him – and that a major problem would be crossing the Rhine.

Buoyed with the idea of freedom, relief at having survived the Germans' departure from the camp, when they could all have been rounded up and shot, and encouraged by the companionship of the women and Boris, Jean-Pierre had not found the day's journey tedious. Now, as by himself he followed a field track pointed out by the villagers in what he hoped was the right direction, he was suddenly overcome by weariness. He was desperately hungry, cold but sweating and on the verge of exhaustion. For the first time since he had left the camp, he realized that pride in his Resistance experience had caused him to overrate his present capabilities, and he was beset by doubts that he would ever reach France.

For Anthea the end of the war was much less traumatic. It wouldn't be true to say that she had been unhappy ever since she had learnt of Jean-Pierre's death. She was young. Her son gave her a lot of joy and, to a lesser degree, so did Peregrine, who had happily accepted her as his mother, though his father was the most important person in his life, in spite of the fact that Keith spent more and more time in London. Her friendship with Meriel also gave her pleasure, and she sometimes went to Ship Street for the weekend while her mother cared for the babies.

Anthea had continued to live at The Elms. Soon after her marriage to Keith old Mrs Stanton had died and it had been easy to adapt the house to suit its new occupants. Keith, who only came down from London for odd days, had raised no objection, and Margaret Grayson was secretly pleased to be rid of the responsibility of Peregrine, as long as she could see as much of her grandson as she wished.

The arrangement had suited Anthea very well, but now, with the

71

end of the war, there were obviously going to be a great many changes, and at least some of them were not going to be for the better. Keith, with his father's help, had bought a house in Marylebone and intended to move Anthea and the boys there as soon as he was demobilized. He was very enthusiastic about the project. 'I got it for a song,' he said to Anthea. 'It needs a fair amount of work, but I can get that done cheaply and we should make a mint out of it. It's really a bit small for us, but it will do excellently for starters, and then we'll buy a better place. Furniture will be a problem – it's not worth buying any of this utility stuff which is all that's available – but I dare say our families will help. They've both got more than enough.'

Anthea found it difficult to share Keith's enthusiasm. Everyone, even Meriel, told her how lucky she was, and indeed she knew this to be true. For most young people finding somewhere to live and setting up house after the war was a major problem, almost insurmountable with children.

But Anthea had lived in Oxfordshire all her life; it was home. She didn't want to move to London, away from her parents and away from her friends, especially Meriel. Meriel too had a new enthusiasm, or rather an old ambition that she now intended to realize. She would soon be losing her job at the Ashmolean when its former holder was discharged from the army, and she planned to open a shop – she proposed to call it a gallery – to sell objets d'art, small furnishings, ceramics, possibly materials, anything decorative.

Anthea, although intrigued by the idea, had thought this was probably a poor time to start such an undertaking but, to her surprise, Keith strongly disagreed. He said people were tired with 'make do and mend', and felt a need for pretty things if they were not too expensive. His opinion, relayed to Meriel, encouraged her to admit that in time she hoped that her business would grow into an interior decorator's, with many of the goods being supplied by the gallery.

Anthea felt flat. Had she been staying in Oxfordshire she might have played a small part in Meriel's new enterprise, but from London this would be impossible, and the life that Keith visualized for her there held little attraction.

She often thought longingly of Jean-Pierre and wondered what would have been happening to them now if he had been alive. She supposed he would have wanted to return to France in order to discover how his parents had fared, and reproached herself because she had almost forgotten about them.

Then, unexpectedly, Keith announced that he was going to France on duty. Anthea appealed to her mother. She was afraid that if *she* asked Keith to make inquiries about Jean-Pierre or the de Mourvilles he would refuse, but it was reasonable that Helen, whose friendship with Chantal de Mourville had led to Jean-Pierre coming to stay with the Stantons in England, should make such a request.

Helen's answer was to embrace her daughter. 'Of course I'll ask Keith, and sooner or later we'll find the de Mourvilles. When we do, darling, I'll see you meet them and that they know about Peter. That's a promise,' she said.

But it was a promise that Helen would be unable to keep.

By a quirk of fate Keith was to reach France and learn how Jean-Paul and Chantal de Mourville had fared during the war before Jean-Pierre reached the château. While Keith was in Paris and planning how he could fit in his private inquiries with his official duties, Jean-Pierre, forced to travel slowly and mainly on foot, had got only as far as Belgium, a long way from home. He had met various groups of soldiers on his way, and seen some convoys; it was with one of these that he had been able to cross the Rhine. But, though these American troops were kind and fed him and permitted him to ride with them for some distance, he had no papers and nothing to prove that he was a British army officer.

In fact, Jean-Pierre had become one of the army of travellers criss-crossing Europe in the aftermath of the war, strangers without identification or money, dirty, unshaven and unwashed. Such people were also unwanted, feared and distrusted – often for good reasons. As a result, though individuals had shown him kindness, he himself trusted no one, not since some half-drunk British soldiers had refused to listen to him and had threatened him with the local police when he had approached them.

And now he was ill. Too little food, too many nights in the open, often in bad weather, and too much stress had taken their toll of a constitution already weakened by life in a German detention camp. Jean-Pierre had woken this morning shaking with fever and unable to get up from the hard floor of the shed where he had been sleeping under a couple of sacks. His forehead was burning, his body cold, his throat raw, his mouth like sandpaper and he had to accept that no amount of willpower was going to help him on his way.

73

He curled himself up under the sacks and prayed that a day's rest would enable him to continue his journey. Meanwhile, he could only hope that no one would come to the shed and, finding him, drive him away.

As the morning passed he dozed fitfully, and felt a little better. In spite of not having eaten for thirty-six hours or even longer he wasn't hungry, but he was dreadfully thirsty. He yearned for a glass of water, a yearning which seemed stronger each time he woke. Once or twice in his need he groaned aloud, though he wasn't aware of this.

It had been dark when he reached the shed and he had no idea how close he might be to a house, but he had heard no sounds until, shortly before what he judged was noon, the barking of a dog disturbed him. Then, soon afterwards, he heard an animal snuffling at the door. He propped himself up on an elbow and held his breath. He waited. Someone called to the dog. The snuffling stopped. Jean-Pierre relaxed.

His relief was premature. Without warning the door of the shed was suddenly flung open to reveal a red-eyed German shepherd which growled deep in its belly and, beyond the dog, a bulky figure carrying a shotgun. The weapon was pointed directly at him.

NINE

If it had not been for Maria Poirier and Denis, her father, Jean-Pierre might well have died. Together they supported him from the shed to the farmhouse, half-carrying him. In the big kitchen that smelt of cider apples and was clearly the hub of the household, they took off his filthy clothes, washed him and improvised a bed for him near the big stove. Here he lay, sweating into one of Monsieur Poirier's nightshirts. They took turns putting cold compresses on his forehead, making sure that he didn't throw off his blankets and feeding him broth, until gradually his fever subsided.

But the illness had left him very weak, and it was several days before he was able to walk. During this time he continued to receive constant attention; one of the Poiriers always seemed to be within earshot in case he called, and he realized what a burden he was to them. There were only the young woman and the old man to cope with the farm, which in fact was little more than a smallholding, and the work was hard. They did not need the additional trouble of coping with a sick man.

However, Jean-Pierre's health improved steadily, until Maria decided they could leave him for a day. She and her father wanted to drive to the market in their neighbouring town to sell and barter their produce. They would load the cart the night before and leave early the next morning, but the horse was old and slow and they would not be back until late. Would he be all right?

'*Je vous en prie*,' said Jean-Pierre. 'Don't worry about me. I shall be fine.'

'We shall leave you Bruno for company,' Denis said.

At the mention of his name the German shepherd, who was lying near Jean-Pierre, pricked up his ears. He was no longer hostile. He and Jean-Pierre, if not friends, were on amicable terms. And indeed Jean-Pierre was thankful for the dog's company the next day. With Maria and Denis away the place seemed very quiet and time dragged. He was glad when, late in the evening, he heard them returning.

They had a surprise for him. They had acquired – Jean-Pierre didn't ask how – some clothes for him that, unlike those that Denis's own wardrobe could offer, were a reasonable fit. He was touched, but his gratitude was tinged with dismay when Denis quietly suggested that he would soon want to be on his way home, and would need clothing that didn't draw anyone's attention to him. Somehow Jean-Pierre had got so used to living at the farm and being cosseted by Maria that the thought of continuing his trek to France appalled him, at least momentarily.

Maria, who by now was in love with him, sensed this and was ready to take advantage of it. When she slipped into his bed beside him that night she told him not to listen to her father. She had made inquiries about getting him some forged Belgian papers, and if she succeeded he could stay with them indefinitely – perhaps for ever; her father was old and –

Maria did her best to be persuasive, but Jean-Pierre had had time to absorb the idea of setting out once more and was not tempted. He explained as tactfully as he could that he had to find his parents, and anyway there was a girl waiting for him. He had told the Poiriers very little about himself, only that he was trying to get home to France after escaping from a camp in Germany, and he had never mentioned Anthea before.

This revelation changed his relationship with Maria. She made no fuss, but she didn't come to his bed again and, a week later, when Denis offered him a lift to the border in the cart, he accepted with gratitude. Maria packed some food and insisted on giving him a few francs, and he parted from the Poiriers with many expressions of thanks and affection.

And so Jean-Pierre returned to France.

While Jean-Pierre de Mourville was delayed by his illness at the Poiriers' farm, Keith Grayson, Major Keith Grayson, had already arrived in France. He had come equipped with every credential, introduction and authority that might conceivably prove useful, and he had at his disposal a chauffeur-driven staff car. What was more, he discovered that, with his rank and back-up and the fact that he was not attached to any particular unit, he was in a perfect position to do as he pleased – or almost. He was still accountable to Brigadier Beaumont, though this duty was not onerous.

The brief that Beaumont had given him was twofold. He was to form an assessment – inevitably superficial in the time available, but nevertheless useful – of the strength of communism in the country, where it was believed to be deep-seated among former resistance groups, and to attempt to discover the fate of some of Beaumont's people who had been landed in France and had subsequently disappeared. It was a broad brief that gave Keith a great deal of freedom and suited him excellently.

In due course he came to Vire and called on the Colets at their café. At first Henri was very suspicious, but when Keith had satisfied him that his inquiries were genuine and were in no way intended to be dangerous for Henri and his friends or detrimental to their interests, he mellowed. He invited Keith into the room behind the bar where so many plans had been hatched, and offered coffee and the ubiquitous *marc*.

'Your group, Monsieur Colet, has had a very fine record in the war,' Keith said. His French was fluent, though his accent was little better than that of a typical English schoolboy. 'But you had some bad luck in 1943.'

'Bad luck!' Henri snorted. 'Bad luck, indeed! We were deceived, betrayed – and by that man you sent us, the one who called himself Jean-Pierre Morel.'

'Surely not,' Keith protested. 'I agree that you must have been betrayed. It can't have been chance that the Germans were informed in advance about so many of the drops we made to you, but the traitor can't have been Morel. He would never have planned his own capture, his own execution –'

'Why not his own capture – his *so-called* capture? We saw the Germans seize him, but I expect he dined in style with Oberst Becker at the barracks that night. As for execution, who ever said he was executed?'

'We understood –'

Keith was startled, not by Henri's accusation that Jean-Pierre was a traitor, but by the possibility that he might have survived. If for some reason the Germans had spared de Mourville or he had managed to escape from them, he would surely have made contact before now. It was two years or more since all information pointed to the fact that he had been captured, and the war in Europe had now ended. Nevertheless, Henri's remarks were worrying.

'You *thought* you understood, major,' Henri continued. 'You will see. These Fascist types are clever. For the moment they are defeated, but they will rise again – or try to. We socialists must always be on guard. As for Morel, if you don't believe me, make some inquiries in St-Lô. According to my information, he was not executed. He was sent secretly to Germany when Becker was posted back to his regiment, and in Germany he was put in charge of a detention camp. It's a job that would suit him. He liked to give orders, that one. He was a stuck-up bastard, who thought himself superior to us poor peasants.'

Momentarily forgetting where he was and in whose company, Henri spat on the floor in a gesture of contempt. Babette, heavily pregnant, who had just come into the room to offer more coffee, protested, but Keith laughed and made it an excuse to leave. By now he was seriously perturbed. He wanted to get to St-Lô. Somehow Henri's words, in spite of his obvious vindictiveness towards Jean-Pierre, had carried conviction.

At St-Lô, Keith went straight to the Hôtel de Ville where, once he had produced his credentials, he was well received and given every help, but the records were far from complete and a great deal had happened in the barracks that was not known outside. The one fact that Keith was able to establish beyond doubt was that there was no proof – at least in St-Lô – of Jean-Pierre's death. He could have been executed; he could have been sent out of France to a camp in Germany, where he might or might not have died.

'You were here at the time, madame,' Keith said to the clerk who was helping him with the files. 'What is your opinion?'

She shrugged expressively. 'When the barracks were evacuated, I heard that the Germans took the prisoners they had there with them. If this man Morel was one of those prisoners he would have gone then. That's all I can tell you, monsieur. But of course there are many, many stories.'

'Of course,' Keith agreed readily. 'Stories about Morel?' he prompted.

She hesitated. 'It has been said that he worked for the Germans, that he went to Germany to run a detention camp for them. I've heard that he was only a guard there, and also that he was the commandant. It's impossible to know what to believe.'

Keith sympathized. He would have dearly liked clear-cut evidence as to what had happened to Jean-Pierre. But it didn't look as if he was going to get it – unless the de Mourvilles were able to provide it. This, however, was not to be.

Anthea came slowly down the stairs from the nursery. She could hear voices in the sitting-room, her father's voice and her mother's

78

answering, and Keith's. So Keith was back from France. As she passed through the hall she saw his two bags; one was open and seemed to contain some parcels. Presents, she thought, but there was only one present that she wanted – good news of Jean-Pierre, or at least of the de Mourvilles – and she didn't dare to hope that Keith would have brought it.

'Hello, my dear!' Keith leapt to his feet and came forward to embrace Anthea. 'I don't need to ask how you are. I'm told you and the boys are flourishing.'

'Hello, Keith. Did you have a good trip?'

'Yes and no!'

'Look what Keith's brought us!' Helen said.

She displayed the gifts, nylons and scent for herself and Anthea, cigars for David, a bottle of gin, and two small identical teddy bears for the boys. Keith was never other than generous and, Anthea had to admit, he had kept his word as regards the children. Perhaps he gave his own son more love and attention, but at least as regards material goods he treated Peregrine and Peter with strict equality.

'I've one or two things for ma and pa too,' Keith said. 'I thought I'd run them over before supper if that's all right with you.' He looked enquiringly at Helen.

'Fine,' Helen said. 'But bring Margaret and John back with you. I'm sure we can stretch the food to include two more. I was lucky at the butcher's yesterday.'

'Under the counter,' David said. 'I hope all these presents of yours weren't from the black market, Keith. I can't believe the Paris shops are full of such goodies.'

'No, they're not. This stuff all came from the Americans. France is in a bad way, in my opinion, riddled with communism in the country and corruption in the cities. Whether de Gaulle will be able to –'

Suddenly Anthea could stand the suspense no longer. 'Oh, for God's sake!' she exclaimed, her voice strained and high.

The three of them turned and stared at her in surprise. Helen had been looking in some disbelief at the nylons and the scent, and thinking that she had almost forgotten the kind of small luxuries that had made life so pleasant before the war. David was wondering whether, in view of Keith's generosity, he should produce his last two bottles of Chablis for supper. Keith had risen and was halfway to the sitting-room door.

'Stop, Keith,' said Anthea. 'Surely there's no need for us to

79

pretend,' she went on more calmly. 'Keith, Mother asked you to make inquiries about Jean-Pierre and the de Mourvilles. Did you manage to do so, and what did you find out? That's what's really important, isn't it, not – not all this stuff.' She gestured at the gifts Keith had brought.

Keith had stopped, back turned to the others. Now he pivoted slowly on his heels and regarded Anthea without speaking; at that moment he knew that their marriage would never be more than a convenience to her.

Then, 'I'm sorry,' he said icily. 'I didn't want to give you the bad news as soon as I got – *home*. However, as you seem to be so eager to know, my inquiries proved beyond doubt that Jean-Paul de Mourville and his wife Chantal are both dead. They died in a fire at their château in 1944. As for Jean-Pierre, he had been executed as a spy at St-Lô in Normandy the previous year.'

And without waiting for any response, Keith walked out of the room.

TEN

Jean-Pierre de Mourville stood and stared about him at what had once, not so long ago, been his ancestral home. He was temporarily unnerved. The château was a ruin. From the charred remains of wood and fabric it was clear that the place had been gutted by fire, a fierce, violent fire that had overwhelmed it before adequate help could arrive – if there had been any adequate help available, or indeed any help at all.

But how had it happened? It was certainly not the result of an enemy shell. And his father had always been so careful, and had insisted that the servants take every precaution. It was inconceivable that no one had smelt smoke or suspected fire before the flames took such a hold, even if the fire had started at night. And what had anybody done? Where were his parents now? It was obvious that the château had been unoccupied for some time.

Jean-Pierre picked his way slowly and carefully among the debris into the drawing-room, which was a travesty of the fine salon it had once been. It was here, he remembered, that his mother had told him of his parents' wish that he should go to England, and where he had reluctantly agreed. His father had ordered Joseph to bring champagne and they had drunk to him, to the de Mourvilles and to La Belle France. By now all this seemed like a dream.

Sadly Jean-Pierre went through the great hall and out of the château. He needed to find his parents, or someone who could tell him where they might be. Sure that the local priest, Father François, who was a close friend of the family, would know, he made his way to the Église St-Denis, where he had been baptized and received his first communion. It lay on this side of the village and he reached it in a few minutes.

Although he had never before known the main doors to be locked, not even at night, he was not surprised that, as a result of the confusion and looting that must have followed the end of the war, they were now barred. Nevertheless, it was a mild shock – not so dismaying as his first sight of the château had been, but he still felt a chill sense of foreboding. At the back of his mind had been the idea that he would find Father François in the church saying his early Mass as usual.

'*Que faites-vous ici?*'

Jean-Pierre swung round. He was faced by a giant of a man, a priest to judge by his clothes, but not one he had ever seen before. Jean-Pierre was startled. The question had been posed in a most peremptory tone, and the man's attitude was menacing.

'If you were thinking of breaking into the church and stealing the contents of the poor box, you can think again,' the priest said. 'I keep no money in the church.'

'You misunderstand, father,' Jean-Pierre said. It was some days now since he had left the Poiriers' farm and he realized that once again he looked dirty and disreputable, and had been taken for a vagrant. 'I came to see Father François.'

'He's not here. I'm the priest in charge now.'

'Is Father François in the village?'

'Yes. He's living with his sister in the cottage near the café. But why do you want to see him? Is he a relative of yours?'

'No, but –'

'You come from these parts? What is your name?'

Jean-Pierre resented the priest's attitude. 'Yes, father, I come from these parts,' he replied coldly.

'And your name?'

'Jean-Pierre – Morel.'

'Well, Father François won't be able to help you. There's no work to be found here, anyway. If you take my advice, you'll move on.'

Jean-Pierre nodded. 'Would you object if I walked around the churchyard first?'

The priest looked at him suspiciously. 'No-o-o. But don't do any damage!'

Jean-Pierre was willing to concede that from a presumed vagrant his request must have seemed odd. He had made it on impulse, a sudden desire to see that part of the churchyard owned by the de Mourville family, where so many of his forebears had been buried and he had expected to be buried one day himself. But he was not prepared to offer this unfriendly priest an explanation. He was thankful that the man neither refused his request nor insisted on accompanying him, but went into the church.

The churchyard which previously had always been kept in

immaculate condition – his father had paid for the gardener – was now, Jean-Pierre saw, overgrown and neglected. This, owing to the war, was not altogether unexpected. What was unexpected was the sight of a new headstone with the names of Jean-Paul de Mourville and his wife Chantal. Jean-Pierre stared at it in disbelief; though he had known it was possible that his parents might have died while he was away, he had never believed this could be so in reality.

And there was worse. He couldn't read the dates inscribed below the names because they were totally obscured by a couple of swastikas that had been painted on the stone, defacing it. He fell to his knees and wept. He didn't understand. How had they died? They had not been that old. Had they been killed – by the Germans? What did the hideous swastikas mean? The de Mourvilles had never been Nazi sympathizers. The swastikas were an insult, a revolting slur on two honourable people. He shook with grief and rage.

After a while he got to his feet. He left the churchyard and set off for the village. He needed to talk to Father François. On the way he met a couple of people whom he recognized, but who clearly didn't recognize him, older, bearded and shabbily dressed as he was. After the reception he had received from the priest at the Église St-Denis he made no effort to greet them.

'Jean-Pierre! Ah, mon Dieu! Mon Dieu!' The old priest was overcome with emotion as he drew Jean-Pierre into the cottage and embraced him. 'My dear boy! You are alive – and well? But you have suffered. Haven't we all? Terrible times we have been through. Terrible! And they're not over yet.'

Father François was leading the way into the front room of the cottage when suddenly he stopped. 'Jean-Pierre, have you broken your fast today? When did you have your last meal?'

'Yesterday evening, father,' Jean-Pierre admitted; he didn't add that it had consisted of raw vegetables stolen from a kitchen garden, or that he hadn't had a hot meal since leaving the Poiriers' farm some days ago.

'Then let us go into the kitchen. Since the Germans who used to steal our supplies have gone, we do not do badly here. My sister is a clever manager, and there are some in the village who remember their old priest and bring gifts.'

'Where is your sister, father?'

'Right now? Shopping in the village. It is always best to be early.'

'My parents?' Jean-Pierre said at last, as he sat at the kitchen table while the priest busied himself getting breakfast; he felt too dazed to offer to help. 'I saw their graves, the swastikas – and our old home. What happened, father?'

Father François told him. It was a sad story of envy, greed, misunderstanding, pride and plain wickedness. When the Germans overran France the Château de Mourville had been taken over by troops, but Jean-Paul and Chantal had been allowed to continue to live there. Because of this the story was spread in the district that they were collaborators, that they had welcomed the Germans, and that they were living as well as ever, while their fellow-countrymen suffered hardships and shortages.

The truth was quite to the contrary. They had been forced to live in part of the servants' quarters, to act as batman and personal maid to the Oberst and his officers, and to watch their home and their possessions looted and maltreated. What little extra food they received was small recompense.

Nevertheless, the gossip about them grew and flourished. The family had never been especially popular in the village. Before the First World War they had spent much of their time in Paris and abroad, and afterwards they had lived quiet, almost isolated lives at the château. Jean-Paul was too embittered by the loss of his hand and the consequent ruin of his career as a concert pianist to wish for any company other than that of his immediate family. And what good he did in the village, for example, by not inconsiderable charitable contributions, was done by stealth, usually through the church, for he had been a very private person.

'However,' continued Father François, 'in 1944 the Germans went from here. I don't know why. Perhaps they were needed elsewhere. The Allies had landed in Normandy and were pressing forward. It was a great relief. But then the recriminations and accusations began, and there was bitter talk against your parents.'

'Go on, father. Please!' Jean-Pierre said as the old man nearly broke down. 'I need to know.'

'Of course, my son. Of course. But – it's not easy.' He drew a deep breath. 'The bare facts are that one night there was a fire at the château. Jean-Paul and Chantal, your dear parents, died, overcome by smoke.'

'There was no one else there? Joseph?'

'No. All the servants had long gone. Joseph stayed until the Germans came. I think your father made him leave for the south when that part of France was still unoccupied.'

84

'How did the fire start?'

'No one knows for sure, Jean-Pierre, but it was probably deliberate. I'm afraid war brings out the worst as well as the best in people.'

'But didn't anyone protest?'

'Yes, but nothing was done. There's a strong communist element in the village. No one wanted to be accused of being pro-Nazi.'

'I understand.'

It was an automatic response, and in some ways Jean-Pierre, after his spell in the camp and his long trek home, understood better than the priest would have believed. What he found difficult to accept was that this had happened to *his* parents, who had always been the most patriotic of people. He felt anger that they had suffered so unjustly, but he also felt helpless.

Suddenly aware that the priest had been speaking, he said, 'I'm sorry, father. What did you say? I was – was thinking.'

'Yes, you need to think, Jean-Pierre, to consider what you are going to do. You had hoped to come home, but there's no home for you here any more.'

'What do you mean? I know my parents are dead and the château is a ruin, but –'

'There's more to it than that. The whole de Mourville estate has been confiscated – on the spurious grounds that Jean-Paul was a collaborator.'

'But they can't do that!'

'It is done, and there is no hope that you can reclaim your land or property. Indeed, it would be dangerous to try. Believe me, my son, there is nothing for you here. You would be well advised to leave as soon as possible.'

'Surely I have some legal redress.'

'In time and with money, maybe. But not at present. Jean-Pierre, you must realize that no de Mourville is acceptable here now. Unfortunately you are considered as guilty as your father and mother of collaborating with the enemy – of being a traitor to France.'

'A traitor! Me! Dear God!' Jean-Pierre laughed mirthlessly. 'They've no idea how I spent the war.'

'You were sent abroad, to be safe. That was resented, especially when several local boys were killed or maimed. It was said you were living in the English countryside with rich friends of your family who were pro-German, like a lot of English people, and having a good time.'

'Do I look as if I've been having –'

Father François held up his hand. 'Wait! Hear me out. The story goes that at some point you managed to get to Germany, where you were put in charge of one of their hideous camps. There was an English officer here, making inquiries, who is said to have confirmed this. Jean-Pierre, feeling is running high. You are not safe here, my son. You must leave.'

'Yes. I'll leave, father, but first you must listen to the truth.'

Madame Vernet, the widowed sister of Father François, returned to the house as Jean-Pierre finished his story and he had to repeat it for her benefit. She was, Jean-Pierre judged, at least fifteen years younger than the priest and clearly an efficient, capable woman. She listened to what he had to say with interest, nodding her head from time to time in sympathy. But her verdict was the same as her brother's: it was not possible for Jean-Pierre to remain in the district.

'Even some of those who do believe you will pretend they don't, because it would mean giving up what they have stolen,' she said, 'and I think it not impossible that you would find yourself in prison on some trumped-up charge. People in these parts are more aggressive than they used to be, and less charitable.'

'Wicked!' the old man snorted. 'Communists! They are no better than the Nazis.'

Madame Vernet intervened. 'Jean-Pierre, do you have anywhere to go – any family?'

'No. Yes. I'm sorry.'

Jean-Pierre shook his head as if to clear it. It was all more than he could bear. It had been one horror after another. There had been the relief, the joy, of almost reaching home, then the first sight of the ruined château, the unwelcoming priest, the headstone with its dreadful swastikas, and after that the unbelievable account of events that Father François had given – including the absurd accusations that not only his father but he himself had worked for the Nazis. It was too much to absorb at once.

He heard himself say, 'Silly, I know, but I'm the last of the de Mourvilles, at least of those with any connection with this part of France. My mother's family is different. The Rogers come from Paris or the environs. Yes. I must go to Paris.' And then to England, he thought, to the Stantons, to Anthea.

'But not today, Jean-Pierre.' Madame Vernet had been watching him closely, and spoke firmly. 'By the looks of you, you could do with a square meal, not to mention a bath and a shave.'

86

So Jean-Pierre spent the day at the cottage. He bathed in a tin bath in the scullery. Then, while Madame Vernet washed his clothes, he lay on her bed, wearing one of the old priest's nightshirts and a gown. He found it difficult to sleep although he was bone weary; he supposed he was still feeling the aftermath of the fever that had laid him low at the Poiriers' farm. And he couldn't relax. His mind was in chaos as he tried to come to terms with his new situation.

The hours passed slowly. Once or twice he heard strange voices downstairs and knew that Madame Vernet had been right to urge him to keep out of sight during the day. At noon she brought him a bowl of thick vegetable soup, and later, when it was dusk and his clothes were dry, he came down to share their evening meal with them.

'You will sleep in my bed tonight,' Madame Vernet said. 'I will use the couch in the front room.' She brushed aside Jean-Pierre's protestations. 'I will wake you early, and you will be off at first light.'

She was as good as, indeed a good deal better than, her word. When he came downstairs the next morning, expecting to leave at once – he had said goodbye to Father François the night before – he found hot coffee and a bowl of porridge waiting for him, and beside his plate a packet.

'Goat's cheese sandwiches,' said Madame Vernet when he looked at her enquiringly, 'and here are a few francs for the Métro when you get to Paris.'

'Madame, I can't thank you enough,' Jean-Pierre said, 'you and Father François.'

'It will be enough thanks if you are able to start a new life and find happiness,' she said sadly – words that Jean-Pierre was to remember.

Then it was time for him to go, but before she embraced him in farewell, Madame Vernet added, 'Father wouldn't approve of what I am going to tell you. He is an innocent man, and he would say I am tempting you, but God will judge.'

'Madame?'

'On the far side of the café next door to here is a pathway which you may or may not remember. It leads to a shed where Monsieur Rabet keeps his motorcycle. How much *essence* there is in the tank I don't know – petrol is scarce – but he doesn't seem to go short, and with luck it will take you a fair way towards Paris.'

'Madame, you are wonderful.' For the first time since he had seen the shell of the Château de Mourville, Jean-Pierre began to feel lighthearted.

'My brother wouldn't say so. He would say I was a wicked old woman. But my conscience doesn't prick me, and if yours should, Jean-Pierre, you should know that the recent rumours about you being in charge of a camp in Germany seem to have originated from that café, or even if they didn't, Rabet's certainly been doing his best to spread them.'

'Then I shall gladly take his bike with, I hope, a full tank. And God bless you, madame, for telling me about it.'

And not much later Jean-Pierre de Mourville, a packet of goat's cheese sandwiches in his pocket, was heading for Paris on a stolen motorbike, leaving behind him the place he had once considered to be his home.

ELEVEN

Monsieur Rabet's motorbike spluttered, grew silent and coasted to a standstill. Jean-Pierre swore softly, but he had no reason to complain. He was on the outskirts of Paris. Monsieur Rabet had served him well. He dismounted and pushed the bike a short distance along the minor road that he had been traversing until he found an unobtrusive place to leave it. Then he walked. But luck was still with him. He had not gone far before a *camion* drew up beside him and offered him a lift.

The truck driver dropped him in the centre of Paris at the Place de la Concorde, and again he walked, this time up the Champs Élysées, marvelling at how normal Paris seemed. By capitulating in 1940, France had saved her beloved capital from all bombing; what fighting had taken place in the city had been mostly between resistance groups after the Liberation, and this had been mainly with small arms. By now there were few outward signs of war. The city appeared clean and prosperous, much as he remembered it when he had last been there as a boy more than seven years ago.

On an impulse he turned into a café and sat down at one of the outdoor tables. Thanks to Madame Vernet his appearance was unremarkable and he had a little money in his pocket. He ordered a chicken dish which was in fact mainly vegetables, but good, together with a *demi*. He asked for bread and was surprised to learn that *tickets* were required for bread, even in a restaurant. The waiter looked at him curiously but, regardless of his lack of *tickets*, produced a roll. Jean-Pierre ate slowly.

Now that he was in Paris and nearing his immediate destination he had begun to feel nervous. Doubts crowded into his mind. His Roger relations might have moved and he might not be able to trace them. They might not welcome him. They might refuse to help him get to England. They might even be dead. There were so many imponderables. The only way to find out was to go to the house where they had lived on the rue de Longchamps in Neuilly.

Jean-Pierre finished his meal, paid for it and left the café. He walked to the nearby Métro station, now renamed Charles de Gaulle, and took the first train to the Pont de Neuilly. From there it was but a few yards to the rue de Longchamps. The lady who opened the door of what had been the Rogers' house had never heard of them, but suggested that he ask at the shops along the street and the avenue, with whom the Rogers would have dealt.

It was an excellent suggestion. Knowing the French penchant for patronizing a single baker, he tried first at the nearest *boulangerie*. He was told at once that Monsieur Bernard Roger had died early in the war of a heart attack, brought on by news that their son Guy had been killed in action, and Madame had not long survived him. But Mademoiselle Roger still lived in Neuilly, in an apartment building overlooking the Bois de Boulogne, and still bought her bread and pâtisseries from them.

To Jean-Pierre, Mademoiselle Roger was his cousin Ghislaine. When he had last seen her she had been a pretty plump girl of approximately his own age but, in his opinion, far more sophisticated than he was. He assumed she had changed as he had changed, but he wasn't prepared for the woman who opened the apartment door to him.

'*Ghislaine!*' he exclaimed. '*Tu me connais – Jean-Pierre de Mourville?*'

They stared at each other in disbelief. Ghislaine Roger was neither plump nor pretty now. She had become a thin, scraggy woman who looked ten years older than she was. And the man she saw was no longer the attractive, rather withdrawn young boy she had once known, but a gaunt and purposeful stranger.

'Jean-Pierre, is it really you?'

'Yes, really me, but much has happened since we last met.'

For a moment she eyed him doubtfully. Then, convinced, she said, 'Of course. Of course. So much to tell. So much to ask. But I am keeping you on the doorstep. Come in! Come in!'

Ghislaine led the way into a long salon, which was both comfortable and elegant, and waved Jean-Pierre to an armchair. She excused herself for a moment, and disappeared into what was obviously a kitchen, leaving him to look at an array of photographs on a side table, which ranged from studio portraits to snapshots. There were several of a man he didn't recognize; others were of Bernard and Marie Roger and Guy. Ghislaine herself figured in some of them, and so did he in one or two.

'Looking at my picture gallery?'

Jean-Pierre started. He hadn't heard Ghislaine return to the salon. She was standing in the doorway, smiling at him. She carried a tray with two champagne glasses.

'Except for me they are all dead,' she said sadly. 'Guy and Robert were killed in action, defending La Belle France against the Hun invasion. What a farce! But they were army officers and had more sense of honour than our Maréchal Pétain.' She put down the tray and came to sit opposite Jean-Pierre.

'Robert?' he queried softly, anticipating the answer he was to receive.

'Robert Latour. He was a friend of Guy's. We were engaged. We were to be married on his first leave, but we never had the chance. I survived. I was young. When Maman and Papa died soon after – Papa could never accept Guy's death – I sold the house and moved here. I'm not rich, but I'm comfortably off as my needs are small. I have the church, a few friends, books, music and a well-paid job as a secretary to a doctor. It's not the life I'd hoped for, but I've a lot for which to be thankful.'

'Ghislaine, you're only a few months older than I am – in your mid-twenties – but you sound as if – as if – The war's over now, remember. Things will change. You'll meet someone else.'

'No.' Ghislaine Roger shook her head. 'I shan't marry, Jean-Pierre. Robert was the only man I ever wanted or ever will want. But don't be sad for me. I'm not unhappy.'

Jean-Pierre didn't try to argue. He felt it would be an impertinence. It was true that he and Ghislaine were first cousins, but they had never known each other well, and now they had met again almost as strangers.

Ghislaine was standing up. 'I'll fetch the champagne. It's cooling in a bucket in the kitchen. My last bottle. I was saving it for when the war ended, but when it did there was no one to share it with. But you must tell me about yourself, what has happened to you, why you are in Paris.'

'Champagne,' Jean-Pierre said when she returned. 'I haven't tasted champagne since the day my parents told me they were sending me to England. You knew about that?'

'Yes, and I know they are dead too – and what happened to their château. I had quite lost touch with them. I wrote but there was no answer. A short while ago I wrote to the priest. I couldn't remember his name, but I remembered the name of the church. To my surprise

I received a very curt note in reply. I had thought the priest was a family friend.'

'He was. Indeed, Father François still is, as far as there's a family. But he's retired. I've met the new priest, and he seemed to me a most unpleasant character.'

Ghislaine nodded. 'Let us drink to happier days,' she said, lifting her glass. 'Then tell me about England and what you have been doing.'

'But I don't understand! It's preposterous, absurd, contrary to all justice!' Ghislaine said angrily as Jean-Pierre ended an abbreviated account of his last six years. 'I think you've behaved splendidly, been very brave. Your father would have been proud of you, Jean-Pierre, and I'm sure neither he nor your mother ever did anything of which they could be ashamed. I can't imagine how these ludicrous stories started – about them, yes perhaps, because there were Germans living in the château with them – but not about you.'

'Nor do I, really.' This was a half-truth; he didn't want to tell her of his suspicions.

Ghislaine ignored the remark, and concentrated on her own line of thought. 'I can't understand why you didn't get in touch with this Brigadier Beaumont as soon as you escaped from the camp. Wouldn't it have been easier? Then surely it would have been possible for you to contact one of the Allied groups instead of trying to make your way home by yourself. I don't understand,' she repeated.

'No, my dear cousin, I'm afraid you don't understand. When I left the camp I had no money and only the rags I stood up in. I was half-starved and filthy. I knew I was in Germany, but not exactly where, and the local inhabitants were mostly suspicious and unhelpful. I was taken for a vagrant or a deserter. There were quite a few around – thousands of so-called displaced persons, I've since understood. Ghislaine, I had no means of contacting Brigadier Beaumont, and on the occasions I approached British soldiers they either laughed at me or they wanted to arrest me; the Americans were kinder. So I decided it was best to avoid them. My one desire was to get home. I thought that once I was there my problems would be solved. But how wrong I was. Now, apart from the fact that I'm reasonably clean and not positively hungry and I have a few francs in my pocket, I'm in much the same position as I was when I reached home and saw what remained of the château.'

'No, you are not, Jean-Pierre,' Ghislaine contradicted him firmly. 'You are here with me in Paris. This is your home until you can get yourself sorted out, and decide what you want to do. Meanwhile you'll find I'm not a bad cook. So, you have shelter, food, wine – alas, no more champagne after this, just *vin ordinaire* – and we'll buy you some clothes. I assume you don't have any luggage with you.'

'Ghislaine –'

'No, don't thank me. It's what my parents would have wished, what I wish. After all, our mothers were sisters. And that's why you've come to me, isn't it? – for help – as in other circumstances Guy would have gone to your family. Isn't that true?'

'Yes, indeed.'

'I'm glad. For today, relax. Tomorrow you can make contacts – I'm lucky enough to have a telephone – and plans.'

Plans? They were Jean-Pierre's first thought the next morning when he woke in Ghislaine's spare room. He had slept well and felt refreshed. The previous evening he had listened in stunned amazement as she told him of events that were evidently common knowledge. He hadn't known, for example, that Roosevelt had died, that Mussolini had been executed by Italian partisans, that Hitler really had committed suicide or that the Labour Party had come to power in Britain. He had never heard of atomic bombs, of Hiroshima and Nagasaki. He had been living in a small, enclosed world, where all that mattered was personal survival, and now suddenly he felt at a loss, as if he belonged nowhere, as if other people's lives had moved on, coloured by major events.

This was brought home to him later that morning when at last he succeeded in telephoning England and obtained the number of Brigadier Beaumont's country house. A woman answered the phone and he apologized for bothering her.

'I'm trying to get in touch with Brigadier Beaumont,' he said, having prepared his approach in advance. 'It's very important. I used to work for him at one time, but I've lost the number of his Baker Street office.'

There was a long silence, and he wondered if he had lost the connection. Then the voice, now sounding gruff, said, 'I'm sorry. My husband is not here. He had a stroke two days ago and is seriously ill in hospital. I believe a Major Keith Grayson is in charge of the office at the moment, but it's being disbanded or whatever

93

they do to redundant sections in the army when they're no longer needed.'

'I see. I – I'm sorry. I hope the brigadier recovers soon,' Jean-Pierre stammered.

But the line had gone dead before he finished and he still hadn't learnt the number of the Baker Street office. Not that it mattered. He couldn't imagine himself announcing his return to Keith Grayson, and being welcomed home. But what was he to do now?

He had been sure that, once he had been able to make contact with the brigadier, he would be warmly received. He had hoped that arrangements would be made for him to get back to England and that, while this was being achieved, the brigadier would tell the Stantons of his survival, so that when he appeared the shock would not be too great. But this was no longer feasible, and he couldn't hide his disappointment.

Ghislaine tried to cheer him up. 'Jean-Pierre, surely there is no great hurry. It is sad about your brigadier, and you don't seem to think this Major Grayson would be helpful, but you're welcome here for as long as you wish to stay, as I hope I've already made clear.'

'I know. Thank you. But I do want to get to England now as soon as I can.'

'It's because of this girl you were telling me about – Anthea, isn't it?'

'Yes, but we haven't seen each other for almost three years. So much may have happened to her. She would have believed I was dead. And I must put things right with the authorities. At the moment I have no papers, nothing to prove who I am. On a mundane level, there's the question of my back pay, for instance.'

'You could go to the British headquarters here, or the British Embassy.'

'And what do I say, even if I could reach some reasonably senior British officer or official, which is doubtful? The chances are that no one there will have heard of Brigadier Beaumont and his unit. It was all top secret and, assuming I could persuade someone to make inquiries, with the office closing down he would only be told that de Mourville was reported missing, believed executed by the Germans in 1943. Ghislaine, I could spend months in prison as a deserter – possibly accused of trying to take a dead officer's place – before the whole affair was sorted out.'

'Couldn't I vouch for you, Jean-Pierre?'

'My dear cousin, perhaps – eventually. I don't know. But –'

'What is it? There's more, isn't there?'

'Yes. I'm – I'm afraid.'

'Afraid? Why? What of? The war is over. There are enormous problems ahead, I know, but you are still young – absurdly young considering what you have suffered – and you are in one piece, not maimed. Surely you have no need to be afraid of anything.'

'I wish that were true. Unfortunately I'm not sure it is. Ghislaine, when I was working with the *Résistance* at Vire in north-west France, Henri Colet, who ran the group, hinted more than once that he believed I was a traitor. I didn't pay a great deal of attention at the time. I thought he just resented me. But it became more and more evident that there was indeed a traitor, and this was confirmed when I became a prisoner of the Germans at St-Lô. Now, if I am to believe Father François and his sister, as I must, the story has spread and has grown more plausible because of my supposed behaviour in the camp, and because of what happened at the château, that I was that traitor. And I'm scared.'

'You're thinking of what I told you last night that – that people believed to be guilty of war crimes are to be brought to trial. But – but –' Ghislaine shook her head in dismissal of what Jean-Pierre had implied. 'You weren't at home during the war, and you can't be held responsible for your parents' supposed collaboration. As for the camp, others who were there would surely come forward to support you? And anyway, though I hate to put it so bluntly, Jean-Pierre, even if you were guilty, you're surely not important enough to warrant prosecution.'

'Probably not,' Jean-Pierre agreed, 'though according to your *France Soir* anyone who was in charge of a German camp will be held accountable. However, all that's just another worry – almost beside the point. The problem is how I get out of France and into England without papers or passport and without facing a battery of interrogations when I haven't the corroboration which Brigadier Beaumont would have provided. The odds are that I'd land in a prison cell on one charge or another.'

Suddenly Ghislaine stood up. 'Wait!' she said peremptorily as if he were about to take some violent action.

Jean-Pierre waited. Ghislaine hurried out of the salon where they had been sitting. He had no idea what she had in mind, and he didn't care. He felt horribly depressed.

Ghislaine returned in five minutes. She was carrying a collection

95

of papers and what proved to be a French passport. 'Here we are,' she said. 'This is the answer, Jean-Pierre. I should have thought of it before. You can go to England as my brother, Guy Roger – Guy would have been happy for you to take his place. No one will doubt you. Fortunately, the passport's still valid and has never been cancelled; he didn't take it with him on active service. You're near enough like him. I know you're two or three years younger but you don't look it, and there's all the necessary confirmation here. What do you say?'

'What do I say?' Jean-Pierre gave her a long look. 'Ghislaine, I say that you're wonderful, and I shall be eternally grateful to you – and to Guy.'

TWELVE

'The house is perfectly habitable. We *must* move in – soon,' Keith Grayson said, not for the first time.

The move was a long-standing subject of discussion, if not downright argument, between Keith and his wife. Now that London was free from all attacks and was adjusting to peace, there was no reason why the Graysons shouldn't live there as a family, rather than Anthea and the boys staying in the country with Keith visiting them whenever he could. Nevertheless, Anthea continued to raise a string of objections.

She had nothing against the house in Marylebone as such. It was convenient for shops, close to Regent's Park and, if rather small – she called it poky – there was a pocket handkerchief-sized garden at the back where the children could play. She would miss the countryside, her parents, her friends, especially Meriel. But Keith had quite a few friends in London and there would be weekends, holidays; the train service to Oxford was good and as petrol became more available she would be able to drive down to pay visits whenever she wished.

'It's not as if I was expecting you to emigrate to Australia or Canada,' Keith had once said bitterly. 'You're being unreasonable, Anthea.'

She accepted that this was a fair accusation. She *was* being unreasonable, at least according to Keith and everyone else. But she couldn't explain her feelings, not even to Meriel. She had tried and failed.

'Keith, don't you think we should wait until after Karen's wedding?'

Karen Grayson was to marry Bill Overton in the village church at the beginning of December. In spite of continuing rationing and shortages, it was to be a white wedding, with all the usual trappings. John Grayson paid the bills uncomplainingly and Margaret was having a wonderful time organizing the affair. She could talk of nothing except the guest list, the bride's dress, the cake, the gifts the groom

97

should give to the bridesmaids and what the girls were to wear. There were to be no less than eight bridesmaids, and one page – Peregrine; Peter, to his annoyance, was considered to be much too young for such a role.

Anthea, who privately considered that all this was an unnecessary fuss since Karen and Bill had been sleeping together for years, had refused to be a matron of honour, but she had promised to try to coach Peregrine in his duties as train-bearer. This, however, could be done as easily in London as in the country. Karen's wedding was a specious excuse for postponing the move, as Keith knew full well – and he was tired of excuses.

'Anthea, I shall be demobbed by the end of the year. By then I want us to be settled into our new home with as few domestic problems as possible, because I shall be busy with my civilian job and I won't have much time to spare.'

'What sort of problems?'

'There are always problems associated with a house, but until one has lived in it they're difficult to gauge, except of course for the obvious things like plumbing defects.'

Keith pontificated for a couple of minutes. He was fast becoming an expert on property. Quick to see the potential in houses and flats that had been neglected during the war, he was fascinated by the prospect of buying low and, after some minimal restoration had been done, selling high. Although still in the army, he had a while ago joined a small consortium interested in the same type of ventures, and it was already making a profit. Anthea, who didn't really understand the business, had sensed that it was not always as honest as it might have been – she had immediately distrusted the one member of the consortium she had met, the son of a peer with whom Keith had hoped to impress her – and refused to take an interest in it.

'I thought the house you've bought was meant to be our home,' she said coldly.

'For the time being, yes, though I've told you of my plans. And, apart from the house itself, there are other practical questions, Anthea, such as finding a good nursery school for Peregrine, and a cleaning woman. You don't want to do all the housework yourself, do you? What I suggest is that you come up to London with me tomorrow and we make a list of what needs to be done. Then we set things in motion, and plan to move in the weekend after next, and stick to that. What do you say?'

'All right.' Anthea was, and sounded, resigned, completely lacking in interest, but as she caught Keith's glance of exasperation she acted quickly to placate him. 'That would be fine – the weekend after next. That's definite.'

She made some excuse and went out into the garden. She knew now that she was committed. Living at home – to her The Elms would always be her real home – in spite of the two little boys and Keith's fairly frequent visits, she had been able to delude herself that her marriage was ephemeral and would one day, perhaps quite soon, come to an end. She knew in her heart that this wasn't so, that it was a dream, a fantasy, but she had no desire to give it up. But once she and the boys had moved to London, and she and Keith had set up house together, they would be a family unit, which at least in her mind would be indissoluble for the foreseeable future; it would no longer be possible to dream.

She made sure she could not be seen from the house, and tried to brush away a tear. 'Oh, Jean-Pierre! My beloved Jean-Pierre,' she murmured under her breath. 'If only it could have been you and me and Peter, how happy I would have been.'

She had reached the bottom of the garden and sadly she looked back at the house. She felt as if she were already saying goodbye to the past – and the future looked bleak.

Jean-Pierre arrived at Oxford station and took a taxi to the Randolph Hotel. He would have preferred to walk. At Dover he had changed the French francs Ghislaine had given him, but his train ticket had made a bigger hole in the sterling than he had expected. However, his suitcase, made of leather and stamped with the initials G.R., was heavy and he didn't want to draw attention to himself by arriving at the hotel on foot as if he lacked the money for a taxi.

He was following Ghislaine's instructions. She had impressed on him the need to look and act as if he was used to the best and expected good service, and had therefore insisted that he should travel first class on train and boat. Her argument was that this way he would be much less likely to have his credentials questioned than if he appeared wary and shabby. And the ploy had worked. He had had no difficulty in entering Britain as Guy Roger, a Frenchman come to spend a holiday with some English friends.

It had also been Ghislaine who had advised him to come to Oxford and make contact with David Stanton in his office. He had never been close to Anthea's father, but had accepted him as a kind and generous man, and he saw the wisdom of Ghislaine's advice. Nevertheless, as he was driven through a city that looked at the same time familiar and alien, he became increasingly nervous. Wild possibilities skittered through his mind; supposing David were dead or had retired, supposing the Stantons had moved, supposing they had heard the rumour that he had collaborated with the Germans, and he was no longer welcome, supposing –

Thankfully he reached the Randolph, paid the taxi driver and let a porter carry his suitcase. The hotel was not full, and there was no difficulty about a room. As soon as the porter had been tipped and had left him he went at once to the telephone and, sitting on the edge of the bed, riffled through the directory. With a sigh of relief he found the entry for Stanton, Mercer & Webb, solicitors. The address was the one he remembered, and he asked the hotel operator for the number.

'Stanton, Mercer and Webb,' a voice said.

'Mr Stanton, please.'

'I'll put you through to his secretary, sir.'

'Thank you.'

Another voice answered, and Jean-Pierre said, 'I'd like to make an appointment to see Mr Stanton some time today, please.'

'I'm sorry, sir. I'm afraid that's quite impossible. Mr Stanton's diary is full for the little of the morning that's left, and this afternoon he's calling on a client in Woodstock. Would you care to see Mr Mercer or Mr Webb?'

'No! No. I – I – It must be Mr Stanton, and it's urgent. When will he be available?'

The secretary, who had been about to suggest a date the following week, must have caught the hint of desperation in Jean-Pierre's voice, for she said, 'Would twelve-thirty tomorrow morning be convenient for you, sir?'

'Yes, all right. Thank you. Tomorrow morning, twelve-thirty.'

'And your name, sir?'

'Mr – Morel.'

Jean-Pierre put down the receiver. This was not how he had planned his reception, his welcome by David Stanton, though Ghislaine had warned him that problems might arise, and his doubts returned. But until now everything had gone well, and he consoled himself with the thought that this was merely a postponement. An extra twenty-four hours scarcely mattered.

He decided to go for a walk around Oxford. It was a fine sunny day with a nip in the air, and the city was looking its best. He went as far as the Parks, and, feeling hungry on his way back, went into the Lamb and Flag in St Giles' and had a sandwich and half a pint of beer. Afterwards, crossing the road, he spent some time in Blackfriars, thinking of the months that had gone by since he left the camp in Germany, and praying. Then, having lit a candle for those who had helped him on his way, he strolled back past the Martyrs' Memorial, intending to spend a few minutes browsing in Blackwell's, the famous bookshop in Broad Street.

He was outside Balliol College on the north side of the Broad, when the incident happened. He noticed a shop on the opposite side of the street – it called itself a gallery, the Derwent Gallery – and seemed to sell paintings, sculpture, objets d'art, the odd piece of antique furniture and bric-à-brac; he thought he might inspect it more closely on his way back to the hotel, time having to be filled somehow until twelve-thirty the next morning and his appointment with David Stanton.

As he watched idly the door of the gallery opened and a woman in her late twenties with short dark hair came out on to the pavement. She wore a brilliant red dress and made a patch of colour against the shop front and the creamy Oxfordshire stone of the surrounding buildings. She caught his attention. But the next moment he was distracted by the appearance of a second woman.

He was shocked to see that the second woman was Anthea. She had grown her hair, which had been short and curly, and now wore it in a long bob. She looked thinner than he remembered, but there was no doubt about her identity.

Heart pounding at the unexpectedness of the encounter, Jean-Pierre leaned against the wall. He felt physically sick. As in a dream he watched the women lift a double pram over the gallery step. Then they embraced, the woman in the red dress went back into the shop and Anthea pushed the two children along the street away from him.

Weak with relief that he was not to have an immediate face-to-face meeting with Anthea, Jean-Pierre stayed where he was for a full minute. It was not surprising that Anthea should have been in Oxford or that she should be friendly with the woman from the gallery. But who were the children? Even in the brief moments that he had seen her with them, he had noticed that there had been something possessive in Anthea's attitude towards them.

Resolutely he crossed the road to the gallery and went in. Meriel had just seated herself at a desk in a corner of the room. She looked up and gave Jean-Pierre a wide smile.

'Can I help you, or would you like to browse around?'

Jean-Pierre had acted on impulse and hadn't planned what he would say, but the words came naturally. 'The lady with the two small children you were wishing goodbye a few minutes ago – I think I used to know her, but I'm not sure.'

'Mrs Grayson, you mean? Anthea Grayson?'

Grayson? So she had married Keith? One of the children would be Keith and Marcia's – he remembered that they had had a son – and the other – The gallery revolved slowly round Jean-Pierre and he turned his back, pretending that a picture had caught his eye, so that the woman wouldn't see his expression. As from a distance he heard his own voice.

'No, that wasn't her name. The girl I was thinking of was called Elizabeth something. We used to work at Ag and Fish together.'

'Well, Mrs Grayson certainly worked at Ag and Fish during the war.'

'What a coincidence. But still, obviously I was mistaken.' The lies came spontaneously, and Jean-Pierre was glad of them. If the woman should happen to mention his inquiry to Anthea she would never associate it with him.

The woman was saying, 'It's strange how one person can remind you of another.'

'Yes.'

He was yearning to get out of the shop now, but he forced himself to look around and eventually bought a small glass owl. It cost him five pounds, which he could ill afford.

Jean-Pierre lay on the bed in his room at the Randolph Hotel and tried to come to terms with his problems. His instinct was immediately to get away from Oxford and anywhere where he might be likely to meet Anthea or anyone who might recognize him; he certainly wouldn't be keeping the appointment he had made for the next day at the offices of Stanton, Mercer & Webb. But as he would have to pay for his night at the hotel it would have been stupid to leave at once – and where could he go?

He couldn't return to Paris and sponge on Ghislaine. She had already done too much for him and he had some pride left. Besides, he wasn't sure he had enough money to get there. What he needed was somewhere cheap to stay, a chance to try to get a job, any job which would provide him with an interval to consider his situation. Then, when he had reached a decision, he might contact Ghislaine.

He was surprised that he could think so logically when he was consumed by grief for Anthea. He couldn't bear to accept that she was now Keith Grayson's wife, the mother of his child. He was sure that she had loved him as he had loved her – did still love her. So why, why had she married Grayson – Grayson of all people?

After a while his thoughts centred on the question of getting a job, and he considered his qualifications. He had to admit that, apart from a knowledge of languages, they were nil. Even his war experiences must be discounted. Then he realized that he was thinking of himself as Jean-Pierre de Mourville, and that at present his only identification was as Guy Roger. Guy, older by three years, had an honours degree in European history from the Sorbonne, but what use would that be? Jean-Pierre pictured himself in an office with European connections, or in a travel agency, perhaps advising on foreign travel, and realized how absurd were both ideas.

He would have to lower his sights. A reputable employer would ask innumerable questions and would want references. He thought of becoming a waiter in a restaurant in London's Soho, where he had a dim idea that languages might be useful, but what did he know about waiting? He was reminded of Joseph and happy family meals before the war, and he could have wept.

But, determined to be purposeful, he pushed himself off the bed and rescued from the wastepaper basket the *Oxford Mail*, the local paper that had been delivered free to his room. He riffled through the pages, looking for advertisements for employment which he hoped might at least give him some ideas.

He saw it at once. It was in a square box in the middle of the page: 'Because of accident substitute French teacher desperately required immediately for boys' boarding school near Reading. Apply Dr Fitzalan.' A telephone number but no address followed.

Jean-Pierre stared at it in amazement. Here surely, given a little tinkering with the truth, was the perfect job for him – or Guy. At least it seemed so on the surface, especially if the words 'desperately' and 'immediately' meant anything. In his present circumstances he couldn't hope to find anything that might suit him better.

'Mr *Roger*? Roger? Rogers, of course. So sorry. The line's not very good. You're interested in this post, are you, Mr Rogers? It's come up unexpectedly because our last French master was unfortunately killed in a car crash, and we need a replacement at once. You are free right now, Mr Rogers?'

'Yes, I'm free, Dr Fitzalan.' Hurriedly disregarding the misuse of his supposed name and in order to explain why an excellent teacher should be at a loose end in what had to be the middle of the term, he added, 'I've recently been demobilized from the army. I went to see my relations in France, and have just come back to England.' He waited hopefully.

'I understand. Tell me about yourself.'

Jean-Pierre told him an amalgam of truths and lies, mainly about Guy Roger, but also about himself. He took the credit for Guy's years at the Sorbonne, but covered his war service by mentioning his work in Intelligence which he couldn't discuss. He claimed to have taught for a year at a lycée in Paris. He said his father had been English and his mother French. Altogether almost instinctively he made out a convincing case for Guy – pronounced in the English fashion – Rogers, with an 's'.

And Dr Fitzalan's need was clearly desperate enough for him to be convinced. He immediately suggested that Mr Rogers should come 'on approval'. He offered full board and lodging, and half a term's salary. If Mr Rogers liked the school and the school liked him, then the post could be made permanent.

Jean-Pierre accepted. He knew he would have been a fool to refuse, but as he put down the receiver he was beset by doubts. He had agreed to phone the school on his arrival at Reading station the next day, when someone would come to meet him, with an estate car for his luggage.

What luggage? He had absurdly few clothes, and no money or coupons to buy more. He had no books – surely the *sine qua non* of any schoolmaster. He had no ration book, which he had gathered from overheard conversation was essential if one was to eat other than in a restaurant. Peace or no peace, food rationing continued in England. What was worse, he had no British identity card, which was vital if he were to become a British civilian, though he suspected that now the war was over many people had lost their cards or thrown them away. By the next morning his doubts had been resolved; books could have been stored with a friend, and a large bag containing clothes, identity card, coupons and ration book had gone missing or been stolen on the railway. He could always lie his way out; by now he was an accomplished liar. And what did it all matter? He was Guy Rogers now, and Anthea would never know that he had come back for her – too late.

Interlude

1965

For the majority of people the years pass smoothly, almost imperceptibly. The newspapers, with their columns of births, marriages, anniversaries and deaths, bear witness to this. But sometimes for someone there is a year so full of events as to be shattering at the time, and always memorable. For Anthea Grayson such a year was 1965.

In the January of that year Keith, who by now as a result of his property dealings was a very rich man, informed Anthea that he had bought Cherwell Manor, a fine Georgian house standing in ten acres of land not far from Oxford. He had not consulted her beforehand, but such unilateral action was not unusual, even over important decisions such as the purchase of houses.

'This really is it,' he said triumphantly, 'our country place. I'll employ a first-class couple to deal with the household chores. You can get good staff if you pay enough. We'll keep our present town house, of course, but you can spend as much time as you like in the country, and the boys will be happy to bring their friends there. What do you think, sweetie?'

Anthea looked at her husband. Approaching fifty, he had put on weight, the result of too many expense account meals, but he was still in good shape. She could understand why women found him attractive, and she wondered if his willingness to let her spend as much time as she liked in the country was due to the increased demands of his current mistress. She didn't care. If she had been faithful to Keith, it was merely due to personal fastidiousness.

'It sounds great,' she said. 'The boys should enjoy it, especially after working in London all the week.'

In fact, Peregrine and Peter were no longer boys. They had both been to Westminster School, Peter as a King's Scholar – an honour which Keith appeared to begrudge him, presumably on Peregrine's behalf. After school Peregrine had gone up to Cambridge and had become a barrister, but had made no secret of the fact that he intended to go into Parliament; he had recently married Joyce

Carruthers, the granddaughter of a cabinet minister. Peter, more than two years younger, had chosen to go up to Oxford, and was now a Third Secretary in the Foreign and Commonwealth Office.

'I hope you'll enjoy it too, Anthea.'

'I'm sure I shall.' She thought that she would be able to see Meriel more often – Meriel had blossomed from gallery owner to director of a growing interior decorating business – and she would be able to make more casual visits to her parents. 'When do I see the place?'

'Whenever you like, my dear. I was thinking we might have a small house-warming party next month.'

'But will it be ready? What about furniture?'

'It came fully furnished. I bought it from someone leaving England. He's going to live in the States. We can always change things later if we want to.'

'I see. Well, that certainly saves trouble.' She couldn't keep the edge from her voice. Like the succession of houses Keith had bought for her and the family, this was to be *his* house; she was to have little say, even in the furnishings.

'Incidentally, I've persuaded Dad to sell his house. He's been lonely since Ma died, and there's a suite of rooms at the Manor that would be ideal for him.'

'Good,' Anthea said vaguely.

She felt sorry for John Grayson. In spite of losing his wife to cancer two years earlier, and his own retirement, she was sure he had no desire to move. He was happy enough where he was and he would miss being close to her parents and his other friends. But Keith had decided. Suddenly she became aware that the telephone had rung, and Keith had answered it.

'What is it?' she said as he put down the receiver and she saw his expression. 'What is it, Keith?'

'It's Bill – Karen's husband. He dropped down dead about an hour ago outside the National Gallery. Heart attack!'

Keith's house-warming party was postponed; luckily no invitations had yet been sent out. A new date was found in March. Meanwhile Keith helped Karen to deal with Bill's affairs, and discovered that Bill had left far less money than expected. The house in Pinner that he had inherited from his mother was heavily mortgaged, and the pension from the Civil Service which Karen would receive as his widow was not great, since Bill had died so young. Their savings were minute. Karen had always been extravagant.

John Grayson urged that Karen should come and live with him, but this could only be a temporary measure. Keith had already found a buyer for the Grayson house, and the man wouldn't wait indefinitely to finalize the purchase.

'You don't know how lucky you are, Anthea, being married to Keith,' Karen said. 'When poor Bill's affairs are settled I'll count myself fortunate if I can afford a poky little flat in the suburbs somewhere. I hope you'll ask me to spend a weekend at the Manor occasionally.'

'Of course. You'll always be welcome,' Anthea said and, seeing Karen's lips curl at such an obvious lie, felt ungenerous. If only I could afford a small flat, she thought, Karen could have the Manor, but, apart from the war years, she had never worked, and financially she was completely dependent on Keith.

It had been soon after this that Peter had telephoned Anthea and said, 'I want to invite you to lunch, Mama. I must talk to you, and I have a second invitation for you. When?'

'It's not something catastrophic, is it, Peter?'

'Far from it.'

They made a date and on the day Anthea, sensing that this was a special occasion, took extra care over her appearance. She was still slim, a pretty, fair-haired, blue-eyed woman who habitually wore a sad expression. Peter, who loved her dearly, was proud of her and today, delayed at the office and a little late for their appointment, as he hurried across the restaurant to the corner table where she was siting, he thought how charming she looked and how lucky he was to have such a good-looking mother.

'Good morning, Mama. Sorry I'm late.' He pulled out a chair and sat opposite her. 'If I sit on the banquette beside you, I can't see your face.'

'Hello, darling. Why should you want to see my face?'

Anthea regarded her son fondly. He was all she had ever hoped he would be. Thankful that he didn't resemble his father closely in appearance, she was often taken aback when some odd gesture – he used his hands more than most Englishmen – or some fleeting expression reminded her of Jean-Pierre. And as the years passed she had realized that son and father were alike in character. Peter had inherited Jean-Pierre's intelligence, his gift for languages, his occasional moodiness and his natural arrogance. He didn't have Peregrine's driving ambition, nor his easy relationships with people, which Anthea often thought were false, nor his ability to argue a case in which he didn't believe. If someone had told Anthea that she was prejudiced in Peter's favour, she would have admitted it, but until the boys were adults and could make their own choices she had done her best not to be influenced by this inevitable bias.

'Why should I want to see your face?' Peter repeated. 'Mama, I could make all sorts of complimentary remarks, but to be truthful I want to watch your reaction to what I have to tell you.'

'You're not going to give me three guesses, I hope.'

'No, it's too important for games. Let's get ourselves an apéritif and order the food, then we can relax.'

That accomplished, Peter said, 'Mama, I'm engaged to be married. Her name is Anne Giffard. We originally met at Oxford and have continued our friendship in London. She's a year younger than me, intelligent, attractive and – and I love her very much.'

'Darling Peter. I'm so glad for you. That's wonderful news. When can I meet her?'

'She works in a publishing firm, but she's on leave at the moment – making preparations for our wedding next month.'

'Next month? That's rather sudden, isn't it?'

'Yes, but Anne's not pregnant, if that's what you're thinking. This may be the swinging sixties, but we haven't been to bed together yet, surprising as many of our friends would consider it.'

'Darling, I'm sorry. I must admit the thought did cross my mind.'

'Well, you're not going to be a grandmother yet, I assure you. Why it's so sudden is because I expect to be posted in the spring, and I don't want to go abroad without her.'

'Posted?' Anthea tried to absorb all this news: the good – she would welcome a daughter-in-law – she had never been a possessive mother; and the bad – she had known Peter would be posted sooner or later, but she would miss him. 'Any idea where?'

'Probably Norway. It's not too far away, and we hope you'll come over and stay with us.'

'Of course, Peter.'

A waiter came with their food, and another asked Peter to taste the wine he had chosen. After this enforced interruption, Anthea took up the conversation again.

'Tell me more about Anne. She has a family?'

'Her father is Sir Timothy Giffard – a baronet. He lives with Lady Giffard in Greatbourne Hall in Somerset, a house Anne's great-great etcetera built about two hundred years ago. There are two sons, both older than Anne, one a – a horticulturalist who lives at home, the other a local solicitor. Neither is married yet.'

Peter was grinning broadly and Anthea looked at him suspiciously. She guessed he was teasing her. 'Am I meant to be impressed?' she enquired.

'Horribly impressed!'

'You're marrying Anne, not her family.'

'True, but it's good to have pleasant in-laws, and these are exceptionally pleasant. Anne's father and mother – Tim and Gill – are dears. You'll like them. I'm not so sure that Dad will.'

'What do you mean, Peter?'

Peter laughed. 'Well, it all sounds very grand, but in fact Greatbourne is run as a market garden. The Giffards have very little money, and every penny the business earns goes on keeping the old hall in repair and trying to make it a little more comfortable. But they wouldn't part with it for a million, which is probably the value that Dad would put on it.'

There was a note of scorn in Peter's voice as he spoke of Keith and, while she sympathized, Anthea regretted it. The Giffards didn't sound as if they would understand Keith's pride in Cherwell Manor, and she recalled the comments that Meriel, who had gone with her to look over the house, had made after they had left Keith and were driving back to Oxford.

'A lovely house, but prostituted,' Meriel had said. 'If you buy an old place you must treat it with care and understanding, not tart it up without consideration. That may work for a Victorian terrace job or a flat in Surbiton, but not for a fine period piece. And the furniture and furnishings are far from the best, though expensive enough. Obviously money was no object to the previous owner.' Anthea had wondered what Keith would have made of this judgement, but she hadn't repeated it to him.

'There's something else, Mama, something equally important,' Peter said suddenly after their wine glasses had been refilled. 'The Giffards are Roman Catholics. Anne interested me in her religion when we were at Oxford and the attraction grew. Anyway, I've been having instruction and I'm going to be received into the Church in a week or two.'

'You're becoming a Roman Catholic – a Papist?'

'Yes. Dearest, don't stare at me like that. I'm sorry if it grieves you, though I don't know why it should –'

'Peter, darling, it doesn't grieve me. I think it's very – right for you.' For an instant Anthea was tempted to tell Peter the truth about Jean-Pierre; she had thought of him immediately. But Peter had enough to cope with for the moment, and anyway her agreement with Keith still held good. 'I'm not sure how your grandparents will take it – or Keith.'

'Not too well, I expect, but they'll have to accept it. I'm just glad you aren't unhappy about it.'

'No, indeed. On the contrary. Darling, all your news is good, though I'll miss you when you're abroad.'

'I'll miss you too, Mama,' Peter said, and meant it.

It had been quite a day, Anthea thought as Peter hailed a taxi for her. Quite a year, she added to herself, sinking back in her seat, and there would be more to come – her meeting with the Giffards, the wedding, Keith's house-warming party.

But it was not all to be pleasant, though it continued to be eventful.

In the following June, David and Helen Stanton drove up to Scotland to visit their eldest daughter and her family. On the return journey they were involved in an accident. A long-distance lorry driver apparently went to sleep at the wheel, crossed the central reservation into the other lane and hit the Stantons' car head on. They were both killed instantly.

For Anthea this was a bitter blow, how bitter she only realized after the funeral. Peter had immediately flown back to Oslo, and though Keith had urged Anthea's sisters and their husbands to stay for a few days, they were effectively strangers to her, and indeed she was glad when they went. Not that this meant she was alone at Cherwell Manor, even when Keith was in London. John Grayson had moved in permanently, and Karen was there, supposedly until she found a small flat, though it didn't seem to Anthea that she was making much of an effort in this direction.

It wasn't for some months that Anthea was to appreciate that the death of her parents was to alter her life in more ways than leaving a void. The Stantons had always lived modestly, but this had been from choice. When their estate was finally settled, and the amount left divided between the three daughters, Philip Mercer, David's partner in the law firm and his executor, informed Anthea that she would inherit a substantial sum.

'I certainly won't be rich,' she told Meriel, 'but I'll have enough to be independent. I don't need much. A small flat, and I might be able to find a job of some kind. I know I'm not trained for anything, but –'

'You've made up your mind to leave Keith, then?'

'Yes. I hope we can part on good terms. Only his pride will be hurt and I expect he'll call me an ungrateful bitch. But Karen will be happy to take over my job at Cherwell Manor and he keeps a mistress in London. He won't miss me. If he wants he can have a divorce, but I doubt if he will.'

And by the time the fateful year had ended, much that Anthea had foreseen had come about. She and Keith had parted, fairly amicably. It was Karen who had accused her of ingratitude in the face of Keith's kindness to her and her 'bastard'. However, she was not living in a small flat and taking whatever job offered. Meriel had made a counter-suggestion.

'As you know,' she said, 'I'm in the process of expanding the interior decorating side of the business, and this will mean that I shall need someone to take full-time charge of the gallery, someone I can trust. The job's yours if you want it, Anthea.'

So, at the beginning of 1966, Anthea found herself working in the Derwent Gallery and, having abandoned the idea of a flat, sharing Meriel's house in Ship Street. It proved to be an ideal arrangement that neither of them was to regret.

And what of Jean-Pierre de Mourville, who had become Guy Rogers? That is another story.

Part II

1993–1994

THIRTEEN

John Grayson had been duly laid to rest beside his late wife in the presence of his doctor, his lawyer and his family. That there were no friends at his graveside was to be expected; John Grayson had been in his ninety-seventh year, and his friends were all dead.

It was a bitterly cold day, the sky the colour of dirty pewter, and snow started to fall as the coffin was lowered into the ground. The mourners were thankful to hurry to their cars and set off for Cherwell Manor, where they hoped warmth and comfort, drinks and hot food awaited them.

They were not disappointed. A great log fire at each end of the long drawing-room supplemented the central heating. There was coffee for those who wished it, mulled wine and the usual array of drinks, served with hot baby sausages and small stuffed pastries in addition to the customary titbits.

'What! No champagne?' Anne Grayson murmured to her husband, Peter.

'Surprising,' he said. 'Dad always overdoes things.'

'That's not kind.' A cousin whom they didn't know had overheard. 'If you'd come as far as I have, from Yorkshire, for Great-uncle's funeral, you'd be grateful for such wonderful hospitality.'

'Yes, of course,' Anne agreed sweetly, and didn't add that she and Peter had flown in from Brussels where Peter was at present the British ambassador.

The cousin gave them a doubtful glance and drifted away. It could have been any party at Cherwell Manor – Keith Grayson, though in his mid-seventies, still liked to entertain – and old John had lived too long for anyone to feel real grief at his departing. The one who appeared to have most regrets was his daughter Karen, who was enjoying her customary role as hostess for her brother.

'Such a pity Pa didn't live a few more years,' she said. 'Then we'd have had a telegram from the Queen on his hundredth birthday. To miss it by so little is such a shame.'

'Do you really mind, Aunt Karen?'

Karen regarded her great-nephew, Peter's son, coldly. 'Yes, of course I mind, Christopher. It would have been an honour for Pa and for the whole family.'

Verity – a pretty girl, dark-haired and dark-eyed – grinned at her brother. 'I expect the telegrams are all sent out from some office, and the Queen knows nothing about them,' she said. 'I wouldn't call that much of an honour.'

'Of course you wouldn't. *You'd* rather have a telegram from the Pope.' Two spots of colour appeared on Karen's cheeks and she tossed her head angrily before walking away.

'Poor old Karen! I don't think much of her logic.' Christopher, who was a philosophy don at Oxford, tried not to laugh. 'No matter. She means well.'

'If I didn't believe that, coming from you, that was a damning remark, I would disagree,' Verity said. 'Karen doesn't like us, and it's not just because we're R.C.'

'It's because she has no discrimination,' Christopher said.

There was the sound of a muted gong and the buzz of conversation subsided. A white-coated houseman who had been helping the two maids pass around drinks and small eats, announced that luncheon was served, and the guests, no longer pretending they were mourners, filed into the dining-room. There were no place cards – the one concession to informality – and people sat where they happened to be. It was not an altogether happy arrangement.

Joyce, Peregrine's wife, had seated herself at the end of the long table facing Keith at its head, a place usually reserved for Karen. It was unfortunate because Joyce seemed to feel that she should dominate her end of the table, and she had a carrying voice. 'This is an unhappy occasion,' she pronounced over the smoked salmon, to the surprise of her immediate neighbours. 'But the next gathering of the family will be one for rejoicing. You all know that Verity, my niece, is engaged and soon to be married. Come the spring, Cherwell Manor would make an ideal setting for a wedding.'

It was small talk. Joyce was good at small talk. She was not unintelligent, and over the years she had learned that this kind of half-intimate gossip went down well, especially with her husband's constituents, who were able to disdain rather than envy her or were glad to enjoy a feeling of pseudo-intimacy with her. By now, such conversation had become a habit, and formed an excellent cover for her innate shyness.

There was a murmur of approval at the idea of a wedding at

Cherwell Manor. It covered the yelp of pain that Verity had given when Christopher kicked her under the table. She had opened her mouth to say that nothing on earth would induce her to be married from a place that she heartily disliked, and Christopher had prevented the explosion.

But Peregrine had seen her expression and interpreted it correctly. 'Verity may have other plans, Joyce darling,' he said to his wife. He saw no advantage to be gained by having Verity's marriage to Julian Cordel, a young architect, celebrated at Cherwell Manor, with all the fuss and bother it would involve. 'Have you, my dear?'

Anne answered for her daughter. 'Yes. We've made some decisions. It's to be a small wedding, to take place at Greatbourne in Somerset where my family live.'

'What a pity,' Joyce said. 'A wedding here would have been such fun.'

'And we shall have one in June, if Dad agrees. Joyce's cousin, Lady Starminster's youngest girl, wants a country rather than a London wedding, and I thought we might volunteer.'

In fact, Peregrine had just made up his mind. Myra Starminster had been throwing out broad hints for some while, and he had been evading a direct answer. The Starminsters were as poor as the proverbial church mice but Myra, who was better as a friend than an enemy, still had the ear of some important people, and young Starminster could prove a useful ally in the Lords. And wasn't this why he had married Joyce – because of her useful connections?

'What do you say, Dad?'

'Of course, Peregrine. Why not?' Keith responded at once. 'I like Myra.'

'And at least she'll be grateful,' Karen remarked, with a meaningful look at Anne.

By now the pheasant casserole had given way to a raspberry concoction – the cook's speciality – followed by a cheeseboard. There had been a succession of wines, and as the mourners left the dining-room for coffee in the drawing-room several of them were unsteady on their feet.

Karen had certainly been drinking too much. Her face was flushed, and as she and Peter crossed the hall together she had to brace herself by taking his arm. Perhaps she really was grieved by her father's death, he thought charitably, but his charitable feelings were not to last long.

As he and Karen came into the drawing-room Joyce's carrying

voice greeted them. 'Of course, we're glad Grandpa Grayson left his entire estate to Peregrine. It was wise to skip a generation because of taxation, and we can do with the money, though it won't be a great amount. Everyone thinks a Minister of the Crown earns a lot and has all sorts of perks, which is true, but the demands made on one's purse are absolutely enormous.'

Someone made a remark which Peter didn't catch, and Joyce continued, 'I suppose it was unfair not to leave Peter, his other grandson, something, but –'

'Not a bit unfair!' Karen interrupted. 'He didn't have another grandson.' Her voice was loud and slurred. 'Peter's no Grayson. His father was a Frog. If you don't believe me, ask Anthea.'

There was a heavy silence. Keith took half a dozen steps across the room and seized Karen by the wrist. The cup of coffee which the maid had just given her went flying. The liquid stained her dress and burned her hand so that she cried out. Only Peter was close enough to hear Keith say through his teeth, 'Shut up, you stupid bitch!'

'Keith, you're hurting me,' Karen whimpered.

Keith released her. 'Take Mrs Overton to her room,' he said to a maid. 'She's not well.' He turned to the guests, one hand on Peter's shoulder. 'Sorry about that little contretemps, everyone. I'm afraid Karen has had a drop too much of the vino. She was very fond of her old dad, and it's hit her hard.'

There was a murmur of understanding and sympathy. The spilled coffee had distracted attention from what Karen had said. Only one or two of those present could have quoted her verbatim. Conversation resumed and Joyce, laughing, asked what on earth Aunt Karen could have meant about a frog.

Keith's hand tightened on Peter's shoulder before he said, 'A joke, my dear. You know the story of the frog who turned into a prince when the princess kissed him. Well, my marriage to Anthea, Peter's mother, was meant to turn me into a prince. I don't think it did, but then I don't think I was a frog before she kissed me.'

'I'm sure you weren't, Dad,' Peregrine said.

'How would you know? You were hardly in nappies at the time.' There was general laughter. Peregrine pretended to be abashed. And the embarrassing incident was forgotten for the moment.

'I shall drive!' Anne announced and waited for her husband to object, but he didn't.

'It would never do for one of Her Britannic Majesty's ambassadors to be caught driving while drunk,' said Verity, getting into the back of the Rover beside her brother.

'I am not drunk. I've never been more sober.'

Something in Peter's voice halted further comment. They drove in silence. The snow had stopped, but the wet roads glistened with patches of black ice. Luckily there was very little traffic about and they made fair progress to Oxford.

On the outskirts of the city, Peter said, 'It will be no joy driving to London in this weather, especially once it gets dark. I suggest we change our plans and, instead of dropping Christopher off and going on as we intended, the three of us spend the night at the Randolph. What do you say?'

There was no disagreement. Christopher said he was sorry not to be able to put them up, but it was term time and the college was full.

'That's settled then,' Peter said. 'It'll give me a chance to go and see Mama.'

'To ask her about what Karen said? Peter –' Anne didn't like the idea.

'Yes. Karen was tipsy, but she meant what she said, that I was not a Grayson, not Keith's son. Keith was really angry. He swore at her, called her a stupid bitch, and he hurt her. He didn't care that he'd upset the coffee over her. I was standing right there, close to them, and I couldn't have been mistaken.'

'But because he was angry doesn't mean that what Karen said was true,' Anne protested. 'I know you believe Peregrine is Keith's favourite, but that's not unreasonable since Peregrine's mother was killed so tragically when he was still a baby. After all, you've always been closer to Anthea, haven't you?'

'Yes, and Keith's always treated me fairly, I admit.'

'What about your birth certificate, Dad?' Verity asked.

'According to that, Keith Grayson was my father. He and Anthea were married some months before. I was a premature baby, but not illegitimate. However, after Karen's little outburst and Keith's reactions, I'm filled with curiosity.'

'Well, you should stifle it for the moment, Peter. Anthea's not properly recovered from that nasty bout of 'flu – she won't want to be bothered by unpleasant questions. Though I suppose it's fortunate she has been ill, or she would have been at this wretched luncheon today.'

123

'But she'll hear about it. What do you bet? Even though she and Keith are separated, she's very good at keeping in touch with the Graysons. Joyce will certainly tell her, and it's better she should be warned.'

'I'm not so sure about Aunt Joyce.' It was the first time that Christopher, usually prepared to air his views, had made any comment.

'Why do you say that, Chris?'

'The downstairs cloaks was occupied and I wanted a pee, so I nipped upstairs. I was coming out of the bathroom when Grandad – Keith – came out of Aunt Karen's room and in case he thought I was snooping I retreated. But I hadn't shut the bathroom door and he must have turned to deliver his Parthian shot before he left her, because I heard what he said. "You keep your goddam mouth shut in future, Karen. We can't afford to have the past raked up, not now that Peregrine's prospects are so bright." Then he went downstairs, and in due course I followed. But I think he may well tell Joyce to keep her mouth shut too.'

'*Peregrine's* prospects?' Anne queried. 'Are you sure that's what he said, Chris?'

'Positive.'

'It doesn't make sense,' Peter said. 'Oh sure, Peregrine has prospects. He's got every chance of becoming Prime Minister before too long. But even if it turned out that my father was Hitler or Mussolini, which might stop *me* getting a more interesting post, I don't see how it would affect *him*.'

'More likely to be Charles de Gaulle, Dad.'

'You mean just as unlikely, Chris.'

'No, I don't. You know how racist Aunt Karen is – like all the Cherwell Manor lot. It would be typical of her to call a Frenchman a Frog, and one of your given names is de Mourville.'

'That was to please my grandmother.' Peter was impatient. 'She and the de Mourvilles were great friends, and when their only son was killed in the war she thought it would be a kind gesture to commemorate his name in her grandson, and Mama agreed. I've told you this before, Chris.'

'It was just an idea.'

'Anyway, Karen said that if we didn't believe her we should ask Anthea, and that's what I propose to do. I don't like mysteries. I suggest we find out if the hotel can put us up, and if they'll accept us without any luggage. Then you three can have tea or whatever

124

you like and I'll walk around to Ship Street, buying three tooth-brushes on the way.'

'All right,' said Anne, knowing that further argument would be useless. 'But be gentle with her, Peter. Don't make it an inquisition.'

'As if I would – ' Peter feigned amazement.

'Can I come with you, Dad?'

'Chris – ' Peter hesitated. 'Yes. Why not? But no one else,' he added quickly as Verity started to speak. 'Otherwise we'll look like an intimidatory committee and that, as your mother said, is the last thing we want, because whatever – if anything – is behind this accusation of Karen's, I'll back Mama any time.'

'And so say all of us,' Christopher said.

FOURTEEN

Anthea Grayson was curled up in a chair in front of the fire in the little house in Ship Street that she shared with Meriel Derwent. She wore pyjamas and a gown. A book lay open on her lap but she wasn't reading. Although she had only been out of bed for a few hours she felt tired. She was approaching her seventy-first birthday and, after a nasty bout of 'flu which had left her drained of energy, she looked her age.

She was surprised when the doorbell rang. Not expecting anyone, she hadn't bothered with make-up and had merely run a comb through her hair before she came downstairs, so that, half-ashamed of her appearance, she was reluctant to go to the door immediately. But the bell sounded again.

Thinking that perhaps Meriel was home early and had forgotten her key, Anthea pushed herself out of her chair, thrust her feet into her slippers and padded into the narrow hall. She opened the door.

'Peter! Chris! What a lovely surprise. Come in quickly before this horrid cold penetrates the place.'

'You go back by the fire, Mama. We'll hang up our coats and join you in a minute,' Peter said.

'Would you like tea?'

'No thanks. Nothing.'

'We've been eating and drinking since noon,' Christopher explained. 'The hospitality of Cherwell Manor can be somewhat overwhelming.'

Of course, old John Grayson's funeral, Anthea thought. She reproached herself for having forgotten it was to take place today. And, true to form, Keith would have made a great occasion of the obsequies.

'How are you, Mama?' asked Peter anxiously as he and Christopher rejoined her.

'Recovering slowly, but I tire easily. It was a nasty bout of 'flu,' Anthea replied.

126

'Take good care of yourself, then. And if there's anything we can do –'

'No, no. I'm all right really,' she said. 'Tell me about the funeral.'

'The funeral was fine,' Peter said, 'as far as any funeral can be fine. In any case, it was surprisingly simple and short. No one wanted to hang around in a poorly-heated church, and it was bitter by the graveside.'

'The simplicity didn't apply to the "afters",' Christopher added. 'We didn't actually have any champagne toasts, but –'

'Typical of your grandfather.'

'Yes.'

The monosyllable had fallen flat, and Anthea looked from Christopher to Peter. 'I'm sorry. What have I said? I didn't mean to be unkind. I thought we were sharing a – a family joke.'

'Mama, there was an unfortunate incident after lunch,' Peter said. 'Karen was drunk, and when Joyce said that old John Grayson should have divided his estate between Peregrine and me and not left everything to Peregrine, she got very indignant. She said that was rubbish, since Keith was not my father.'

'How – how embarrassing for you, for everyone,' Anthea said slowly. 'How did they take that comment?'

She scarcely listened as they told her. She had always believed that one day something like this would happen. Nevertheless, it had come as a shock. For the moment she didn't know what to say. But she didn't want them to have to ask if it was true. She would tell them without being asked. She wasn't ashamed. She must tell them now, in spite of any objection Keith might have.

'Karen was right,' Anthea said bluntly at last. 'Keith is your stepfather, Peter, not your natural father. We were married when I was several months pregnant.'

'Did he know?'

'Yes, Christopher, he knew.'

'That was pretty noble of him, then, to accept another man's child as his own.'

'So his family thought,' Anthea said coldly.

'Then who was – is – my father?' Peter asked. 'Mama, I realize it must grieve you to talk about it, but now I've learnt half the truth, I must know more.'

'Of course. I understand. Your father was a Frenchman called Jean-Pierre de Mourville, Peter. He was a brave, honourable man. We loved each other very much and would have married, but he

127

was killed in France, working with the Resistance. He was an only child, and his parents, who were friends of my mother, died during the war when their château was burnt down, so you have no close French relations. If there are any cousins, I don't know who they are.'

'I still don't see why you had to marry Keith.'

Anthea looked at her grandson in exasperation, before attempting to explain. 'Christopher,' she said, 'we are talking about fifty years ago, practically prehistory to you and, whatever you may have read or seen on television, it doesn't give you the full picture. Personal problems may not have changed much, but people's attitudes to their solutions have.'

'I don't know what you mean.'

'Christopher, sex isn't something you or your father's generation has discovered. It's been going on for a long time. Girls, even nice middle-class girls like me, have been getting pregnant when they shouldn't for as long as anyone can remember. In 1943 I thought I had a choice of either having a nice, quiet illegal abortion, or having the baby adopted. But I *wanted* my baby, Jean-Pierre's baby, and I'm glad I kept him.'

Anthea's voice broke and she started to cry. Peter was out of his chair, kneeling beside her, cradling her in his arms. He was near tears himself.

'Dearest Mama, I'm glad you did, too. Very glad.'

Anthea blew her nose and gave him a watery smile. 'Let me explain. Eventually, there turned out to be a third possibility – to marry Keith. He wanted me. He always had, but I'd always refused; I wasn't and never had been in love with him, but now was his chance. I know that sounds uncharitable, but that's how it was. Keith acquired the wife he had always wanted, and a mother for Peregrine. He promised to claim Peter as his own and bring him up like his natural son. Thus he avoided any gossip that I had only married him because I was pregnant by another man, which would have hurt his pride. For my part, I was saved from disgrace, and in those days producing an illegitimate child *was* considered disgraceful, at least among families like the Stantons and the Graysons and their friends. What's more, the wretched child was stigmatized too. That's something that's changed for the better, thank goodness.'

Christopher thought for a moment, and then said, 'You mean if it became known it wouldn't make any difference to Dad's career?'

'I very much doubt it, Chris.'

'And Peregrine? How might it –'

'Enough questions for today, Chris,' Peter interrupted him. 'Your Gran is looking tired, not surprisingly after this rotten 'flu, and our – our unexpected news.' He gave Anthea a hug. 'I'm sorry about all this. We'll leave you in peace now. We can talk about the de Mourvilles another day.'

'Yes, of course, darling.' Anthea returned Peter's embrace. 'It would give me a lot of happiness. But before you go I'll run upstairs and get some snapshots I'd like to show you. They're old and rather poor, but they're all I have so I've treasured them.'

Alone, the two men grinned at each other in relief, and Peter murmured, 'She took it well, thank God.' Christopher nodded. There was no time for more before Anthea returned – clearly she had known exactly where to find the snapshots.

'Here we are,' she said. 'It's a pity there aren't more, but film was scarce during the war, and of course the quality wasn't anything like it would be now.'

There were a couple of dozen prints, brown and faded. Peter and Christopher passed them to each other in silence. Except for two, which showed Jean-Pierre in the uniform of a second lieutenant, they looked as if they could all have been taken on the same occasion. The setting was the same – Peter recognized the Stantons' garden – and Jean-Pierre could have been wearing the same slacks and shirt. But though a little stiff, they had a certain charm, and what was striking was the resemblance of Jean-Pierre to his grandson, Christopher. 'It's an extraordinary likeness, Mama. Hasn't anyone ever commented on it?'

'No one else has seen these photographs to make the comparison, no one who knew Jean-Pierre. Remember, he died in 1943, the year you were born, Peter.'

Anthea passed a hand wearily over her face and Peter looked at her anxiously. 'Mama, are you all right to be left?'

'Yes, of course. Off you go. I'd like to be alone, and Meriel will be home soon anyway. Bless you both.' She smiled from her son to her grandson. 'I don't know what I'd do without you.'

When Meriel Derwent returned to Ship Street she found Anthea, her face wet with tears, staring into the fire. Scattered around her were the old snapshots of Jean-Pierre de Mourville.

'I'm going to make us a strong whisky each. Then you can tell

129

me what's happened,' Meriel said firmly, and when Anthea had told her of Karen's drunken indiscretion and its aftermath, she added, 'My dear, I realize this must have brought back a lot of memories for you, but does it really matter? Of course it was a shock for Peter and his family to learn of the doubts about his parentage – especially in that way, but they're all adults now, and the general climate has changed so much. No one would hold it against you or him these days.'

'It matters to Keith.'

'To Keith? Too bad!' Meriel had never had much sympathy for Keith Grayson. Then she had second thoughts. 'Anthea, why should it worry him so much after all this time?'

'I don't know, but it does. He's just telephoned me. He wanted me to promise that if Peter started asking me questions I would swear there was absolutely no truth in Karen's accusation, and I told him he was too late. I had already admitted it.'

'And then?'

'He gobbled, Meriel. There's no other word for it. The sound came clearly over the line and I had a wild desire to laugh. But Keith was serious. He said it could prove disastrous if the media got hold of the story, but at first he wouldn't explain why, except to suggest it could damage Peregrine's prospects.'

'Peregrine's? What about Peter's?'

'It's Peregrine who matters most to Keith. You can't blame him for that. Anyhow, when I pressed him he said there was something he had never told me. When he was in France at the end of the war he found out that it was the French who had set fire to the Château de Mourville, and thus caused the death of Jean-Pierre's parents.'

'The French? But why should they –'

'During the occupation the Germans took over the château, but the de Mourvilles were allowed to go on living there. According to the locals they had made the Germans welcome – they had always been pro-Nazi, it was claimed – and they did very well for themselves as long as the enemy was there to safeguard them. When the Germans left the locals took their revenge. It's not a nice story.'

'No, not nice – if true. But I still don't understand why, even if all this should become public knowledge, it should affect Peregrine. He's not remotely related to the de Mourvilles, and therefore any scandal connected with them should be irrelevant as far as he's concerned.'

'You say – if true. Are you suggesting that Keith was lying?'

'No-o, though I wouldn't put it past him if he wanted to be unkind. But what I was thinking was that during the war France, like other occupied countries, was a hotbed of rumours. People paid off old scores, sometimes new ones. Heavens, Britain wasn't immune. It's possible that this tale Keith was told about the de Mourville's Nazi sympathies was merely the result of spite.'

'I suppose so.' Anthea was tired. She was still weak as a result of her recent illness, and the visit of Peter and Christopher with their questions about Karen's accusation had been more of a strain than she had realized. 'Anyway, I don't think I should repeat it.'

'To Peter or Christopher? Definitely not.' As she had grown older, Meriel's opinions were apt to be definite. 'It would do no good, and might do some harm. I'd agree with Keith. On the whole it's better not to rake up the past.'

But the past, thanks to Karen's drunken indiscretion, had already been raked up, Anthea thought, and she knew that it had always been lying there, waiting to be revitalized. Now it had happened and she was afraid, though she had no idea why.

'Well, no one can say that it hasn't been an exciting day,' Peter said.

The four of them – Peter and Anne, Christopher and Verity – were sitting in the bar of the Randolph Hotel, discussing what Anthea had told them. They were all disturbed or intrigued, though in different degrees.

'It's a most romantic story,' Verity said.

'Not all that unusual in wartime,' said Peter. 'But I admit that when you're one of the characters involved it's far more interesting.'

'Well, I hope your curiosity is satisfied, Peter.'

'My dear Anne, doubtless Mama will tell us more about Jean-Pierre as she remembers him, and I shall be delighted to listen, but I agree that the "Mystery of the Frog" is now solved.'

'Except for how it concerns Uncle Peregrine.'

'Chris, it can't concern Peregrine. He's only two and a bit years older than I am. He was a baby at the time and he's not related to the de Mourvilles.'

'You must have misheard what Grandad said to Karen, dear.'

Christopher shrugged. He hadn't misheard, but it wasn't important. He wasn't prepared to argue the point, and he certainly wasn't going to question Keith or Karen on the subject. Let Jean-Pierre rest in peace. He looked at his watch. He was dining in Hall, and it was time he went back to his college.

'I must be off,' he said. 'As Dad said, it's been an exciting day.'

FIFTEEN

There, apart from some idle conversation, the matter might have rested, had it not been for Celia Bingham. Celia was Christopher Grayson's current girlfriend. She was twenty-five, the same age as Christopher and also an Oxford don, though she didn't live in college. She had a small garden flat in North Oxford, which they both found extremely useful.

They had been going together for nearly a year and, though the subject of marriage hadn't been discussed, they had each wondered if theirs might be a lasting relationship. They were physically attractive to one another and they had a great deal in common, not only their academic work, but other interests such as music and the theatre.

Nevertheless, they hesitated. Christopher had never met Celia's parents and her two younger brothers, who all lived in Scotland, but he knew from what she said that they were staunch Presbyterians. For her part, Celia claimed to be an agnostic, and she and Christopher carefully avoided religious controversy. However, the one occasion on which he had taken her to Ship Street to visit his grandmother had not been a success. Celia had later commented on the crucifix in Anthea's bedroom, and had added, 'I suppose at her age religion is some compensation for a lack of sex.'

This defect in perception had jarred on Christopher, and he had not invited Celia to Ship Street again. It had been left to her to come to a decision and make the first move towards encouraging their relationship to become more formal. She had suggested that during the Easter vacation she and Christopher should drive up to Scotland and perhaps drop in on her parents for a day or two. Christopher, not deceived, had agreed, albeit reluctantly.

It was the Saturday morning of the last weekend of term, and all the arrangements for the trip had been made. Christopher and Celia, still wearing their night clothes, were having a late breakfast in the kitchen of the flat when the post came. There was a letter from Mrs Bingham.

Celia glanced at it. 'Mum says she's looking forward to meeting you,' she said.

'Good.' Christopher looked up and put another piece of bread in the toaster.

Celia finished reading her letter, drained her coffee and rose to her feet. 'I'm going to have a shower and dress.'

'Okay.' Christopher was listening to the World Service on the radio. 'I'll wash up the breakfast things before I change.'

'Right.'

Fifteen minutes later when Christopher, his chores completed, went into the bedroom he could hear Celia singing in the shower. She had a pleasant contralto voice, and he smiled at the sound. Brushing against the bed by accident, he knocked Mrs Bingham's letter, which Celia had left on top of the duvet, on to the floor, and he stooped to retrieve it.

Carelessly stuffed into the envelope, the pages had become loose. Christopher had excellent eyesight and Mrs Bingham's writing was clear. He had read half the letter before he could stop himself. It was enough to make him read the whole, and he swore aloud.

'What is it? What are you doing?' Celia had come silently into the bedroom. She snatched the letter from Christopher's hand. 'How dare you read my mother's letter? Do you make a habit of reading other people's correspondence?'

'Do you make a habit of telling lies?' rejoined Christopher angrily. 'How dare *you* tell your mother I'm your fiancé? How dare you let her arrange a party for me to meet "all the family" – and over Easter, too? I told you Easter was out.'

'You don't understand. She and Dad would have been shocked at the idea of us travelling around together if they hadn't believed we were engaged. And why not Easter? They won't stop you going to your church. They're not bigoted like some people.'

Christopher thought for a moment. Then he said, 'I bet you haven't told them I'm a Papist.'

The argument continued and developed into a full-scale row. Meanwhile, Christopher had been dressing quickly and considering the situation. Now he collected the few personal belongings, such as a razor and a clean shirt, that he kept at the flat. He found his bag and threw them into it. He hadn't washed or shaved, but that didn't matter; it could wait till he got to college.

Celia stared at him. 'If you walk out now like this, you needn't come back,' she said.

'I don't intend to.' Christopher tossed the key of the flat on to the dressing table. 'You can write and tell your blessed parents that we are disengaged, and I shan't be present at their party.'

'You – you –'

But Christopher wasn't listening to whatever invective Celia could produce. He was letting himself out of the flat and resisting an impulse to slam the front door.

He found that it was a cold, raw morning with a hint of rain in the air, and he walked fast down the Woodstock Road, his sole purpose to get to college, where he could have a hot bath, make lots of coffee and think what he was going to do during the Easter vacation, which was almost upon him.

There was a choice. He could stay in college and continue with research for the book he hoped to write. He could join his parents in Brussels. He could sleep on the sofa in the London flat that Verity shared with two other girls, and go to plays and films and concerts. None of these possibilities appealed to him.

It was not until late in the morning, when he was eating a solitary lunch in his rooms that the thought occurred to him. There was nothing to prevent him from taking his car to Europe and driving to the part of France that had been home to the de Mourvilles for so many generations.

As Christopher's second-hand BMW, which he had been lucky to afford, consumed the kilometres of the autoroute that was taking him across France to the Château de Mourville, he wondered why his grandmother had been so averse to this expedition of his. He had dropped in to see her on the last day of term to say goodbye and tell her he was going to France, not Scotland, for his vacation. She hadn't questioned his choice until he had explained his purpose. Then she had said it was pointless.

'There's nothing to see, Chris. The château was looted and burnt down during the war and, as I told you, there are no de Mourvilles left. Keith was able to find the place in 1945 and, at my mother's request, made some inquiries. That's almost fifty years ago now. I doubt if anyone will even remember the de Mourvilles, except perhaps for a few old people.'

A few old people, Christopher had thought, such as yourself and Keith and Karen; there was no reason to believe the French were more forgetful than the English. But he hadn't wanted to worry Anthea, and though it was news that Keith had made inquiries on

135

the site at the end of the war, it was no help. In the circumstances he didn't think Keith would welcome questions. Not that it mattered. He was on his way and could ask his own questions.

As he turned off the autoroute and eventually drew near to his destination Christopher experienced a sense of *déjà vu*, which he knew to be false. He had never been in this part of France before. But his feelings of elation lasted. Even when the exterior of the Auberge St-Denis, the only inn in the village, proved not particularly impressive, it was still an improvement on the expected café, with possibly a room to let. In fact, the bedroom to which he was shown was clean, with a bath in one corner behind a curtain and a feather bed that promised a good night's sleep.

Christopher unpacked a few things and then went downstairs to the bar, where half a dozen men were seated around a table drinking. Aware that, as a foreigner, he had aroused their interest, he ordered a *demi* and inquired the time of supper. His French was fluent, though accented, but he was surprised when the *propriétaire*, a Monsieur Rabet, asked him if he was German.

'No. English.'

'We don't see many English here. May we ask your business, monsieur?'

'I'm a teacher, on vacation, touring around France.'

'Alas, there's not much to see in our poor village, but the countryside is fine,' one of the drinkers said.

'You have an old church, I believe, and the Château de Mourville is close by,' Christopher said. 'I thought I might visit them in the morning. I'm interested in the de Mourville family.'

There was a sudden heavy silence. Christopher saw one of the drinkers stop with his tankard halfway to his mouth before he replaced it on the table. His hand must have been shaking, for the beer spilled.

Rabet said, 'There is no de Mourville family any more, monsieur. They are all dead, and the château is a ruin, burnt to the ground.'

'But some people must remember them. You, monsieur, would be too young, but –' Christopher gestured towards the men sitting at the table, but they all shook their heads, though he would have sworn that at least two of them were well over seventy. 'Well, what about the priest?'

'He's only been here a few years.'

'He's not a local man.'

'And old Father François is long dead.'

Christopher nodded in acceptance of this chorus of explanation, of denial. He noted that old Father François, who had previously known the de Mourvilles, was remembered, but not the family who had lived in the nearby château and who must have had contact with the people from the village, and probably employed some of them.

'Your supper is ready, monsieur, if you would care to go through to the dining-room.' The *propriétaire* pointed to a beaded curtain at one side of the room.

'Thank you.'

Christopher slid off the bar stool. Obviously there were to be no more chances to ask questions about the de Mourvilles at present. He went through the curtain as directed, and paused, wondering if he should have offered to pay for his drink or if it would automatically appear on his bill.

And the voice came clearly to him. 'English he may be, but he's no teacher, that one. He's a *flic* like those French *types* last month – the ones who wanted to interrogate everyone about the bloody de Mourvilles.'

He was in a small dining-room, containing no more than half a dozen tables. They were all unoccupied, as it was early. The dining-room, like his bedroom, was spartan in appearance but immaculately clean. And the food was excellent – vegetable soup, roast pork, apple tart; everything, Christopher had no doubt, was home-produced or at least the produce of a neighbour. This, he reminded himself, was still a small, inward-looking community. And, with a bottle of adequate wine, Christopher would have enjoyed his meal if he had not been disturbed by what he had overheard. He couldn't imagine why the French police should be making inquiries about the de Mourvilles, or why the locals should be subjected to such inquiries.

After the meal he went through to the bar, which was now crowded, nodded goodnight to Monsieur Rabet and climbed the stairs to his room. As soon as he entered he knew that someone else had been there, someone who had smoked and had been careless enough not to put out his or her cigarette before opening the door. There was no sign that the visit had been on legitimate business – for instance, the bed had not been turned down for the night. Indeed, except for the faint but unmistakable smell of a Gauloise there was no sign of an intruder. Christopher inspected the things he had unpacked, and the remaining contents of his bag. Nothing was missing. Even the gloves he had stuffed into his raincoat pocket were still there. But he hadn't been mistaken. Someone had been in the room. Uneasy, he got ready for bed.

It wasn't until he picked up his current book – Iris Murdoch's latest novel – which had been lying on the bedside table, and started to read that his suspicions were confirmed. He hated dog-eared pages and always used a bookmark. The bookmark was there, but at the beginning of a chapter he had already read. Presumably the book had been knocked off the table and the bookmark misplaced.

Christopher slept fitfully. He was disturbed by the noisy exodus from the bar below at closing time, but otherwise the night was uneventful. In the morning he paid his bill, parted on seemingly good terms with Monsieur Rabet and collected his car. He inspected the BMW carefully, but there was nothing to suggest that anyone had tried to enter it or tamper with it. He shook his head, dismissing his suspicions, Then, not in the least sorry to leave the village, he drove past the Église St-Denis, which he intended to visit later, and on to the Château de Mourville.

The château was no longer the grim and blackened horror that Jean-Pierre had seen almost fifty years ago. Time and weather had been kind to it. Rain had cleansed it. Moss and lichen had softened its contours; grass had covered its slopes. Even man, picking over the rubble, had tidied the area. Nevertheless, it was still a bleak monument compared with what it had been, the more so since a cluster of small houses had encroached on the grounds, and without isolation the ruins lacked dignity.

Saddened, Christopher returned to his car. Anthea had been right. There was nothing for him here. It held no memories for him, and the characters with whom his imagination tried to people it – Jean-Paul and Chantal de Mourville – lacked reality. Jean-Pierre, his grandfather, he could visualize, but only in England, in Oxfordshire or possibly even in France fighting with the Resistance, not in this place – the ancestral home of the de Mourville family.

He drove back to the church. Except for an elderly woman sweeping the floor and another arranging a cloth on the altar, it was empty. He crossed himself and inspected the building. It was in perfect condition, well kept and well polished. He knelt before a statue of the Virgin Mary and said a brief prayer, then lit two candles, one for his grandfather Jean-Pierre, and the second for Anthea, his grandmother. Afterwards he walked around the churchyard, which was once again well cared for, the paths free of weeds, the graves tended, the flowers all reasonably fresh.

He had no difficulty in finding the place where the de Mourvilles, including Jean-Paul and Chantal, were buried, and was peering at some unclear marks on their stone when he heard heavy limping footsteps behind him. He turned to face an old white-haired man whom he judged to be in his late seventies.

'*Bonjour, monsieur*,' he said.

The old man didn't reply. His mouth had fallen open and he was staring at Christopher as if he had seen a ghost. '*Ah mon Dieu! Mon Dieu!*' he gobbled, his Adam's apple going up and down.

Christopher was alarmed. '*Tout va bien, monsieur?*'

The old man pointed to the de Mourvilles' grave and then at Christopher. '*Je m'excuse, monsieur, mais vous –*'

'Of course!' said Christopher, suddenly grasping the reason for the old man's confusion. 'It's my likeness to Jean-Pierre, isn't it? You knew Jean-Pierre de Mourville, and seeing me here by the de Mourvilles' graves – The two together.'

'*Oui.*' The old man nodded. 'I knew him and his dear parents. I am Joseph – Joseph Flemand. I worked at the château as did my father before me, until the Germans came. The de Mourvilles had sent Jean-Pierre to England, and now they sent me away to what they hoped was a safe part of France, so I do not know exactly what happened here. But I would swear they were never collaborators. Monsieur de Mourville hated the Germans. He had lost a hand in the First World War, and with it his hope of becoming a great pianist.'

'Were they accused of being collaborators?'

'Oh yes! There was a lot of bitterness. When the Germans left the château was burned down – that is how the de Mourvilles died. Some say it was an accident, but I have heard that a party of villagers set the fire. There was a strong communist element in the village, led by Denis Rabet.'

'Rabet? The *propriétaire* of the inn? But surely he must be too young –'

'It was *Denis* Rabet. He is dead. It's his son, Claude, who owns the Auberge St-Denis, and one wonders where the money came from to transform their old café into this inn. Loot from the château, perhaps. But I don't know. I was a long time in hospital where they cut off my leg.' He banged his left thigh, which gave off a metallic sound. 'When I got back here the de Mourville estate had been confiscated, and even the graves desecrated. Those marks you see there were swastikas. I have tried and tried but I can't remove them completely.'

'That – that's a dreadful story.' Christopher was stunned.

'I fear there were many such throughout Europe, monsieur, and even now it's necessary to be careful not to ask too many questions, not to rake up the past.'

Christopher nodded. At least he understood why the owner of the Auberge St-Denis had taken such an interest in him, though not why he had been mistaken for a policeman. He asked old Joseph, who said he had no idea; he lived with his wife, who was the priest's housekeeper, in the presbytery, and these days rarely went into the village. He had heard nothing of the *flics* making inquiries about the de Mourvilles.

'Monsieur,' he said, '*je m'excuse*, but I must ask. You are – connected with the family? It surely cannot be by chance that you are so like Jean-Pierre as I remember him – and you are visiting his parents' graves.'

Christopher hesitated. 'I will tell you, monsieur, but you will appreciate it is in confidence.'

'Monsieur, I give you my word. Not even my wife shall know,' said the old man.

And when Christopher had explained briefly, he murmured his sympathy. 'I am happy to know the truth. There have been many rumours about Jean-Pierre, as you might guess. It has even been said that he was a Nazi-lover like his parents, and that he betrayed a Resistance group near a place called Vire in north-west France. I never believed any of it. There are people who will say anything.' He turned away, and spat to show his contempt.

'Joseph! Joseph!' A woman had come out of the church and was waving to the old man.

'Monsieur, that is my wife. I must go. I am so glad we have met.'

They shook hands, and on impulse Christopher embraced him. 'Goodbye, monsieur.'

'Goodbye and God bless you. Always be proud of the de Mourville name.'

SIXTEEN

Christopher sat in the car, thinking. He felt at a loss, unsure what to do next. He told himself that he had been naïve. In spite of Anthea's warning that a visit to the de Mourvilles' ancestral home would be fruitless, he had looked forward to seeing where they had lived and had hoped to learn more about the family from people who remembered them with affection. He had not expected to be met with distrust, even hostility, or to hear such a shocking story concerning them as old Joseph had retailed.

How much of it was to be believed, he wondered? Had the de Mourvilles collaborated or seemed to collaborate? Had the Germans as a last act of spite set fire to the château, or was this the work of communists led by Denis Rabet? Had the deaths of his great-grandparents been accidental, or had they been deliberately murdered? And the rumours about Jean-Pierre – had they any basis in fact or had they been invented to lend credence to the supposed Nazi collaboration of his parents?

Christopher had no doubt whatever of Joseph's sincerity, but Joseph had only hearsay and his prior knowledge of the de Mourvilles to go on. He had not been living in the village at the time of the German occupation or for some while afterwards. But Keith, Christopher suddenly remembered, had made inquiries about the de Mourvilles soon after VE Day. What had he learnt or not learnt about them? How much had he told Anthea? Had he concealed anything from her? Certainly there had been no suggestion in what she had told Peter or himself that the de Mourvilles had been other than honourable and patriotic, and understandably she had depicted Jean-Pierre as something of a hero.

Jean-Pierre? Christopher had told Joseph that Jean-Pierre had joined the British army, which was true. He had not mentioned that the Frenchman had returned to France to work with the Resistance. It was Joseph who had referred to the Resistance, and in particular to a group based near Vire.

Christopher examined his Michelin book, and then started the engine. Vire was a old Norman town, not far from Caen in the north-west, still relatively small, but not an ingrown village. If there had been a major betrayal of a resistance group there in 1943, the year Peter had been born and Jean-Pierre was believed to have been killed, surely it would be remembered and he would be able to find someone – perhaps a priest, a doctor, a fellow-worker – who would be prepared to talk about it. At least it was worth a try. He would go to Vire, but not today. It would be a long drive, and the morning was already spent. He would go as far as Paris, have a good dinner and break the journey there. After the last twenty-four hours he felt that he deserved a rest from the de Mourvilles. He must not let them become an obsession, but must remember that this trip was part of his vacation.

It was noon the next day when Christopher, having driven along the autoroute from Paris to Caen, and then turned south to Vire – a route similar to the one traversed by Jean-Pierre in much less comfort so many years earlier – entered the centre of the town by the Porte-Horloge. He had decided on a new and different approach to his inquiries, but a bar still seemed the best place to start. Besides, he could do with a drink and some food; his breakfast, of coffee and croissants, had been early.

A café, obviously well patronized by locals, attracted him; he parked the car and went in. He sat down at one end of the bar, and ordered a *demi* and *andouilles*, the rough-cut sausages for which the region is famous. The woman who served him – a large, generous blonde in her fifties – was more than willing to talk to him when business slackened a little, and Christopher took the opportunity to explain himself.

'*Je suis écrivain*,' he said. 'I'm writing a book about the Resistance during the last war. I've heard there was a group – a *réseau* – working out of Vire, and I wondered if you could direct me to someone old enough to remember, someone who could tell me some details about it.'

'*Bien sûr, monsieur*. You are in luck.' She pointed to an elderly couple sitting together at a table. 'Monsieur Henri Colet, who was the mayor of our town for many years, and his wife, Babette. He owned this café at the time, and it is said that more than one plot against the Hun was hatched in the back room here.'

Christopher regarded the couple with awe. To him they looked incredibly old, well over eighty, but they were obviously enjoying their food and wine and were having an animated conversation. The woman had shiny black hair piled high on her head and a plump face heavy with make-up; Babette seemed a singularly inappropriate name for her. The man appeared to be about half her size, a dried-up nut, though it was with an imperious gesture that he ordered more wine. Their clothes, Christopher noted, were expensive. The former mayor and his wife were not poor people. He wondered how he should approach them.

This problem was solved for him. The generous blonde, who appeared to have taken a fancy to him, asked if he would like her to have a word with Monsieur Colet as an introduction, and Christopher gratefully accepted. Five minutes later he was sharing the Colets' wine.

Henri Colet was not averse to reminiscing about the war and the exploits of his group, and when he paused Babette prompted him. All that Christopher had to do was listen and, after the wine was finished, buy a couple of rounds of Calvados. But though several names were mentioned, there was no reference to Jean-Pierre de Mourville. Eventually, Christopher began to wonder if he was wasting his time.

Tentatively he said, 'Sometimes you must have had disasters, been betrayed, lost some of your mates.'

'Yes, indeed,' Colet agreed. 'We were nearly wiped out once, thanks to that traitor from England.'

'An Englishman?'

'No. He was French all right, but he'd been living in England and he was one of the people parachuted in, supposedly to help us. In fact, he almost destroyed us. I began to suspect when the Germans from the barracks outside St-Lô always seemed to know when and where there was to be a drop. Then a safe house was raided, and we lost good people and a lot of equipment. A German we captured admitted the source of their information was Jean-Pierre Morel.'

'Jean-Pierre Morel?' For a moment Christopher didn't know whether or not to be disappointed.

'Oh, that wasn't his real name. He let slip once that he came from some aristocratic family with a big estate not far from Paris, and had been brought up in a château.'

The similarity was too great for it to be coincidence. Christopher controlled his excitement. Of course Jean-Pierre would use some kind of cover name, and there could be little doubt that Colet was speaking of Jean-Pierre de Mourville, but how could this be

143

reconciled with his bald statement that Morel had been a traitor? It was difficult to disbelieve him. He had spoken with considerable certainty, and he had been in a position to know. Undoubtedly he believed the story himself. Nevertheless –

'What happened to this Morel?' Christopher asked.

'That is what the Americans used to call the sixty-four thousand dollar question,' replied Colet. 'There was to be a big drop for replacement of our equipment and personnel. Morel had been in England to organize this, and he insisted on the utmost security, but I didn't trust him. I was right, too. The Germans were waiting. We didn't give Morel the support he'd expected so we got away, but he was captured.'

'Captured?'

'Supposedly. In fact, I bet he was dining with Oberst Becker – the German officer in charge of the area – at the barracks that very night. Anyway, we never saw Morel again. In spite of the evidence, some still say he was not a traitor, but was executed. Others that he was sent to Germany, where he ran a concentration camp.'

Colet excused himself to go to the urinals and Christopher asked Madame Colet if she agreed with her husband's opinion of Jean-Pierre Morel. 'Women are often more perceptive than men,' he said.

Babette Colet gave an expressive sigh. 'Monsieur, Jean-Pierre Morel was a most attractive man but, alas, yes, I feel he did betray us.'

'And what do you think happened to him, madame?'

'If he is still alive I imagine he is living somewhere in Germany, monsieur.'

'The authorities believe he *is* still alive, *chérie*.' Colet had returned. 'Otherwise they wouldn't be making all these inquiries about him.'

'There have been recent inquiries?' Christopher said, remembering what he had heard at the Auberge St-Denis about the *flics* asking questions about the de Mourvilles.

'Yes. With the renewal of neo-Nazism in Europe – you'll have read about it, monsieur – there have been fresh demands that all war criminals should stand trial. It is suspected – and in several cases has been shown to be true – that some who committed dreadful atrocities have changed their names and are living – indeed for years have been living – prosperous and respected lives.'

'You believe Jean-Pierre Morel could be one such, monsieur?'

Colet shrugged. 'I do not know. I would have helped the authorities if I had been able. I believe the man was a traitor to our cause. But I could tell them no more than I have told you.'

'I think we should forgive and forget,' his wife, who had been studying the bottom of her empty glass as if reading tea-leaves, said suddenly. 'It was all so long ago. What good will it do to put old men in prison, even if we are sure of the identifications? And what about their children and their grandchildren, who are totally innocent? There's no doubt that this witch-hunt into the past can ruin many lives.'

Henri Colet smiled ruefully at Christopher. 'Women,' he said. 'They are so sentimental.'

Christopher returned the smile, but he was thinking of himself, his father, his grandmother, Verity. If Jean-Pierre de Mourville was brought to trial as a war criminal, innocent or not, at best it would be unpleasant and at worst devastating for the family.

After he left the Colets, Christopher drove the forty kilometres north-west to the larger market town of St-Lô, rebuilt since its destruction in 1944. His feelings were mixed. He was certain that Henri Colet had not deliberately lied about Jean-Pierre Morel; he saw no reason to change his opinion that Colet believed what he had said, that his Resistance group had been betrayed by Jean-Pierre. But it made no sense that Jean-Pierre, who had made his home with the Stantons in England and had become Anthea's lover, should risk his life being parachuted into occupied France, only to betray his fellow Frenchmen.

Nevertheless, the accusation had to be taken seriously. Henri Colet was no Denis Rabet. He had nothing to gain from spreading false rumours about the de Mourvilles and he had mentioned the names of Claude Le Sohiér and Auguste Maque who had been members of his group, who had worked with Morel, and would, he said, substantiate Morel's betrayal. Christopher hadn't thought it worth while to seek them out to ask further questions. He might well be stirring up a beehive, amd with no chance of gaining from it.

He had reached his own conclusion – a possible explanation of the seeming contradictions between what he had been told and what he knew. There had been treachery; he didn't question that. But he did question whether Jean-Pierre de Mourville, known as Morel, was guilty of it. Colet and his close companions, he believed, were mistaken. Somehow both they and Jean-Pierre himself had been tricked. However, even assuming he was right, to prove it after all this time would be like asking for a miracle, and barring such a miracle it seemed likely that the de Mourvilles would go down in a footnote to history as collaborators and traitors.

Suddenly despondent, Christopher wondered if it was even worth trying to get at the truth. What decided him to continue was the fact that he had nothing better to do with his vacation. He thought of Celia and her family in Scotland, and was glad he was not with them. But it was going to be a very lonely Easter.

There was another reason for pursuing his inquiries, Christopher realized as he found a parking space opposite the Hôtel de Ville in the new civic centre, the Place du Général de Gaulle, and, taking his bag, went to find somewhere to spend the night. Official inquiries were already being made, and if accusations were to follow the more he knew the better his position would be to refute them, or at least to mitigate them. Besides, he was curious; Jean-Pierre de Mourville had been his grandfather.

Ignoring the obvious tourist hotels Christopher found a small establishment in a side street within easy walking distance of the Place. A restaurant next door, at present heavily shuttered, promised an excellent dinner if the menu, displayed outside in accordance with French law, was to be believed. And Christopher reminded himself again, there was no reason why he should allow the de Mourvilles to overshadow his vacation completely.

He had a leisurely bath and changed his clothes. He tried to read, but the book didn't hold his attention. It was still light. The days were drawing out, and so far south of Oxford this was noticeable. He opened the window and leaned out. After a few minutes, he imagined he could smell spring, even early summer, and decided to go for a walk.

It was a beautiful evening and a stroll around the Promenade des Ramparts, with its gardens and its massive bastions welded into the rock, delighted him. Later, returning to the Place du Général de Gaulle. he discovered the big Église du Sacré-Coeur on the rue de Neufbourge, and was reminded that he had not yet done his Easter duties.

Christopher would not have called himself a devout Catholic. He would have said that he took his religion fairly tolerantly, but he was punctilious about its practices. Now, he went into the church with the intention, if possible, of going to confession. He was about to join the small queue waiting beside the confessional when he saw

146

an old white-haired priest come through a door in the rear and limp into a side chapel.

Sacré-Coeur had been almost totally destroyed during the war and had been rebuilt. It had not occurred to Christopher that any of the present priests might have been there at that time. But now, influenced by the obvious age of the priest, and perhaps by his limp which could have resulted from a war wound, Christopher got to his feet and hurried to the side chapel. The old man looked up from his inspection of the candlesticks.

'*Mon père, je m'excuse, mais –* ' Christopher didn't know where to begin.

'Father Damien is in charge here, my son. He is hearing confessions at the moment, so if you need help –'

'Father, it's you I would like to talk to – that is, if you were in St-Lô during the war.'

'Yes. I am Father Vincent, and I was the priest in charge here for much of the war, until my poor old church of Sacré-Coeur was destroyed. During that time I heard the confessions of and gave communion to French, Germans, British, Poles, even the odd Russian and Italian. If that makes me a collaborator, too bad. I would do the same again. So, what do you want to know? I thought I had answered all your questions.'

'Father, you misunderstand. I am not from the authorities. I am not accusing anyone,' Christopher said quickly. 'On the contrary, I am hoping to prove the innocence of my French grandfather, who was Jean-Pierre de Mourville, known in the Resistance as Morel.'

'Jean-Pierre de Mourville, yes. That was one of the names the men from Paris mentioned.'

'They were from Paris, your interrogators?'

'Yes. I demanded to see their papers. They were officials all right – from some security organization. They said they were making inquiries about war criminals who might be still alive, living under different names, who could be charged with crimes against humanity.' The old priest peered hard into Christopher's face, then took him by the arm. 'Come with me.'

He led the way through the door from which he had first appeared, along a green-painted corridor, through another door, along a covered path, and into an adjoining building where eventually they arrived in a small cold parlour, smelling of furniture polish and dominated by a huge crucifix. Father Vincent bent and switched on an electric fire, then waved Christopher to a chair.

'Tell me about yourself, my son, and your grandfather.'

Christopher kept his story as short as possible and the priest listened without interruption, merely nodding his head from time to time. 'Can you help me, father?' Christopher concluded. 'It is a personal matter, as I'm sure you understand.'

'I will tell you what I know, which isn't much, my son.' Father Vincent said slowly. 'I met Jean-Pierre Morel once. I found him asleep in my church one morning. He told me little except that he was on the run from the Germans. I made him breakfast and lent him an old bicycle, but he was caught and taken to the barracks just outside the town, where various special prisoners were kept. After that I have no idea what happened to him. I heard various rumours – that he was executed, for example, or was taken to Germany with the other inmates when the barracks were temporarily evacuated in 1943. I never understood why this was done, but a lot of strange happenings took place during the war.'

The old priest paused, lost in his memories, and Christopher prompted him. 'Have you any idea where in Germany they might have taken him?'

'A German guard told his French girlfriend they were going to a camp at Ansbach, just this side of Nürnberg – but it may not have been true. There were so many rumours. I'm sorry, my son, but I'm afraid that's not much help. Personally, I can't believe your grandfather is still alive.'

'No, it doesn't seem very likely,' Christopher said sadly, and thought that probably this was to the good, certainly if there was any chance he might be traced and tried for crimes against humanity. 'Well, thank you, father,' he said, rising to his feet.

'There is one thing I would like to add before I take you back to the church. My son, when one gets old memory plays strange tricks, and often one remembers clearly an incident that happened fifty-odd years ago, but not one that happened last week. I remember your grandfather with great clarity. For what it is worth, I am sure he was a good man and never in any sense a war criminal.'

SEVENTEEN

Christopher lay in bed and tried to sleep, but his mind was too active. Even a bottle of wine and an excellent dinner hadn't enabled him to relax. It had been an extraordinary day, a day of contradictions, from Henri Colet's vivid condemnation of Jean-Pierre, which demonstrated that there was no doubt in his mind, to old Father Vincent's equal certainty that Jean-Pierre, on the run from the Germans, had been a good and honourable man. Christopher knew whom he believed, whom he wanted to believe, but he couldn't simply disregard Colet's accusations in favour of his own inner convictions; there had been a certain ring of truth about them, and now they haunted his thoughts.

There was another and vitally important point. His quest for information about his grandfather was no longer strictly personal. He was worried about what the so-called official inquiries might produce, true or false, and he thought of what Father Vincent had said. When he had suggested that it was all so long ago, and that it seemed pointless for the authorities to pursue fifty-odd years later those who had supposedly been traitors or collaborators or even war criminals, the priest had provided a valid explanation for the official reaction.

'I believe it is due to fear,' the priest had said. 'As you must be aware, throughout Europe there is at present a revival of Nazi sympathy, resulting in renewed attacks on Jews, which have in some countries spilled over to include attacks on any foreigners, indeed of almost anyone of different colour or creed. As a consequence of this the authorities, frightened that such behaviour could lead to a new Hitlerism, with its concentration camps and all that went with them, are doing their best to demonstrate that the guilty are never safe and will eventually pay for their crimes. It is an attempt at prevention – damage limitation, if you like. The trouble is that in their enthusiasm the authorities may accuse some who were innocent.'

It was a frightening thought, though scarcely believable. Christopher turned and twisted, knotting the bedclothes. Then the telephone rang. Surprised, he switched on the light and lifted the receiver. The time was twenty minutes past two. It had to be a wrong number.

'Hello,' he said.

'Monsieur Grayson?' It was the voice of the night clerk who had given Christopher his room key and wished him goodnight on his return from the restaurant. *'Ne quittez pas. On vous demande.'*

There was a series of clicks and clangs on the line, which made Christopher think it might be a long-distance call. But he couldn't imagine who would be phoning him in the middle of the night, especially as he had told no one where he was staying, not even Father Vincent.

'Christopher Grayson?'

This time Christopher didn't recognize the voice, but it was authoritative and he instinctively resented its tone. 'Yes,' he said shortly. 'Who are you?'

'It is not important to you who I am. I have a message for you. Go home, Mr Grayson. Cease these inquiries you are making about the French side of your family. Otherwise –'

'Otherwise what? Are you threatening me?'

'Yes.' The caller allowed the monosyllable to carry its full chilling weight before he continued. 'Take this as a warning, Mr Grayson. Be sensible. Forget your quest, or whatever you consider it to be. It will bring only trouble for you and everyone.'

There was a final click as the caller replaced his receiver, and another one as the night clerk dealt with the switchboard. Christopher drew a deep breath. He was shaken. There had been something curiously cold-blooded about the call. But it wasn't merely what had been said. It was the fact that someone seemed to have been following his movements, someone who spoke standard English with the slightest of accents, which he couldn't place. Not French, Possibly German.

Christopher slid out of bed and went to the bathroom. He relieved himself and drank a glass of water. He didn't believe that he would get any sleep now, but in fact he fell into a deep slumber almost at once.

He woke with the sun streaming through the window, and a sense of well-being which proved only temporary. The telephone was burring again and, expecting it to be the early morning call for which he had asked, he lifted the receiver.

'Monsieur. This is the concierge. There are two, two – gentlemen – here who insist on seeing you. Indeed, they are no longer here. They are on their way up to your room. *Je regrette, monsieur, mais* – I couldn't refuse. They showed me their identification. They are from Sécurité, monsieur.'

Christopher acted spontaneously: he just had time to leap out of bed, pull on a robe and run his fingers through his hair before there was a sharp knock on his door. '*Un moment,*' he called, a delaying tactic to enable him to catch his breath. He opened the door, and the two men moved forward simultaneously. They didn't exactly force Christopher back into the room, but they crowded him so that he stepped back voluntarily.

They were not big men. They were of medium height, straight-backed, purposeful, clearly military or ex-military types in spite of their civilian clothes. They didn't look dangerous, but they gave the impression that they expected to get their way.

After a formal greeting they immediately produced identity cards and handed them to Christopher, who studied them carefully, comparing the photographs with the originals, and then returned them. There was little doubt that they were genuine, and he assumed these men were the same pair who had interrogated Father Vincent. He told himself that it was ridiculous to feel afraid.

'We would like to ask you a few questions, monsieur.'

'What about?' Christopher sat on the bed and gestured to the two chairs. 'I am English, a tourist in your country. Would you like to see my passport?'

'Please.'

The more junior of the two took the passport, glanced through it and handed it to his superior, who studied it carefully before saying, suddenly, but with an assumed casualness, 'Why are you so interested in the de Mourvilles, monsieur? Are you thinking of writing a book about them?'

It was a temptation to acquiesce – they couldn't prove it a lie – but Christopher resisted it. 'No, not my discipline,' he said with a confidence he didn't feel. 'The de Mourvilles were friends of my family on my grandmother's side. Jean-Pierre was sent to England to stay with the Stantons when war seemed inevitable and . . .'

He told the story straight, omitting the relationship between Anthea and Jean-Pierre, and stressing that Jean-Pierre had always been considered something of a hero by the family, who had been most upset when he went missing.

'My plans for my Easter vacation fell through, and on the spur of the moment I decided it would give a purpose to my trip if I tried to find out more about what did happen to Jean-Pierre. I must admit I am shocked that anyone should think he would betray the French Resistance.'

Christopher was glad he had told the truth, albeit in an emasculated version, when he saw the senior security man give a nod of acceptance. He had no desire to fall foul of the authorities.

'Monsieur Grayson,' the man said, 'you seem to have chosen an unfortunate time for your inquiries. France, indeed the whole of Europe, is unstable economically and politically at present and there is a great rise in nationalism and xenophobia as a result, which is most deplorable. Your inquiries may be innocent but they can cause – complications, and there are enough of those already.'

It was an enigmatic remark, and all Christopher could think of to say was, 'I'm sorry. I simply do not understand. It was all so long ago, and –'

'Monsieur, there is no need for you to understand. But I will tell you a story. A few weeks ago a young girl committed suicide. Her fiancé's family had called off the wedding because they had discovered she was the granddaughter of Armand Lejeune, a baker here in St-Lô, and they wouldn't allow their son to marry her.'

Christopher looked at him. 'I'll ask the obvious question, monsieur. Who on earth is Armand Lejeune? I've never heard of him.'

'I've told you he was a local baker. But he was also a traitor to France. He used to bake cakes for the Germans at the barracks just outside the town here, and he sent messages in his cakes to Oberst Becker, the commandant, telling him about the movements of the local Resistance.'

'What – what happened to him?'

'He shot himself at the end of the war after he learned that his son had been killed. It's possible to feel grief for him. Poor man, he had believed that by acting as a go-between he was making life easier for his son in a POW camp.'

'A go-between, you say?'

'Yes. He received the information by telephone and passed it on. According to his wife, to whom he confessed before he died, he never had any idea of his source.'

'And *you* don't know, monsieur?'

'Not yet. We hope to find out. But I tell you the story, monsieur, to illustrate that the past, even the past of fifty years back, can have a profound effect upon the future. So I would advise you to forget your quest for the de Mourvilles until a more propitious time. And now we'll bid you *au revoir*.'

It was a thoughtful Christopher who shut his bedroom door behind the two security men and phoned for his breakfast to be sent up. Replacing the receiver, he realized that he had not asked them if they were responsible for the warning call he had received in the small hours. Somehow he didn't think they were; it was not that they weren't devious. The story of Armand Lejeune and his grand-daughter raised several questions.

Was it true? Probably. If so, what, apart from the one stated, was the reason for telling it? Was it to put into Christopher's mind the nagging worry that they believed the information the baker was said to have passed on to Oberst Becker originated from Jean-Pierre de Mourville? Was it to suggest a parallel between the Lejeunes and Christopher and Jean-Pierre, which meant they knew Jean-Pierre was his grandfather? Was it even a vague threat to Verity's coming marriage? The Cordels wouldn't appreciate a scandal, but he couldn't imagining Julian abandoning Verity, or vice versa. Whatever the purpose, the undeniable facts were that within the last twelve hours he had received two warnings to stop his inquiries about the de Mourvilles, and especially about Jean-Pierre. So, what was he to do?

He could go home and spend the rest of his vacation in Oxford or London. He could join his parents in Brussels. But there was a streak of obstinacy in him – the same streak which, together with curiosity, made him a good academic – and by the time he had finished breakfast he knew what he was going to do. He was going to Germany, to make inquiries about the Nazi concentration camp at Ansbach, near Nürnberg, that Father Vincent had mentioned.

Again Christopher stopped over in Paris, this time for three nights. He didn't want to arrive in Nürnberg during the Easter weekend. On the Saturday afternoon he went to the Musée National d'Art Moderne, and in the evening he had a good dinner. On Sunday morning he went to High Mass at La Madeleine, and in the afternoon he walked in the Bois. Later he dined in the same restaurant as the previous evening.

Monday was equally peaceful. He hoped that if he was being watched he was giving the impression of a sober young man who, although he hadn't made straight for the Calais–Dover ferry after the warnings he had been given, was nevertheless content to do no more now than enjoy his vacation. And indeed, in spite of earlier misgivings, he found he was enjoying his solitary Easter. He had seen nothing to suggest that anyone was taking a personal interest in him, and driving around the *périphérique* on his way out of Paris he would have sworn he was not being followed, though it was hard to be absolutely certain. Thanks to the autobahn he arrived in Nürnberg in good time, and went straight to the Rathaus. Here his difficulties began.

His German, unlike his French, was not fluent, and there seemed to be no one on duty in the Town Hall who spoke English. Somehow, he gave the impression that he wanted information about the Nürnberg trials of war criminals, and when at last he made it clear that his interest was centred solely on the concentration camp that had existed outside Ansbach he was met with dismissive shrugs. The camp had been relatively unimportant and was now in ruins, its commandant had not been charged with any war crimes and if there were any records of its former inmates still extant they would probably be in Bonn.

Disappointed, Christopher returned to his car. He had hoped that in a large town like Nürnberg, with its close involvement with the trials of war criminals, the information he sought would be easily available. If he had known this was not so, he would have gone straight to Bonn. For that matter he could forget Nürnberg now. He had no desire to visit its fine Gothic churches, not even the famous St-Sebaldus-Kirche, or tour the town's ramparts; for some reason, quite unfairly, he had taken a dislike to the place. He could drive to Bonn right away. But Ansbach was so close and the chance to visit the site of the concentration camp where his grandfather might have been a prisoner and had perhaps died, was surely not to be missed. Heaven knew when he would be in this part of the world again. He had to take this opportunity.

When Christopher arrived in the small Frankish town of Ansbach he was hungry, and ready for a late lunch. But by the time he had finished his meal it was mid-afternoon, and he wished he had settled for beer and sausage. He decided not to bother with a hotel for the moment – his waiter said the town was not unduly full in spite of the Easter holiday – but to go first to inspect the old camp, and he asked how to get there.

The waiter consulted with the owner of the restaurant and between them they gave Christopher directions. He was far from sure he would be able to follow them, even with the help of a map scribbled on the back of the restaurant's bill, but, hoping for the best, he thanked them profusely. He was leaving the restaurant when a man he had noticed at a neighbouring table accosted him.

'*Mein Herr*, if you will pardon me, I heard you asking about the old concentration camp. It isn't easy for a stranger to find, but if you would permit me to take you there –'

'*Danke. Danke*. But I couldn't impose on you.'

'It will only take an hour, which I can easily spare and it will be a pleasure, not an imposition, *mein Herr*.'

'But surely you have –'

'This is a small place, and when one lives here as I do it is always enjoyable to speak with a cultivated stranger. Incidentally, I am Doktor Boris Hueber.'

Christopher introduced himself and shook the hand that was proffered to him. He felt strangely reluctant to accept the Herr Doktor's kind offer, though he had begun to doubt his own ability to find the camp site. He looked sideways at the man as they walked along the street to where he had parked his car.

Boris Hueber was well-dressed, and had been eating at a comparatively expensive restaurant. It seemed unlikely that he would ask for money; he hadn't suggested that he should receive any quid pro quo for the service he was prepared to offer. But why should a reasonably attractive man in his late thirties, as Christopher judged him to be, give up a lovely spring afternoon to take a stranger to see the ruins of an old concentration camp? It was scarcely one of the sights of Ansbach, and Hueber seemed proud of the town.

It was only when they were out in the country that Christopher realized that Hueber's description of Ansbach's fourteenth-century castle with its porcelain gallery and its Room of Mirrors, and the St-Gumpert-Kirche with its chapel of the Knights of the Order of the Swan sounded unreal, as if he had no personal knowledge of these places, but was reciting passages from a guidebook. Cursing his folly, Christopher wished he had been firmer and refused to let Hueber be his guide.

But at last, after turning and twisting down several lanes, they seemed to have arrived. Hueber said they would have to walk the rest of the way, and pointed to a path that led across a rough field to a wood. They had almost reached the first belt of trees when Hueber appeared to lag behind as if tired.

155

If Christopher hadn't come to distrust the Herr Doktor the outcome of what happened next might have been very different. But he was on his guard, and the sudden movement behind alerted him. He threw himself sideways and the cosh landed on his upper arm, doing minimal damage. Then he went on to the attack.

The fight was brief. Christopher was of slight build, but he had studied karate, and Hueber didn't stand a chance. Seconds later, while the Herr Doktor lay panting on the ground, Christopher picked up the cosh and ran for his car. Hueber could make his own way back to Ansbach. Personally, he intended to drive straight to Bonn.

EIGHTEEN

It was late when Christopher arrived in Bonn. After his abrupt departure from Herr Doktor Hueber he had become confused in the minor lanes. His one desire had been to get out of the district and foolishly he had not stopped to consult a map. Upset by what had happened, he had not been thinking very clearly and only recovered his sense of direction when he found himself on the main route to Frankfurt and Wiesbaden, from where it was but a short drive up the Rhine to Bonn.

In Bonn he had made straight for a hotel in the Clemens August Strasse, where he had stayed before with his parents. It was a large establishment, part of a widespread chain, and offered twenty-four-hour room service. He ordered soup and an omelette and a half-bottle of Niersteiner to be sent up, and while he waited for the waiter to come, he raided the minibar for whisky.

He was not exactly proud of himself. His precipitous flight from Ansbach now seemed stupid, an act of panic. At least he could have returned to the town and discovered if Hueber was indeed a resident there, and perhaps learnt something about the man. Because the main questions remained unanswered – who the hell was Hueber and what had been his purpose?

Christopher drank his first whisky quickly and opened another miniature bottle. He considered the possibilities. The most obvious was that Hueber was a common thief, in search of an opportunity. He hadn't looked or sounded like a thief, but the cosh he had produced suggested that his original approach to Christopher had been with a view to robbery or violence. He could hope that the *Engländer* had a fat wallet; he certainly had an expensive car with which, leaving his victim stunned on the ground, he could make his getaway. For surely he hadn't intended to kill. The guessed-at prize wouldn't have been worth the intensive inquiry that would follow the murder of a foreigner on German soil.

Christopher fingered the lump that had resulted from the blow on his upper arm. It was a nasty bruise and it hurt. But he doubted if the blow would have killed him even if it had landed on his head. He took the cosh out of his pocket and examined it. It was small and rubber-covered and when he weighed it in his hand he confirmed that he would have been unlucky if a single blow from it had caused his death. However, it could easily have rendered him unconscious for a while, allowing his aggressor to strip him of all valuables and steal his car. He had had a lucky escape.

And he could take it as a salutary lesson about consorting with strangers, except that he remained far from convinced that the so-called Herr Doktor Hueber was merely a casual thief. The attack could easily be considered as a forceful reminder that he should not ignore the verbal warnings he had received to forget Jean-Pierre de Mourville and go home. Or was this fantasy? He couldn't imagine French Sécurité organizing the incident, but the voice on the telephone was another matter; it had carried a direct threat.

Christopher's thoughts were interrupted by a knock on the door and the arrival of his supper. When he had eaten it he pushed the trolley out into the corridor and got ready for bed, He did not expect to sleep, but the excitement of his confrontation with Hueber, the drive to Bonn and the half-bottle of wine on top of the whisky he had consumed had drained his nervous system. Exhausted, he slept solidly.

It rained overnight and the next morning the streets of Bonn were glittering with moisture, the trees dripping sadly and the mist from the Rhine rolling in over the city. Christopher walked to the Rathaus, a pleasant pink and grey rococo building, from where he was redirected to the Public Records Office. Here he met with disappointment. After a great deal of telephoning between various departments of government, he was told that there were no records of the camp that had once existed outside Ansbach; they had all been destroyed before the camp was abandoned. There was no point in him approaching any other department; a thorough search had been done in response to a request from the French government.

He was turning away when the clerk who had been dealing with his inquiry called him back. '*Mein Herr*, is it important for you? You say you are trying to trace someone. Is it a personal matter?'

'Yes, very much a personal matter. A relation – my grandfather. Would it make any difference if it were some kind of official inquiry?'

'As we told you, there was an official inquiry from French Sécurité a while ago, but we could not help. There are no records.'

'So you said.' Christopher looked puzzled. 'I don't understand.'

'*Mein Herr.*' The clerk had pulled a note pad towards her, torn off a sheet and was busy writing. 'This is the address of a Herr Richmann, who lives in Bad Godesberg which, as you may know, is a superior suburb on the Rhine to the south of Bonn. It is possible he could be of assistance to you. He was himself in that camp when he was a boy.'

'Thank you. Thank you very much.' Christopher took the piece of paper she was holding out to him. 'I'm most grateful.'

'Perhaps you would be good enough not to mention how you came by this name and address. In the usual way, I should respect Herr Richmann's privacy.'

'Of course. *Danke. Danke schön*,' Christopher repeated.

'*Bitte, mein Herr.*'

Christopher was indeed grateful – and excited, though he knew it was more than likely that Jean-Pierre de Mourville had never been in that camp or, if he had, that it was not at the same time as Herr Richmann. But there was a chance that they might have known (or known of) each other, and that Herr Richmann, who by now would be only in his middle sixties, would remember Jean-Pierre. It was certainly a chance not to be missed.

He was doubly grateful for the implicit assurance that French Sécurité had not been informed about Herr Richmann, for if the man had not already been bothered by an interrogation, he might be more willing to submit to questioning. But the persistence of the French, who always seemed to be ahead of him, worried Christopher, and there was the still unsolved mystery of Herr Doktor Hueber. He told himself that he had better be careful.

Drawing in deep breaths of cold, damp Rhineland air Christopher walked back to his hotel. He went to the garage to collect a map of Bad Godesberg, and was surprised to find a man cleaning his BMW. 'Sorry, *mein Herr*. I'm a little late this morning. I'll be finished in a minute.'

'I never asked for my car to be cleaned,' Christopher said mildly.

'It's all part of the service, *mein Herr*.' The man opened his mouth as if to add something, and shut it again. He was grinning. 'I just want to get a map,' Christopher said.

'*Mein Herr*, it is not my business . . .' the man began hesitantly, but he had decided to speak. 'You do know that your car has a bug?' His grin had widened.

'A bug?'

The man took Christopher to the rear of the BMW and pointed under the off-side wing. 'The electronic sort that makes it easy to follow another car, *mein Herr*,' he said as Christopher pulled off a round magnetic object the size of an overcoat button and inspected it. 'Someone must have been eager not to lose touch with you.'

'Yes, indeed.' Christopher was thoughtful; he wondered how long the bug had been there. He took a note from his wallet and gave it to the man. 'Thanks for finding it. Make sure there's not another one, will you?'

'I will, *mein Herr*, I will. You won't be needing the car at once?'

'No, not until this afternoon.'

'It will be ready for you then, *mein Herr*, and meanwhile I'll make sure no one comes near it.'

'Yes, you do that – and thanks,' Christopher was grateful that the man seemed to consider the bug something of a joke; perhaps he thought an irate husband was trying to catch out his wife with her lover.

Personally, Christopher was not amused.

At the hotel Christopher went straight to his room. There were several Richmanns in the telephone book but, given the address, he found the number of Boris Richmann easily. A woman answered but made no difficulty about bringing Herr Richmann to the phone.

As he waited Christopher found that his mouth had become dry. He rehearsed carefully what he wanted to say, but somehow when he started to speak the words came out in a jumble of broken German, and Herr Richmann stopped him.

'*Mein Herr*, I think perhaps my English is better than your German. Shall we try again?'

Christopher didn't try to be subtle. He said he had recently discovered who his grandfather was, and he was trying to trace what had become of him. When he mentioned Ansbach there was a sharp intake of breath on the line, and he paused.

'Yes, I was there,' Boris Richmann said, 'and I remember the place, though I was only a boy at the time. I remember it well, too well. I still dream of it sometimes.'

'Sir, I am sorry. It must be painful for you to speak about it, but –'

160

'What was his name, your grandfather?'

'Morel – Jean-Pierre Morel,' Christopher answered tentatively. There was another pause before Richmann said, 'Yes. I knew him. He was a good deal older than I.' His voice, which had been sounding weak and old, strengthened. 'Listen, I think you should come out to see me? I am busy this afternoon with a directors' meeting, but I shall be free at six. Would you be prepared to pay me a call about that time?'

'Yes, of course, with pleasure. Thank you, sir.'

'Right. *Auf Wiedersehen*, then.'

Delighted with the prospect of meeting someone who had actually known Jean-Pierre Morel at the Ansbach camp, Christopher spread out the plan of Bad Godesberg on his bed and pored over it. Unfortunately it was on a fairly small scale and he couldn't find the street he sought. This was annoying since he did not want to ask at the hotel desk. After the bug on his BMW he proposed to take every precaution not to be followed when he kept his appointment with Boris Richmann that evening.

However, he knew that in the lobby of the hotel there was a giant wall map of Bonn, extending as far south as Bad Godesberg, and he hoped for better luck there. Buttons beside the list of *Sehenswürdigkeiten* or 'Sights not to be missed' caused indicator lights to appear and Christopher tried the Schaumburg Palace, the Rhineland Museum and Beethoven's birthplace. But in reality his eyes were checking for the street where Herr Richmann lived. He found it without much difficulty and memorized the immediate neighbourhood. He was already impatiently waiting for evening.

Christopher did not take his car. In the afternoon, thankful that the weather had cleared, he walked to the university and strolled among the old trees of the Hofgarten. Then, after a while, he made his way through the streets past the Rathaus to the marketplace, where he lingered among the gaily-coloured stalls. He was not as relaxed as he appeared. He was constantly on the watch to make sure he was not being followed.

When he was reasonably confident he took a taxi from a rank and asked the driver to take him to the centre of Bad Godesberg, where he walked beside the Rhine, watching the barges glide by and admiring the romantic peaks of the Siebengebirge on the far side of the river. Many other people seemed to be taking the same form of exercise, but he saw nothing to rouse his suspicions.

Later he went to the restored thirteenth-century castle in the centre of Godesberg, which was now part of a hotel. He had a quick drink in the bar – to his surprise he was feeling nervous – went to the cloakroom, and waited for a taxi to deliver a passenger.

The villa where Boris Richmann lived was more imposing than Christopher had expected, with a circular drive and lawn and flowerbeds in front. The door was opened by a middle-aged woman in a black skirt and white blouse which suggested a uniform. She showed him into a large sitting-room, over-full with heavy, stuffed furniture, but comfortable enough.

Boris Richmann rose from a deep armchair and came to meet Christopher, hand outstretched. 'Good evening,' he said, in English.

'Good evening, sir. It is kind of you to see me.'

For a moment they studied each other. Christopher saw a tall, good-looking man with a lot of grey hair, large brown eyes and a wide, smiling mouth. For his part, Richmann saw a ghost of the past.

'You are very like your grandfather as I recall him,' he said at once.

'You knew him well?'

'No, not really. He was a very private man. He spoke little about himself. But he was kind to me and my mother, and I remember him with affection. My mother was French, as he was, and it was a bond. They talked about Paris. You know, I hadn't thought of Jean-Pierre for years, not until nine months ago when I buried my dear wife. I was standing at her graveside, and I remembered my mother's death. She died at the camp, and it was Jean-Pierre who dug her grave and said a prayer for her.'

'You mean he was some kind of official?'

'Good God, no! He tried his best to keep out of trouble, as did we all, but he did the commandant and his men no favours. Of course there were those in the camp who did. We were a mixed bunch of races, religions, real criminals, fools and innocents, a sort of dustbin of a camp where it was best not to question your neighbour. And, though our circumstances were bad, they were not unspeakable as they were in some places. Nevertheless, the vulnerable – the old, the infirm, the sick – they died, and the strong or comparatively strong, for what with the poor food and dreadful hygiene we were all scarecrows, were forced to dig their graves and bury them.'

162

Abruptly Boris Richmann pushed himself out of his armchair and went to a cabinet, from which he produced various bottles and glasses. 'Let us drink to those who died for us,' he said. 'My mother used to give me half her rations and Jean-Pierre would sometimes risk stealing from the cookhouse for me and for others, though rarely for himself. He was a good man.'

'There are those who think otherwise,' Christopher said sombrely, and told Richmann about Henri Colet who believed his Resistance group at Vire had been betrayed by Jean-Pierre.

'Rubbish! Absolute rubbish!' Richmann dismissed the idea. 'Jean-Pierre was never a traitor or a collaborator. I would bet my life on it.'

Christopher wondered if he should tell Richmann that, rubbish though it might be, French Sécurité was taking a close interest in Jean-Pierre and his wartime activities. He decided against it, on the grounds that it could worry Richmann if he believed his own past might be scrutinized. However, he did tell him about the warning telephone call he had received, the bug on his car and the attack by Hueber at Ansbach, incidents which he admitted could possibly be unconnected with each other.

'Can you think, sir, of any reason why anyone should try to prevent me from finding out what happened to my grandfather fifty-odd years ago?'

It had been intended as a rhetorical question, but Richmann was nodding his head. 'Yes. It seems to me there are two possibilities. Someone gained enormously when Jean-Pierre went missing and either he or his descendants don't want to give up anything. Or whoever betrayed that group at Vire is afraid you'll discover that he, and not Jean-Pierre, was the traitor.'

Christopher considered these suggestions while Richmann went to tell his housekeeper that his guest would be staying for supper. Rabet, who had inherited the café from his father, and probably many others in the village had done well out of the looting and the subsequent sequestration of the de Mourvilles' estate. Were they afraid that he and Verity, as the grandchildren, might try to prove they had behaved illegally and claim back what they had seized? It seemed very unlikely that he could prove Jean-Pierre had been innocent, so they had little to fear.

'Everything is arranged.' Richmann had returned.

'Thank you very much,' Christopher said.

'It is my pleasure. I only wish Jean-Pierre could be with us. You know, for several years after the war I hoped that he would get in touch.'

'After the war? But I thought – I understood you to say he died in the camp.'

'No! No, you misunderstood me. My English, perhaps. No, we left the camp, together with Frau and Fräulein Hauler, who were killed in a car accident some years ago. They were to bring me to Bonn where I found my uncle and other members of my family, but not my poor father, who had been accused of dealing on the black market and had died in prison. Jean-Pierre wanted to go to France, and we parted company when we came to a village where the locals would only allow women and children to enter. The country was in a dreadful state, you must remember. There were a lot of displaced persons and a lot of marauders around, men who would murder for a loaf of bread. I wanted to go with Jean-Pierre, but he wouldn't let me and I wept when we parted.'

'And you have no idea what happened to him?'

'No. I did make some inquiries, but that was some time later, and they were for Jean-Pierre Morel. I didn't know his real name until you told me. I can only imagine he would have gone to his parents.'

'They were dead, sir, and their château destroyed.'

'Did he have no other relatives?'

'None close, as far as I know.'

'I had the impression he had cousins in Paris. I told you that he and my mother used to talk about the city, but I do not recall him mentioning any names. Surely it's possible your grandmother might remember?'

'Yes. I will certainly ask her. Thank you for the information, sir.'

Richmann had been so kind and hospitable that Christopher hated to appear ungrateful, but he was not hopeful. Nevertheless, it would be worth asking his grandmother. It was time he phoned the family, anyway. It wasn't really so long, but he felt as if he had been out of touch with the real world for ages.

NINETEEN

'Christopher, darling! Where are you?'

'In Bonn.'

'Bonn! What on earth are you doing there? Oh, Chris, I hope it's not in connection with the de Mourvilles. Your grandfather is furious, and he blames you. He says you've been stirring up a lot of trouble.'

Christopher poured himself a last cup of coffee. He was having breakfast in his hotel room and had put through a call to Anthea. He proposed to go on to Paris later in the morning, though this was to some extent dependent on what she had to say.

'Why should he be furious? What am I meant to have done?'

'Some men from MI5 came to see him. I gather they were not very pleasant. They interrogated him about Jean-Pierre. One of them said that French security had been forced to warn you off because you were getting in their way. Chris, have you seen any English newspapers recently?'

'No, I haven't, but – I don't follow, Gran.'

'You knew the government was doing badly. Everything seems to be going wrong for them. Well, there's been another couple of scandals in the last fortnight and ministers have resigned. Keith's terrified for Peregrine. The tabloids seize on anything these days, and if they manage to come up with the connection between Keith and the de Mourvilles –'

'What connection?' Christopher interrupted. 'Peregrine's not related to Jean-Pierre.'

'Not really, but Keith did marry me when I was carrying Jean-Pierre's child, and Peter has always been accepted as Peregrine's half-brother.'

'Gran, I'm tempted to say "so what?", except that it would sound rude. This is the slightest, the most tenuous, of connections, and I can't see why the media should be in the least interested. There's nothing in it for them.' Christopher tried to sound reassuring. 'By now it's just a rather sad love story. I don't understand how it could possibly harm Peregrine.'

'If there's a scandal concerning Jean-Pierre, if he's accused of having been a war criminal, it will affect all the family, but Peregrine will bear the brunt of the publicity because he's a Minister of the Crown, and what's more on the right wing. The left will go to town on the tale, and of course it will get twisted and falsified. It could ruin his chances of becoming Prime Minister.'

'I – I suppose it could.'

Christopher was doubtful; he believed that Anthea, having suffered Keith's anger, was exaggerating the potential damage that could be done to Peregrine's career and to his prospect of being Prime Minister, if that were really on the cards. But he was startled that Anthea had learned – presumably from Keith who had got it from the MI5 men – that there was any serious possibility of Jean-Pierre's being accused of crimes against humanity, which would be the official charge.

'Don't worry, Gran,' he said. 'It's extremely unlikely there'll be any scandal involving Jean-Pierre. I've met several people who say he was a brave and good man, and they would vouch that he was never a traitor. As for a war criminal, that's absurd.'

'I only hope you're right, Chris.'

'What about his family on the French side? You said there were no de Mourvilles left, but what of his mother's relations? Do you know anything about them?'

'Chantal's parents would be dead by now, and she was an only child. There could be some cousins, I suppose, but –'

'You must remember what Chantal's maiden name was.'

'Yes. It was Roger. But Chris, please stop these inquiries about the de Mourvilles. You just seem to be causing trouble.'

'You're quite right, Gran. I'm going to forget the de Mourvilles. I'm leaving Bonn today and making for Paris, fine French food and wine, look up some friends, enjoy myself.'

'Good.' Anthea was clearly relieved. 'I'm sure that's sensible. Chris, I must go. I'm on duty at the gallery this morning. Meriel's attending a sale at some great country house. We oldies keep going, you see. 'Bye for now, dear.'

Christopher's conscience pricked him a little – he didn't like lying to his grandmother – but not much. After all, most of what he had told her was true. He was leaving Bonn for Paris, he did indeed intend to enjoy himself there, and, if he wasn't about to forget Jean-Pierre de Mourville, his immediate purpose was to track down a Roger relation.

166

This proved to be no simple matter. There was a list of Rogers in the main Paris telephone directory, any or all – or none – of whom could be related to the de Mourvilles. After lunch Christopher went to his hotel room and started at the top of the list. It was a frustrating pastime. Sometimes the phone rang and rang, and there was no answer. Once or twice a maid or a housekeeper answered. On one occasion a Madame Roger said she knew nothing of her husband's relations – and had no wish to. On another the receiver was banged down. Christopher began to despair.

It was not until late afternoon, on his second attempt to call one of the previously unanswered numbers, that his luck changed. The female voice was old, but businesslike. Christopher explained himself and the reason for his call. There was a long silence. He was afraid she was about to hang up.

'*Madame, ne quittez pas, je vous en prie.*' he said quickly.

'*Mademoiselle,*' she corrected him. 'Ghislaine Roger. My mother and Chantal de Mourville were first cousins.'

'Then we are related, if somewhat distantly. Please, Mademoiselle Roger, may I come and see you?'

'Yes, I – I suppose so.' She was a little hesitant. 'But it is too late today. Tomorrow morning I am busy in the church. There's to be a wedding and I shall be doing the flowers. After lunch I always have a rest these days. Alas, I am an old woman. Tomorrow afternoon, three o'clock, would suit me, if it is convenient for you.'

'That will be fine. I'll be there. Thank you very much.'

At precisely one minute past three the following afternoon, having been announced by the concierge on the internal telephone, Christopher stood outside Ghislaine Roger's apartment and waited for her to open the door. He was carrying a sheaf of spring flowers and a bottle of vintage champagne; he could only hope these gifts would be acceptable.

The door opened and there she stood, a woman in her seventies, tall, thin, but with a certain distinction. In other circumstances, Christopher might have found her a little forbidding, but she was the sole relation of Jean-Pierre de Mourville whom he had been able to trace, and she was clearly moved by the sight of him. The next moment they were embracing.

'Come in! Come in!' She took the champagne and the flowers from him. 'How lovely! Thank you!'

Ghislaine Roger led the way into the salon, a long elegant room

167

whose far windows overlooked the Bois de Boulogne. Christopher was not to know that the furnishings had scarcely changed since his grandfather had been there. There was the same side table laden with photographs, and he went to look at them while Ghislaine took the flowers and the champagne to the kitchen.

'My picture gallery,' she said as she returned. 'You recognize Jean-Pierre? He was about the same age as you are now, and there's a marked resemblance between the two of you.'

'So I've been told. My grandmother has shown me some photographs of him.'

'Your grandmother? The woman he was in love with? But she married someone else.'

'She believed he was dead. He was reported missing in 1943 when she was pregnant with my father, Jean-Pierre's son.'

'He was not dead, though he came near it several times. He was in a detention camp in Germany. When the war ended in 1945 and he was freed, he went first to his family's home, but his parents had died, the château was destroyed and the property confiscated, so he came to Paris and found me. He was in a dreadful state, but he was determined to get to England, to the girl he loved. This was not easy. His health was poor. He needed rest and good food. He had no papers, nothing to prove where he had been or what he had been doing. He tried to reach his English brigadier on the phone, but the unfortunate man was dying, and Jean-Pierre didn't trust the one who was now in command.'

Ghislaine paused. Christopher had made an involuntary sound. The man who had taken over from Brigadier Beaumont had been Keith Grayson. But why should Jean-Pierre not have trusted him? Was it perhaps because of Anthea? Christopher dismissed the idea for the moment.

'And he didn't want to spend months arguing with officials in Paris – British or French,' Ghislaine continued. 'He wanted to waste no more time before getting to England. Of course, he didn't know that his girl had married.'

'How did he find out? Did he get to England?'

Ghislaine explained how she had helped Jean-Pierre by giving him her brother's papers and passport, so that he could take on Guy Roger's identity, and Christopher listened in amazement. She didn't mention money or clothes or how she had cared for Jean-Pierre until he was fit enough to travel, but Christopher could imagine the situation and her reaction to it.

'Jean-Pierre eventually reached Oxford, and by chance he saw your grandmother in the street with two small children.' Ghislaine said sadly. 'It's ironic that he didn't know one of them was his own son – your father. Anyway, he made inquiries and discovered she was married. I know this because he phoned me and I remember how sorry I felt for him. He said he wouldn't ever try to break up her marriage; he had nothing to offer her and he was going away.'

'Going away?' Christopher was aghast. 'He didn't – You don't mean – he –'

'Committed suicide? Of course not. Jean-Pierre was a devout Catholic. No, I understood that his intention was to leave that part of the country where your grandmother and her family lived. Indeed, I expected him to return to France, but he didn't. A few months later I received another call. He said he was all right, that he was teaching in a boys' school and considering the future. Then there was silence.'

Ghislaine passed a hand over her face and gave a tired smile. 'I am sorry, but I am an old woman, and the excitement of meeting you and recalling those sad times has wearied me more than I expected. Christopher, would you mind very much if I asked you to leave me now, and return tomorrow? There is still much we have to say to each other. I must tell you about the security men who came and questioned me about Jean-Pierre –'

'French Sécurité? They questioned *you*?'

Ghislaine nodded slowly. 'I wouldn't have been worried about it, except – Oh, leave it until tomorrow, please.'

'Of course.' Christopher tried not to sound reluctant. He was filled with curiosity, but he couldn't insist. 'When would you like me to come?'

'Come at noon. We'll have lunch together and drink your champagne.'

'That sounds great.'

Christopher kissed her goodbye and left the apartment. As he hesitated outside the door before moving to the lift, he heard her putting up the chain. An elderly woman in the deep black of widow's weeds that have ceased to be popular in France stared at him curiously as she passed him in the corridor and, as he entered the lift, he saw her opening the door of the apartment opposite Ghislaine's; obviously they were neighbours.

On his return to his hotel Christopher went straight to his room. His mood was one of exhilaration. He yearned to share his news with someone, to say he had met a cousin of Jean-Pierre's, that Jean-Pierre had survived the war, had gone to England in search of Anthea, that it was possible he was still alive. His imagination pictured a great family reunion before commonsense took over and he accepted that he was in no position to judge everyone's reactions. He could guess that Keith would not welcome Jean-Pierre, but what about his father Peter, his grandmother – and Jean-Pierre himself? There could be innumerable reasons why he wouldn't want to be reunited with the Graysons after all these years.

TWENTY

The spring flowers and the champagne had been a success, and Christopher didn't feel he should go empty-handed on this, his next visit to his French second cousin. He bought a small jar of caviare, which Ghislaine could store, and some stuffed vine leaves to which he was partial and which could probably be added to their luncheon. Pleased with his purchases, he parked his car without difficulty and, early for his appointment, decided to take a short walk in the Bois.

It was a beautiful day and Christopher walked further than he had intended. He had to hurry to complete his circuit of the Mare St James, but arrived at the entrance to Ghislaine's apartment block as a nearby church clock was striking twelve.

In the lift he met the lady whom he had taken to be Ghislaine's neighbour the previous evening. Again she was dressed all in black, but on this occasion, instead of staring at him curiously, she gave him a little bow and a toothy smile. She introduced herself as Madame Le Breton. As Christopher had surmised, she was a neighbour and – she would like to think – a friend of Mademoiselle Roger, though they were not close companions.

'And monsieur?' she enquired.

Christopher gave her his name, aware that it would mean nothing to her, and added, 'I am a distant relation of Mademoiselle Roger.'

'*Vraiment?* But you are English.'

'Yes.'

Christopher had no intention of giving her any further information, and luckily by now they had reached their floor and the lift had stopped. They walked together to their respective doors. Madame Le Breton searched for her keys in the bottom of her capacious black bag.

'*Au revoir, madame*,' he said.

And, turning away from her, he inadvertently knocked against the door of Ghislaine's apartment. Of its own accord the door creaked open. Christopher found himself staring through the hall, a small square room, into the salon, where all the lights were on.

Ghislaine Roger was lying on the floor. She was wearing a night-dress and gown. Her feet were bare.

'Oh, God!' Christopher said, and ran to her.

Hearing his exclamation of distress Madame Le Breton abandoned the search for her keys and followed him into the apartment. They knelt one on either side of Ghislaine's body, regardless of the blood on the carpet. With surprising presence of mind, Madame Le Breton took a small mirror out of her bag and held it to Ghislaine's mouth.

'*Dieu merci*! It has clouded over. She is alive.' Madame Le Breton scrambled to her feet. 'I will phone for an ambulance and the police.' She looked hurriedly around her. 'Thieves! It must have been thieves, but why did they have to hurt her?'

Thieves? Christopher too stood up. There was nothing he could do for Ghislaine. It was best not to move her, not even to put a pillow under her head. Following Madame Le Breton's example, he looked about him. The salon was in disarray, tables and lamps knocked over, Ghislaine's collection of photographs and the contents of a small bureau scattered on the floor, a vase broken, but the television set and video recorder had not been taken. To Christopher the room suggested that an attempt had been made at intimidation or was the work of vandals, rather than thieves.

He walked through the rest of the apartment, which might have been subjected to a quick search. Otherwise, it appeared untouched, but the lights in the corridor were bright, and in what was obviously Ghislaine's bedroom the lamp on her bedside table was switched on, the bedclothes thrown back as if she had got out of bed hurriedly, perhaps in response to the persistent ringing of her doorbell.

As if in answer to his thoughts, he heard the doorbell ring, and 'Monsieur Grayson! Monsieur Grayson!' Madame Le Breton was calling him.

Christopher collected his wandering thoughts and hurried into the salon. The police had arrived and the ambulance. He was impressed by their speed and efficiency until he realized that time had passed while he had been allowing his imagination to run riot.

He found Madame Le Breton sitting at the dining-table, which was placed horizontally across one end of the salon. Opposite her sat two plain clothes police officers, one of them with a notepad in front of him. Through the door into the hall, he could see Ghislaine, who had been lifted on to a stretcher, being carried carefully out of the apartment. The senior police officer gestured to him to sit beside Madame Le Breton.

'You are English, monsieur?' he enquired.

'Yes,' said Christopher.

'Do you understand our procedures, which are quite different from yours, I understand?'

'Yes, I do, a little. I imagine you're from the Police Judiciare, and I must say you've got here pretty quickly.'

'That's because Madame Le Breton had the sense to phone directly to the Sûreté, thus by-passing the local police.'

'I see.'

'Now a few questions, please, madame, monsieur.'

'Of course,' they replied in unison.

The questions were polite and stereotyped. Names and addresses and relationships to Madame Roger. When had they last seen her? How had they come to find her? And here Christopher was glad he had not been alone.

There were peepholes in the doors to all the apartments; would Mademoiselle Roger have opened her door to a stranger? 'Not late at night,' said Madame Le Breton positively, and Christopher volunteered that he was sure he had heard her put up the chain after he left the previous evening. These remarks were greeted in silence but with great interest.

There was a further ring at the doorbell, and one of the officers opened it to admit a team of men, some in uniform. Photographs and measurements were soon being taken, handles and likely surfaces dusted for fingerprints. Neither Christopher nor Madame Le Breton objected to their own prints being taken 'for the purpose of elimination', and Madame Le Breton provided the names of other visitors to Ghislaine's apartment of whom she was aware – the cleaning lady who came in twice a week, the priest, one or two other casual callers, but no close family.

'She led a very quiet life,' said Madame Le Breton.

The senior police officer nodded his understanding; elderly spinsters were expected to lead quiet lives. He got up from the table and consulted for a moment in a low murmur with the officer who seemed to be in charge of the investigating team. Christopher tried to hear what was being said, but caught only an odd word. He was still impressed by the quiet efficiency of the police.

'At least on the surface,' the officer said, returning, 'it would appear that this was an attempted burglary which was interrupted

173

by Mademoiselle Roger. Perhaps she threatened to scream and one of the thieves hit her. Then they panicked and fled.'

Somehow it didn't ring true to Christopher; it was not how he had read the evidence. 'How do you think they got into the apartment?' he asked tentatively.

'Admittedly, that is a difficulty, Monsieur Grayson. You might have been mistaken about Mademoiselle Roger putting up the chain on the door after you left, but there are no marks on the lock or the door to suggest that anyone broke in. However, we shall continue with our inquiries, I assure you, before we make a report to a *juge d'instruction.*'

There were a few more questions. Madame Le Breton, requested to look around the apartment, couldn't swear that anything was missing. Christopher explained the presence of a bag containing a jar of caviare and some stuffed vine leaves in the bedroom; he hadn't realized that he had left his gifts for Ghislaine there. And eventually, warned that they would have to sign written statements later, they were allowed to leave, Christopher having agreed to stay in Paris for another few days; he would certainly be needed to give his evidence to the *juge d'instruction.*

At Christopher's request the senior police officer used his authority to obtain information from the hospital – l'Hôpital Pasteur, across the Bois in the 15th arrondissement – about Mademoiselle Roger's condition. Apparently the prognosis was not good. She had not regained consciousness and was at present being prepared for an emergency operation. It was believed she had a fractured skull and other injuries and of course she was not a young woman. But there would be no definite news for four or five hours.

'*La pauvre, pauvre Ghislaine!*' Madame Le Breton said quietly. 'None of us is safe these days.'

She was so obviously upset that Christopher, who would have preferred to go to the hospital or to his hotel to mull over the events of the morning by himself, agreed to have lunch with her. He insisted she should have the gifts he had brought for Ghislaine and they lunched off the vine leaves, an omelette with a mixed salad, cheese and fresh fruit and an excellent bottle of wine. Christopher enjoyed the meal and, unexpectedly, Madame Le Breton's company.

In spite of her widow's weeds and innumerable photographs of her late husband in the salon, which was very similar to Ghislaine's, she proved an intelligent and sympathetic companion. It was also clear that, although she reaffirmed that she had not been an intimate friend of Ghislaine's, she had been fond of her.

'She was a lonely woman,' Madame Le Breton said sadly. 'I don't think she had anyone really close to her, poor dear, and of course she had never married. Her fiancé was killed in the war, as was her brother and I know she had no near relations. But she was extremely devout and found a good deal of consolation in her religion and church affairs.'

'If she had seen someone through the peephole who looked like a priest, would she have opened the door to him, even if she didn't recognize him?' Christopher was still worried about how the intruder had got into the apartment.

'Possibly, Monsieur Grayson,' Madame Le Breton gave a Gallic shrug. 'But that would mean it was someone who knew quite a lot about her.'

Christopher nodded. It was, he thought, an astute remark, and it made him wonder to whom else Ghislaine might have opened her door late at night. Someone she knew, however casually, such as a workman or a shop assistant? Someone she recognized as living in the neighbourhood? Someone in a uniform whom she would trust? There were too many possibilities.

Madame Le Breton was frowning. 'Monsieur, may I ask you a question? You came to see Ghislaine yesterday I know, but when did you first get in touch with her?'

'Just earlier in the day, madame, when I arrived in Paris from Bonn.'

'Ah! That is interesting. Then Ghislaine wasn't speaking of you. I was having coffee with her one morning two or three weeks ago, when she had a telephone call. I couldn't help hearing some of it. She addressed the caller as "*Mon cher*", and asked how he was and said she was well. Otherwise it was mostly, "*Oui, je comprends*", as if she were receiving instructions. Then she said goodbye and, "*Dieu te bénit*".'

'So it would seem to be someone she knew very well. But it certainly wasn't me,' Christopher said. 'Did she offer you any explanation?'

'Yes. After a pause to recover herself, for she seemed quite shaken by the conversation, she said it was an old friend from whom she'd not heard for quite a long time. That would account for her surprise, for she was desperately surprised – shocked, you might say, or that

175

was my impression. I also had the impression, though I can't say why, that it was a long-distance call.'

'And you think it might be connected with this break-in and the attack on Ghislaine?'

'It sounds absurd, I know. I've no reason to think there's any connection, but – monsieur, my first reaction was that there had been a burglary, Ghislaine had interrupted a thief, and he had panicked and fled without stealing anything. However, now I've had time to consider the situation, taking into account my knowledge of Ghislaine, your assurance that she put up the chain after you left and the fact that there were no marks on the lock or door, I have wondered if she had let in someone, someone she knew, and perhaps – perhaps there was a connection with whoever phoned her. Because there is no doubt she was very shaken by that call.'

Christopher sat in the waiting-room of the hospital, where he had gone on leaving Madame Le Breton. He was accompanied by a uniformed officer from the Sûreté, who was not permitted to be any closer to the patient. He had promised to let Madame Le Breton know as soon as there was any news of Ghislaine, but so far there had been none; she was still in the operating theatre, where she had been for more than three hours. He was determined to wait, at least until the operation was over, although both a young doctor and a nurse had tried to persuade him to go home. He preferred the bleak waiting-room to his hotel room. He wanted to be near Ghislaine in the hope that it might be possible to speak to her, if only for a moment.

There was one all-important question to which he needed an answer. Was the 'old friend' whose unexpected telephone call had shaken Ghislaine really Jean-Pierre de Mourville? According to Madame Le Breton, Ghislaine had addressed her caller with affection, using the familiar second-person, and given him her blessing. But if it was Jean-Pierre, why had he suddenly contacted her? Was it connected with the inquiries of the French Securité?

Christopher swore softly under his breath. Ghislaine had been on the point of telling him about these inquiries when she had been overcome by tiredness. She had said she would tell him the next day when he came to lunch, but by then – Who on earth had she let into her apartment late at night? Who had assaulted her? Was that telephone call from Jean-Pierre? Was he still alive? Was there any connection between the telephone call and the assault?

Christopher's teeming thoughts were interrupted by the arrival of a nurse. The operation was over. Mademoiselle Roger was in the recovery room, she had regained consciousness and her condition was as good as could be expected. Monsieur Grayson might see her for a minute, but not the officer. The nurse chatted all the way along long green corridors, up in a lift, more corridors. Christopher had always hated hospitals, even the aseptic smell of then, and he heartily distrusted the cheerfulness of the nurse.

As he looked down on Ghislaine's face, grey-blue against the whiteness of the pillow, Christopher was sure he was right. The distant relation he had just found did not have long to live. He bent over her. Her breath was no more than a whisper on his cheek and her eyes remained closed.

'Cousin Ghislaine,' he murmured. 'It's me, Christopher.' He waited but she made no response. 'Christopher,' he repeated.

'She can hear you,' said the doctor who was standing behind him. Suddenly Ghislaine's eyes opened. They were dull and clouded, and she seemed not to recognize him. Disappointed, he straightened himself. Then he saw her lips move and bent over her again.

'Christopher, I didn't tell them where he was. I couldn't. Thank God, he didn't say, or I would have told them. They hurt me so much.'

'Who were they?'

'I don't know. They were dressed as gendarmes, but they weren't police.'

Ghislaine's breath was coming in short gasps, and her face was wet with sweat. It was obvious that she had to make a great effort to speak. The doctor put a hand on Christopher's shoulder and gently pulled him back.

'Enough,' he said. 'I'm sorry, but she can't take any more. Tomorrow, perhaps.'

'Yes, of course. I understand.'

Christopher had noted that the doctor had made no promises about the next day, and sadly he gave Ghislaine what he thought might be a last look before he started to turn away. But unexpectedly she thrust her arm out of the bedclothes and seized his hand, digging her nails into it with surprising force.

'What is it?' he said. 'What is it?' Once more he bent over her.

The words came hesitantly and so softly that Christopher just caught them. 'Jean-Pierre warned me. Tell no one – about – Guy.'

177

'I won't,' Christopher promised at once, without understanding, but he doubted if she heard him.

When Christopher returned to his hotel – the doctor had said it was pointless for him to stay at the hospital as Mademoiselle Roger had to be allowed to rest – he found two men waiting for him in the lobby. He recognized them at once. They were the two French security men who had questioned him before he went to Ansbach, and had warned him off making inquiries about the de Mourvilles.

'You remember us, Monsieur Grayson? We met last in St-Lô.'

'Yes, I remember you, messieurs,' Christopher said, and wondered if these were the same grey-faced men who had interrogated Ghislaine a few weeks ago. 'You get around.'

'It is our job. But not yours, monsieur, as we tried to make clear before.' The senior man looked around him; there was a certain amount of activity in the lobby. 'Perhaps we could go somewhere more private for a little talk.'

Christopher yearned to say that he didn't want 'a little talk'. He was tired almost to the point of exhaustion after the events of the day, and certainly his brain wasn't working at its best. His mind was confused by the words that Ghislaine had whispered to him, and by what they implied. The last thing he wanted to do now was to have a fencing match with the two Frenchmen, whose authority and intelligence he didn't doubt. He was also scared of what they might trick him into saying. But he had no choice.

'I can't imagine what we have to talk about,' he said, 'but if you insist you had better come up to my room.'

Christopher collected his key and the three men went up in the lift together in silence. The pause gave Christopher a minute or two to think. A lot would depend on how much his interrogators knew, but whatever they knew or guessed he must not betray Ghislaine's confidences.

'Please sit down,' he said when they reached the room, 'and tell me what you want.'

'Monsieur, we would like to know why you have claimed to be a cousin of Mademoiselle Ghislaine Roger, which would automatically make you related to the de Mourvilles? You didn't mention this when we last met.'

Christopher had been expecting this question. 'I didn't know then. What I told you about Jean-Pierre de Mourville being sent to the Stantons at the beginning of the war was quite true, but it seems he and my grandmother, Anthea Stanton, became lovers. My father is their son, though by the time of his birth my grandmother had married Keith Grayson. This makes Chantal de Mourville, Jean-Pierre's mother, my great-grandmother. I have only just learnt that her maiden name was Roger, and as I was in Paris I decided to call on my distant cousin, Ghislaine Roger.'

'Interesting, Monsieur Grayson.'

It wasn't clear to Christopher how much of this family history his interrogators already knew, but it didn't matter. What did matter was that they should remain in ignorance about the phone calls from Jean-Pierre, and about his use of Guy Roger's name and credentials – or at least that was how Christopher interpreted Ghislaine's whispered instructions.

'And perhaps unfortunate for Mademoiselle Roger.'

'What the hell do you mean?' Christopher's temper flared. 'Are you blaming me for the attack on her? You know about that, of course.'

'Yes, of course. And no, no, monsieur, we do not blame you. You were probably a contributory cause, but the blame if anyone's is ours. We have been keeping a watch on Mademoiselle Roger, but obviously not closely enough. Unfortunately there is always a shortage of operatives.'

Christopher stared at him. 'Why should you – keep a watch on Mademoiselle Roger, I mean?'

The question was ignored. 'I regret to say I fell down this afternoon, too. I should have insisted on a man at Mademoiselle Roger's bedside, but the doctor was difficult. Only relatives – and only one – could see her, and you, the long-lost cousin, were there. What did she say to you?'

The last words were snapped out, making Christopher start. 'She didn't say much,' he said. 'She had just come out of the anaesthetic and she was very weak. The doctor will tell you. She said there were two men in the uniforms of gendarmes, which is why she opened the door to them. She told them to take whatever they wanted, but they started to assault her – and that's all.'

'They didn't ask her about de Mourville?'

'Not as far as I know,' Christopher lied. 'Why should they?'

'Because, Monsieur Grayson, someone is determined to find out what happened to Jean-Pierre de Mourville, and equally determined to prevent anyone else from doing so. What is more, whoever it is seems to be becoming more and more desperate, and is not going to stop at murder.'

And when Ghislaine Roger died in her sleep at two o'clock in the morning, murder had indeed been committed.

TWENTY-ONE

Christopher drove at a steady pace along the autoroute to Brussels. He didn't bother to check if he was being followed; it couldn't matter less. If anyone was interested they would soon realize that he was merely going to join his family at the ambassador's residence.

Family? He thought of Cousin Ghislaine, who had been so pleased to welcome him. She had been family, too. He had been a fool, a criminal fool. He had gone to great lengths to avoid being followed to the home of Herr Richmann in Bonn after the bug had been found attached to his BMW in the hotel garage, but he had taken almost no precautions before visiting Ghislaine Roger. Because he had seen no signs of a tail he had prided himself that he had got the better of the opposition. How could he have been so stupid? The French security officer's heavy hint that by contacting Ghislaine he bore some of the responsibility for the attack on her appalled him, but he was forced to accept it as justified.

Tired and depressed after two fairly sleepless nights he arrived at the residence shortly before noon. He gave Sanford, the butler, his bags to be taken up to his usual room, tidied himself in a downstairs cloakroom and went along to the drawing-room, where he was told the family was gathered. Unobserved for a minute, he stood in the doorway and listened to the conversation.

'The Brussels embassy, or anywhere else where I happen to be the ambassador, is not a holiday home or even a weekend cottage for members of my family,' Peter Grayson was saying.

'Oh darling, don't be so pompous.' Anne claimed a wife's privilege to speak bluntly.

'If I'm not welcome here, I'll go to a hotel. Probably I should have taken Karen's advice and done so in the first place.' Keith Grayson was clearly not in the best of tempers. 'I certainly haven't achieved anything in the forty-eight hours I've been here. I came to talk to you, Peter, to persuade you to use your influence over Christopher, but you're always too busy to spare any time for me.

Whenever I corner you your secretary demands your presence or you're wanted on the phone. It's hopeless.'

'I'm sorry, but I have a job to do, an important job.' Peter was irritable too. 'And I'm particularly busy at present, so, to be frank, I could have done without a succession of visits from the family. First there were Peregrine and Joyce –'

'Peregrine came on an official visit with a parliamentary delegation,' Keith snapped.

'I know. I was only too well aware of the fact. He expected the red carpet to be laid out for him, a special dinner party, Joyce to be entertained while he was at his wretched meetings,' Peter said curtly. 'Then Anthea came. Now you. All with the same request, or should it be demand? I must stop Christopher from the absurd inquiries he's making about de Mourville.'

'Not me,' said Verity flippantly. 'I've just come to buy some classy clothes.'

Her father ignored her attempt to lighten the atmosphere. 'Look, Keith. Christopher is a grown man, not a boy. I cannot give him orders. I wouldn't even if I could. Why should I? I understand his curiosity about Jean-Pierre, and frankly I can't see why you should make all this fuss about it.'

'You would if you had had MI5 interrogating you, the way they did me,' said Keith, and hurried on as if he regretted the remark. 'Anyway, it could be dangerous. They as good as hinted that was so, and I'm fond of Christopher. Peregrine and Joyce aren't going to have any children, and Chris is all I have in the way of a grandson. At least he bears my name.'

'And they say listeners never hear any good of themselves.' Christopher decided that he had been eavesdropping for long enough, and spoke as he stepped into the room.

'You can only have overheard the good part, Christopher. You really have been making a nuisance of yourself. It's no joke,' Keith said harshly. 'Dear Jean-Pierre de Mourville, whom the Stantons thought such a hero, was probably working for the Germans all the time, and now it seems there's a possibility that when he went to Germany he ran a Nazi camp. He is not an acceptable relation for this family, Christopher, so why do you go on insisting on involving us with him?'

Christopher opened his mouth to contradict the accusation against Jean-Pierre and to point out that, whether Keith liked it or not, Jean-Pierre *was* a relation, indeed Peter's father and his own grand-

father, and personally he was not ashamed of the fact. Anne fore-
stalled him and prevented what she feared would turn into a violent
argument.

'Chris, how good to see you. We've been wondering where you
were. Ring the bell, will you, there's a dear? It's time for drinks
before lunch.'

Christopher grinned at his mother. When she liked Anne could
be a forceful woman, getting her own way without making a furore
about it or causing any embarrassment. Even Keith accepted that
there was not to be a row between himself and Christopher, at least
not for the present.

Christopher, who had not been pleased to find Keith staying at the
embassy, seized his opportunity after lunch, when Keith went to
have a rest, to give the others a fairly full account of his time in
France and Germany. He did not mention what had happened to
him at Ansbach; he still thought that Hueber's attack could have
been coincidental and he didn't want to worry his mother. But there
was no disguising what had befallen Ghislaine Roger.

'Poor woman!' Anne said. 'So you didn't have much of a chance
to talk to her, Chris?'

'Not as much as I'd have liked.' Christopher hesitated, remembering his promise not to mention Guy Roger; luckily no one had
asked how Jean-Pierre had managed to get to England.

'And poor Jean-Pierre!' said Verity. 'How ghastly for him to see
Gran with two children like that – Peregrine and you, Dad.'

Peter nodded. 'It's a strange thought, I must admit – and it must
have shaken him.'

'Do you think Gran will be upset to learn about it?' Verity asked,
looking at Anne.

'It was a long time ago, dear, but I would guess she'd shed a tear
or two. They loved each other very much. I'm not sure it wouldn't
be best not to tell her – or Keith. And I wonder what happened to
Jean-Pierre after that. What bad luck Ghislaine wasn't able to tell
Chris more.'

'Was it luck, Chris?' Peter asked.

'No, Dad, The French security people suspect – and I know,
because she told me – that the men who assaulted her tried to make
her reveal where Jean-Pierre was. She couldn't tell them because
she didn't know.'

This information was greeted by a long silence. Then Peter and

Anne started talking together. Their intention was the same, to save Christopher from coming to any harm.

'Here's where you stop, Chris. This is serious.'

'Darling, you must forget your inquiries at once.'

'It's one thing to irritate MI5 and the French Sécurité, but quite another to get yourself involved with some third party which doesn't seem to draw the line at murder.'

'No more, Chris. Please! As Peter says, it's become dangerous, though heaven knows why.'

'I think –' Christopher began.

'You believe, like those men, that Jean-Pierre is still alive, don't you Chris?' Verity said.

Not for the first time Christopher was displeased by his sister's perceptiveness. 'Possibly,' he said.

'Dear God!' Peter said. 'Don't say I'm suddenly going to be confronted by a long-lost father? That would be interesting. But Chris, I don't want to gain a father and lose a son.'

'I doubt if the chances of either are very great,' Christopher said.

'Didn't Jean-Pierre ever contact Ghislaine again, although she'd been so good to him?' Verity was curious. 'What did he do for a living in England? Did he have any money?'

'She gave him some money, and he telephoned her a couple of times,' Christopher said. 'He told her he was going to start a new life, that he hoped to teach.'

'That's all you know?' Verity persisted.

'Yes,' Christopher lied.

'So there's nothing more you can do?' Anne was relieved.

'I shall have to return to France, to appear before the *juge d'instruction*, but that will only be a formality as far as I'm concerned, and I hope to go to Ghislaine's funeral. I gather she has no close family.'

'What do you plan to do in the meantime?' Peter asked. 'You can stay here if you like.'

'Thanks, Dad, but no. I told the French authorities they could contact me in Oxford, so I'll go back to college and quietly wait to hear when I'm wanted.'

This was less easy to accomplish than Christopher had expected. Waiting was onerous. He tried to work, but couldn't concentrate. He went for long walks by himself, up to Cumnor, along the towpath out to Iffley. He made a duty call at Ship Street and gave his grandmother a greatly expurgated version of his 'holiday' in Europe. He wondered if Celia Bingham was in Oxford, or if she was still in Scotland, but he made no attempt to get in touch with her. He longed to hear from the French authorities. The days passed slowly. Then Keith telephoned to ask when he was returning to France and whether he had heard any more about Ghislaine's death. Keith was aggressive and Christopher short-tempered. It was an acrimonious conversation on both sides and it didn't have the desired result. Christopher was annoyed that Keith should check up on him and, because of his annoyance, instead of taking no further action, he decided to follow up an idea that had been at the back of his mind for some while.

It was not an idea in which he put much confidence, but *faute de mieux* he planned to try it. He would advertise for Guy Roger, if not completely anonymously, which was next to impossible, at least tactfully and with circumspection. He didn't want to bring down Keith's wrath on him, or to worry his mother. Equally importantly, he didn't wish to arouse the authorities on either side of the Channel, or whatever group had caused Ghislaine's death. He refused to be nervous for himself, but he was prepared to take reasonable precautions. He inspected his car each time he drove it although it was in a lock-up garage owned by his college, and when he went for long walks he kept Herr Doktor Hueber's handy little cosh in his pocket. Sometimes he wondered what the Oxford police would make of a peaceful don who carried a blunt instrument. The thought amused him temporarily.

But in general he was not amused; Ghislaine's death had affected him more than he had realized at the time, and he could only hope that by advertising for Guy Roger he wasn't violating his promise to her. He worded the advertisement with the utmost care.

It read: 'Information urgently required for legal reasons re Guy Roger, last heard of teaching – ' He thought for a moment, tapping his teeth with his pen; then he decided on Jean-Pierre's most likely subject ' – French in a boys' school in the mid-1940s. Anyone who remembers him or has any knowledge of him, please phone (0865) xxxxxx, reversing the charges'.

Christopher was pleased with the finished product. The 'for legal reasons' gave it, he thought, an authentic touch. His only doubt was the telephone number, his own, for it made a direct link with him, but a newspaper box number would have been too slow and less likely to produce a result. Someone who might be prepared to

185

lift a receiver might not bother to write a letter, and the chances that the advertisement would be seen by anyone, such as Keith, who was familiar with his phone number, were slight.

Christopher arranged for the advertisement to appear for three days in *The Times* and the *Telegraph*. He would have liked to put it in a local paper, but he had no idea where.

On the first day there was no response. On the second Christopher's heart leapt as a man's voice said, 'Are you the party who put an advert in the paper about Guy Rogers?'

'Yes, I am,' Christopher said, noting that the man had added an 's' to Roger, and pronounced the name in the English way. 'Can you help?'

'Well, that depends on what's in it for me, mate.'

'You mean you expect a reward?'

'Sure thing, mate. You don't get somethink for nothink these days.'

'What sort of information do you have?'

'This Rogers character was shacked up with me ma until last year when he died, so I can show you where he's pushing up the daisies.'

Christopher thought quickly. It could be relevant, but his instinct was against it. 'Phone me again tomorrow,' he said. 'I'll know then how much my firm is willing to offer for further information. Okay?'

'Sure thing, mate.'

The line went dead, and after a minute Christopher telephoned Verity in London. Luckily she was available. Christopher explained what he needed, and she agreed to check at St Catherine's House for any Guy Roger or Rogers who had died the previous year at an age which meant that he might be Jean-Pierre de Mourville.

'Thanks,' Christopher said. 'I'll owe you.'

'I'll settle for an explanation when we meet. I assume this is just between us.'

'Definitely.'

'I'm lunching with Julian, and I'll go to St Catherine's House after that. I'll phone you as soon as I get home.'

Verity was as good as her word. She phoned Christopher at three o'clock. No Guy Rogers or Roger of a suitable age had died last year. Christopher was not disappointed. He had not put much trust in his 'mate'.

His second caller, who gave his name as Martin Rogers and said that his father had been christened Guy, but was known as Charles,

186

proved equally useless. After a brief conversation it was clear from the dates that Mr Guy Charles Rogers could not possibly be Jean-Pierre. Martin Rogers said goodbye and wished Christopher luck. He did not call Christopher 'mate'.

But on the morning of the third day when, after a hostile conversation with his 'mate', Christopher was thinking that his ploy had been a mistake, luck did favour him. The voice on the line was elderly and apologetic. The caller, whose name was Arthur Brent, expressed the hope that he wasn't wasting the advertiser's time, but he had been taught French by a Guy Rogers shortly after the war ended. 'I remember him with affection,' he said. 'If it had not been for him I would never have gone to Oxford, and my life would have been very different.'

'Mr Brent,' Christopher felt excitement rise in him; surely he had found a genuine link with Jean-Pierre. 'Mr Brent, I would like to meet you if that's at all possible. Where do you live? My name is Christopher Grayson, and it's a family matter.'

'I live quite close, if your telephone code is anything to go by, in Charlbury, in an old house facing the Green, and, if you would care to, you're more than welcome to visit.'

'This afternoon? As you guessed, I'm only in Oxford. I could easily drive over.'

'All right. Four o'clock. Come to tea. I hope what I have to tell you about Guy Rogers will make it worth your while.'

And from general interest the visit was indeed well worth while. Christopher learned that Guy Rogers had arrived at St Michael's College near Reading in mid-term after the regular French master had been killed in a car accident. He had been something of a mystery. He never received letters and he spent his holidays at the school. He had few clothes or possessions, not even a gas mask, which he said he had lost, together with his ration book and his identity card.

'I don't know if the Head believed him, but we were in desperate need of a French master and Rogers was not only totally fluent in French, but also an excellent teacher and one who could keep order. Neither did he mind how much time he spent in extra coaching. If it hadn't been for him I'd never have got my Oxford scholarship.'

'Did you keep in touch with him after you left school?' Christopher asked hopefully.

'Yes, until he went to North America.'

'North America? What part of North America?'

'I don't know, Mr Grayson. It was just a note in a Christmas card saying he was going to emigrate. I never heard from him again.'

The disappointment was the more bitter for Christopher because his hopes had been raised so high. But now, as he drove back to Oxford, he faced the fact that at last he had really come to a dead end. North America had swallowed up Jean-Pierre de Mourville.

TWENTY-TWO

It was not exactly raining, but it was not dry either. The air was thick with a damp swirling mist that kept visibility to a minimum and made breathing unpleasant, almost as if one were living under water. It was a day to stay at home by a fire, not to stand beside an open grave in a churchyard, huddled under umbrellas, while the priest hurried as quickly as decency permitted through the rest of the burial service.

There were not more than a dozen mourners and everyone was thankful when at last the soil rattled on to Ghislaine Roger's coffin, the final prayers were said and they were free to leave. They shook hands with the priest and, in twos or threes, left the graveside, chatting quietly. Christopher knew none of them apart from Madame Le Breton. She had gone ahead, in earnest conversation with a small, sharp-faced man whom she seemed to know well. Christopher followed and, as he reached the gates of the churchyard, he became aware of two men standing under one umbrella, seemingly deep in discussion. He recognized them.

'*Bonjour, messieurs*,' he said, and wondered why the security officers had bothered to attend Ghislaine's funeral. Reluctantly he concluded that they were curious as to who else might be there, but the question of 'why' remained.

'*Bonjour, Monsieur Grayson – et adieu*,' came the reply.

Noting the *adieu*, Christopher grinned wryly. They wanted to see the back of him, and probably they had. After he had given Madame Le Breton lunch, which he felt was the least he could do in the circumstances, he would catch the bus to Charles de Gaulle and his flight to Heathrow. He must settle down in his academic groove in Oxford once more – the Trinity term would soon be upon him – and leave the pursuit of the myth of the man who had been Jean-Pierre de Mourville to other interested parties.

Madame Le Breton and her companion had stopped beside a car. Christopher caught up with them and Madame introduced him. Her companion was a *juriste*, a Maître Dornet, Ghislaine Roger's lawyer and legal executor, who, Madame Le Breton explained, had been kind enough to offer them a lift.

Christopher shook hands with him, and he said how pleased he was to meet a relative of Mademoiselle Roger, however distant. They all got into the car and the lawyer drove at what to Christopher was alarming speed to the little restaurant – the choice of Madame Le Breton – where they were to lunch. Monsieur Dornet, though urged, declined an invitation to join them, pleading pressure of work.

Inevitably, once they were having an apéritif and had ordered their meal, Madame Le Breton started to talk about *la pauvre Ghislaine*. She was touched, she said, touched. She had not realized that she had meant anything to Mademoiselle Roger. She had been a neighbour, a casual friend – but no more. Now Monsieur Dornet had told her that, according to the terms of Mademoiselle Roger's will, she was to receive an amethyst brooch for which she had once expressed admiration.

'I shall treasure it in her memory, not that I need it in order to remember her,' Madame Le Breton said sadly.

Christopher made the conventional response, but a thought had occurred to him. There were, among Ghislaine's cherished possessions, one or two that he would love to own, and which, worthless to others, he was sure she would gladly have bestowed on him – the photographs which included the de Mourvilles, especially Jean-Pierre. The more he considered the possibility of getting them, the more he wanted them, and on returning to his hotel to collect his overnight bag he telephoned the lawyer's office.

Maître Dornet's secretary sounded charming, but adamant. It was impossible for Monsieur Grayson to see Maître Dornet before the next morning or even to speak to him on the telephone. Maître Dornet was not in his office. If monsieur wished she could make an appointment for eleven o'clock the following day.

Reluctantly Monsieur Grayson agreed. It meant changing his plans, but in the event this presented few problems. His hotel room was available for another night, his bag took only a minute to unpack, no one was expecting him at home. However, it proved more difficult to change his travel arrangements. He had to settle for the last British Airways flight out of Charles de Gaulle to Heathrow, which would mean spending the whole of the next day in Paris and arriving late in London. It was a nuisance, but he was sure it was worthwhile if it could lead to the acquisition of even one photograph of Jean-Pierre.

The next morning Christopher arrived at the office of Maître Dornet promptly at eleven o'clock and was shown at once into his inner sanctum. Maître Dornet came around his desk to offer Christopher his hand, then waved him to a chair.

'What can I do for you, Monsieur Grayson?' he asked affably. Christopher looked around the room. It was small and rather dark, the shelves heavy with legal tomes, but he was encouraged to see on the desk the photograph of an attractive woman approximately the same age as the lawyer, and another of two girls in their teens, presumably the lawyer's wife and daughters. Maître Dornet was clearly a family man.

'Maître Dornet, although I was a distant relation of Mademoiselle Roger I'm sure I don't feature in her will, but –'

'That's correct, Monsieur, not even in her new will.'

'New will?'

'Yes, she made a new will a few weeks ago. To be more exact she made a slight alteration to her old one, in the form of a *codicille*. The bulk of her estate still goes to her church. It's not a vast estate, but I'm sure the priest will find a good use for it.'

'Otherwise there were some small personal bequests, I gather. Madame Le Breton tells me she is to receive an amethyst brooch. She is extremely pleased because of the sentimental value she attaches to the gift.'

'That is very understandable.' The lawyer nodded his approval. 'Sentiment is not to be despised. I believe it was because of sentiment that Mademoiselle Roger decided that her personal jewellery, other than the amethyst brooch, should be left to another friend, a Madame Delancourt, rather than sold and added to the estate, as she had originally intended.'

'Madame Delancourt? An old friend?' Christopher queried. Madame Le Breton had said that Ghislaine had no close friends. 'Does she live in Paris?'

'Yes, in the 16th arrondissement.'

'You know her, maître?'

'No. I'd never heard of her until Mademoiselle Roger decided to make this bequest.' Maître Dornet glanced at his watch. 'I do not wish to hurry you, Monsieur Grayson, but I have another appointment and you've not yet told me your business.'

Christopher explained that he was very eager to possess at least one or two of the photographs that had belonged to Mademoiselle Roger. 'For family reasons, you understand, maître. They would mean nothing to anyone else, but to me they are beyond price.'

The lawyer considered the request seriously for a full minute, until Christopher was afraid he was about to refuse. Then he nodded abruptly. 'Yes, why not? As executor, I have a certain amount of discretion, and I think your request would have been in accordance with Mademoiselle Roger's wishes. It shall be arranged, monsieur. If you will give me your address, the photographs will be sent to you when the estate is probated. As to the frames – many of them silver, I think – it would seem a pity to separate them from the photographs, but they have some financial value. Would you perhaps give me a small cheque to recompense the church?'

Christopher agreed readily, and wrote a cheque at once. He hadn't expected to get hold of all the photographs, but he thought it a fair bargain. They could always be shared with his grandmother or other members of the family. He thanked Maître Dornet and bade him goodbye.

By now it was noon. Christopher found a pleasant-looking café, where he had a drink and a *croque-monsieur* and wondered what he should do with the rest of the day until it was time to go out to the airport. He thought of Madame Delancourt, Ghislaine's old friend to whom she had bequeathed her jewellery, and on impulse he telephoned Madame Le Breton, who was surprised to discover that he was still in Paris. 'Delancourt? No, Monsieur Grayson. I know of no one by that name. Certainly Mademoiselle Roger never mentioned her. Perhaps they were friends long ago, who quarrelled and have recently become reconciled.'

It was a conceivable explanation and, if he had not had so much time to spare, Christopher might well have dismissed the thought that had occurred to him of paying a personal call on Madame Delancourt. Maître Dornet had not mentioned her address, but he had said she lived in the 16th arrondissement and, thanks to the telephone directory, Christopher had no difficulty in finding four possibilities.

Of these, two proved to be out and the third regretfully denied any knowledge of a Mademoiselle Ghislaine Roger. Christopher believed her, although her appearance suggested that she was about Ghislaine's age and could easily have been a friend of hers. The fourth possibility he was tempted to forget, as it was a fair distance away, too short for a taxi, but a longish walk.

He started to look for a taxi to take him back to his hotel. Then he noticed a woman with a shopping basket whom he could have sworn he had seen earlier in the afternoon. He realized that in ordinary circumstances he would not have been so observant, and the idea that she had been following him wouldn't have crossed his mind. Now he was not so sure. He accepted that, thanks to his inquiries about Jean-Pierre de Mourville, which he had begun in all innocence, his situation was now other than ordinary. And the last thing he wanted to do was involve someone else, who could be quite unconnected with the affair.

Christopher went into a flower shop and, while constantly glancing out of the window, spent a lot of time sending his mother some flowers by Interflora. When he came out the woman had disappeared. He told himself he had been mistaken, and he decided to change his mind; he would visit the fourth Madame Delancourt, but he would go carefully, and he kept a close watch around him until he reached the apartment block where she lived. He walked past the entrance, doubled back, and quickly slipped into the hall.

The concierge was not in evidence and without being questioned he was able to consult the list of tenants and run up the stairs to the first floor. He rang the bell and waited, conscious that he was being examined through the spyhole. Then the door opened.

'Madame Delancourt?' He hoped she would deny it, but she nodded. '*Madame, je cherche une Madame Delancourt, mais –*' How to explain to this pretty blonde blue-eyed girl in her early twenties who stood looking at him enquiringly, that she couldn't be the Madame Delancourt he sought, the 'old friend' of Ghislaine Roger? '*Madame, je m'excuse.* My name is Christopher Grayson and I'm looking for a lady who was a friend of Mademoiselle Ghislaine Roger.'

Christopher stopped abruptly, startled by the effect his words had had. The girl had paled. Her eyes had grown wide and she had put a hand up to her throat. She looked frightened.

'I'm so sorry. Are you all right?'

'Yes. I'm all right. Why shouldn't I be?'

Without thinking Christopher had spoken in English and she had answered in the same language. For a moment they stared at each other. Then she started to shut the door, and instinctively he put a foot into the closing gap.

'Madame, please,' Christopher begged. 'Did you know Ghislaine Roger?'

'No! No! I've never heard of her. Go away or I'll call my husband and the police,' she said in English.

Christopher withdrew his foot as she relaxed the pressure on it a little, and she slammed the door. He heard her put up the chain, and he hurried down the stairs. The girl had sounded hysterical. She might call the police, and if she did he would be in an embarrassing position. He did not want to have to explain why he was trying to trace a Madame Delancourt.

The concierge was still missing from her post when Christopher left the apartment block. He hesitated on the pavement outside, as if unsure which way to go. There was a young couple on the opposite side of the street, strolling happily along, arms around each other, stopping to kiss; Christopher envied them. A woman pushing a pram walked past. Two cars went by. But to his relief Christopher could see nothing suspicious.

Next to the apartment block was a small courtyard, of which the windowless side of the apartments formed one wall. Opposite was a church – apparently the Église St-Sulpice – and across the back of the courtyard was what Christopher took to be the presbytery. Because he wanted to think about the girl who had claimed to be Madame Delancourt, and who had reacted so strangely to the mention of Ghislaine's name, he went into the church and sat in a pew at the back. But he could think of no reason why the girl should have behaved in a way that he sensed was out of character. She had been prepared to open the door to him, a stranger. She hadn't looked or seemed timid. She had conducted herself perfectly normally, reasonably, until – She had been suddenly shocked, frightened, and she had lied. If she hadn't known Ghislaine she had certainly heard of her. What was the connection? Who was she? Who could he ask? Madame Le Breton had never heard of a Madame Delancourt in relation to Ghislaine; nor, before the alteration to Ghislaine's will, had Maître Dornet heard of her. They couldn't help. But he had to find out more about her. The concierge? No, she would immediately refer his inquiries to the Delancourts and would probably tell him nothing. The priest? If Madame Delancourt was a Catholic it was most likely she would go to the church next to where she lived, and would be known there. He could explain that he wanted to get in touch with his cousin's friend, and perhaps elicit some information. At least it was worth a try.

Christopher rang the bell of the presbytery, and a woman who was obviously the housekeeper opened the door to him. He asked if he might see the priest; he would keep him only a few minutes. To his disappointment the housekeeper shook her head. She explained that this was the afternoon that Father always went to the hospital to visit the patients. If monsieur cared to return shortly before five when Father heard confessions, she was sure he would spare him a little time then. Christopher agreed. It was inconvenient but not impossible, and he gave the housekeeper his name. She had shut the door when it occurred to him that he might have asked her about Madame Delancourt. It was too late now.

He decided to take a taxi back to his hotel, where he had left his bag. He remembered seeing a rank close by and as he came out of the courtyard he quickly turned in that direction, nearly bumping into a couple in conversation on the pavement. Muttering an apology he hurried on. He was sure – almost sure – that the woman was the one he had seen twice before that afternoon carrying a shopping basket. The man he had not recognized.

TWENTY-THREE

The side door of the hotel where Christopher had been staying in the St-Germain des Prés area of the left bank gave on to the rue Jacob, as did the main doors, so there was no means of leaving without being observed from the street. This was particularly annoying as he had intentionally chosen this small and obscure hotel rather than his usual haunt in an effort to avoid being followed, either by the pair of Sécurité men or by anyone else. He decided on the same ploy that he had used in Bonn.

Allowing himself plenty of time he walked to Notre Dame. He spent a few minutes in the cathedral, then caught a taxi which took him to the Place de la Concorde. From there he went by Métro to the Pont de Neuilly, once getting out of the train and waiting on the platform for the next one. The trains were full, people standing, and the platforms crowded, so that in spite of his precautions Christopher couldn't have sworn that he hadn't been followed all the way from the rue Jacob.

As he headed in a taxi for the 16th arrondissement and the Église St-Sulpice he mocked himself. What did he think he was doing? He had set off on a holiday with the intention of finding out more about his grandfather. Now he seemed to be playing a leading part in a bad movie, except that the role was for real. He had only to remember Ghislaine to be reminded of that fact.

He arrived at the church and went to sit in a pew near the back, as he had arranged with the housekeeper. Several other people came in, forming a vague queue in the seats near the confessional. Christopher moved close to them, intending to move forward and catch the priest as soon as he appeared. He waited.

The priest was late. When Christopher was beginning to think that he might not come and it was useless to wait further, he bustled in, a small, grey-haired man, eager to get on with his business. Christopher stood up, but the priest had already gone into the confessional and switched on the small green light to show that he was ready to receive the first penitent. There had been no opportunity for a single word with him.

An elderly woman stepped forward to take what she considered her rightful place, but a man brushed past her. The light above the confessional turned red, and the woman returned to her seat, clearly annoyed that she should have been pushed aside so brusquely, but unable to protest.

Another couple came in and Christopher decided to leave; there was no knowing when the priest would be finished with confessions and available to talk to him. Then, as he moved out of the pew his gaze was attracted to the light above the confessional. There seemed to be something wrong with it.

In fact, it was flashing on and off. Christopher stared at it. Three long flashes, three short, then three long again – SOS, the universal signal of distress. It had to be accidental, a faulty connection. If the priest was feeling ill he could appeal to the man whose confession he was hearing. There would be no need for this dramatic signalling. Christopher half turned away. But the red light was still flashing, three long, three short, three long. No fault could produce such consistency. Something was wrong.

Christopher glanced at the other people in the church. No one else seemed to have noticed the errant light. They were all on their knees, deep in prayer, except for the elderly woman who was glaring at him, daring him to go into the confessional ahead of her, like the man who had pushed her aside. Why had he – ?

Thoughts tumbled through Christopher's mind. He thought of the man's determination, the way he had treated the elderly woman, shouldering her away with careless brutality; people about to seek absolution for their sins did not as a rule behave like that. Then there was the flashing light, the signal of danger or adversity, surely the only means at the priest's disposal if he couldn't walk out of the confessional. Clearly he was in trouble.

To leave the church and ignore the incident was impossible. Christopher knew that if he did this the deed would haunt him. But what should he do? The one thing he didn't want was to make a fool of himself by creating an unnecessary fuss. Nevertheless – Gritting his teeth he moved swiftly to the door on the priest's side of the confessional box, and opened it.

'*Tout va bien, mon père?*' he started to say.

He stopped. He had seen the hole in the mesh which separated the confessor from the penitent, and the barrel of a gun poking through it. Simultaneously the priest took immediate advantage of the interruption Christopher had caused. He flung himself through the open door, and there was the soft plop of a silenced gun as a bullet missed him by inches and buried itself in the woodwork of the confessional.

Christopher, caught off balance by the violent impact of the priest's body, fell backwards, knocking his head on the carved end of a pew. For a moment, while the priest sprawled on top of him, he lost consciousness. Then he became aware of shouts, a woman screaming, willing hands helping him and the priest to their feet. He felt dazed and staggered a little. Someone helped him into a pew. Someone else went to fetch him a glass of water. Someone picked up his overnight bag and put it beside him. There was talk of calling the police, a doctor.

But in the general mêlée, the pseudo-penitent had had no difficulty in making his escape.

An hour later Christopher was sitting in the parlour of the presbytery of the Église St-Sulpice, talking to Father Anselm and drinking Pernod, which he didn't really like. The police had come and gone, taking with them the bullet that had been prised from the back of the confessional, and a variety of contradictory descriptions of what everyone seemed to assume had been a madman. Christopher had been congratulated on his perspicacity in recognizing the priest's cry for help, and had been treated as a minor hero. He had also been examined by a doctor for signs of concussion, but luckily there were none and the only result of hitting his head on the end of the pew was a nasty bruise. Now he was trying to extract more information as to what had happened from the priest.

'Father, you say the man must have been mad, but didn't he make any demands of you?'

'He wanted to know where some men were – Mourville and Morel were the names, I think. I said I'd never heard of them, and he replied, "Yes, you have. Don't lie and don't try to be funny." Then he asked if – who was it? – a Ghislaine Roger came to St-Sulpice, and I said, perhaps, I don't know everyone who comes to Mass here. At that point, thanks be to God, you intervened, my son.'

'You didn't tell the police all this, father?'

'No. I was pretty shaken at the time. I'm not a young man and I've never been shot at before. But I doubt if it mattered. I'll be surprised if they catch the chap unless he tries the same crazy game again, and I certainly couldn't identify him. Could you?'

Christopher shook his head. 'No! I – I scarcely saw him.'

'I can't help wondering if he really would have shot me. I know he fired his gun, but I think that was just a reaction when you opened the door of the confessional so suddenly, and I dived out.'

Christopher didn't contradict the priest, but he thought of Ghislaine and felt guilty. He had been forced to accept Father Anselm's thanks and gratitude, but he was sure that he was the cause of the attack which could have ended in the priest's death. In spite of the precautions he had taken, he must have been followed, now and earlier in the day, and the erroneous conclusion drawn that the priest had information concerning Jean-Pierre. But he couldn't explain any of this; it was much too complicated.

'What I don't understand,' the priest was saying, 'is why he chose to make this crazy attack on me in the confession box, of all places.'

'That could have been chance, father. He could have expected you to go through to the vestry, but you didn't.'

'No. I was kept late at the hospital. A street accident. The man died.' The priest was silent for a moment. 'As a rule I like to have a few minutes to myself before hearing confessions, but today it was not possible. I came straight into the church.'

'So you haven't spoken to your housekeeper since you returned?'

'No. Why do you ask?'

Christopher said he was trying to trace a Madame Delancourt, a friend of his late cousin. He did not mention the name of the cousin, nor the circumstances in which he had heard of her friend. He thought that the less the priest knew, the better. But how could he explain that he had not asked the lawyer for Madame Delancourt's address? He was not sure himself. True, at the time he had been intent on obtaining the de Mourville photographs, and the opportunity had passed, but he could have phoned afterwards, except that it would have made too much of the matter, possibly aroused Maître Dornet's curiosity and thereby the curiosity of the Sécurité, who were bound to be in touch with him because of Ghislaine.

'There are some Delancourts who live in one of the apartments next to the church,' said the priest. 'Richard and Chantal, a charming couple. I married them three months ago. But she isn't French. She's a Canadian, and I do not think –'

As Father Anselm paused, looking enquiringly at Christopher, Christopher thought of Chantal de Mourville, née Roger,

Jean-Pierre's mother and his own great-grandmother. It couldn't be coincidence that the girl who had reacted so violently to the name of Ghislaine Roger had been christened Chantal.

'Indeed, father, I called on her this afternoon, but she said she didn't know my cousin and couldn't help me. I noticed she spoke French with an accent. Does she come from Montreal? You said she was a Canadian.'

'I gather her mother came from Montreal originally, but the family live in Ottawa now – her parents and her sister Jane, who's a doctor at the Civic Hospital. But of course they're not Delancourts.'

'No.' Christopher waited, hoping the priest would volunteer Chantal Delancourt's maiden name, but he didn't. 'Is there a senior Madame Delancourt, father? My cousin was not a young woman. She was in her seventies and I would expect a friend to be of much the same age.'

'I know that Richard's mother is dead. She died young – cancer, I believe. And I know of no other. I'm sure there were none at the wedding, which was a small, private affair. Apart from some young friends of the couple there was just a handful of Richard's relations. Of Chantal's family, there were only Madame Rogers and Jane. Unfortunately her father was unwell and couldn't face the journey from Canada.'

Christopher nodded. He felt too stunned to speak. Madame Richard Delancourt, born Chantal Rogers in Canada, had to be the granddaughter or daughter of Jean-Pierre de Mourville, who was believed to have emigrated to North America. She bore the same Christian name as his mother, and before marriage had had an adaptation of the surname he had borrowed from his cousin, Guy Roger. Moreover, in spite of her denial, Chantal Delancourt *had* recognized the name of Ghislaine Roger and Ghislaine wouldn't have bequeathed her jewellery except to someone who, for some reason or another, she held dear.

There was also the time element. According to Father Anselm, Chantal Rogers had been married to Richard Delancourt three months ago. In the last few weeks Madame Le Breton had been present when Ghislaine had received a telephone call, conceivably from Jean-Pierre, that had shaken her, and in the last few weeks she had added a codicil to her will leaving her jewellery to Madame Delancourt.

In the circumstances it was not unreasonable to assume that this was the sequence of events, and the conclusions to which it led were shattering.

'. . . getting on, my son.'

'I'm sorry, father. For a moment my thoughts were elsewhere.'

The priest nodded. 'I won't ask questions. You have told me what you wished, and what I don't know I can't repeat. But what I was saying was that time was getting on. I don't want to speed you on your way. In fact, I wish you could stay to have supper with me, but you said you had this aeroplane to catch.'

'I most certainly have, father.'

And Christopher arrived at Charles de Gaulle after a hectic taxi ride just as Passenger Grayson was being called to take his seat on the British Airways flight to London. He was hurried through the formalities, and caught the aircraft, still trying to come to terms with what he had just learnt.

TWENTY-FOUR

'But you can't, Christopher. You can't,' Verity protested. 'You're my only brother. You must be at my engagement party. Julian will be awfully hurt, and his parents will be offended if you're not there. If Dad can bother to fly over from Brussels –'

'I'm sorry, Verity. Truly sorry. But I can't make it.' The two were having lunch in a small restaurant in Soho. 'I have to go to Canada. I'm due back in college at the end of next week, and really I should be there earlier.'

'Can't you wait until next week to go?'

'No. I don't know how long my business will take. I've booked a flight for Wednesday and I intend to be on it.'

'Why Wednesday?'

'Because it's one of the days when there's a direct flight to Ottawa.' Christopher stopped abruptly. He was saying more than he had intended. 'Look, Verity, I am terribly sorry, but –'

'Why are you going to Canada, anyway?'

Christopher had been expecting this question and had his answer ready. 'I need to interview a man who's been teaching at Carleton University and might want to come over to Oxford.'

'I see.' Verity regarded her brother quizzically. She sensed that although he might not have told a direct lie he had not produced the whole truth. 'I was afraid you were still hunting our dear grand-father.'

'Why afraid?'

'Because it's become dangerous, Chris. Peregrine said you were lucky to have come out of it unscathed and that your luck might not hold if you persisted in going on with this quest of yours.'

'Peregrine? What's it got to do with him?'

'Oh, it was just dinner party chat. Joyce asked Julian and me to dinner. I wasn't too keen, but Peregrine knows a lot of people and could put work in Julian's way.'

'I still don't understand why you had to gossip about me. Who else was at this party?'

'Only Keith and Karen and some chum of Peregrine's and his wife. I never got the name. Blackwood or Blackpool – something like that.'

'I thought Keith was keen that no one outside the family should know about Jean-Pierre.'

Verity shrugged. She looked at her watch. 'Chris, that was a lovely lunch, but I must be off.'

'Half a minute.' He stayed her. 'Verity, you remember going to St Catherine's House for me and looking up a Guy Rogers, who was said to have died last year in his seventies. You didn't mention that, did you?'

'No! Of course not.'

'Are you sure?'

'Yes, quite sure. It was a good party. Champagne flowed and we all got a bit tight, but no – I'm certain I never mentioned Guy Rogers.'

As he drove back to Oxford, Christopher wished he could be as certain. He didn't blame Verity. He thought she had been set up. Joyce and Peregrine weren't in the habit of giving cosy dinner parties for their relations, and the hint that Peregrine might put some work in Julian's way had been a heady temptation; young architects didn't find it easy to come by commissions. But why had Peregrine bothered? Presumably in order to find out what Christopher had been doing, though why this was important to him – or to Keith – remained a mystery.

Nevertheless, Christopher was annoyed that Verity had mentioned the name of Guy Rogers, as he so strongly suspected she had, and in the event his suspicions were confirmed that evening, when he went to Ship Street to pay a visit to his grandmother and Meriel Derwent. As soon as he told the story of the dinner party, Anthea expostulated, 'Christopher, you told me you weren't going to continue your inquiries into Jean-Pierre, but it seems that wasn't true. You've found a cousin of his in Paris.'

'Yes. Ghislaine Roger. How did you know?'

'I had a long letter from your mother. She said she thought it was the best way of breaking the news to me that Jean-Pierre had survived the war.' Anthea gave a sad smile. 'I wept when I read the letter. But it was a long time ago, and it's useless to cry over what-might-have-beens. I only hope he had a happy life.'

'I don't know, Gran. I don't even know if he's alive or dead. He lost touch with Ghislaine.' Christopher shaded the truth. 'She didn't know what had happened to him.'

'He could easily be alive,' Meriel Derwent said. 'He'd only be in his early to mid-seventies, younger than me.'

'What I don't understand is why the authorities are so eager to find him. I simply don't believe he was a traitor or a war criminal or anything like that, whatever Keith may say.' Anthea sounded angry.

'It's strange he doesn't come forward if he's got nothing to hide.' Meriel was ruminating, ignoring Anthea's obvious exasperation. 'Of course, it need have no connection with his war activities. It's also strange that someone is eager to prevent the authorities from finding him.'

'Why do you say that?' Christopher asked.

'I gathered it from what Keith *didn't* say.' Meriel smiled; she didn't like Keith Grayson. 'Incidentally, Chris, he *did* say that if you persist in your inquiries you'll be in real trouble. It could be a warning.'

'Thanks! But what makes you think I haven't abandoned the project?'

'But it's true that you haven't, isn't it, darling?' Anthea interposed. 'Otherwise you wouldn't be interested in Guy Roger, would you?'

Damn Verity, Christopher thought. Damn all gossiping women! But they could be dangerous. And he decided to lay a false trail, to give them something to gossip about.

'Ghislaine told me that her brother Guy had come to England and had been teaching in a school, but she hadn't heard from him for ages. Then a friend of hers said he had died last year, and I promised to have it checked at St Catherine's House,' Christopher lied fluently.

'Oh dear! Poor Ghislaine!' Anthea said.

Meriel was more practical. 'And had he died?'

Christopher hesitated, wishing he knew what Verity had said. 'Verity checked for me and she didn't find his name. A wider search might find it – the friend was pretty definite – but I shan't bother now.'

'So at last you're abandoning your search for Jean-Pierre?' Meriel was quizzical.

'Sure! I can't imagine what else to do. Can you?' Christopher asked coolly.

★   ★   ★

On Wednesday as the aircraft levelled out at its cruising altitude, Christopher settled comfortably into his aisle seat – he always preferred an aisle to a window seat – and loosened his safety belt. The seat beside him was empty. He got a book from his briefcase and started to read.

'Excuse me!'

Christopher looked up, suddenly aware that a girl in a shocking pink suit was standing beside him. She was tall and slim with short red hair and a white skin. She reminded him of Celia Bingham, his ex-girlfriend. But her eyes were green, not blue, and when she smiled her dimples were deep.

'Excuse me,' she said again. She had a soft, gentle voice. 'Would you mind terribly if I came and sat beside you? The man I'm sitting next to reeks of tobacco and beer. It's horrible.'

'On the contrary,' said Christopher, getting up, so that she could pass in front of him. 'I shall be delighted to have such an attractive travelling companion.'

The green eyes sparkled and the smile widened, but the girl didn't comment on the compliment. Nor, once she was settled, did she attempt to make conversation. It was Christopher who started to talk, asking if she always preferred orange juice to champagne. After that they chatted, exchanging casual information.

Christopher learned that her name was Heidi Fielding, her mother was Austrian, her father English. She was a secretary to a high-powered businessman, who had given her a week's holiday in Canada, where he had many interests, as a bonus. As she had never been to North America before she had decided Ottawa would be a good place to start.

'What about you, Mr Grayson. Are you on holiday or –' She glanced at his briefcase. 'Business?'

'Christopher, please,' he corrected her. 'Actually it's nearly the end of my vacation and I'm planning to round it off by visiting friends.'

'You're not staying in a hotel, then?'

'Yes, I am. I much prefer hotels to staying with people. It gives me more freedom and there's no question of imposing on anyone.'

'The Château Laurier?'

'Yes.' Christopher raised an eyebrow. 'How did you know?'

'An easy guess.' Heidi laughed. 'I'm told it's the best and most central hotel in Ottawa. It's where my boss booked me in, anyway, and he's an expert on hotels around the world.'

'In that case, may I offer you a ride in my taxi from the airport – unless of course your boss has laid on a car to take you into the city?'

'No, he hasn't, and thank you. I should love a lift.'

'Good. That's settled then.'

Later, when the door of his room closed behind the porter who had brought up his bag, Christopher wondered why he hadn't asked Heidi Fielding to have dinner with him. He was sure she would have liked to be asked, and confident she would have accepted. He had been tempted, but he reminded himself that he was here for a purpose. There were phone calls to be made, and it was just possible that, if he managed to trace Dr Jane Rogers, she would be prepared to meet him that evening.

He tried the telephone book. There was no problem. Dr Jane Rogers was listed under two numbers, office and home. Her home number corresponded with that of G. L. P. Rogers and E. S. Rogers who lived in Rockcliffe, which Christopher knew to be an expensive and superior district of Ottawa. He tapped out the office number first, to be answered by a secretary who informed him that Dr Rogers didn't come in on Wednesdays, which was one of her hospital days. She asked if he wanted to make an appointment and, on being told no, abruptly cut the line. There was no answer from the home number; presumably everyone was out. But, surprisingly, he got through to Dr Rogers at the main hospital – the Civic – after only a short delay.

'Dr Rogers here. Who is this?'

Christopher hadn't been asked for his name, and he wondered for a moment if the doctor was always so accessible to anonymous phone calls. With the tip of his tongue he wet lips that were dry. He felt stupidly nervous.

'Dr Rogers, you won't know me. My name is Christopher Grayson, and I'm over here from Oxford where I teach. But I've been in Paris recently and, as the result of an absurd happening, have become friendly with Father Anselm of the Église St-Sulpice in the 16th arrondissement. When I told him I was coming to Ottawa, he suggested I might get in touch with you.' Christopher stopped; the silence at the other end of the line was palpable, or he was imagining it. 'I – I hope you'll forgive the intrusion.'

'You have a message from Father Anselm, Mr Grayson?'

The voice was cool and dispassionate, but not unfriendly. He tried to imagine the young woman who would fit the voice, but could only picture Chantal Delancourt.

'Scarcely a message, Dr Rogers. He asked me to give you and your family his best wishes and affectionate regards.'

'How kind of him – and of you to bother to deliver the message, Mr Grayson.'

There was no doubt that she was amused, and momentarily Christopher felt annoyed – annoyed enough to be reckless. At once he said, 'I have another motive for calling you, doctor. I don't know anyone in Ottawa, and I was hoping I might persuade you to have dinner with me one night.'

'One night? How long are you staying in the city? Indeed, why are you here at all?'

'I'm not sure. A few days. I hope to visit colleagues in Carleton University and the University of Ottawa. I told you I was an Oxford don.'

'You implied it, anyway, Mr Grayson. Well, I'm sure you'll find a lot of your fellow professors happy to entertain you.'

'Does that mean you won't have a meal with me? What about tomorrow? Please!'

'Tomorrow?' She appeared to muse. 'Yes, that would be possible. Where would you suggest?'

'Wherever you like. Tell me and I'll book a table.'

'There's a French restaurant in Hull, across the river. It's called L'Oiseau Bleu. The food is excellent. I'll meet you there at seven-thirty.'

'That will be wonderful.'

'Until tomorrow then.'

The line went dead and Christopher let out a shout of triumph. He couldn't believe his luck, that the ploy of using Father Anselm's name had worked. But as he recalled his conversation with Dr Jane Rogers he began to have doubts. Could she have heard of him before his phone call? Could the name of Grayson have had some meaning for her? She had been extraordinarily composed, and surely it was unusual for a presumably busy doctor to be prepared to give up an evening to have dinner with a stranger.

No longer so pleased with events, Christopher caught himself yawning. It had been a tiring day's journey and, although according to the clock it was still early, he yearned for bed. He decided to have some supper sent up to his room. At the same time he ordered a rental car for the next morning, and asked to be called with breakfast at eight o'clock.

While he waited for the food to arrive he helped himself to a whisky from the mini-bar and studied the map of the district and other useful information provided by the management. He found Acacia Avenue in Rockcliffe, where Dr Rogers and her family lived, and located L'Oiseau Bleu in Hull in Quebec, on the opposite side of the Ottawa River. It was highly rated as a restaurant, and thankfully he saw that it took American Express cards. He wanted no embarrassment about paying the bill.

And, as he contemplated the morrow, he decided that it was going to be an interesting day. In the event, it proved more stimulating than he had expected.

Christopher saw Heidi Fielding coming out of the coffee shop in the hotel. This morning she was wearing a jade green suit, with an exceedingly short skirt which drew attention to her beautiful long legs. Christopher was not the only male who watched her with admiration.

'Good morning,' he said as she approached and gave him a dimpled smile. 'Did you sleep well?'

'Too well. It must have been jet-lag. I've just had breakfast and look at the time.'

Christopher laughed. Then on an impulse he said, 'I've rented a car. Would you like to come for a drive with me, and perhaps find somewhere for a drink and lunch?'

'Would I not? I wouldn't dare drive in this city myself. So many of the cars are so huge, and they go on the wrong side of the road. But to be chauffeured would be great.'

They agreed to meet in fifteen minutes, and spent the rest of the day exploring Ottawa and the outlying suburbs, where there was still snow on the ground and large mounds of it, now dirty brown, at the sides of the highways where the ploughs and snow-blowers had deposited it. Although officially it was spring, it was surprisingly cold and they were glad of the powerful heater in the car. But Heidi was good company, as she had been on the plane, and it was far from being a wasted day from Christopher's point of view.

He drove twice past the house on Acacia Avenue in Rockcliffe where Dr Jane Rogers lived. It was a large and imposing mansion, like most of the houses in the district, with a circular drive and a three-car garage. Outside the front door there was a blue Cadillac, and the second time they went past Christopher caught a glimpse of a short plump woman in a fur coat and hat getting into the driving seat. He easily found L'Oiseau Bleu. It was a small, unpretentious place in a side street, which might have been difficult to track down without his map.

They got back to the Château shortly after six, later than Christopher had intended, but they had lost their way at one point and found themselves heading for Montreal. Heidi thanked him and said she had had a marvellous day.

'I can't remember when I've enjoyed myself more,' she said. 'Can I stand you a drink now, Chris, before dinner?'

It wasn't clear to Christopher whether she expected them to dine together, but she was obviously disappointed when he refused the drink and pleaded a prior engagement.

'Perhaps tomorrow?' she said.

'Perhaps. I can't promise. It depends what comes of my meeting this evening.'

She didn't press him any more, and Christopher hurried to his room where he showered and shaved and spent considerable time choosing a tie. But still he was early. He had decided to allow half an hour to get to the restaurant, in the expectation that Jane – he found that he now thought of her as Jane – would be punctual, and he would be there a few minutes ahead of her.

Idly he turned on the television set and, flicking through the innumerable channels, was suddenly surprised by a picture of Piccadilly Circus appearing on the screen. The area was thronged with a mob of angry demonstrators, fighting both among themselves and with the police who were all in riot gear. There was stone-throwing, and petrol bombs. An elderly man was knocked to the ground and others trampled on him. There was a close-up of a youth, his face streaming with blood, who was being dragged to a waiting police van by two officers.

The voice of the newscaster said, 'This was the scene yesterday in the West End of London, England, where a bunch of the new right-wing so-called National Party, a neo-Nazi group, was attacked by left-wing opponents. Three people were killed and many injured. The police seemed unable to contain the violence, which has also flared up in other parts of Europe. In Germany right-wing extremists recently burned down a synagogue and in France –'

Christopher switched off the set. He was not politically-minded. In the last election he had voted for the Conservatives, but his views were generally liberal. He hated the fascist kind of racism that both

209

the Graysons, Keith and Peregrine, seemed to espouse, though since Peregrine had become a minister they were less inclined to express their opinions, at least in public.

Anyway, it was time to leave for his appointment with Dr Jane Rogers.

As Christopher had expected, Jane was punctual, but until the maître d' brought her to his table he didn't recognize her; she bore no resemblance to her sister Chantal. In fact, she was tall and dark with an oval face and eyes which, he was to discover were of an extraordinary violet colour. She was beautiful, not pretty like her sister, nor attractive in the same way as the vivacious Heidi Fielding. But, simply dressed in a plain green dress and without any jewellery, she took his breath away.

He managed to stammer a greeting, and they shook hands. Jane appeared quite composed. She immediately began to ask him questions, but they were polite queries of the kind that casual strangers might ask, and not in the least intrusive. She enquired about Oxford, his work, his supposed visit to colleagues at the local universities, his first impressions of Ottawa. In return he asked her about the hospital and what Ottawa was like as a place to live in. Inevitably, as the meal progressed, they touched on their respective families. Christopher spoke of his parents, his sister, his brother-in-law to be – all safe subjects. But the only fact of any importance that he learned about Jane Rogers which he didn't already know was that her father was in his seventies; his mind boggled at the thought of what their relationship must be if her father was his grandfather.

It was towards the end of dinner that Jane, having refused the sweet trolley and settled for cheese, brought about an abrupt change in their conversation. Without warning she said, 'Now, Mr Grayson.' He had twice asked her to call him Christopher, but she had ignored the suggestion. 'Perhaps you'll tell me why you were so eager to meet with me. The truth, please. No nonsense about Father Anselm sending greetings. To prevent any more lies I'll tell you I've had Chantal, my sister, on the phone from Paris. She said you called at the apartment and questioned her about someone by the name of Ghislaine Roger. Neither she nor I have ever met this Mademoiselle Roger. Is that clear?'

'Quite clear,' Christopher said mildly. Although Jane's tirade had been unexpected it had lasted long enough to give him time to get over his surprise at her sudden attack. 'I didn't imagine that either

Madame Delancourt or you had met Ghislaine, who happens to be a distant cousin of mine.'

'Then why – ?'

'Have you told your father about any of this?' He knew she was bluffing; they might never have met Mademoiselle Ghislaine Roger, but Chantal had certainly heard of her.

Jane stared at him. 'No. Why should I worry Dad about something that has nothing to do with him, with us? Let me tell you that, if I'd not checked that you really were an Oxford don, I'd think you were crazy.'

'The two are not necessarily incompatible.' Christopher's smile was wry. 'However, I am not crazy. I'm trying to trace my natural grandfather, Jean-Pierre de Mourville, and I believe your father may be able to help me.'

'Why?'

'I believe they were – companions in the war.' Christopher leaned across the table. 'Jane, please! This is terribly important to me. Will you ask your father to meet me, and have a talk with me? That's all I want, I swear.'

'I don't understand. Dad taught in a boys' school during the war. It was a reserved occupation. He's unlikely to have met your grandfather.'

'My *natural* grandfather! I believe he did know him. Please will you ask him to see me?'

'Yes. All right. I will ask him, but he may not agree. He's not a young man and his health is not too good.'

'Thank you.' Christopher wondered why Jane looked so worried. He was not to know that when she had told her father that she was dining with a Christopher Grayson from Oxford, she had thought for a moment that he was about to collapse.

TWENTY-FIVE

As Christopher returned to the Château Laurier after his surprising dinner with Dr Jane Rogers, his feelings were mixed. He was confident that he had at last found Jean-Pierre de Mourville, his grandfather. But to meet him face to face and talk with him was another matter, and yet it was essential. He was not the only individual searching for Jean-Pierre, and sooner or later the others would catch up with him, whatever name he chose to use. If Jean-Pierre was not already aware of their determination, he needed to be warned.

Christopher had hoped that through his acquaintance with Jane – Canadians being noted for their hospitality – he would be able to invite himself to the Rogers's house, and give Jean-Pierre no choice but to meet him. This was no longer possible. His supposedly cunning plan had misfired. Indeed, he was in a worse position than if he had rung the doorbell at the Rogers's house and, unknown to any of the family, presented himself. The old man, now forewarned, could easily disappear again, at least temporarily, and his own time was limited; he had to be in Oxford for the beginning of the new term.

In spite of Jane's advocacy – and Christopher was far from sure that she would speak on his behalf – he was very doubtful if he, a Grayson who claimed to be the grandson of Jean-Pierre de Mourville, would be made welcome in the Rogers household. And what was he to do if, when Jane telephoned as she had promised, she said her father was too busy or too unwell to meet strangers, or had unexpectedly gone out of town. What if she didn't phone at all?

No, Christopher decided, she would phone; she was not the kind of girl to break a promise. As he collected his room key at the desk, said goodnight to the porters on duty, and crossed the foyer to the elevators, he thought about Jane Rogers. He had never met anyone quite like her. She was astonishingly beautiful and she was intelligent, but she was also distant. He wondered if this was because she distrusted him, perhaps disliked him. He wondered if she had a lover.

'Chris! Chris!'

He had stepped into an elevator but he held the door as Heidi Fielding came running towards him. She was wearing a black dress and a short fur jacket and her face was flushed. She almost threw herself into Christopher's arms.

'Oh, Chris, I'm so cold. I've been to the Arts Centre to see the ballet. It was lovely in there, but it was too near to take a taxi. I had to walk back across Confederation Square and it's freezing outside.'

'Poor old Heidi!'

Christopher hugged her. It was the natural thing to do. And she *was* cold. For a moment he thought again of Jane Rogers, but he couldn't imagine the composed doctor acting with such exuberance, however chilled she might have been.

'What you need, sweetie, is some hot coffee with a good dollop of brandy in it. There's brandy in my little refrigerator. We'll get the coffee sent up. How does that sound?'

'Oh, Chris, that sounds blissful.'

Christopher woke from a deep sleep. His alarm clock was ringing. He put out a hand to turn it off, but it wasn't there. Then he realized it wasn't his alarm clock, but the telephone – and he was in a hotel, the Château Laurier in Ottawa, Canada. As his brain, befuddled by sleep and too much to drink the previous evening, began to work again he was sitting up in bed, thrusting aside Heidi's arm lying across his chest and reaching for the phone which was on her side of his three-quarter bed – which they were sharing.

'Hello!' he said breathlessly. 'Hello!'

'Good morning, Mr Grayson. This is Jane Rogers. I'm sorry to have disturbed you.'

'Jane!'

'Dr Rogers,' she corrected him.

'I beg your pardon, Dr Rogers.'

He was so pleased to hear her voice that he was scarcely aware what he was saying or, until Heidi began to move beneath him, that in order to reach the telephone he was lying astride her and they were both naked. Heidi moved her hands, rhythmically caressing him, and he gritted his teeth so as to resist her and concentrate on what Jane was saying.

'What – what did you say?' he muttered into the receiver.

'Mr Grayson, are you drunk – or what?' Jane asked sharply.

The answer was 'or what', but he couldn't explain. 'I'm sorry,' he said. 'I only woke up when the telephone rang.' He put his hand over the receiver. 'Heidi, stop it! At once! This is important to me!'

'Oh Chris, darling,' she sighed.

'Be quiet! And stay still!'

'Mr Grayson, are you not alone?' There was an edge to Jane's voice.

'No, the maid just brought in my breakfast,' Christopher lied convincingly, but the lie was spoilt by a suppressed giggle from Heidi.

There was a short silence and Jane said coldly, 'Well, if you still wish to meet my father, Mr Grayson, I'll pick you up at your hotel at two-thirty today and drive you out to our summer cottage in the Gatineau Hills north of Ottawa for the weekend. Is that convenient for you?'

'The weekend?' Christopher was stunned. He had hoped to be asked in for a drink which, if he was lucky, might stretch to a meal. But a whole weekend was beyond his wildest dreams, especially as Jane had not sounded in the least friendly. 'The weekend would be fine. Thank you very much,' he said.

'Right. Two-thirty.' She didn't bother to say goodbye.

Heidi snuggled closer to Christopher. 'You're going away for a dirty weekend. Oh, Chris, must you? We could have such fun together – like now.'

'It's not a dirty weekend. I'm going to meet her family.'

'You mean it's serious? You're going to ask Papa for her hand?' Heidi mocked him.

'Don't be silly.' Christopher tried to push her away, but she was strong and he didn't want to use force. 'Let me go.'

'Not until we've made love. There's time, isn't there? Or will it take you too long to get to wherever your rendezvous is?'

'I'm not being picked up till after lunch, at two-thirty, but I've various things to do first.'

'They can wait.'

And wait they did, but at two-twenty-five Christopher was standing under the portico at the entrance to the Château Laurier. He had paid his hotel bill, booked a flight home via Montreal for Monday, bought himself a warm padded jacket, suitable for wearing in a cottage in the Gatineau Hills, and promised to be in touch with Heidi before he left Canada. He had also pondered over the problem

214

of what he should take as a present to his host and hostess, but the difficulty had proved insoluble; he knew nothing of their tastes, and impersonal gifts, flowers or chocolates, seemed somewhat inappropriate in the circumstances.

Precisely on time Jane Rogers drew up in front of Christopher and, without getting out of her seat opened the door for him to sit beside her. He threw his bag in the back next to hers, and got in, doing up his seatbelt.

'It's very good of your father to see me,' he ventured.

'According to him, he had no choice.'

'I don't understand.'

'Nor do I. He said he would explain after he had talked to you and found out what you wanted.' She hooted savagely at a pedestrian who had stepped off the sidewalk almost in front of her car. 'But I'll tell you one thing, Christopher Grayson, if you mean Dad any harm you'll have me to deal with.'

'I don't wish him any harm. Why should I?'

'I've no idea. He's a wonderful man, kind, intelligent, generous. I couldn't have wished for a better father.' Surprisingly, Jane's voice broke. 'And if he did something to be ashamed of in the past – though I can't imagine what on earth it might be – I don't give a damn!'

Christopher looked at her profile, at the long, slender neck and the determined set of her jaw, and thought she was even more beautiful than he had remembered from the previous evening. But the weekend was not beginning well.

'I assure you he has nothing to fear from me.'

Jane glanced at him sideways before turning her eyes back to the road. 'I wish I could believe you. But you've already worried him so much that he can't sleep. Last night, after we'd arranged for you to come to the cottage for the weekend, he was prowling about the house until three or four in the morning instead of getting some rest. I got up to see if I could help him, but he sent me away.'

Christopher was silent. There was nothing to say. Clearly he had upset the Rogers's peaceful household, but the arrival of some unwelcome visitors couldn't have been completely unexpected – or why had Jean-Pierre telephoned Ghislaine and warned her not to mention the name of Guy Roger? He must have known that inquiries were being made about him.

The silence lengthened. By now they had passed through Hull and were heading north towards the hills. The highway was bare and dry, but lined with melting mounds of snow, and there was snow on the fields. In spite of the sunshine and a flawless blue sky, the countryside looked bleak and cheerless to Christopher. He didn't envy the people who lived in the solitary farmhouses that dotted the landscape, or even the inhabitants of the straggling villages through which they passed. He thought how harsh the land looked in comparison with the rolling countryside of Oxfordshire, with its cosy Cotswold towns.

To break the silence, he said, 'Wouldn't it have been more convenient for everyone if your father had agreed to see me at your house in Rockcliffe instead of driving all these miles?'

'Why should we change our plans for you? These days, this is the weekend we always open up our cottage for the summer. It's more or less winterized and at one time we used to go up there for the skiing during the winter and have great parties. But nowadays we just use it for five months or so in the year. Meanwhile, the Nortons who have a house not far away keep an eye on it for us.'

'The cottage sounds like fun.'

'Yes, it was.' She sounded sad. 'And it could be very peaceful, too. It was lovely to sit on the veranda overlooking the lake on a summer's evening, and listen to the cry of the loons.'

'You speak as if it is the past tense?'

'I'm afraid it is. Dad talks of selling. He and Ma are getting old, Chantal's living in France, and I'm too busy to spend much time out of town.'

Again they fell silent, but now it was a companionable silence, not hostile, and Christopher thought how wonderful it would be if they had been going to spend the weekend alone together.

The 'cottage' was a surprise to Christopher. It stood at the top of a steep and narrow lane, built of wood that had mellowed over the years to a silver-grey, and was much larger than he had expected. He was to learn that in addition to a huge living-room where a log fire was burning, it contained four bedrooms, a kitchen and two bathrooms, and was surrounded by a wide screened balcony where in summer everyone relaxed and ate meals and even sometimes slept in the open air.

'Not as primitive as you expected?' Jane said as, having parked her car in the double garage beside the Cadillac that Christopher had seen outside the Rogers's house in Rockcliffe, she led the way in. 'Some of the cottages *are* primitive – outside loos half a mile across a field. But we have a generator that gives us electricity and allows us to pump water up from the lake and from a deep well for drinking water. Very civilized.'

A voice interrupted them. 'My dear Jane, you sound as if you're trying to sell the place.'

Jane laughed. 'My mother, Mrs Rogers,' she said, gesturing to a grey-haired woman, still pretty in her early sixties, who had come into the room. 'Mr Grayson.'

Elizabeth Rogers bowed her head in acknowledgement of the introduction, but she didn't offer her hand. 'Mr Grayson, I don't wish to appear rude, but I'm an outspoken person. We Rogers are a close-knit family. We stick together for better or worse, and as I understand it your presence here may not be good news for us. That being said, you are our guest. Jane will show you to your room. My husband is resting at present, but he'll see you before supper and perhaps he can discover what it is that you want of him, and how he can satisfy you.'

'Thank you,' Christopher said carefully, and thought resentfully that the damned woman was treating him as if he were a potential blackmailer.

Seething with anger, he followed Jane to what was to be his room. It was small and cold, and had the barest necessities, a bed, a chair, chest of drawers, and a row of pegs in a corner behind a curtain. There was a strip of carpet on the wooden floor beside the bed, which when he bounced on it proved to be surprisingly comfortable.

'I'm afraid it's rather spartan,' Jane said, 'but there are lots of blankets, and we all have hot-water bottles at this time of year.'

'Thank you,' Christopher said again.

'Come along to the fire when you're ready. Your bathroom's two doors along the passage.' She opened her mouth as if to add something, and shut it again. But at the door she turned. 'Dad's an old man. He may not have that much longer to live. And we love him dearly. You can't expect us to welcome you – or anyone else who may pose a threat to him.' She was gone before he could expostulate.

If the bedroom had been warmer Christopher might have lingered there, but the idea of the blazing log fire and the comfortable furniture in the living-room was enticing. He visited the bathroom, then went along to the big room. No one was there, but he could hear voices from the kitchen, Jane and Mrs Rogers. He drew a chair up close to the fire and warmed himself.

'Good afternoon, Mr Grayson,' a voice said behind him.

Christopher leapt to his feet. 'Good afternoon, sir.'

The two men, so alike in spite of the forty-odd years that separated them, assessed each other. Secretly they were both impressed. Christopher thought that his grandfather had aged well. He was still upright, still slim – unlike the fat, pot-bellied Keith – and even in his casual clothes he had a certain elegance. For his part, the old man thought that in different circumstances he would have welcomed Christopher as his grandson, but as it was –

Abruptly he said, 'Mr Grayson, Jane tells me you have been trying to trace your natural grandfather, a Frenchman, and you believe I might be able to help you. Why?'

Christopher made no attempt to be other than blunt. 'Because after the war, in 1945, Jean-Pierre de Mourville returned to England carrying the passport and identity papers of his cousin, Guy Roger. When he discovered that my grandmother, Anthea Stanton, had married Keith Grayson, he got a job teaching French in a boys' school. Later, with a slight change to his name, he came to Canada as Guy Rogers.'

The old man gave a sardonic smile. 'Can you prove this accusation?'

'If it were necessary, yes, sir. A lot of people are still alive – Anthea, Keith, Boris Richmann who was at the camp outside Ansbach with you, Arthur Brent whom you taught at St Michael's College, and others. But the question of proof doesn't arise. This, sir, is in no sense an accusation. Who am I to accuse you? And what of? I had been hoping – but the whole thing has got out of hand, grown complicated and gone awry.'

'You mean you haven't satisfied your masters? You seem to me to have been pretty efficient.'

'Masters? I don't understand.'

'Who are you working for, Mr Grayson? MI6?'

'I'm not working for anyone, dammit! A few weeks ago and quite by chance I learnt that my grandfather was not Keith Grayson, but had been a French aristocrat called Jean-Pierre de Mourville, believed killed in the war, a romantic figure, something of a hero. I decided to try to find out more about him during my Easter vacation. It was a personal matter, you understand, a family matter! Then I discovered other people were also interested, that he might not have been what he seemed. The French authorities told me I was being a nuisance, meddling in matters I knew nothing about, and that I should go home. And then there was the lot –'

218

Christopher controlled his emotion. 'The lot who killed Ghislaine.'

'I knew Ghislaine was dead, but – There was a connection with me? Surely not! Chantal just said that Ghislaine had interrupted thieves who had attacked her, and that she had died in hospital.' The old man was visibly shocked. 'I had told Ghislaine that if she ever needed to get in touch with me she could do so through Chantal, and I told Chantal that Ghislaine was a family friend, who might contact her. Christopher, what did happen?'

Christopher told him. 'I blame myself.'

'No, it's not your fault. It's the past catching up with the present, because of a possibility of history repeating itself.' Jean-Pierre de Mourville sighed. 'You don't know what I mean by that, do you? Well, I'll try to explain. But this is all going to take some sorting out, so first let us have a drink. It's not every day I acquire a grandson.' He smiled sadly, and suddenly Christopher felt overwhelmed with love for him.

TWENTY-SIX

They would have talked far into the night, but at eleven o'clock Betty Rogers intervened. It had been a long day for all of them and an emotional one; it was high time they went to bed.

Jean-Pierre de Mourville, who admitted that by now he thought of himself as Guy Rogers, had done most of the talking. He had told them how he had been sent to England by his parents immediately before the outbreak of war, and how he and Anthea had fallen in love. He had glossed over his experiences with the French Resistance, except to say that he had been taken prisoner and spent the rest of the war in a prison camp in Germany,

His wife and Jane, to both of whom all this was news, listened with rapt attention. Christopher, on the other hand, was more interested in the omissions, in what he didn't tell the women.

'You mean that at the end the guards just left the gates of the camp open and everyone walked out?' Jane said in amazement.

'Yes, but it took a while to get home. Europe was in a dreadful state. And when I got home I found that my parents were dead and the estate had been confiscated,' said Jean-Pierre, and hurried on before they could question him. 'I went to Paris, to my cousins, whose name was Roger. My mother had been a Roger. Ghislaine gave me the papers of her brother Guy, who had been killed in the war, and I went to England illegally, only to find that my Anthea had married Keith Grayson.'

'You must have been devastated,' Betty said sympathetically. 'But why didn't you go home then, back to your relations?'

Jean-Pierre shrugged, and glanced at Christopher. 'There were complications. Anyway, if I had returned to France, I would never have met and married you, my dear Betty, and had two beloved daughters.'

'My husband was a colleague of Guy's at the University of Montreal,' Betty said to Christopher. 'He died young, and I was left a widow with a small daughter.'

'So I acquired two for the price of one,' said Jean-Pierre. 'A very good bargain.'

'You mean that Jane isn't – isn't –' Christopher stammered.

'Isn't your aunt, Chris?' Jane laughed. 'Chantal is, but you and I are not relations, except distantly by marriage.'

'That's certainly interesting,' Christopher said, more coolly than he felt.

And later when, lying in bed under a heap of blankets and hugging his hot-water bottle, he mused on the events of the day, he thought that it was the most interesting fact he had learnt. By now he knew that he was half in love with Dr Jane Rogers, and he was looking forward to the next day.

Christopher woke reluctantly. Someone was shaking his shoulder. As the possible significance of this percolated to his sleepy mind he became fully awake and sat up.

'What is it?' he asked anxiously.

'Nothing to panic over. I've brought you some coffee.'

Jean-Pierre put the mug down beside Christopher. 'It's still early. Not much after six. The women aren't awake yet. But I thought it a good idea that you and I should have a private talk.'

'Yes.' Christopher propped himself up against his pillows. 'Thanks for the coffee, sir.'

Jean-Pierre pulled his chair closer to the bed and sat down. 'The walls aren't too thick,' he said softly. 'Now, Christopher, first I want to thank you for being so tactful yesterday. My story – you could call it a tragic love story because that was what it was – was enough of a shock for Betty and Jane without learning about the darker side of my life. As you must have realized by now, the two were to some extent tied together.'

'Yes, I understand that. But, sir – I don't believe either Jane or Mrs Rogers believe it was quite as simple as you implied. They're both worried about you. They've gone out of their way to impress on me how important you are to them. They're not fools and I'm sure they must suspect there's more that you're hiding from them. They had already suspected something, for wasn't it odd that Chantal should have been so upset that she telephoned Jane from France because someone – actually it was me – suddenly called on her and asked if she knew Ghislaine Roger?'

'I didn't know Chantal had done that.'

'It made Jane very suspicious of me, but not, I'm sure, because

221

she thought I was about to put in a claim for Ghislaine's jewellery.'

'Oh dear!' Jean-Pierre suppressed a grin, then became serious. 'Christopher, you noticed the question I didn't answer yesterday. When Betty asked why I hadn't returned to France when I discovered Anthea was married to Keith Grayson –'

'Yes. You said there were complications, sir.'

'You have no idea what they might be?'

'None. Admittedly, the Château de Mourville was destroyed and your estate lost, but Ghislaine would have been delighted to share her apartment with you. And you must have had friends in France. You could have re-established yourself in Paris. Surely it would have been easier for you than making a new – and, you must admit, illegal – life in England. Was it because of Anthea, sir? Were you afraid she might discover you were alive, and it would cause her more unhappiness?'

'Chris, I regret to say you have too high an opinion of me. No! That may have influenced me, but it was not the deciding factor. I was afraid to go back to France.'

'Afraid?'

'Yes, afraid. I couldn't tell Betty and Jane all this, but after my time in that prison camp, I couldn't bear the thought of being incarcerated again, and I was fearful that might happen if I returned to France. Christopher, you have met Henri Colet, who ran the resistance group centred on Vire in Normandy. He would have named me as a traitor – *the* traitor. Because again and again his group was betrayed and lives were lost. If I had had any doubt about this, the commandant of the barracks at St-Lô, Oberst Karl Becker, confirmed it to me when I was finally captured.'

'Did the Oberst name the real traitor?'

'Not in so many words.' The old man was silent, lost in thought. 'The worst disaster was at the farm, which was a sort of unofficial headquarters for Colet's *réseau*, and kept very secret – but seemingly not secret enough. The Germans raided it. They found a store of weapons and a wireless, and they took the whole family away – the farmer, his wife and their two sons, and his brother and *his* wife and daughter. They had all been enormously brave and taken great risks for the Resistance, and it was an awful blow to Colet and his group.'

'What happened to the farmer and his family?'

'God knows, Christopher. They were sheltering a Jewish family, which made the betrayal worse.'

'Did Colet blame you for it – the betrayal, I mean, sir?'

'He blamed me for everything that went wrong. He even thought I was laying his wife, which I wasn't. But that isn't all. You don't know this, and again I certainly wasn't going to worry Betty and Jane, but when I first reached home, where I had hoped for a welcome, I found the villagers hostile, my parents condemned as collaborators, their graves desecrated and accusations being made against me. It was said that not only had I betrayed my country and caused the death of French and British patriots, but that I had gone to Germany when things became too hot for me, and had become the brutal commandant of a camp where many had died. An English security officer had been asking about me, and he had implied that charges would be brought if I could be apprehended.'

'Was that true, sir? About the English security officer?'

'Certainly a British major did made inquiries about me, and, according to an old priest and his sister, whom I visited, did nothing to discourage rumours about me.'

'But people who had been in the camp with you, people like Boris Richmann, would have said what rubbish they were, and surely your brigadier – Brigadier Beaumont, wasn't he? – would have supported you.'

'Boris was just a boy, and I didn't know where he or anyone else who had been in the camp with me had gone. We all scattered and lost touch. You have to remember that Europe, especially the countries that had been occupied and fought over, were in a dreadful state – an administrative nightmare – at that time.'

'What about your unit and the brigadier?'

'Unfortunately for me, when I telephoned from Ghislaine's apartment in Paris before I went to England, I learnt that the brigadier had had a stroke and that while the unit was being disbanded Keith Grayson was in charge.'

'And he wouldn't have helped you?'

'Christopher, what do you think?'

'No, I suppose he would have been afraid that Gran would have left him for you.'

'Possibly, but there was more to it than that. Grayson knew that if I could prove myself innocent I might have been able to prove him guilty. Of course, what he didn't know was that once I had learnt he was married to Anthea and, as I believed, had a son by her, he was safe. He must have had an anxious time after the war wondering if I would reappear. His visit to my home and doubtless other inquiries he made in France must have reassured him.' The old man's voice was hard. 'But even then in his role of security officer he took every opportunity to blacken me and my family.'

'Sir!'

Christopher was aghast. He felt no great affection for Keith Grayson. If he had been honest he would have admitted that he rather disliked his racist and extreme right-wing views. Nevertheless, he had acknowledged all his life that Keith Grayson was his grandfather. He bore the name of Grayson, as did his father. Yet now he was being asked to accept that Keith had behaved despicably, and had not only been a traitor but had put the blame for a series of betrayals on another man, out of personal jealousy.

'I find all this difficult to believe, sir,' he said.

'Yes. I can understand that.'

'Do you have any proof? You said that the Oberst at St-Lô didn't name his source.'

'That's right. His immediate informant was the local baker, but the man was only a go-between. The Oberst didn't know the originator, but suspected he was British.'

Christopher nodded. It was what the French security man had told him when they were trying to warn him off. 'Is there any evidence that it was Keith who supplied the information?'

'Circumstantial. The last drop, the one I met when I was taken prisoner, was put forward twenty-four hours at the last moment. This was agreed before I left England. Only the brigadier, Keith and I knew this was to happen. Henri Colet was not to be told until the morning of the night that the drop was to be made. As it was, I had trouble persuading him I was telling the truth and he didn't trust me. He provided no back-up, which in the circumstances was lucky because the Germans had been warned and were waiting in force.'

'But what about communications? Surely one could hardly pick up a phone in London and speak to occupied France?'

'Of course not. I imagine he used some military net and spoke to a cut-out who spoke to another cut-out, who got hold of the baker. That wouldn't have been so difficult.'

'It sounds complicated.'

'Maybe, but it would be a safeguard against the original source being traced. Anyway, I gather that the baker received a telephone message early that morning and passed it on as usual. The Oberst

224

was surprised and even cross-questioned him. But he was surprised at the very short notice of the drop, not that the date had been changed; he wasn't aware that a drop had been expected twenty-four hours later. The baker's very reliable source hadn't mentioned it, perhaps deliberately so as not to cause confusion, or perhaps he saw no need. Either way it was a mistake.'

'And only three people knew what was to happen,' Christopher said slowly. 'Why did the prime source wait so long to give the right date if he knew it in advance?'

'I don't know. Perhaps it was to cast suspicion wider than the three of us if things went wrong. After all, Keith couldn't guarantee I'd be captured or killed, and if I hadn't been I'd have been in a position to ask a lot of awkward questions. But, in the event, I was captured and the disaster could be put down to bad luck, or negligence or worse on my part.'

Christopher shook his head. 'Could you possibly be wrong about Keith, sir?'

'No, Christopher. I had plenty of time to consider the situation after St-Lô, and there were a lot of small pointers, straws in the wind, you might say, that suggested Keith.'

'But why, sir? For heaven's sake, why?'

'He was pro-Nazi. He always admired the Germans, their efficiency, their orderliness, their thoroughness – and he disliked the French. He believed the British had far more in common with the Germans than with any other European country. Even the Royal Family was of German descent. And of course, his dislike of me – the Frog as he and Karen called me, even to my face – turned to hatred when Anthea fell in love with me.'

'You speak of it so dispassionately.'

'It was all a long time ago, and I'd come to terms with the situation – until recently. Now the past has caught up with the present. I had hoped I was safely hidden here, but if you can find me, others will, and I hate to think of the consequences.'

'As far as the authorities are concerned, isn't there a period of twenty-five years after which war crimes can't be tried?'

'Yes, but not so-called "crimes against humanity". As I told you, the family at the farm were Jewish and so were some of those at Ansbach. I could be extradited to France, Christopher, and made to face a trial. It'll be even more difficult now to prove my innocence than it was then. And imagine the scandal, what it will mean to Betty and Jane and Chantal – and, if I accused Keith, to the Graysons.'

225

'It would certainly be a *cause célèbre*. The tabloids would go to town on it, and the media would have a field day.'

Christopher thought of his parents, his grandmother, Verity and Julian. The publicity would be hideous. None of them would escape it. In different ways it would affect each one of them and would stretch beyond to friends like Meriel Derwent and relations of his mother, and Julian's family.

It was a full minute before he thought of Peregrine. 'Dear God!' he said aloud.

'What is it?'

'I've just remembered. When Karen got tight after old John Grayson's funeral and let slip that Dad was not Keith's son, Keith was absolutely furious. He swore at her and knocked her coffee over her, and made one of the maids take her to her room. But the point is that it wasn't because of Dad, but because of Peregrine that he was so angry. A bit later I overheard him threatening her. I can't recall the exact words but the meaning was that, for Peregrine's sake, the past must not be raked up, not when Peregrine's future promised so much. It didn't make much sense at the time.'

'But it does now?'

'Yes, after what you've told me. The scandal might do Dad no good, but it would certainly ruin Peregrine's chances of becoming Prime Minister.'

'If his views are anything like his father's that would be beneficial for the country,' Jean-Pierre said cynically.

'Yes. I agree he'd be a disaster, especially if he had a large majority.'

They were silent for a minute, each concerned with his own thoughts. Then the old man said, 'Perhaps I have been too pessimistic about the French authorities. They may not have enough evidence against me to put me on trial. But this other lot, who seem determined to trace me, are terribly worrying. If they'd get their thugs to kill poor dear Ghislaine and threaten the priest –'

'Have you any idea who they might be, sir?'

'I can only guess that they are neo-Nazis – probably members of the British National Party, but more likely crypto-fascists who of course don't do their dirty work themselves, but merely pull the strings.'

'Do you think Keith could be behind it, that he believes you know more than you actually do, and if the French authorities found you, you might ruin Peregrine's prospects?'

Jean-Pierre had no time to answer. There was a brief knock on the door and Betty poked her head into the room. She was already dressed.

'Breakfast in fifteen minutes, gentlemen. Jane is putting on the coffee right now.'

The day had begun, and all was horribly normal.

TWENTY-SEVEN

In other circumstances Christopher would have enjoyed the day, which on the surface was distressingly ordinary. In the morning he helped with the household chores, brought in wood, cleaned out a birdbath, peeled potatoes, fed a chipmunk. After lunch he and Jane set off across country where there was still enough snow to make skiing possible.

Throughout the entire proceedings, everyone studiously avoided speaking of what was uppermost in their minds, Jean-Pierre de Mourville's past and how it might affect the future. Betty and Jane talked about themselves and Chantal, Jean-Pierre about Canada and its economic and political ills, Christopher about his parents and Verity's forthcoming marriage. But, underlying this seemingly casual conversation was a constant feeling of restraint, of doubt, almost of trepidation.

Then after tea Betty said that she would be going out later and, when Christopher expressed some surprise, she explained. 'Not very far, just down the hill to the Nortons' house. Mrs Norton dropped by this afternoon and I promised to make up a fourth for bridge. But I've made a casserole for your supper, so you won't starve. Jane knows what to do with it.'

The time passed pleasantly. Betty came in to say that she was off and goodbye. Her husband told her to drive carefully and not to be too late; it was obvious they were very fond of each other. Christopher heard the front door shut, and minutes afterwards the sound of a car going down the steep lane. It seemed to be a signal. Jane went to put the casserole in the oven, and Jean-Pierre to serve drinks.

When Jane returned, she said, 'Dad, I know you don't want to worry Ma, but I think you should tell me the truth, not just half of it. You were troubled before Chris turned up, weren't you? And you still are. What *is* the matter? It's not only that you came to Canada with false papers. I'm sure after all these years that can easily be fixed.'

Jean-Pierre looked questioningly at Christopher and shrugged.

'Okay, Jane. I have to admit there is a little more to it. Shall I tell her, Chris?'

'I think you should, sir – and Mrs Rogers, because the problem isn't going away, is it? Either you'll have to take some action or it will be taken for you, and it could be dangerous.'

'Dangerous?' Jane was horrified. 'Do you mean physically dangerous?'

'I regret to say yes, my dear Jane,' Jean-Pierre said sadly. 'And Chris is right. You and Betty should be told the whole truth. I did intend to tell you when I had decided what I should do. However, now is possibly as good a time as any. I'll make a point of explaining to Betty later. So . . .'

They discussed the situation throughout supper, but without reaching any conclusions. The only new suggestion was that Christopher should tell his father the whole story and seek his advice.

'Do you really think he might be able to help?' Jane asked as she and Christopher did the dishes together.

'He'll certainly know what it's best to do,' Christopher said, 'and he may be able to pull some strings, though it's a difficult position because of Peregrine.'

The washing-up done, they returned to the big room. Jean-Pierre was snoozing in a comfortable armchair in front of the fire. Jane regarded him with affection.

'I should hate anything to happen to him,' she said.

'So should I,' Christopher agreed.

There was a knock on the front door and the old man started awake. 'That will be Betty. She's early. She must have forgotten her key.'

'I'll go,' Jane said.

She left the door of the big room half open, and Christopher heard the murmur of raised voices in the hallway. A minute later Jane returned. She was not alone. With her were two men. One of them held Jane in front of him like a shield. He had twisted her arms behind her back and was propelling her before him while he pressed a knife into the side of her neck.

The other man held a gun, swinging it between Jean-Pierre and Christopher. A girl, who appeared to be unarmed, accompanied them. It was Heidi Fielding, or at least that was the name she had given Christopher.

'Hello, Chris,' she said. 'We meet again. First on the plane, then at the hotel and now here. Isn't that nice? Or didn't you expect me?'

Momentarily Christopher shut his eyes. The look of shock and disgust on Jane's face told him what she believed of him, and this was more than he could bear. And he cursed Heidi, then himself. He had been a fool, an utter fool. Even after Ghislaine's death he had not learnt his lesson. He had allowed himself to be picked up on an aircraft by an attractive girl, had entertained her, had gone to bed with her, had mentioned Jane's name in front of her and told her about his planned weekend at the cottage up in the Gatineau Hills. He had made it easy for them. But, he suddenly wondered, how had they known he would be on that flight?

'Sit down!' Heidi ordered. Jean-Pierre and Christopher had automatically risen to their feet as Jane was marched in. 'Sit down!' she repeated as they both remained standing.

They sat. She motioned to a chair between them and the man with the knife half threw Jane into it. Close to her Christopher could see a thin trickle of blood creeping down her neck. He felt sick with anger and frustration.

'And what do you propose to do with us?' Jean-Pierre asked calmly.

Heidi did not answer. Instead she said to the man with the knife, 'Search the place. Make sure there's no one else around.' It was obvious she was the dominant member of the trio.

Watching the man leave the room, Jean-Pierre said, 'They are going to kill us, all of us, not just me. Take in what I'm saying, Chris – and Jane. They intend to kill us; they're not the kind of types to give us a chance.'

'Shut up!' Heidi said.

Jean-Pierre paid her no attention. He glanced at Chris. 'There's no point in waiting.' he said. 'There won't be a better time than now, so let's make it – *now*!'

The last word was a shout, a command. Christopher had been expecting something like this and he knew what to do. He was the nearest to the man with the gun, and had already used his eyes to measure the distance between them. It was too great. Even given the element of surprise, the man would have shot him before he was within reach. Nevertheless, he braced himself. It was Hobson's choice; either he died now or later – Jean-Pierre had spoken the truth – and perhaps by some miracle Jane might be saved.

As these thoughts flitted across his mind Christopher launched himself forward. Simultaneously Jean-Pierre, who had, unseen, closed his hand around a piece of Inuit sculpture that sat on the table behind him, hurled it at Heidi. Luck was with them both.

The Inuit piece, a primitive bird with a sharp beak, made of ironstone, struck the girl in the face. Jean-Pierre had thrown it with all the force he could muster and it was heavy. It broke her nose and the point of the beak pierced her eye. Blood poured down her chin. She staggered back, hands pressed over her eyes, stumbled and fell. She lay on the ground, curled herself into a foetal position and screamed with pain.

Christopher heard the screams but didn't register the source, for he didn't see what had happened. He had moved a fraction of a second after Jean-Pierre and had hurled himself across the intervening space at the man with the gun who, distracted by the attack on the girl, fired wildly.

Christopher had been right. He had been in no way near enough to reach the man and would most probably have been killed if the aim had been true. As it was he felt a searing pain in his left shoulder, but was scarcely conscious of it. He knocked the gun out of the man's hand with a vicious backhand blow, and out of the corner of his eye saw it skitter across the floor.

Nevertheless, Christopher was a couple of inches shorter and considerably lighter than his opponent, so it would still have been an uneven contest had it not been for his training in karate. It had stood him in good stead at Ansbach against Herr Doktor Hueber and it did the same now. The man, who had expected no difficulty in dealing with him, was taken by surprise by the ferocity of the attack and went flying, pursued by Christopher.

The struggle was brief. Christopher staggered to his feet. Heidi had stopped screaming and was moaning softly. Jane had picked up the gun and was holding it awkwardly, as if she had never held a weapon before. She was pointing it with an unsteady hand at the door. Christopher swung round.

Jean-Pierre shouted, 'Look out, Jane!'

The second man, who had been ordered by Heidi to search the cottage, was standing in the doorway. In his hand was a knife and his arm was raised in a throwing position. His target was Jane, who held the gun.

Christopher reacted with a jumble of emotions to Jean-Pierre's warning shout. He flung himself at the man, not in the expectation of being able to achieve anything, but in some wild hope of

231

protecting Jane from an attack. At least he succeeded in the latter. The knife caught him in the chest. Then there was the sound of two shots, and for a moment as he collapsed on the floor and blacked out with an excruciating pain that seemed to travel through his body he believed he had been hit.

It was almost a couple of days before the doctors at the small hospital in Wakefield, the nearest Quebec town to the cottage, were certain that Christopher would live. The knife had slid off a rib and punctured a lung and he had lost a lot of blood from the bullet wound in his shoulder. That he didn't die was probably due to the fact that Jane, who was by now an experienced doctor, had taken immediate care of him, and that help from outside had arrived so quickly.

By the end of a week his condition had stabilized and he was transferred to the Civic Hospital in Ottawa, still in intensive care and under sedation. For his relations and others who loved him – Peter and Anne had flown out to Canada and were in constant touch with Verity and Anthea in England – it had been a period of anxiety, and their eventual relief was enormous. Christopher was scarcely aware of any of this. He was living very much in a world of his own, a world of pain, of shadowy figures, of nightmare sleep. He had no idea that he had been in hospital in Wakefield; he had never even heard of the place.

But after a day or two in Ottawa he began to have periods of clarity. He was conscious of doctors and nurses, of his mother and father and Jane, and of brief visits from Betty and Jean-Pierre. His pain eased and, as his sedation was decreased he became more aware of where he was and what was happening around him. But he had no desire to talk or to ask questions. He was content that Jane and Jean-Pierre were obviously safe and well, and he knew that he himself was growing stronger. He was undoubtedly recovering, and he was moved from the intensive care unit to a private room, but he was still weak. He lay in bed in a semi-somnolent state which was strangely akin to happiness.

By the middle of the third week, however, he was much improved. His curiosity sharpened. He remembered the events at the cottage, but not their final outcome, and he wondered what had befallen Heidi and the two men – if they had been arrested, for example. He would have asked Jean-Pierre, but Jean-Pierre no longer seemed to be around. His father too had gone – Peter had had to return to his post in Brussels – and his mother, who was still staying at the Rogers's house in Rockcliffe, appeared not to know. She had told him that she believed one of the men had been drowned, which was palpably absurd.

It was the Sunday afternoon when Jane, who was off duty and therefore not too busy to talk, came to see him, and he learned what had happened both on the night of the attack and subsequently. And to his amazement Anne's seemingly absurd remark about one of the men having drowned proved to be true.

'I nearly shot you, Chris,' Jane said. 'Not on purpose, I assure you. By then I had realized you had no connection with those ghastly people. But I was aiming at the guy with the knife when you so gallantly threw yourself between us. I fired – twice.'

'You didn't hit me. Did you hit him?'

Jane shook her head. 'No. I was nowhere near either of you. One shot went into the ceiling, the other into the wall, yards from the door. It was absolute chance – I didn't know what I was doing – but it scared the guy and he bolted. He took the car they came in and tore down the hill, which would have been dangerous at any time, but at night for a driver who wasn't familiar with the route it was madness. He failed to take the last sharp bend and went straight into the lake. They fished him and his car out next morning.'

'Well, I'm damned,' Christopher laughed, but it hurt and he quickly desisted. 'Ma said one of them had drowned and I didn't believe her.'

'Dad tied up the other guy, though he didn't show much resistance, and the girl was too badly hurt to care about anything except herself. I was attending to you to the best of my ability, but I knew it wasn't going to be enough. We needed help and we needed it fast, but there's no telephone at the cottage. Dad would have to go to the Nortons. They were our nearest neighbours with a phone. Then the miracle happened.' Jane smiled at Christopher fondly. 'I must have been praying hard for you without realizing it.'

'What miracle?'

'Ma arrived with Frank Norton and his brother who had been visiting with him. They had left Dorothy phoning the police – that's the Québec Provincial Police – and an ambulance.'

'But – but how did they know?'

'That's the miracle. The four of them were playing bridge. Mother was dummy and she got up from the table to stretch her legs and look out of the window at the night sky. She saw an automobile come hurtling down the lane much too fast, and she guessed there was something badly wrong up at the cottage, even before the automobile went into the lake.'

'They didn't try to get him out?'

'No. It would have been an impossible task for them. They came straight up here. And were Dad and I ever glad to see them, and especially to know Dorothy was on the phone.' Jane paused. 'Calling the police was obvious enough, and she included the ambulance because of the driver in the lake. Chris, that's enough for now. You're looking tired.'

'I'm all right. Anyway you can't stop there. What happened next?'

'The police arrived and the ambulance. You and the girl were taken to Wakefield hospital. I insisted on going with you. Dad said the police kept him up half the night asking questions and the next morning we both had to make statements. You'll have to make one as soon as you're a little better.'

'What do I say?'

'Tell it straight, starting with the intruders. We said we had never seen them before and –'

'But I can't say that. It's not that I mind lying, but I was seen with – with Heidi at the Château Laurier. I'll have to admit she picked me up on the flight from England.'

'So what does that matter? Boy meets girl. You may appear a bit of a fool, but –'

'I *was* a fool.'

'We'll let that go.'

'But how did she know I was going to be on that flight?'

'Your mother discovered that. You told your sister Verity you were going to Ottawa on a *direct* flight, of which there aren't all that number. She told her Julian – she was upset about some party – and by chance he mentioned it to Peregrine Grayson, who seems to have been cultivating him.'

Christopher groaned. 'Yes. It fits.'

'The second man, whom the police took off to prison, swore they never meant to harm us. He said they hadn't expected anyone to be there; they'd hoped to steal whatever they could from half-a-dozen cottages.'

'Did the police believe him?'

'I think they have their doubts. So far the girl has refused to speak. A lot may depend on what she says or doesn't say. Incidentally, Dad has gone to France.'

'What?'

234

But Christopher was going to have to wait to hear more. An irate matron bustled into the room, saying, 'Doctor, you should know better than to tire my patient.' Christopher didn't mind. It was true he was tired, and Jane bent and kissed him on the mouth before she went.

TWENTY-EIGHT

It was his mother who brought more news the next day. Anne was looking pale and tired, with dark circles under her eyes. Relieved of anxiety concerning Christopher's recovery, she was nevertheless worried about him. She had no wish to leave him to recuperate in Ottawa without her, even though Betty and Jane both assured her they would take every care of him and make sure he had everything he wanted.

But there were other demands on her. Indeed, she was being torn four ways. First was Christopher, then there was her husband, who had just learnt that in the autumn he was to be moved from Brussels and appointed ambassador to France, a post to which he had always aspired; he was extremely busy and needed her support. There were the preparations for Verity's wedding, which was to take place in six weeks' time. And finally there was the fear that at any moment her pleasant world might disintegrate.

A sensible woman, Anne didn't allow her mind to dwell on this last point. Peter had told her that a great deal would depend on the outcome of Jean-Pierre de Mourville's confrontation with the authorities in Paris, and she knew that if things went wrong Peter's posting, which had not yet been officially announced, might be cancelled, Verity's wedding might be ruined, and unhappiness might engulf many of those whom she held dear. But there was nothing she could do about all this.

What she had done, however, was to speak to Christopher's doctors. For some days Christopher had continued to gain strength steadily. He was now allowed to sit in the armchair in his room, and even to dress. She had explained the circumstances and asked if there was any medical objection to his flying straight back to Europe in a day or two. They had said no, as long as when he got there he didn't walk long distances or get overtired; they had offered to provide explanatory letters to his physicians or surgeons. In short, they had been very helpful.

This was part of the news that Anne brought to Christopher, who was pleased, though somewhat annoyed at being prevented from spending more time with Jane.

Then Anne said, 'Chris, I had a long talk with your father on the phone. He sends you his love. So does Jean-Pierre.'

'Jean-Pierre? I thought he was in France.'

'He's staying in Brussels with us, and being driven over to Paris every day. After all, it's not far and Peter can advise him, keep an eye on the proceedings and, if it seems desirable, perhaps pull some strings. Besides, there's the added advantage that they'll get to know each other properly – an opportunity I'm sure they are both welcoming.'

'How are these so-called proceedings doing?'

'Moderately well, I gather, Chris – at least as far as Jean-Pierre is concerned.'

'What do you mean?'

'Peter had to be careful what he said on an open line, and there's every possibility that this could turn into a *cause célèbre*, which of course is the last thing we want. It's already an international affair. For instance, that girl Heidi – if that's her real name – is likely to be extradited to Germany where it's believed she's wanted for murder. She belongs to some neo-Nazi group which, among other atrocities, has burnt down a synagogue and attacked the homes of foreign workers.'

But Christopher didn't want to think about Heidi. 'How does that affect Jean-Pierre? No one can suggest that he's a neo-Nazi. As I understand, it was the neo-Nazis who were so eager to find him and kill him that they were prepared to torture Ghislaine and –'

'Chris, don't get so excited. It's bad for you. Peter believes that Jean-Pierre is in the clear. There doesn't seem to be any question of bringing him to trial for crimes against humanity, as he feared at one time. The authorities aren't interested in his past, except that he's a potential witness.'

'I see – or do I?'

'The French Sécurité have been very active. With the help of other security services they've amassed a mountain of evidence to prove that in France, Germany and Britain there's a growing swell of neo-Nazi sympathy and sympathizers, and behind them, encouraging them and providing financial backing, are people like certain influential politicians, senior civil servants, bankers, leading business men, all of whom keep well in the background. A few of them are old, with their Nazi sympathies going back to the war and

237

Hitler. What's more, they will stop at nothing. One or two of the potential witnesses against these unpleasant characters have died mysteriously or unexpectedly, believed murdered, before they could make an official statement. And it was very possible this could have happened to Jean-Pierre.'

'Dad didn't mention any names?'

'No, but from what Jean-Pierre told us about Keith – he said he'd already told you – Peter's train of thought was obvious. If Jean-Pierre's suspicions are justified, then Keith's past and Peregrine's present may equate. In other words, they may both espouse the Nazi cause.'

'And even the only grandson to bear the name of Grayson would have to be sacrificed if it ensures Peregrine getting into Number Ten.' Christopher was bitter. 'God, what a stink there's going to be if all this becomes public!'

'I don't think any of the governments are too keen to air their dirty linen in public. But you've received some publicity, Chris, and not only here in Canada.' Anne searched in her handbag and produced a newspaper cutting. 'Verity sent me this. She said you were also mentioned on television. Such is fame.'

Christopher took the cutting. There was a photograph of himself which he remembered had been taken five years ago; it made him look young and innocent. The heading of the brief news item that accompanied it read, 'Oxford Don Nearly Killed in Quebec'.

The piece gave a short account of Christopher's career and said that he had been staying with friends, Mr and Mrs Guy Rogers and Dr Jane Rogers, in their country cottage in the Gatineau Hills north of Ottawa for some late skiing when armed thieves broke in. In the scuffle that followed, Mr Grayson was attacked with a knife and badly wounded, but was now out of danger. The thieves fled.

'Not what you could call accurate,' Christopher said, 'but fair enough, I suppose. What newspaper was this in?'

'*The Times*, but Verity said an almost identical item appeared in the *Oxford Mail*. It may have been in the English tabloids too, but as Canada doesn't get much publicity in the English press, and you're not exactly a celebrity, darling, it's not very likely.'

'Good! But Keith will have seen it?'

'Most probably. Anyway, he knows. We discussed it with Jean-Pierre when we were afraid you – you might not live, and we decided that he had to be told. After all, it couldn't be kept a secret. Anthea and my parents had to know and it seemed sensible to include Keith.

238

We had no idea how much or how little publicity there would be, and we didn't want anyone connected with the family to learn about the – the incident from the media.'

'I suppose Keith didn't ask who the Rogers were? It would have been the natural thing to do.'

'No, he didn't ask. But when he heard you had started to recover he did say that if you would like to recuperate at Cherwell Manor you would be welcome.'

'He must have been joking!'

Anne laughed, but without much enthusiasm. 'Darling, I've arranged for you to go down to Greatbourne as soon as you're back in England. Somerset will be lovely at this time of year, and you'll be right there for Verity's wedding.'

'That will be great.' Christopher was fond of his mother's family and always enjoyed staying with them. 'Incidentally, I've had a letter from the Provost – very kind. The college is farming out my work for this term, and they don't expect me back till October. That's a relief. I was afraid they might take a dim view, because of the burden of exams that I'm escaping.'

'Good. Everything seems to be working out nicely.'

'Yes, indeed.'

The two exchanged rueful glances; neither of them was over-optimistic.

In the afternoon Christopher had two unexpected visitors. They had come all the way from the UK, and identified themselves merely as members of the British Home Office. They produced evidence to substantiate their claim, including a letter signed by the Home Secretary to say he would be grateful for any help that could be given to them in their inquiries. Christopher, who was dressed and sitting up in an armchair, regarded them with some awe which he did his best to hide. He had no doubt they were Security Service officers, and they made little pretence to be otherwise. It crossed his mind to wonder why they were not accompanied by someone from the Canadian Security Intelligence Service or even the RCMP, but that point was soon to be explained.

Having asked him if he was feeling better and able to answer a few questions, the older and more senior of the two, whose name appeared to be Carter, said, 'Mr Grayson, it's somewhat unusual that we should be here, but we are in Canada with the knowledge of the Canadian authorities and indeed of the French authorities. We

239

have been working very closely with the French and the Germans concerning what is a matter of internal security for each of us.'

Christopher didn't answer. He stared from Carter to his colleague, a man apparently called Bergson, who was a slightly thinner version of his senior. They both wore grey suits and sober ties. They were both of medium height. They both had brown hair, pale eyes and nondescript features. Christopher thought them slightly frightening.

'Mr Grayson,' Carter went on. 'We appreciate that you have given the Quebec Provincial Police a simple statement of what occurred at the Rogers's cottage, but perhaps you would care to elaborate on it for us?'

'Elaborate? In what way? I don't remember a great deal.'

'But you do remember the girl who called herself Heidi Fielding. You know that she and her companions were no common thieves. They had come to assassinate Guy Rogers and were prepared to kill anyone else who happened to be in the cottage.'

Christopher sighed. 'I met her on the flight over here. I'd never seen her before. She made an excuse to sit by me – and you can guess the rest. It was my fault. In a sense, I led her to the cottage. Not on purpose, God knows, but as a result of my stupidity in not keeping my mouth shut.'

'You shouldn't blame yourself, Mr Grayson. You've been an amateur playing against professionals and you don't seem to have done too badly.' Carter allowed himself a thin smile. 'But you're lucky to have come out of it alive.'

'You speak as if it's all over.'

'It will never be that,' Bergson said. 'We thought that the Nazi beast had been killed for good after the Second World War, but we were wrong. We've learnt from bitter experience that it's still alive and flourishing, and it's the more dangerous because mostly it's covert and often in high places.'

'But one particular aspect is almost over,' Carter said. 'Mr Rogers has told the French authorities all he knows and suspects, so he is no longer a danger to anyone and, we trust will be able to resume his normal life in Canada, which is what he wishes to do, as soon as the bureaucracy is sorted out. You know, Mr Grayson, both you and he made the same mistake. The French wanted to find him, not to accuse him of any crime against humanity or anything else, but to ensure his safety and pick his memory. That, mainly thanks to you, they have been able to do, and Mr Rogers has made only

240

one further request of them. He has asked that the headstone on the graves of Jean-Pierre and Chantal de Mourville, which was defaced by swastikas, should be replaced and that it should be made clear to the villagers that this is an official action and that the rumours concerning the family were due to malicious falsehoods.'

'And this can be done? That's great!' Christopher was genuinely pleased. 'But –' He didn't know how to frame the questions he wanted to ask.

'Mr Rogers does not really concern us any more,' Carter said. 'By us, I mean the British Home Office. However, our task, as you know, is to prevent anything that threatens the security of the realm, such as fascism and racism. Of course this is an international problem; it's impossible to separate one country from another or, it seems, the past from the present. You understand what I'm saying, Mr Grayson?'

'Yes.' Christopher nodded. He understood only too well. They were not concerned with Jean-Pierre any more – their interest was now nearer home. He wished he knew exactly what Jean-Pierre had said about Keith. 'I think so, Mr Carter – Mr Bergson. I hope you're not questioning my loyalty.'

'No, indeed, Mr Grayson. We accept that you and your father are beyond reproach. However –'

In the event, though it took some time to tell his story and to respond to all the questions he was asked, Christopher found it less of an effort than he had expected. On the contrary, it was something of a relief. But by the end he was exhausted, and he was glad when the two men left, and he was able to undress and get back into bed to doze and watch television until it was time for his supper.

By the end of the week Anne had made the necessary arrangements and took Christopher back to England. Betty and Jane drove them to Mirabelle, Montreal's airport, where to Christopher's chagrin a wheelchair was provided for him. Jane insisted on pushing it.

Waiting for his mother and Betty to catch up with them at one point, Christopher turned in his chair and said suddenly, 'Jane, I know this is a ridiculous place to ask you, but would you consider marrying me?'

'I'd consider it, yes,' Jane said lightly, though the huskiness in her voice betrayed her.

'Jane, I'm serious.'

'I know you are, Chris, but we don't know each other very well,

241

and we've both been under a strain. Our circumstances have been peculiar, to say the least. Wait till you come and stay with us after Christmas as you've promised. Maybe then –'

And with that Christopher had to be content, but he was not discouraged. He would wait. Meanwhile he must get completely fit. There was the summer to enjoy, Verity's wedding and, with luck, an end to all anxiety about Jean-Pierre. For a moment he recalled with bitter regret the death of Ghislaine, and he was reminded that there could still be – indeed, probably would be – an appalling family scandal if accusations were made against Keith. Then he turned his thoughts again to Jane.

The flight was uneventful. Christopher slept much of the way, and was less exhausted on arrival at Heathrow than he had expected. Nevertheless, he was pleased to find Verity and Julian waiting to greet them and drive them to Durrant's Hotel where they were to spend a night before going down to Somerset the following day.

'You'll never guess what I've been doing,' Verity said, as Julian coped with the traffic on the M4 to London. 'I've been to Paris with Gran!'

If she had wanted to surprise her mother and brother, Verity had succeeded. Why Paris, they asked, and why on earth had Anthea gone with her?

'Paris rather than Brussels,' Verity said, 'because Dad's up to his eyes in work and he has the Foreign Secretary staying at the embassy with his wife and some other members of a delegation. They're having a succession of meetings. It was a time for family to keep away, and anyhow, as you may or may not know, Jean-Pierre has gone on to Paris for a week or two.'

'Verity, do start at the beginning,' Anne said.

'All right. It seemed a pity that with Gran and Jean-Pierre within an hour's flight of each other they shouldn't meet. He'd be going back to Canada soon and this might be their last chance. Neither of them is exactly young. So I phoned Ship Street and put it to Gran, who pointed out that Jean-Pierre was my grandfather, and I should take the opportunity to meet him too. It was difficult on the phone. I couldn't work out whether she was keen on seeing him or not.'

'But you persevered,' Christopher said.

'Yes. I got hold of Meriel, who assured me Gran had been taken by surprise, but would very much like to have a reunion with Jean-Pierre. So I called Dad's secretary, who told me Jean-Pierre had gone to Paris to stay with his daughter Chantal. She gave me the

Delancourts' phone number, and I spoke to Jean-Pierre himself. To cut a long story short, Meriel, who wanted to do some shopping in London, drove Gran up from Oxford and took us both to Heathrow. I stayed two nights with the Delancourts, who incidentally are both absolutely charming, and came home yesterday, leaving Gran there.'

'And the answer to the big question,' Anne said. 'Was the reunion a success?'

'I didn't see the actual reunion. Chantal tactfully arranged that Gran and Jean-Pierre should meet for the first time alone, but when they joined us they were bright-eyed and smiling, and they were obviously terribly happy to be together. It was as if the years between had dropped away, and they weren't strangers. Gran told me afterwards they had both wept in each other's arms. I suppose for what might have been.'

'It's strange to think what a difference it would have made to all our lives if what might have been *had* been,' said Christopher.

'Better *not* to think about it,' said Julian, who was a practical man. 'Here we are at the hotel.'

The manager in his black morning coat and striped trousers came out to the car as the hall porter helped unload their bags.

'Mrs Grayson?'

'Yes. Good morning.'

'Good morning. Mrs Grayson, your husband's secretary has phoned. Your husband wishes to speak to you urgently.' He looked at the three young people; he wasn't sure of their relationships. 'Perhaps you'd care to wait in the lounge while Mrs Grayson telephones. I'll arrange for coffee to be sent in.' He ushered them into the hotel and took them into a lounge. When they were comfortably installed, he took Anne to a telephone booth.

The porter brought in their luggage and told Julian he would put the car in the mews behind the hotel and keep an eye on it.

'Might something have happened to Gran – or Jean-Pierre?' Verity wondered, worried.

'It's no use guessing,' Julian said firmly. 'We'll soon know. Just wait.'

They waited. The coffee appeared and behind the waiter came Anne. She sat down heavily and took the cup of coffee that Verity had poured for her.

'Bad news,' she said. 'Keith was found dead early this morning. The circumstances suggest it could have been suicide.'

Postlude

The Colombury coroner's court was half-empty. No special publicity had been given to the inquest on Keith Grayson of Cherwell Manor, Oxfordshire. Nevertheless, there were three or four local journalists present, plus the usual public scavengers who haunt such places, members of the dead man's family, including Anthea who had come with Meriel, and Karen who considered herself the star witness. Among the other witnesses were Keith's doctor, police, a forensic expert, business friends and, seated in the back row of the court, two men whom Christopher would have recognized as Carter and Bergson from the Home Office.

It was a hot, sunny day, not the sort of day to be cooped up in an airless courtroom. Before the proceedings had begun the coroner had ordered that all the windows be opened, but the routine identification of the deceased had scarcely been completed when he was compelled to order them to be shut again; the noise from the traffic outside made it impossible to hear what was being said. So everyone sat on the hard uncomfortable benches and sweltered in the heat. There was no doubt as to how Keith had died. His manservant testified that he had been drinking heavily all the evening but, encouraged by the coroner, modified this statement to add that the amount he had consumed was probably not more than usual, as 'Mr Grayson liked to do himself well'. However, there had been a glass and a half-empty bottle of whisky on the bedside table, which suggested that Keith had had at least one drink – probably strong – as a nightcap on the night he had died. He had also, according to the autopsy, taken at least three times the number of sleeping capsules prescribed for him. This, the doctor assured the court, might easily have happened if Mr Grayson had been a little fuddled with drink and sleep.

'At least three times the prescribed amount?' the coroner asked sceptically.

'It's been known to happen.' The doctor refused to have his opinion queried. 'I always advise my patients, especially the elderly, not to leave their sleeping pills beside their beds.'

The inquest continued. Meriel whispered to Anthea that the coroner looked as if he were dozing, but he woke to stress the point that no suicide note had been found. The maid who had taken up Keith's early morning tea had seen no note. Nor had Karen, whom the maid had summoned when she failed to rouse her employer.

'But I don't think that's necessarily important,' Karen said, when she came to give her evidence. 'Keith wouldn't have wanted to cause me grief. He was such a kind and good person. He would have thought I would be happier if I believed it was an accident.'

There was a stir in the court. The journalists sat up. Karen, pleased with herself, looked around, then concentrated her gaze on Anthea. In spite of the summer weather Karen was dressed completely in black except for a touch of white at the throat – more like a widow than a sister.

'This woman could be dangerous,' Carter muttered to his colleague. Evidently the coroner had a similar thought, for he said smoothly, 'Mrs Overton, I agree that the lack of a note *proves* nothing, but it is an indicator. Has your brother ever threatened to take his own life?'

'No-o,' Karen admitted, 'but he wasn't happy; I could tell. He felt neglected in his old age. His son, Peregrine Grayson, is an important man, a minister, a member of the Cabinet, and really can't spare the time to visit him often, and the rest of the family don't seem to care a great deal. His granddaughter has refused to have her wedding reception at his house and – '

'Mrs Overton! Mrs Overton!' The coroner overrode her. 'Mr Grayson was a widower, was he?'

It was an unfortunate question. It set Karen off again. She glared at Anthea. 'He might as well have been. His wife, to whom he was devoted, left him years ago to live with another woman.'

There was a murmur of real interest in the court. The reporters scented scandal. Anthea had to put a restraining hand on Meriel's arm to prevent her from leaping to her feet and denouncing the implied canard. Carter and Bergson sat, grim-faced, their hope for an uneventful, uninteresting inquest fast disappearing. But they had underestimated the coroner.

Seizing on the opportunity that Karen had unwittingly given him, he said, 'As you remarked, that was years ago, Mrs Overton, and no longer seems relevant. Mr Grayson, who after all had you as a companion, must have become used to the situation. So let us be practical. To your knowledge, did your brother have any business worries?'

'No! He –'

'Good! We know from his doctor that for his age his health was excellent.' The coroner hesitated. He didn't want to ask the next question but, if he didn't, it might be noticed. 'Did he have any other worries that you know of, recent worries?'

'Well, he wasn't entirely happy, as I said earlier, and I'm sure he was worried about something in particular, but he didn't confide in me.'

'I see. So it was just a feeling you had. Well, thank you, Mrs Overton. Perhaps our next witness can throw more light on the matter.'

The two men from the Home Office relaxed. They knew the man who was taking the stand, and a word in his ear had ensured he would say the right thing. He was the last witness, and ten minutes later it was all over. The coroner, thankfully sitting without a jury, recorded a verdict of accidental death.

The inquest sparked off a brief appreciation of Keith Grayson in *The Times*, which appeared as a supplement to his obituary, but this caused no stir.

His funeral too was uneventful. It was strictly private. The mourners, almost exclusively relatives, met at the church. They included Peregrine and Joyce Grayson, Karen, Peter and Anne Grayson, Christopher, Verity and Anthea. The service was short, as was the formality of the interment, and the steady summer rain gave everyone an excuse to say brief goodbyes afterwards and then hurry to their respective cars without appearing to be unsociable. The mourners were not asked back to Cherwell Manor as they had been after the funeral of John Grayson, Keith and Karen's father, but there was not one of them who did not reflect on that day.

'Thank heaven that's over!' Peter said as his immediate family got into their car.

'It wasn't as embarrassing as I thought it might be,' said Anne who was once again driving.

'Peregrine and Joyce know how to hide their feelings, but an outburst from Karen was always possible.' Peter was grim.

'She was the only one who cried,' Anthea said sadly. 'She genuinely loved Keith.'

'He did take his own life, didn't he,' Christopher said, 'in spite of the coroner's verdict?'

'Yes. I don't think there's any doubt,' Peter agreed. 'There was no possibility that he could have been prosecuted for his wartime activities. Jean-Pierre said he wouldn't give evidence against him, and anyway it would have been difficult to prove his guilt. But he was aware that they were known to the authorities, and he was warned that if he didn't stop his financial support of his neo-Nazi chums there would be serious trouble. MI5 can be tough on occasion.'

'So this is the end of the affair,' Verity said. 'No almighty scandal, which is what we all feared.'

'That is indeed something to be thankful for,' Anne said. 'Your future in-laws wouldn't have liked it, Verity. No more than any of us.'

'You think we really are safe, Dad?' Christopher asked.

'Yes. The powers-that-be have damped everything down. None of the governments involved want publicity for their unsavoury citizens because it reflects on them. But I'm sure there's a lot going on behind the scenes, and there will be repercussions.'

'Peregrine?' Anthea said.

Peter smiled at his mother, but ignored her question. He had been told what was to happen to Peregrine, but it had been in strict confidence. Others would have to learn that Peregrine was to be allowed to resign his seat in the Cabinet on the grounds that he would now have to attend to his late father's business affairs, and would not stand again in the next election. It hadn't been hard to persuade him, since the alternative was that he would be dropped without official explanation in the Cabinet reshuffle expected in late summer, and the rumour spread that this was because he was a neo-Nazi and a covert supporter of the British National Party.

Seemingly Peregrine had got off lightly but, knowing the strength of his ambition, Peter felt sorry for him, especially as he himself had been so fortunate. To distract Anthea, he said. 'Incidentally, I've news for you all. It's now official that I'm to be Her Majesty's Ambassador to France, and before I'm actually accredited I shall become Sir Peter.'

This was a surprise to everyone but Anne, and there was a chorus of congratulations. Amid them, the Right Honourable Peregrine Grayson PC MP was forgotten.

And for a little while they drove in companionable silence. Peter and Anne were thinking of Paris, Verity of her forthcoming wedding, Christopher of Jane and his visit to Canada in the New Year. They were almost all looking forward to the future. It was Anthea alone who was thinking of the past, of Jean-Pierre de Mourville and how much they had loved each other.